THREE WAYS TO DISAPPEAR

A NOVEL

KATY YOCOM

Ashland Creek Press

Three Ways to Disappear

A novel by Katy Yocom

Published by Ashland Creek Press

www.ashlandcreekpress.com

© 2019 Katy Yocom

ISBN 978-1-61822-083-7

Library of Congress Control Number: 2018964454

The excerpt of Jorie Graham's poem "Prayer" is from *Never*. Copyright © 2002 by Jorie Graham. Used with the permission of HarperCollins Publishers.

Cover design by Matt Smith.

To Jeff, with love

The longing
is to be pure. What you get is to be changed.

—JORIE GRAHAM, "PRAYER"

QUINN

IN THE YEAR AFTER MARCUS DIED, their mother stopped loving people, one after another. Her minister, her tennis coach, her friends. Daddy. On a day dripping with the end of the monsoon, she clicked shut the brass latches on her daughters' suitcases and supervised as Ravindra loaded them into the car. In the courtyard, beneath the peepal tree, Daddy clutched the girls to his chest. Quinn, at eleven, was the responsible one; Sarah, at eight, the remnant twin: widowed by Marcus when he died, if *widowed* was the word for it, which it wasn't. There was no word for it. Thin mud soaked their shoes as he kissed their cheeks and begged them not to forget him. It was a terrible thing to hear him say because it opened up the possibility that they could. His voice had gone high with pain, which embarrassed Quinn for him. She didn't think men were supposed to feel that much.

Mother pulled the girls away, leaving their father to stand alone in the filtered sunlight, arms dangling at his sides as if he didn't know how they operated. Daddy was a doctor, the reason they lived in India, and India, according to Mother, was the reason Marcus was dead. Daddy's mouth curled down, and he cried silently as his daughters watched. Behind him, Ayah wept, rhythmic and soft like singing. Beyond Ayah, the watchman stood: the courtyard a chessboard, the adults the game pieces isolated in their separate squares. Ayah's weeping turned ragged, and Quinn and Sarah ran and clung to her until Mother pried their fingers from Ayah's damp turquoise sari and pushed the girls, stumbling and crying, into the car. Their shoes muddied the floor mats, but Quinn didn't care.

Ravindra opened the wrought iron gate and nosed the car into the inchoate, horn-honking flow of Delhi traffic. In the back seat, Quinn turned around and watched their home grow smaller. Before it vanished altogether, she raised her hand to it and said goodbye. Goodbye to everything and everyone and everywhere. Goodbye to Daddy. To Ayah. To every friend, enemy, household staff member, shopkeeper, schoolteacher, gymnastics instructor, swimming coach. It seemed easy for Mother: She had shut down her heart. But she still loved her girls. The proof was that she took them with her.

The other proof was that she hadn't believed Quinn when she tried to confess her role in what had happened to Marcus. Quinn said the words, but Mother had let them fall to her bedroom floor, where they scuttled under the bed and vanished. Which meant that the secret was still Quinn's to carry. She had spent a long time considering the consequences before she told Mother what she'd done, but this possibility had never occurred to her.

"Remember, young ladies. Always be good," Ravindra said at the airport curb, his eyes streaming. Sarah and Quinn hugged him hard. They cried. But when Mother told them to leave him, they left, dutiful girls. They boarded an enormous jet and flew west across India, Pakistan, Iran, Iraq, Turkey. Across all of Europe, to Paris. Over the ultramarine Atlantic Ocean and down the Eastern Seaboard to New York. From there to Louisville, Kentucky, the town where Mother had grown up. They were leaving their unhappiness as far behind them as the planet would allow.

Quinn thought she felt it happen. When the plane lifted off from the Delhi runway, she felt an invisible force push her body back into the seat and flow through her, a tide running in the direction of India and the ground. So Mother was right: It *was* possible to leave things behind, events and stories and history. With a sense of relief, as the plane shuddered around her, she lifted up her secret and offered it to the tide. She would go to America, and she would be free.

She was twenty-eight years old on the day she stopped believing in this magic. Twenty-eight and bare-bellied on an examining table, her husband's fingers interlaced with her own. The ultrasound tech ran a wand over her midsection, and in a haze of black and gray, the two children inside her revealed their identities: a boy and a girl, just like Marcus and Sarah. Sarah was twenty-five at the time. Marcus was still seven, if he was anything at all.

As she looked at the hazy images of the children inside her, she felt it again: the weight of the plane lifting off and pushing her down. And she knew then that distance and years were nothing, that no matter what their mother said, their histories traveled with them, stitched into their DNA.

•

Peacock blue, she thought at first, but that was wrong. Mineral blue, like larimar. A sky color.

On a stool in front of Quinn, her son kicked his feet. It was the day before Nick and Alaina turned seven, and he was sitting for his portrait, to match the one of his sister that Quinn had completed that morning. Quinn's eyes wanted to linger on the curve and color of his peachy little cheek, to slow everything down. She wasn't ready for the twins to be seven. She had known it since the day of that ultrasound: She would never be ready for them to reach this age.

"How come you're using pastels instead of real paint?" Nick asked. By "real paint," he meant acrylics. In art school, Quinn had loved oils, but she hadn't allowed them into her studio since the day she'd learned she was pregnant. Too many noxious fumes in the paint thinners and brush cleaners: bad for the babies.

"I want to get you down fast so you don't have to sit so long," she said. The cerulean blue of his T-shirt reflected into Nick's eyes, which were a cool, deep hue, nearly periwinkle, pebbled with white. She touched oil pastel to paper to add the reflected color, just a couple of tiny arcs. Barely there at all.

The work absorbed her as it always did. She registered only vaguely the aroma of applewood smoke that meant Pete was heating the gas grill on the deck below. Giggles from the twins' room meant Alaina had commandeered her auntie Sarah, who was back in Louisville between reporting assignments. Sarah had come for a meal and to spend the night; Alaina had brokered the latter part of that deal. Quinn paused for a moment to listen. They were arguing playfully over whether their card game should be called Crazy Eights or Crazy Aunts. Sarah was advocating for the latter.

"What kind of cake are you making?" Nick asked.

"Chocolate with chocolate frosting. Just like you asked for." She stepped back to assess the drawing. Getting close, although she wanted to do a little more around his mouth and nose. So many complicated curves in that part of the face.

"Mom? Can we be done?"

"Sure, kiddo. You did great." Before she finished the sentence, he shot out the door, eager to fill Alaina in on the proceedings of the past half hour, no doubt. "Twin summit" was the family term for this mandatory briefing after every separation. "Like heads of state," Pete had once said as he and Quinn stood watching their children, bemused.

Quinn had begun straightening her studio when Sarah ambled in. "My services were no longer needed," she said, nodding toward the room across the hall. She straddled the stool and twined her long legs around it, giving the effect of a rider on horseback. "So my last assignment didn't go so well."

"No? Where were you?"

Sarah made an impatient noise. "Crappy little dictatorship. Continent beginning with the letter A." Sometimes she answered questions that way, to avoid scaring her family, Quinn assumed. "I was doing a series on government reforms to help with the refugee crisis. It all looked pretty impressive. I filed a long story about how things were turning a corner, the aid initiatives were working, et cetera. But the day I'm supposed to leave, all the flights get canceled because of a coup attempt, so I come back to the city. On the way, something tells me to stop by one of the sites where I'd been reporting. And it's gone."

Quinn stopped cleaning and tried to gauge her sister's expression. "Gone? Like a massacre?"

"Gone, like it never existed. Poof. They'd struck the whole damned camp like a movie set." Sarah dismounted the stool and paced to the window. "I'm out there with my driver, walking around this empty field, and the only things I'm seeing are some tent stakes and a bunch of empty Pepsi cans. And I'm realizing I've been played. And then my so-called government liaison shows up, and the next thing I know, I'm being detained."

"Holy hell, Sarah." Quinn settled her hips against her worktable and glanced involuntarily at the door, but the Lego noises coming from the bedroom said the twins were otherwise occupied.

Sarah peered out between the mullions like a prisoner. "They took my cell phone and laptop and parked me in this hotel room with a guard outside my door. In the middle of the night, I hear a scratching at my window, and it's two guys I know, journalists, and we sneak out of there to this little dirt-track airfield and take a puddle jumper to the next country."

Quinn blanched. "What would have happened if they'd caught you?"

"By that point, the government had bigger things to worry about than me."

This *Year of Living Dangerously* stuff: It knotted Quinn's stomach. "You must have been terrified."

Sarah turned around. "I'm pissed, is what I am. That"—she

glanced at the doorway and lowered her voice—"that fucking little dictator used me as a mouthpiece. Turned us all into his propaganda whores."

Quinn wiped her hands on a paper towel. "It's not your fault. He set you up."

"But who's to say this is the first time? Every time I've gotten access to some site or some person who was supposedly off-limits, maybe it was the same thing. And the damage is done. The stories have already run."

"You can retract them."

Sarah shrugged one shoulder. "People remember the story. They never remember it got retracted. Anyway, that's it for me. I'm done."

"What do you mean, 'done'?"

"Done. With journalism."

"Because of one story? That's a little impulsive even for you."

"Because of that story, and the one before it, and the one before that. Like the boy soldiers this summer. People read a story, and the next day it's forgotten. Nobody wants follow-up. Nobody cares. Or at least that's what the people in charge of the budgets believe."

Or they care, but they feel helpless, so they look away. Quinn considered the set of her sister's mouth. "You're shedding a lot of layers these days," she said. Sarah's divorce had been final less than a year. It had been a short marriage, but still, it had exacted a toll.

"You know me. I don't like to mess around."

Quinn recognized that breezy tone: a classic Sarah deflection. "It's hard to imagine you without journalism. I'm really sorry," Quinn said, and for Sarah's sake, she wanted to mean it, but she couldn't. No more wondering when she'd get the phone call saying her sister had been killed on assignment. "So you're coming back home, then?"

Sarah turned, planted her hands on the windowsill, and squinted up into the walnut tree. She was tall and blond like Quinn, but Sarah spilled over with half-contained energy. The way she walked, rangy and loose. People watched her wherever she went, a fact she never seemed to register. "Actually, I got a job."

"Really! Where?" The local newspaper, Quinn hoped.

"India."

Quinn dropped a tray of pastels, sending sticks of pigment skidding across the floor. She knelt to gather them and came up clutching gaudy fistfuls. "Why would you do that? Why would you go back there?"

"I'll be doing media work for a conservation NGO. Getting their story out. Fundraising. Whatever they need me to do." As if that were what Quinn had asked. "I'll be in Sawai Madhopur," Sarah added. "Ranthambore."

"Ranthambore," Quinn said. "Tigers?"

Sarah nodded.

"You always did love the big cats." Quinn recognized the expression on her sister's face: full of the future, in love with the next thing. It stung her that Sarah seemed perfectly content to remain a special guest star in the twins' lives. She didn't know how they idolized her, how they imagined her life the way some people imagined the lives of celebrities. "What the hell are you doing, Sarah?"

"I'm going where I'm needed."

"You think *we* don't need you?"

Sarah looked almost amused at that. She spread her arms to encompass the modest but lovely 1920s bungalow, the good husband making dinner downstairs, the two perfect children in the next room. The whole package: That was how it must look to her. "There's a crisis going on."

"There's always a crisis somewhere. Did you ever once think about getting a normal job like a normal person? Like, here in the States?"

"How are the States any more normal than the rest of the world?"

Quinn smacked the pastels onto her worktable. "You think I'm small, don't you? Living my small little life with my small little family while you're out there risking your life and saving the world."

Sarah laughed. "Come on, Quinnie."

The twins appeared in the doorway. "Auntie Sarah, are you going to go live in India?" Nick asked.

Sarah scooped him up in a hug. "I am!" she exclaimed, as if it were the best news in the world. "But not till January, so we still have three whole months together."

"How far away is India?"

"Do you have a world map? I'll show you." And the three of them disappeared into the twins' room until Pete called up to say dinner was ready.

At the table, the talk was all India. "Will you get to pet tigers?" Nick asked.

"If I petted a tiger, it would probably eat me for dinner."

"Whoa!" Alaina laughed through a mouthful of chicken. "Don't do that."

"I won't. I promise."

Pete said something about the guy he worked with from Bangalore at the tech start-up. Nobody mentioned the DeVaughan family history, or the years that would likely pass before the twins saw Sarah again. It was all just pleasant table talk.

After dinner, the children played with Sarah until Quinn sent them into Pete's office to say good night. He turned away from his monitor and scooped up Alaina, then Nick, for a hug and kiss. "Almost finished," he said to Quinn, turning back to his database as she ushered the twins from the room. When she and Sarah said good night at eleven, Pete was still clackety-clacking away at the keys. She went to bed and turned off the lights.

Later, she woke to the sound of Nick's coughing. Pete lay next to her. She hadn't heard him come in.

In the twins' room, light seeped in, dim and blue, around the edges of the blinds. On the nightstand, the digital clock read 2:15. She touched her son's cheek. "You okay, buddy?"

He nodded, covering a cough. She dosed him with the albuterol inhaler, waited, had him blow into the peak flow meter. Seventy percent, middle of the yellow zone. They sat up together on his bed, her back to the wall. Nick leaned against her, dozing between fits of coughing. She ran her hand over his silky hair.

"Mom?" he murmured.

She kissed his head. "Yeah, sweetie?"

"You grew up in India, didn't you?"

"Till I was eleven."

"What was it like?"

"Oh," she said. "Packed."

"You mean crowded?"

"Yes, but … more like being inside a great big kaleidoscope. Everywhere you looked, there were a million things to see. Beautiful bright colors. People. A million things going on all at once."

"Like that time we went to the carnival?"

"A lot like that."

Across the room, Alaina slept on her back, arms flung over her head.

Nick fell quiet, his forehead wrinkling as he tried to puzzle something out. "Mom? Are you Indian or American?"

"I'd say I'm American."

"What's Auntie Sarah?"

She smiled. "Auntie Sarah is a citizen of the world."

His readings stayed in the yellow zone. Just another interrupted night. At five o'clock, the meter showed 82 percent—back in the green—and he drifted into a sleep that held. Quinn slipped back to bed.

At seven, she pulled her blond curls into a messy ponytail and stumbled into the kitchen, where she found Sarah rummaging through cupboards, her duffel by the door. It was still dark out. The windows reflected back the overhead lights.

"In the freezer," Quinn said.

Sarah threw her a glance. "You okay? You look like hell." She pulled open the freezer, came up with a bag of Italian roast, and thumped the door shut.

"Nick was up coughing. He's still asleep."

"Sorry. I'll be quiet."

When the coffee finished brewing, they stood together cradling hot mugs of it, hips propped against the counter. It was a family trait, standing when other people would sit. "Hey," Quinn said. "I'm sorry about that thing I said yesterday."

Sarah glanced at her curiously. "Which thing?"

"About you thinking my life is small."

"I don't think it *is* small," Sarah said. "It fits you perfectly."

Quinn squeezed her gritty eyes shut. "God! Can you hear yourself?"

"Aw, Quinnie." Sarah set her mug on the counter and cuffed Quinn lightly on the shoulder. "We're different people. So what? I got a job I'm excited about. Can't you be happy for me? Just a teeny bit?" She held up her palms and peeked between them. "Pretty please? Just that much?"

Quinn laughed in spite of herself. It irked her. Sarah would do exactly as she pleased, so why did she want Quinn's blessing? It seemed greedy. Yet some tender spot inside her was grateful for the request. Sarah was not one to ask for things.

She considered her sister's laughing, hopeful expression. Sarah was so elusive to her, always had been: first because she was a twin, then because she was grieving, then because she was gone. "All right, you," she said, because what else could she say? "Do what you want. Go save those tigers."

Sarah grinned. "You're the best." She picked up her mug for a last gulp of coffee and set it in the sink. Then she gave Quinn a surprising kiss on the cheek, and she was gone.

SARAH

THE WATER BEARER was staring at her breasts.

For the five-hour train ride from Delhi on the Golden Temple Mail, Sarah had dressed modestly, as she always did when in transit: a purple-and-gold gypsy skirt, sturdy ankle boots, a short brown jacket over a white T-shirt woven thick enough to conceal any trace of her bra. Eleven years as an itinerant journalist had taught her never to overlook that last part. She was a traveler, not a tourist. But she was traveling alone, and wherever she went in the world—including this small, dusty platform at the railway station in Sawai Madhopur— certain men saw that fact as an opening.

"*Bhaiya*," she began, addressing the teenaged water bearer politely, "do you have a sister?" He pushed an overhang of hair off his pimply forehead and said he did. She asked in Hindi, "Do you like it when men stare at *her* breasts?" then collected her bags and walked away. She knew how to tell men off in twelve languages. In Hindi, the most direct way to say it was *Jao*, which meant simply, *Go away*. Her favorite was Italian: *Lasciami in pace, maiale*. It sounded beautiful rolling off the tongue. It meant: *Leave me alone, pig*.

She also knew how to say, "Wait—I have a condom." It had come in handy from time to time.

Sawai Madhopur. She'd been here when she was seven, with Marcus and Quinn and Mother and Daddy, visiting the Ranthambore tiger reserve. They'd made their way together down this very platform as a family, intact and squabbling amiably. Three months later, Marcus was dead.

And now here she was, a week into the futuristic-sounding year 2000, starting her life over in the land of her birth. So much had changed since she'd been here, and so little. India was as thoroughly, soaked-to-the-roots India as she remembered it, only with the addition, in certain quarters, of cell phones and the internet.

Quinn had surprised Sarah by giving her blessing, however reluctantly, for Sarah to come back here. Mother had tried to talk her out of it, relying on her usual bag of tricks: guilt, hurt feelings, icy withdrawal. Somehow, in Mother's twenty years as executive assistant to the head of a law firm, she had failed to acquire effective arguing skills. But Sarah had been traveling since she was twenty-two, and there was nothing to keep her in the States. She had business to attend to here, a new mission to replace her old career, even if it was only half-formed in her mind. Things would become clearer, she was sure, as she settled in and committed herself to one purpose, one dot on the global atlas.

Her suitcase wheel began to stutter. Glancing down at it, she nearly crashed into a man. She smiled a brief apology without making eye contact, but he said her name, a question, and she looked up into his face: a white man, older, so worn and grizzled that it took her a second to recognize him. "William Amesbury." She extended her hand and shook his warmly. She'd expected someone much younger, but of course she was picturing him as he'd been in his nature documentary days. "I'm a huge fan. I grew up on your films."

He said a few words of welcome and smiled briefly with half his mouth. Maybe he thought she'd just called him old. Or maybe something had happened to him, a stroke, an illness. It might explain why he hadn't made any new documentaries in the past half-dozen years, why he was now working in obscurity for a conservation NGO. The journalist in her wanted to ask. She filed away the questions: things to find out later.

From the railway station, William steered the silver Tata Sumo SUV over the viaduct, past low buildings and billboards, to a neighborhood of two- and three-story apartment complexes intermixed with small houses. He pulled up to a gate and parked. She would be living just above him in the block of flats. Her younger self couldn't have imagined she'd end up as William Amesbury's upstairs neighbor.

"Let's get you settled in," he said. "You must be ready to drop." But then the gate swung open, and a lanky woman in an elegant beige salwar kameez galloped to his door. Geeta Banerjee, the head of Tiger Survival: Sarah recognized her from the magazine articles she'd read while researching her new employer.

"Quickly. We must hurry." Geeta scrambled into the back seat. "There's been a tiger accident. A man dead."

A tiger accident. In the Indian vernacular, it meant a tiger had attacked a human.

"You're joking." William reversed onto the road. "Which village?"

"Vinyal."

"Sod's law." William navigated through an intersection, adding for Sarah's benefit, "It's one of the less welcoming, shall we say, of the district's villages."

"Do you mean violence?" she asked. "Or just the cold shoulder?"

Geeta glanced at Sarah. "Hard to say, given that we represent the interests of the killer." She didn't introduce herself.

The drive took them far out into the countryside, to a village of low whitewashed buildings scattered over a nearly treeless plain. A crowd had gathered in front of a mud-and-thatch house. Some of the villagers stared openly at Sarah as she approached, presumably because she was white, and a stranger. But for Geeta they stepped back.

So no violence, at least for the moment.

In front of the house, a woman knelt, keening, over the body of a thin man. A rag covered his face and a blanket draped his body, leaving visible his dust-cloaked bare feet. Three small children clung to the woman, crying, and a teenaged boy sat on the ground, staring at nothing, his oversized hands dangling between his knees. The tiger had eaten the man's buttock and thigh, judging from the bloodstained blanket. Sarah caught a glimpse of the man's throat: purpled but intact. The tiger had crushed his windpipe without breaking the skin.

A tall man in Western clothing approached. Sarah recognized him as Sanjay Prakash, the third Tiger Survival staffer. "I spoke with some of the men," he reported in a low voice. He glanced at Sarah, but again they didn't bother with introductions. "It's Sunil. The one we caught poisoning the water holes last dry season. He slept in his field last night as usual, to protect his crop from antelope and boar. When the other men woke to start a fire and boil water for tea, he didn't join them. His son found his body, dragged a little way from where he'd been sleeping."

Sarah glanced at the boy with the dangling hands and vacant stare.

"He was wearing a white *dhoti kurta*, sleeping on a white blanket," Sanjay said. "The tiger probably mistook him for a bullock. Ninety percent chance the tiger hadn't eaten in days. Otherwise, he wouldn't have been out here in the first place."

So the attack hadn't been the action of a surprised or threatened tiger, as Sarah had imagined, but of one who'd made a fundamental error in its choice of prey. Geeta and William exchanged a look. "One of the subadults from the Semli Valley," William ventured. "They're twenty months. Just the age when they start to disperse. They've no experience. No territory."

Except that now this tiger had discovered that humans made easy prey.

A murmur ran through the crowd as the widow began to speak. "She says the tiger who did this should be killed," Sanjay said. "Everyone comes to save the tiger, but who was there to save her husband? She says she and her children are as good as dead now, but no one cares."

How many times had Sarah documented some variation on this scene? Natural disaster, war—the cause didn't matter; the outcome was the same. It bothered her not to be scribbling down notes, shooting pictures. She didn't know what her role was in this situation, and she felt like a voyeur. She approached the smallest child, a girl of four or five, and crouched before her. *"Aap ke naam kya hai?"* Sarah asked gently. *What's your name?*

The girl snuffled. "Piya."

"Piya," Sarah murmured. "Good girl, Piya." The girl thrust both hands into Sarah's blond curls and stared, openmouthed, till her mother stepped forward to take her. Piya gazed back at Sarah over her mother's shoulder as they walked away.

"I'll talk to the sarpanch," Sanjay said.

"Tell him we'll do what we can to help," Geeta said. She nodded to William and Sarah. "Come on. We're going. I'll drive."

They rode in silence down the dirt track heading out of the village. Fields of yellow-flowering mustard stretched away on either side. Who knew what animals were sheltering in that chest-high crop. Ground squirrels, spotted owlets, herds of blackbuck antelope. A lone tiger, invisible.

"Poisoned the water holes. Bah," Geeta said. She glanced at Sarah in the rearview mirror. "The forest guards had to fill them in with a backhoe. God knows how many animals died of thirst." She grimaced. "So the man who tried to bag a tiger got bagged instead. I guess you could call that justice."

William shot her a look, and she raised her chin. "I'm sorry for his family," she said. "Truly, I am. Padma, his wife—obviously, she's distraught. She's in a terrible position. In theory, the government will compensate her for her loss, but it won't be much, if it comes through at all." She shook her head. "I promised her we'd do what we could.

But I cannot feel sorry there's one less poacher in the world."

"Geeta," William said reprovingly. It surprised Sarah to hear him use her name like that, no honorific, despite the fact that she was his boss. Maybe it was because he was British. An Indian would have called her "Geeta Ma'am," and Sarah, as her employee, intended to follow suit.

Geeta growled. "You're right. If anyone needs to be eaten, it's the bloody dealers, not the poor sods like Sunil who do the dirty work for the price of a secondhand motorbike. You think I'm joking about the dealers," she added for Sarah's benefit. "Do this work for a few years and see if you don't feel the same."

Sarah leaned forward between the seats. "What will happen to the tiger?"

"Officially, nothing, unless there's another attack on a human. It's called a 'tiger accident' for good cause. There's no reason to assume it will happen again." Geeta steered around a swaying camel cart piled high with firewood. "But the widow wants revenge. And God knows how many men in that village are listening to her say the tiger should die. And thinking how it could have been them instead of our friend Sunil."

She flicked the wipers to knock dust off the windshield. "Well. This was not quite the introductory meeting I'd planned." She sketched out Tiger Survival's mission. Protecting tigers mostly involved getting humans to leave them and their habitat alone. For the villagers, that meant reducing their dependence on the park's resources. William headed up lake-building efforts. Sanjay served as resident naturalist, educator, and jack-of-all-trades. He hailed from Sawai, so he had community connections and the trust of the villagers. He also served as translator; the dialects changed from village to village. "I'm afraid my role has become mainly administrative," Geeta said. "My most important task is to consult with Project Tiger officials in Delhi on matters of policy and with the police on anti-poaching efforts."

She didn't mention what Sarah had read about her in a

conservation magazine: that she'd been more or less born to the work. She came from a prominent Calcutta family, her father a well-known naturalist who'd spent his life advocating for tigers long before most people recognized their endangerment. After completing her education at Cambridge, Geeta had followed the same path. She was famously relentless in her work. She'd been called authoritarian, the interviewer noted. Authoritative, she'd countered. That exchange had made Sarah like her.

Now Geeta glanced over her shoulder. "Rules and regulations. We do not interfere with anything inside the park. If we stumble across a poacher setting a trap, we radio the forest guards. If we find a tiger in a trap, we radio the forest guards. If we see an animal in trouble in any manner that is not human inflicted, we leave it strictly alone. Nature is the boss inside the park, and what nature doesn't manage, the park director does. We have excellent relations with him, and this is how we keep those relations good. We respect his territory. We do not interfere. Understood?"

"Understood," Sarah said.

The road curved as it entered Sawai Madhopur, with its collection of low brick buildings and billboards. Geeta waved a hand. "You see the problem, of course."

"Population," William said. "And proximity to the park."

Sarah nodded. She'd read about the hordes of school groups and weekend sightseers, the tourist hotels, the villages drawing on the park for water and firewood and fodder grass. It added up to a ready-made disaster, and the park directors, along with nongovernmental agencies like their own, could hold it off for only so long. "It's the reality of our work, unfortunately," William said. "We all cope in our own ways."

"Stubbornness is a useful tool," Geeta said.

"As are a few sharp edges," William added. "And a touch of denial."

Geeta stopped in front of their building and killed the engine. "Well, Sarah. What else is there to say." She drummed her fingers on the steering wheel, frowning. "Ah, yes. Welcome to Sawai Madhopur."

•

Thirty hours of travel and then the tiger accident. Sarah lay in bed but couldn't sleep. A day like that deserved a wake of its own—drinks with friends and a chance to say, or not say, the obvious things: that being a poor man in rural India was a life-threatening occupation. That being a tiger trying to make a living in this decimated world was at least equally dangerous.

She fidgeted beneath the sheets, her arms on top of the covers. It was a habit she'd developed in her traveling years. No one had ever actually invaded her room at night, but you never knew, and if your arms were tucked in, you had no way to fight them off. She wondered if Geeta slept with her arms out. It seemed a pretty good bet that once or twice in her decades of conservation work, Geeta had found it necessary to run off some drunken bureaucrat who'd decided to pay her a visit in the middle of the night. Or maybe her upper-class status insulated her from behavior like that. Still, Sarah could picture storklike Geeta sticking her long neck out the door, peering down over her beaky nose at some weaving, hopeful suitor and flapping her bony arm to shoo him away so she could settle herself, with much folding of legs and rustling of nightgown, back into bed.

She got up and made a cup of tea. Sanjay had arrived at their building around dark to visit William. Sarah could hear their voices murmuring downstairs now. She wished William had invited her down, but maybe it wasn't going to be like that. Or maybe it would eventually, but not yet. These things were delicate. She couldn't just assume she'd be welcome in any conversation. In her reporter/photographer days, she'd never had to stare down an empty evening. They'd all gathered in the hotel bar at the end of the day and swapped stories over beer.

The temperature had dropped sharply since the sun went down. She dressed in jeans and a sweater, stepped outside, trod lightly on the wooden steps down to ground level, and looked around the courtyard for a place to sit. A bench stood empty on the front porch, between William's flat and the landlord's, but she didn't want to claim that spot till she got the lay of the land. Someone had left a low stack of bricks next to the courtyard wall: That would do. She sat, the cold instantly seeping through the denim of her jeans. Ivory light spilled from William's front window, and she could see the two of them in there, saying their goodbyes.

William's door creaked open, and Sanjay stepped through, laughing at some parting exchange, but the night air took his breath in a wordless exclamation as he closed the door. He hunched his shoulders and crossed the graveled courtyard toward her.

She said hello, and he jumped, not seeing her. She stood, apologizing, and he namaskared and introduced himself.

"I know who you are," she said, and she saw that her words startled him, as if she'd just announced she could read his thoughts. "I recognize you," she clarified. "From the village."

"So. Sarah DeVaughan." He recovered himself with a smile. His black hair shone in the buzzing streetlight. "What on earth makes you want to sit outside on such a cold night?"

She had embarrassed him just now. She thought she owed him an honest answer. "I'm seeking clarity."

"On a stack of bricks? I've never found it there, myself. Rats and snakes—now, that's a different story."

She took a hop-step away from the pile. "I've been wondering when it's going to hit, that's all. The fact that I'm here for the long haul."

"*Achchha,*" he said, a multipurpose word that meant *okay* or *I understand.* "You were a journalist. Always on the go." His breath clouded white.

"Exactly. And now I'm not." She liked him, found him familiar somehow. Maybe they had met before. Maybe when she was seven, when her family had visited the park.

They mounted the front steps to the porch, and though Sanjay left room for her on the wooden bench by the door, she chose instead to stand facing him, hips balanced on the porch railing. The streetlight threw her shadow across him. "What about you? Have you lived in Sawai all your life?"

"Oh, yes. I'm a mud hut—I'm made of this place; you can't move me. Actually, I did go to university in Mumbai and stayed on for a few years, working for the Bombay Natural History Society, but I came back first chance I got."

"The BNHS," she said, impressed. "You must have been at the top of your class."

He laughed. "Actually, I got my foot in the door there before university. I won an essay contest in senior secondary school. The prize was a spot at a summer conservation institute."

"So you're a writer."

"Not like you are. I'm a devotee of this park. That's why I left Mumbai. I couldn't stay away. And of course my family were here, but I would have come back regardless." He paused. "People say it's one of the most beautiful places on earth. We're taking you there tomorrow. You can tell me if you agree."

"I've been here before, actually. As a young girl."

"Really? Here? So Sawai called you back, too." He pronounced it *Savai*.

"Ranthambore did." She hesitated. "I have this recurring dream. I'm standing alone in a thick fog, and I don't know how to get out. That used to be the whole dream—I was just stuck. But a few months ago, a tiger appeared out of the fog."

"Very auspicious," Sanjay said. "Unless it wanted to eat you."

"No. It wanted me to follow it."

"And where did this tiger lead you?"

She spread her hands. "Here, I think."

He laughed. "Let me tell you. You must be Indian, to make such a big decision based on a dream. We're famous for that sort of nonsense."

"Really? Most of the Indians I know are very practical."

"Sixty percent. Maximum seventy. The rest wander about with their heads in the clouds."

"Then I guess I can stop seeking clarity," she said. "Looks like I've landed in the right place."

"No doubt about it. You're made for this country."

He smiled at her and stood to go. She watched him leave. *Had* they met before? In 1974, India had only just discovered that the tiger had all but vanished from the subcontinent, had only just begun establishing its network of tiger preserves. Her father had decided the family should go have a look. They'd ridden through the park in an open jeep beneath the forest canopy until they came upon a tigress resting in a grove of kulu trees, washing her face. To Sarah's eyes, she didn't look endangered at all. In fact, she seemed to be smiling and enjoying her bath. Her head moved in a graceful ellipse, tongue out to wet her wristbone, tongue in when her paw swept over her cheek and around her ear. Sarah wanted to sink her fingers into that soft, thick fur.

The tigress stopped her grooming, her paw halted in midair. She looked directly at Sarah and said, "Hello, you." Or not that, exactly. The message was languageless but definitely an acknowledgment. The tigress *saw* her, recognized that she existed: not prey, not competitor, just an odd creature passing through her territory—migratory perhaps.

Maybe there had been another jeep there, one with an Indian family in it, Sanjay a boy of ten or so. Or maybe the two of them had sat at adjacent tables on the hotel verandah, watching each other curiously, as children will do. Or maybe in another life. Who knew?

Or maybe she was making the whole thing up because he was good-looking and he clearly liked to play. Her favorite kind of man. She rested her chin in her hand and smiled, considering the possibilities.

The landlord's door creaked open, and a girl of fourteen or so stepped out. "Hello!" the girl said. "May I join you?"

"Of course! If you don't mind the cold."

"I'm bundled up." She nodded to the shawl wrapped around her shoulders. "I'm Drupti. I was hoping I'd have the chance to meet you. It's very exciting to have a new person in the building. Especially you."

"Why especially me?" Sarah asked. Drupti wore her hair in two long braids. Maybe she was sixteen. Hard to tell.

"Because you're living alone," Drupti said. "In India, it's terribly rare for a woman to be allowed to live alone. It seems quite glamorous."

Sarah laughed. "Nice to meet you, Drupti. You're in … school?" She didn't want to guess her age wrong.

"Yes, law school, in Jaipur. I'm home on holiday." She laughed at Sarah's reaction. "I'm twenty-one. It's hard for us to tell Westerners' ages, too."

Sarah smiled. "How old do you think I am?"

Drupti cocked her head and squinted. "Mmm … twenty-five?"

"Thirty-three."

"Close," Drupti said. "I'm glad you're here. We've been talking about nothing else for days. And tomorrow, William and Sanjay are taking you to the park, I think. Thin walls," she explained. "It's going to be terribly cold tomorrow; you'll have to wear your warmest clothes. And speaking of which, it really is freezing out here, isn't it? I think I'll go in, but I'm glad I got to meet you. Knock if you need anything; someone's always here." And she disappeared inside.

•

Sarah awoke before dawn to a chilly apartment. She dressed in her warmest clothes and carefully made her way down frost-slicked stairs to the courtyard, where Sanjay and William and their driver waited in an open jeep. The night was black, the air cold as iron, but her introduction to Ranthambore would proceed according to plan.

On the wind-whipped drive to the park, Sanjay pronounced the cold weather highly auspicious. "The animals will teach us something new today," he shouted to William and Sarah, who sat in the back seat, wrapped tight in buffalo plaid blankets, eyes watering from the assault of frigid air. The driver—a kind-faced, barrel-chested man named Hari—slowed the jeep only when they turned off the macadam of Ranthambore Road onto the dusty track into the park. The jeep shuddered and snorted white exhaust into the freezing predawn blackness. Around them, hills rose blacker than the sky.

The Aravalli Hills are the oldest in the world. So began a passage in a book Sarah had slipped into her pocket as she left her flat. Now she flipped to a dog-eared page and read as best she could by penlight on the bumpy road. *They, along with the Vindhya Mountains, form two spines that define Ranthambore. It is a place of dramatic terrain: cliffs where leopards prowl at dusk, vine-draped ravines where tigers raise their cubs, mirror lakes reflecting summer palaces and temples built a thousand years ago. The ground is dust and stone.*

She glanced up. They had entered thick woods, and on either side of the track, every leaf and twig to a height of three feet glowed ghostly in the headlights, as if the foliage had been doused in bleach. It was dust, she realized, that created the eerie effect: ordinary dust kicked up by every jeep that had passed that way since the last rain.

On the tawny hillsides, gnarled acacias claw against the landscape, failing to reach the sky. Dhok trees hunker sere and lifeless until the monsoon comes, and then their spindly branches unfurl leaves of transparent green, the first tree in the forest to wither in the heat, the first to revive in the rains. Near the stony nullahs, wild date palms scent the air, and flocks of rose-ringed parakeets pour, crying, across the sky.

She lowered the book. The wind had died, and the headlights caught a herd of spotted chital deer nibbling sparse grass beneath a fig tree. "My father taught me the concept of camouflage beneath that very tree," Sanjay said. "The chital were grazing just as they are now. The white spots on their backs looked like sunlight through leaves." He turned in his seat. "Please remember, Sarah. Even if you don't see a tiger today, you can be sure the tiger sees you." Half aphorism, half consolation, his breath puffing out in white clouds, preparing her for disappointment. But everything seemed a wonder to Sarah. The way the world smelled of ice, of living things pulled in tight. The way the forest creatures came awake when the sky began to gray in the east. Animals rustled and hooted and *krr-krrrr*ed.

The jeep rumbled out of the wood and crested a hill. Rajbagh Lake lay spread out below, its shining black surface exhaling streamers of white mist. In the dark, the water gave up nothing but the liquid reflection of headlights, though Sarah remembered it as a gem of a lake, ringed by reeds and ornamented on its far shore with a summer palace built a thousand years ago.

Crowning it all is the clifftop fortress, its millennial ramparts golden at sunrise and late in the day. In its thousand-year history, its seven gates have withstood innumerable sieges, their strategic placement at switchbacks in the steep path rendering them all but impervious to elephants and battering rams. In 1301, when the fortress was under the control of the Rajput king Hammir Singh, it came under siege by the sultan of Delhi, who managed to turn one of Singh's generals against him. Enticed by the promise of his own kingdom, the traitorous general accomplished from inside the stronghold what armies and elephants could not manage from below. In secret, he raised the orange flag, which the king had decreed was to be flown only in defeat. Seeing the coded sign that all was lost, the five thousand women and children of Ranthambore flung themselves into fire.

In the face of this catastrophe, the Rajput king lost all heart and surrendered to the sultan, though not before finding and killing the traitorous general. The execution was utterly insufficient as an act of revenge, but it was the only thing Hammir Singh had left to him.

Now the fortress belongs to the tiger.

Sarah closed the book. Sanjay murmured something to Hari, and they drove on, past a uniformed forest guard who sat on a rock near the lakeshore, peeling an apple with a pocketknife. The headlights caught him, and he pressed his palms together in a long-distance namaskar. Nothing about him suggested that he was afraid of being on foot in the tigers' domain, but even from a distance, Sarah could see that his face bore signs of an old injury: the nose misshapen, the cheekbone caved in.

"It happened last dry season," Sanjay said. "Herders. He and his partner caught them grazing their cattle illegally in the park's core area." He glanced back at Sarah. "He was the lucky one. His partner died from the beating."

Sarah had heard stories like this before. Too many people, too few resources, everything out of balance. The reason NGOs like Tiger Survival existed.

All around, bird chatter rose up amid the bustle of bodies moving in the trees, the blunt sound of feathers against air. Whoever thought the countryside was quiet had never been around birds in the morning. Sanjay identified their calls: white-bellied drongo, Asian paradise flycatcher, rufous-tailed shrike. Sarah sat back and listened, both to learn a few things and to enjoy the cadences of Sanjay's voice, the British cast of his vowels, the *v*'s instead of *w*'s: *jungle varbler.* "When I was a small boy," he said, "I thought the birds sang the stars to sleep. I don't know where I got that idea. My father, probably. He taught political science, but he was a naturalist at heart. He spoiled me for any other kind of work."

A peahen mewed. Night thinned to gray, and Sanjay gestured for Hari to wheel the jeep onto a track leading into the forest. A few dozen yards in, where blackness still held, Sanjay murmured, "*Bas,*" and Hari stopped in the middle of the road, killing the engine but leaving the headlights on to illuminate the track.

"Claw marks." Sanjay pointed to scratches in a tree trunk at the edge of the headlights' reach. "But he hasn't been here in three or four days. Maybe today he makes his rounds again."

Sarah and William exchanged a hopeful glance. She was curious about him. On film, William had always been the narrator. In person, he seemed contained and respectful of Sanjay's authority in the park. Humble, really, a trait she found surprising and rather endearing.

For forty minutes they waited in the biting air. Sanjay and Hari exchanged a few quiet words about Hari's children, then fell silent so as not to scare off the animals. The engine ticked intermittently as it cooled. Sarah thought the membranes inside her nose might freeze and shatter. For a time, she listened to the pressured pulsing in her ears to take her mind off her fingertips, burning with chill despite her gloves.

A hoopoe stalked across the road, its headdress of black-tipped feathers swaying. Sanjay handed Sarah his copy of *Birds of the Indian Subcontinent*. As she read the field guide by the red beam of her penlight, something shifted in the atmosphere to her right.

Without moving, she slid her eyes in that direction. And there he was: a tiger, standing alongside the jeep. She could have reached out and touched him.

In the gray half light, his body blended into the forest like a ghost. He turned his head and looked right into her eyes. Then he stepped past her into the headlights, and Sanjay whispered, "*Tigertigertiger!*" and the four of them rose to their feet. In the light, he was no ghost but a big, glossy male, long and lean, close enough that Sarah could see the individual hairs in his fiery orange coat. His breath turned to smoke as it hit the air. Without taking her eyes off the animal, Sarah raised her camera.

Something about the angle of the tiger's shoulder seemed eloquent, as if all his power and grace originated there. The backs of his black ears sported white spots that stared back like eyes, then disappeared as he flicked his ears backward to judge the jeep's proximity. He had registered their presence, that much was clear, but he had already measured them up and decided they weren't worth bothering about.

He sauntered down the middle of the track, unhurried but purposeful, stopping every few feet to spray his scent on a tree or bush. Twenty feet past the jeep, he reared up and placed his forepaws on a tree trunk, stretching easily six feet up. In profile, his eye glowed amber, as if lit from within. His tail swished the dust as he pulled his claws through the bark, which squealed and groaned under his mauling.

Hari started the engine, and the tiger turned his head, his eyes transforming into an unearthly electric green. He pulled his black lips into a demonic snarl, wrinkling the skin of his nose and cheeks. His long canines gleamed. Then he dropped silently to all fours and disappeared into the trees.

Sanjay turned to Sarah and grasped her hand in victory. "God is smiling on you," he said, and, in fact, so was Sanjay himself. "That was Akbar, the resident male. To see him in your first hour in the park—it's unheard of."

She beamed, crinkling the corners of her eyes. "I'm lucky." But she quickly closed her lips. It was too cold to keep one's teeth exposed for long.

Later that morning, back in her apartment, she thought about that moment. *God is smiling on you.* People didn't usually talk to her that way, but she liked that Sanjay did. Throughout the morning, he had seen everything and known what it meant. Not only did he spot pugmarks—paw prints—from a moving jeep, he could tell how old they were. If dewdrops had fallen into a pugmark from the trees, the track had been made before dawn. Three times, he heard noises that Sarah didn't even register. Once it was a tiger's far-off roar, barely more than a vibration in their chests. Sarah took a photo of him at that moment: one hand in the air for quiet, lips slightly parted, a searching look on his face.

In the bedroom, she peeled off her clothing, scattering whitish dust onto the tile in an irregular circle, like unbleached flour. It was too cold to shower, so she wiped herself down with a washcloth and dressed as quickly as she could. She figured it was maybe forty-five degrees Fahrenheit in her apartment. The tile floor didn't help matters. Still, she had a space heater and warm clothes, which put her in the privileged class. On the predawn drive to the park, they had passed a farmer wearing a thin *dhoti kurta* and a turban. He clutched a shawl around his shoulders, but his legs and feet were bare to the bitter cold. India was a hard place to live, a hard place to make anything change. A hard place to get past the tragic and the absurd.

She picked up her camera and flipped through the morning's shots. That tiger! She opened up her laptop and wrote up the encounter in an email to Quinn. She wrote one more paragraph, hesitated, deleted it, and pasted it back in:

> What hit me was not so much the majesty of the animal but the practicality of it all. For the first time, I understood the tiger as a creature with a job. His work this morning was to patrol his territory, the way a person might start the workday by catching up on email. For the first time in my adult life, I saw a tiger in the wild, and I found myself shocked to discover that he and I have something in common. That the tiger's untamed nature does not exempt him from routine and responsibility. That wildness and freedom are not the same thing.

This was not the way Sarah normally wrote. On assignment, she reported; she didn't interpret. Her editor, Hal, used to say, in the sardonic way of old-school newsmen, "If your mother says she loves you, check it out." What he meant was, take nothing at face value. Verify everything, and find a statistic or an official to quote. Do not compare your life to a tiger's.

But this tiger had looked straight into Sarah's eyes. The way she saw it, that eye contact gave her permission to write it any way she wanted.

She sent the message and moved to the front room, where she'd placed a few photos in a niche above the low madras plaid couch. A shot of her skydiving. A photo she'd taken of the boy soldiers after their surrender. A faded snapshot of Marcus and her leaping off the back of a sofa, knees bent, feet pedaling the air. They'd linked arms, both of their free arms flinging outward like wings, as if they were one flying creature with two backlit blond heads.

There must have been a reason she had lived and Marcus had died. They both went into the creek that day; they both came down with cholera. But maybe she was made of more resilient stuff, the same quality that had made her the older twin by ten minutes. Or maybe it was Sarah's fate to cause her brother's death. They lived in a houseful of adults plus one older sister, yet in the moment she had lured him outside, they had managed to slip beneath the notice of every single person charged with their care. The sheer unlikelihood of that achievement seemed to argue that its outcome was fated.

Or maybe the universe didn't make it its business to pay attention to naughty seven-year-olds, or to anyone else, for that matter. In her adult life, Sarah had seen plenty of evidence to support that hypothesis. In which case, the adults should have been paying vastly more attention.

She sat down on the low sofa with a pad of notepaper and began composing a classified ad to place in the *Times of India*.

IT WAS 1974, she wrote. WE WERE THREE AMERICAN CHILDREN. YOU WERE OUR AYAH.

QUINN

GO SAVE THOSE TIGERS, she'd told Sarah.

She should have begged her not to go back there. Especially not now, with Quinn's own twins the worrisome age of seven. It was inauspicious, Ayah would have said. A terrible idea.

Go save those tigers. What a coward she'd been.

Three days after Sarah left for India, Quinn checked her email and found a long letter waiting. A vivid description of a close-up tiger sighting, and then a surprising, thoughtful summation: *That the tiger's untamed nature does not exempt him from routine and responsibility. That wildness and freedom are not the same thing.*

Spoken like a woman in the act of contemplation. Like a woman finally settling down.

So maybe India was what Sarah needed after all. Maybe Quinn should be happy for Sarah to find her feet on the ground, even if she was half a planet away.

She spent the afternoon in her studio, working on a commissioned piece for the city's Olmsted Parks Conservancy. She'd chosen to paint a beech tree from a low perspective, looking up through a canopy of branches as would a picnicker, or a child. She wanted to evoke a feeling of steadfastness and protection, of being enfolded in strong, maternal arms.

Downstairs, Pete and the kids swirled into the house. The twins galloped upstairs and poured into her studio like a pack of puppies.

She hugged and kissed them, asked about their day, followed them into their bedroom, and plopped down on Alaina's bed. They piled on top of her for a snuggle. "Airplane ride!" Alaina shouted, and Quinn planted her feet under Alaina's stomach and lifted her into the air. Another year or two and they'd be too big for this. She set Alaina down and lifted Nick up. He made motor noises, and they grinned at each other.

Something about his coloring caught her eye. She set him down and peered into his face. And there it was: the white ring around his mouth.

He coughed.

"Go get your peak flow meter," she said.

"It was one cough."

"But your mouth. You're turning white."

The meter read 112 liters a minute: 80 percent of Nick's personal best, the boundary between his green and yellow zones. His next two tries didn't make it out of the yellow.

"Let's get you on the nebulizer," she said.

But Pete called up from the kitchen, and Nick turned and raced downstairs. "I'll do it after we eat."

"What's going on?" Pete asked from behind a cloud of white steam. He was draining a pot into the sink. Bad timing. The nebulizer took fifteen minutes.

"I don't like cold spaghetti," Nick announced. "Or reheated spaghetti, either."

"He blew eighty percent," Quinn said.

"Let him eat. He'll be done in ten minutes anyway."

Pete believed their children were safe, always had. He moved through life convinced that on any given day, they would live to see the sun go down and wake safe in their beds in the morning. Most days, Quinn tried to pretend she shared his conviction, if only in the hope that it would become self-fulfilling.

Alaina bounded into the steamy kitchen and declared herself

starving. The air hung rich with the aroma of tomato sauce. So, for the sake of convenience, and because 80 percent was borderline green, and because Quinn's magically secure husband had said everything would be all right, she said, "Fine. Let's eat."

They sat down to dinner, and Quinn ate in silence, willing everyone to finish quickly. But Nick only picked at his food, and in the space of ten minutes, the white ring around his mouth turned gray, and he began struggling for breath. Quinn ran upstairs to grab the albuterol inhaler while Pete had Nick blow into the peak flow meter again, and this time it showed 55 percent: five points from a medical emergency.

They buckled the kids into the car and sped to the ER—five minutes away, quicker just to go than call an ambulance. Nick coughed uncontrollably in the back seat as the skin at the hollow of his throat sucked in with every breath. When Alaina asked if he was okay, he couldn't answer. Quinn rode facing backward, staring into her son's pale, panicky face. The late-afternoon sunlight threw it all into high relief: the sweat beaded on his upper lip, the fear in his bulging eyes. At a red light he coughed so hard he vomited up what little food he'd eaten, spattering his shirt with bits of spaghetti and sauce. His eyes brimmed with tears, Alaina began shrieking about the vomit, and Quinn found a napkin and tried to wipe up the mess. The skin around his mouth turned blue, like the underside of a storm cloud, a blue more dreadful than she'd ever seen. When the light changed, Pete accelerated so fast the force threw them all backward.

At the ER, the admitting nurse ordered them straight back, and another nurse put Nick on a nebulizer and hooked him up to a hydrocortisone drip. With the mask covering his nose and mouth, Quinn couldn't monitor the color of that sullen blue ring, which was her son's body speaking directly to her eyes. She stood helpless, listening to him gasp, watching medicine escape the nebulizer with every racking cough.

The IV machine began beeping. Pete and Quinn locked eyes. "What's that?" Alaina asked.

Quinn's heart galloped past the implacable beep. No one came.

In the hallway, three nurses in blue scrubs stood at the station, singing "Happy Birthday" to the nurse at the desk. Quinn stormed up to them, her rage turning to sweat and tears as it hit the air. For a moment they looked at her stupidly. Then one of them sprinted to Nick's room, Quinn close behind. When they got there, the nurse said "Oh" in an ordinary voice. She pressed something on the IV machine, and the noise stopped. She turned to leave the room, but Quinn begged her to tell them what the beeping had been.

"Nothing," she said. "Just an indicator to add another medicine if we needed to, but we don't." Quinn wanted to weep. Her ignorance about how to save her son's life was total. Maybe fatal.

The adrenaline ebb left her muscles shaky-weak. The nebulizer hissed with Nick's breaths, a loud, white, comforting noise. His coughing had subsided. Over the mask, his pebbled eyes met hers, and she smiled at him. That blue ring around his mouth. She'd never seen anything more terrifying.

As a child, she'd asked Ayah why Krishna's skin was blue, and Ayah explained that someone had wanted Krishna dead when he was a baby. A demon assassin named Putana fed him poisoned milk from her own breast, and though Krishna survived, his skin turned chalky blue.

She pictured Nick at her breast, pink and healthy. Breathing in and out while he looked into her eyes with utter trust.

She ran her thumb down her son's pallid cheek. Its earlier hues of rose and apricot had drained away, leaving his skin the color of skim milk. A nasty, bruised purple arced underneath his eyes. But when the nebulizer stopped and she slipped the mask off his face, the blue ring had disappeared. Thank God.

And now came the part where they waited four hours to see

if the treatment held. Pete took Alaina home. Quinn stayed with Nick, her body aching in the hard plastic chair. Nick, keyed up on hydrocortisone, bounced his leg against the thin mattress as the fluorescents flickered and buzzed.

She stroked his arm. "Doing okay, buddy?"

His eyes went bright with tears. "Mom? I couldn't breathe."

"I know, babe. Can I get in there with you?" He scooted over, and she climbed into the bed and cuddled him close, thinking about Krishna. After the demon tried to poison him, he killed her in revenge.

Sometime after midnight, a resident with her hair in a bun showed up and unloosed a torrent of words at Quinn. She took notes, but nothing she wrote down held much comfort. *Just watch him*, she wrote. *Keep the emergency inhaler handy.*

In Delhi, when Sarah and Marcus had been babies in the house on Cornwallis Road, Ayah used to scatter salt in the corners of the nursery to protect them from ghosts. "Nothing but an old wives' tale," she told Quinn, "but why not? It's just a little salt. What can it hurt?"

So salt, maybe.

Mother's champagne-colored Lexus waited for them outside the hospital. Quinn buckled Nick into the back seat and slid into the front seat with Mother, whose face shone with night cream, her blond coif slightly disheveled. Quinn thanked her for coming to get them so late. There was no telling what payment Mother would exact for this favor later. Quinn would have called a taxi except for the likelihood of a chemical air freshener dangling from the rearview mirror. As it was, the car smelled lightly of roses and cold cream: a potential trigger she had forgotten to take into account. She looked worriedly into the back seat, but Nick sat wilted, eyes closed, breathing peacefully.

"Poor little fella," Mother said. "Did they say what caused it?"

Quinn shook her head, staring out at the black night as Mother pulled out of the hospital compound. "We told the doctor everything we could think of that he might have been exposed to. You know what she said? 'Sometimes you never do figure out what caused an attack.'" It had seemed cavalier to Quinn. Offensive.

"Could it have been your paints?"

"Nope," she said flatly and turned away to look out the side window.

At home, she carried Nick upstairs, put him in pajamas, and tucked him into bed. He never woke; nor did Alaina. She watched him most of the rest of the night from the twins' bedroom door. Pete got up at about four o'clock, took her by the shoulders, and steered her to bed. After thirty minutes of lying rigid with the effort of listening, she got up and dragged a pillow and blanket into the twins' room, where she fell asleep on the floor. A couple of hours later, a sunbeam touched her face, awakening her. Pete stepped out of their bedroom, looked at Quinn without speaking, and went downstairs.

In the kitchen, they barely made eye contact. Quinn surveyed the counter through a glaze of exhaustion. Pete had done most of the dishes but left the pasta pot unheeded. She scraped rubbery, candle-colored spaghetti into the garbage disposal and ran water into the saucepan to soak away red curls of dried tomato sauce. She poured a cup of coffee and stood staring into space. Pete fixed bowls of cereal. She ate half of hers, then went back to the twins' room and watched Nick breathe.

When she went back downstairs, Pete came into the kitchen and stood in front of her till she had no choice but to give him her gaze. Lavender tinged the skin under his eyes. He looked old. "I know you think this was my fault," he said.

She folded her arms beneath her ribs. Exhaustion had hollowed her out. "You couldn't have known he'd go downhill so fast."

"*You* knew," he said. "I know you did."

"Not really. I just had a bad feeling."

"Well, next time, insist, okay? Argue with me."

"When I argue with you, you tell me I'm overreacting."

"Next time I won't." The look on his tired face was all innocence.

•

When she was seven, Quinn had asked her father why he took care of poor people at his medical clinic. They were in the courtyard that fronted the house on Cornwallis Road, sitting on a wooden bench beneath the peepal tree, sharing an orange and spitting the seeds on the ground. "Because people need help," he told her, "and I can give it to them. I can't pretend they don't exist."

"Yes, you can," she said. "You can pretend anything."

They ate oranges as a ritual whenever they were available. "Never, ever eat an unwashed orange," Daddy admonished them dozens of times. "And never, ever eat an orange that's been washed with unboiled water." The cook boiled water regularly for drinking and kept stores of it in the pantry.

The oranges served as a survival mechanism. Every morning and evening, Delhi's air turned gray and prickly with woodsmoke from millions of cookfires. In the DeVaughans' neighborhood, it merely hazed the air, but elsewhere it got so thick, sometimes airplanes couldn't land.

Daddy held out an orange section but didn't release it. "You're right," he said. "We could look away from people's suffering. But that won't make it go away. Do you understand?" Only when she nodded did he let her have the fruit.

She had thought about his words afterward. Daddy couldn't look away, but Mother could. Every Sunday, she ushered the children up the church steps right past people with their hands out. And nearly every time they went out into the city, a painfully thin Indian woman would tap on the car window, gesturing to her baby's mouth to show their hunger. The children would clamor to help, but Mother vetoed them. "This country is overrun with poor people," she always said. "We can't help them all."

"We could help *this* one!" the children cried. But Mother had already ordered Ravindra to pull away. As the adult, she could just decide to leave, and *voilà*, they were on their way, beelining it to some other, less accusing place.

When Quinn was eight, Mother took the children on an overnight trip to watch the Taj Mahal transform from an ethereal predawn gray to glowing ivory when the sun came up. To the twins, at age five, it seemed plainly evident that before the first rays touched the Taj, it wasn't quite there. The sun made it solid. In the evenings, their guide told them, the marble turned pink, or sometimes gold. "Psychedelic," he added, this being the early 1970s. Quinn begged to stay all day and watch this magical building turn colors, but Mother said they'd have to come back another time.

In the car on the way back to the hotel, Mother entertained them with a rhyme: "Hogamus higamus, men are polygamous. Higamus hogamus, women monogamous."

"Did you make that up?" Quinn asked.

"Ha," Mother said. "It's old as the hills."

"Teach us," Sarah said, and Mother did, till the children could say the words perfectly, even if the finer points of the concept eluded them.

The next morning they took the train back to Delhi. On the railway platform, a tall, bone-thin man dressed in rags crawled past like a swimmer doing the freestyle in a shallow pool, his knees and elbows banging against the bottom with every stroke. The children were accustomed to seeing people who didn't move like they did—just the day before, they'd been sitting at a café when a man with no legs had walked past, using his hands and muscular arms as crutches, *plant plant swing, plant plant swing.* But this swimming man was painful to look at, flailing spastically across the concrete platform at incredible speed, like an injured spider. Sarah and Marcus gaped at him, though they knew better than to stare. Quinn watched him because she thought she owed it to him to imagine his suffering, even though she couldn't make it go away.

"Stop gawking." Mother's tone brooked no dissent. And so the children snapped their eyes forward and marched along behind the man Mother had hired to carry their luggage to the car.

Predictably, the incident piqued Sarah's curiosity. She'd always been interested in questions of why. Now she asked why the man had been walking on his elbows and knees, and why he had a spine deformity. Quinn followed her questions with interest. The answers depended on the person asked. Daddy: Probably the root cause lay in a vitamin deficiency in the mother's diet, followed by the lack of a simple surgical procedure when he was young. Mother: Because plenty of people in the world aren't as fortunate as we are. We're lucky to be Americans. Ayah: Because that man was unlucky. Most likely he did something evil in a previous life, and he's now suffering the consequences. But if he's virtuous in this life, then his next life will be better.

For weeks, when Quinn closed her eyes at night, she saw the elbows-and-knees man swimming on bent limbs, bone on concrete, his dark head dipping and rising. She included him in the prayers she had learned at First Presbyterian, though she knew it did no good. There were too many people in the world, too many poor and sick and suffering, and even at age eight she could see that God didn't take care of everyone. After a few weeks she stopped praying for him. She told herself that such a misfortune would never happen to a family like theirs. That kind of thing didn't happen to Brahmins, and it didn't happen to families who were white and rich with parents from America.

Of course, two years later, Marcus was dead, and a year after that, their family blew apart and landed on different continents. Daddy came to visit every couple of years until his car ran off the road during the monsoon, killing him. By then the girls were American, but that fact hadn't saved them from anything.

•

"Mommy?" Nick said. She opened her eyes. They were curled up together on the couch, his skin pink and pearly as the inside of a seashell. "We fell asleep."

She made chicken noodle soup and sliced a Granny Smith apple for lunch. Goldfish crackers. She sat down with the children and folded her hands under her chin to keep her head up.

•

The year of the cholera outbreak, Doordarshan India TV network had shown *Born Free* over and over. It riveted Sarah. She gazed into the lions' faces the way a baby gazes at its mother. When Joy Adamson crooned, "Elsa, Elsa," Sarah said it right along with her, her seven-year-old voice rich with love and heartbreak.

"You're too close to the TV, runny babbit," Mother said. "Scoot back."

The monsoon came, and the power flickered on and off every day, and sometimes the house went dark right in the middle of *Born Free*. Marcus pestered Sarah to go outside and play with him, rain or no rain. At least once, they did go outside together. Quinn knew because she saw them sneak back in.

Their parents had hosted a party the night before. From the nursery window, the children watched guests arrive, their cars gleaming in a steady rain. Partygoers disappeared through the front door, drivers around the side of the house to the kitchen, where the cook was preparing them dinner.

After the arrivals tapered off, the children slipped out of the nursery to watch the goings-on from between balusters on the staircase. Grown-ups filled the living and dining rooms and central foyer, women dressed in fashionable shifts, men in slacks and short-sleeved dress shirts, everyone chatting and sipping drinks. There were doctors and nurses from Daddy's clinic, tennis-playing ladies from the club. There was bald Mr. Chatterjee, who ran the international school, eyes magnified behind thick horn-rimmed glasses. Servants slipped unobtrusively through the rooms, collecting empty glasses and replenishing appetizer trays. Vikram, their housekeeper's son, had been assigned the role of disc jockey and stood proudly at his station by the credenza with the built-in record player.

Quinn had a ten-year-old's crush on Vikram. He was fourteen and cute and seemed to be concentrating hard, the tip of his tongue sticking out of his mouth as he pored over album covers: Aretha Franklin, Stevie Wonder, Paul McCartney, ABBA. The children danced on the staircase, Sarah and Marcus trying to knock each other down the stairs while doing the bump. Mother circulated, looking beautiful in her Pucci minidress with its swirls of pink and green. Daddy stood by the bar, talking with Dr. Rao and Dr. Upadhyay from the clinic and the young Irish nurse with the pixie cut, whose name the children couldn't pronounce. Mother and Daddy smiled and laughed with their friends but didn't talk to each other. There'd been raised voices in the master bedroom before the guests had arrived.

Gradually the sound of rain grew to an insistent hush, overpowering the voices and music in the house. Vikram turned up the volume and played "Rainy Days and Mondays," winning nods of appreciation for his cleverness. Egged on by the approval, he followed with "Who'll Stop the Rain" and then, in a moment of triumph, "It Never Rains in Southern California." Appreciative laughter swept the room. Partygoers clapped and danced and sang along. On the stairs, the children grinned into one another's bright faces and bellowed out the lyrics until the song finished and Mother emerged from the crowd on the arm of Pastor Mark from First Presbyterian.

She seemed unsteady on her feet. The pastor steered her to the staircase and sat her down. She spotted the children on the steps above her and shooed them back upstairs. A lock of blond hair partially hid her face, but when their eyes met, Quinn saw her mother's anguished expression and wet cheeks.

The next morning, Mother didn't appear at breakfast. The children ate with Ayah at the dining room table amid the dregs of the party. The house reeked of cigarette smoke. Vikram and his mother, Leela, moved in and out of the room collecting dirty dishes and paper napkins and colored toothpicks. After breakfast, Ayah sent the children to play in their rooms so the servants could finish cleaning up.

In her bedroom, Quinn rummaged for the book she was reading. Slowly she registered a sound coming from down the hall. Mother was crying.

Quinn tapped on her parents' bedroom door. No answer. She pushed open the door and peered inside. Mother lay in bed, disheveled, her cheeks streaked with last night's mascara.

"Why are you crying?"

"It's nothing, honey. Go back to your room." Tears clogged her voice.

"But why are you crying?"

"I had a fight with a friend." It sounded like a lie.

Quinn returned to her room as instructed just as Leela appeared at the top of the stairs, looking nervous. The servants did not fare well when Mother was upset. She didn't like being seen to cry, and inevitably she turned angry. Through her bedroom doorway, Quinn watched the flow of traffic in the hallway: first Leela, who entered the master bedroom only to flee ten seconds later with a look of alarm; then Vikram, clearly unhappy that he'd been charged with delivering a cup of tea. When he entered Mother's bedroom, she said something harsh. He emerged teacupless, looking shaken.

Quinn motioned him over. "What's going on?"

He shook his head. "Ma'am is really upset. She turned over a chair."

Quinn blanched. "She didn't throw it at you, did she?"

"No, no. It was upside down when I went in."

Mother yanked her door open and glared. Vikram disappeared down the stairs. Quinn ducked into her bedroom and pressed her ear to the door in time to hear quick footsteps descend the stairs. Mother's voice in the hallway, not loud, but focused to a sharp point. Someone else weeping. The back door thumping open and closed, open and closed. Then quiet.

Quinn padded down the hall to the nursery. A scuffle of footsteps told her Marcus and Sarah were hiding themselves behind the half-open door. Quinn knew they were there by the dull gleam of their eyes and the sound of their breathing. They watched her through the crack. She thought she should say something but didn't know what. She turned and left them there.

Downstairs in the library, she found her copy of *The Cricket in Times Square*. The cigarette smell was not so bad in here, and the room felt pleasant. Watery squares of sunlight fell onto the carpet through the tall windows overlooking the backyard. She settled into a chair and opened the book.

She didn't know how much time had passed when something brought her back—a noise, a sudden movement. When she looked up, there were the twins, tiptoeing past the doorway, soaked and covered in mud.

Later she couldn't reconstruct the logic behind her actions. She knew the twins had been somewhere forbidden, not just the courtyard but somewhere much worse and wilder, somewhere dangerous. A gully ran behind the house, dry and dusty most of the year, but running with filthy water during the monsoon. Even in the dry season, the children were absolutely forbidden from going there because bad men liked to roam such places, just waiting to snatch children. Quinn had always dismissed the warning about bad men, given that the gully lay within the walls of their property; even the waterway itself was fenced to keep intruders out. Still, dirty water was a terrible danger, and there was a cholera outbreak going on. They'd been in the gully, she felt sure of it; it was the only place on the property they could have gotten so muddy. They would be in extreme trouble as soon as the adults found out.

Even so, when she looked back, she couldn't fathom why she felt responsible for fixing the situation by herself, why she felt compelled to keep this transgression a secret even from the servants. Whatever her reasons, the sight of the twins jolted her into action. She caught them on the stairs, rushed them to the bathroom, and stared at the faucet. Ayah or another servant always ran their baths. But she had seen it done. She twisted the handle experimentally and watched, mesmerized, as water came gushing out of the faucet in a twisting silver stream.

It took her a minute to realize the level wasn't rising. She seized the rubber stopper and shoved it into the drain.

"Take off your clothes," she ordered, and, shockingly, the twins obeyed. Quinn read alarm in their faces. Her stomach hurt. One of the servants would come rushing in any minute to see what was going on, and Quinn would be in unimaginable trouble. How many times had she heard Ayah say, "It's my duty"? All the servants said it anytime they were thanked, and it wasn't just a way to say, "You're welcome." Duties belonged to one person only. You didn't step into someone else's territory.

Marcus dipped a finger into the water. "It's freezing," he complained, and Quinn's despair mounted. Hot water came from the kitchen, carried down the hall by a servant and dumped into the tub to mix with cold water from the faucet. Defeated, she twisted off the tap and rushed to the kitchen, skidded through the doorway, and pulled up short. The room was vacant. No cook. No Vikram. She'd never seen the kitchen empty. It looked fake, the silent appliances staged as if on a movie set.

She ran from room to room, calling for Ayah, ready to confess and beg for help. Any adult would do, even Mother. Quinn couldn't imagine her fury when she found out what was going on.

No one came. The twins yowled doleful complaints from the bathroom.

She ran back to the kitchen and stood before the stove, confronted by a confusing set of knobs. She'd never once bothered to figure out how they worked. Even if she'd wanted to, the cook would have shooed her away. With a sweaty hand she grasped a knob and twisted. A hiss, a smell of gas. A series of loud clicks that went on and on. The gas smell grew stronger.

She twisted the knob one way, then the other. A whoosh of blue flame made her jump back in terror. Her heart quieted as the fire settled into a steady ring. She adjusted the knob to its highest setting, filled a copper pot with water, and hoisted it out of the sink. Its weight shocked her. How did the cook manage to lift waterpots like they were nothing? She wrestled it onto the stove, soaking her shirtfront in the process.

After an eternity, the water reached a boil. She grasped the handle, screamed, and snatched her hand back as the vessel teetered at the edge of the stove. She grabbed a dishcloth and shoved the pot back onto the burner. When she held up her hand, a red stripe ran across the insides of her fingers.

She knew first aid. Cold water was what was needed. As long as she kept water running over her hand, the pain wasn't too bad.

"Hurry up!" Sarah yelled.

Quinn found pot holders and lugged the vessel down the hall, her arms shaking with its weight. The twins sat naked on the bathroom floor, wrapped in towels and playing with little plastic monkeys they must have retrieved from the nursery. They glared at her as she set the pot on the lip of the tub and tipped its contents out.

Sarah stuck her hand into the water. "It's still too cold."

Quinn tried not to cry.

Back in the kitchen, she filled three pots. She pulled a wobbly wooden chair to the stove and climbed up to maneuver the smallest saucepan to the back burner. Heat scorched her belly, and she realized she was leaning over an open flame. She startled and nearly fell off the chair.

She wanted Ayah, the cook, anyone. She didn't care if she got into trouble. While the pots heated, she sat down on the floor and cried.

Somehow she managed to lift the scalding vessels off the stove and haul them, sloshing, down the hall. It took all three containers to make the bathwater hot enough. She wiped sweat and tears from her face and ordered the twins into the tub, and they climbed in and hopped from foot to foot, howling that now it was *too* hot. She washed them as if they were two bundles of filthy laundry, scrubbing them with Lux till red streaks welted out all over their fronts and backs, prophesying how angry Mother and Daddy were going to be.

But when she dried them, she fell silent. In the nursery, she stepped back and watched as Ayah dressed them and bundled their dirty clothes.

This was the part that, later, she could never work out. When had Ayah come? How had she just appeared, silently, like a ghost materializing? It felt like a dream. No tears, no shouting, not even a moment of outcry when she discovered the catastrophe. Just— suddenly, almost inevitably—Ayah.

"You children," Ayah said, her voice frightened. "You must never, never sneak out of the house again. If I tell your parents how very-very bad you have been, they will smack your bottoms like you have never been smacked before. You won't know it was possible to hurt so much or cry so hard. Promise me, children."

Marcus and Sarah whimpered that they promised. Ayah turned to Quinn, her eyes searching. They both knew she was asking Quinn something different. "I promise," Quinn said.

Late that afternoon, Quinn came upon Mother standing at the

telephone table in the hallway, stroking the cradled black receiver with one finger as if she couldn't decide whether to place a call.

"Where did you go?" Quinn asked.

Mother looked at her. Even in the dim light of a monsoon afternoon, Quinn could see her eyes were puffy from crying. "Church," she said in a scratchy voice.

Two days later, the twins woke up fevered. Midmorning, Marcus leapt up from the dining room floor, where he'd been playing lethargically with his Matchbox cars, and ran into the bathroom. They heard him retch. Mother turned to Quinn. "Go check on Sarah," she ordered.

Quinn raced upstairs and found her sister in the bathroom, pants soaked. Footsteps thumped beside her, and Leela ordered Quinn aside, stripped off Sarah's filthy clothes, and sluiced her down under the bathtub faucet as Sarah wailed and shivered. Mother appeared at the doorway, took in the scene, and vanished. A minute later Quinn heard her on the phone. "I need to speak to Dr. DeVaughan. It's an emergency."

Within minutes, Mother and Ayah were bundling Sarah and Marcus into the car. Ayah and Quinn watched as Ravindra drove them away in the pale-yellow car, the twins visible as two little blond heads in the back seat, flanking their mother, her face white above them.

After the car disappeared, Ayah took Quinn's hand and led her down the hall to Ayah's own room, where she stayed some nights when it was too late for her to go home. "Take off your shoes," she said gently. In their sock feet, they stepped into the room, which Quinn had rarely entered before. It was simply furnished: a single bed with a white-painted iron frame, a tall dresser, a desk and chair. No decorations except two framed prints on the wall, a god and a goddess Quinn couldn't name. From the corner Ayah pulled a small prayer rug and unfurled it onto the floor. On the puja tray on her dresser top, she lit the diya lamp and a stick of incense and rang a small brass bell, causing the smoke to part and curl. She sank to her knees on the rug. "Come," she urged. "We're going to pray to Lakshmi to keep the little ones safe from disease."

Quinn knelt. "Do Sarah and Marcus have a disease?"

Ayah clasped Quinn's hand. "Pray with me."

Night had fallen by the time the car returned from the clinic. The headlights swept across the face of the house, illuminating the peepal tree, washing through Quinn's bedroom window. She and Ayah ran to the courtyard to meet them. Ayah whispered in Quinn's ear, "Remember, they must stay very, very quiet. Your duty is to be gentle with them."

They emerged from the car in slow motion: first Ravindra, from the driver's seat, moving as if underwater. He closed his door with a muted thump and opened the back-seat door, reached in, and emerged with the sleeping form of Sarah in his arms. As if an afterthought, he shifted Sarah to one side and held out his hand. Mother's white hand emerged like a hooded cobra from the dark interior. Her pale fingers gripped Ravindra's, and she stepped into the light, her face blank, hair in disarray. She moved toward the house as if her feet were not quite connecting with the earth.

Ravindra's arms were already full with Sarah, but Quinn thought he would reach into the car one more time. When he pushed the door shut, she felt a cold confusion, a dread she didn't understand. "Ravindra," Quinn called softly. "What about Marcus?"

And then she saw Ravindra was crying. And Ayah's hand tightened on her shoulder. And Mother glided past them like a ghost.

Cholera is a deceptive disease: easily curable with a simple rehydrating solution, if caught early enough, but capable all the same of killing in a matter of hours. Children especially. First the diarrhea and vomiting, then convulsions, then death. That was what had happened to Marcus. That was what had happened to their family.

Quinn still remembered the disbelief as Ayah and she clung to each other in the courtyard: that a thing so simple could have undone them.

It dawned on her gradually that this was what Mother had feared. All those times she had marched them along, eyes forward; all those prayers murmured in hard wooden pews; all the times she reminded them of their good fortune, she had been trying to protect them from the other India. She had realized all along what Quinn learned only as she stood in the courtyard that night: that their house on Cornwallis Road was such a small island, a speck, really, and all this time the other India had been a sea lapping at their shore, needing only the slightest rise in tide, the slightest ripple of wind, to rise up and bear them away.

SARAH

ACCORDING TO TALK IN THE VILLAGE, Sunil had injured his knee the day before the tiger found him. He could have asked for help climbing onto his sleeping platform that night, but instead he had spread his white blanket in the field and lain down on it wearing his white *dhoti kurta*. He'd chosen, in fact, to spend the night on the ground, looking—not that he would have realized it—like a slumbering bullock. A hungry young tiger had come along, and that was that.

Sanjay told this story to Sarah on a cold, sunny morning the week after the accident as they drove to the village to check in on Padma, Sunil's widow. According to the villagers, the entire sequence of events had happened because Sunil had taken to saying *bagh*, the Hindi word for *tiger*, aloud. That carelessness had attracted someone's attention (*someone* being the villagers' deliberately vague term for the tiger), and Someone had killed Sunil.

"Not the most forgiving worldview, is it?" Sarah said.

Sanjay moved his head in the distinctively Indian way, not quite a nod and not quite a shake. "When I was a boy, I used to wonder why tigers would ever hunt anything but humans." He steered carefully around an oxcart entering the road from a field of millet. "Most of us are completely distracted ninety percent of the time, regretting the past or worrying about the future. We would be the easiest prey in the world."

"Funny, isn't it," Sarah said. "Every religion I can think of would have us think we're higher than the animals, and yet look what we need to do to advance spiritually. Quit being so distracted. Be in the now. Be like the animals."

"Which itself is a bit simplistic," he said. "Animals plan. They remember; they strategize. I wonder if we like to think of them as living in the eternal now simply to convince ourselves we're different from them."

They rolled into the village, and Sanjay parked near a scrubby young tree—Sarah hadn't seen a tree in this village that *wasn't* scrubby and young—and a pack of children came running to meet the vehicle, calling out *"Ramram!"* When they saw Sarah, the shouts changed to "White lady! White lady!" and one of the girls asked, *"Aap ke nam kya hai?"*—*what's your name?* When she told them, the children pounced on the name like a new toy, confusing the sounds with delighted abandon as they buoyed their visitors like two corks to the tidily whitewashed home of the sarpanch, the village's leader. His wife was bent over a jug of water near the door. She straightened, drew her dupatta over her head, flapped the indigo-and-gold hem of her *lehenga* to shake off the dust, and offered a wide smile that included them both. Sanjay had advised Sarah that Vinyal women were generally easier to get along with than the men.

The sarpanch's wife greeted Sanjay, then glanced over at Sarah and asked a question in the local dialect.

"A new colleague," Sanjay said. Sarah had come on this visit partly to observe but mostly to become a familiar face to the villagers. She was certainly making an impression among the children, several of whom were petting her hair. One of the girls caught hold of a lock and gave it an experimental yank. Sarah returned the favor quickly but lightly, making the children laugh. A girl of six or seven in a red gingham dress offered her a shivering newborn goat to hold. Sarah took it, marveling at the heat pouring off the little body and the strength of its slamming heart. She wanted to say something but couldn't come up with the Hindi word for *goat*. Fortunately, she knew how to solve that problem. "*Kutta?*" she asked innocently—*dog?*

The children threw their heads back and roared with laughter. The sarpanch's wife gave Sanjay a sidelong glance.

"Come on now," Sanjay said. "She was making a joke."

Next the sarpanch's wife asked the inevitable question. "She wants to know where your husband is," Sanjay said to Sarah, not quite meeting her eye. No one at Tiger Survival had ever asked about her marital status.

"Tell her I'm traveling solo," Sarah said. But the woman smiled at Sarah and asked the question herself in the local language. For clarification she pointed to the red-dyed line at the part in her hair, then to her heavy silver bangles, the marks of a married woman. The girls craned their necks to see Sarah's response.

Sarah answered, "*Nehi*," and bore it like a soldier when the sarpanch's wife clucked her tongue in pity. "Don't feel sorry for me," Sarah said in Hindi. "I like it this way." The woman laughed, clearly both amused and unconvinced.

Sarah caught Sanjay's eye and gave him a private grin, an invitation to laugh with her, but he turned away. It caught her off guard. Maybe she'd been too friendly.

Earlier, on the drive to Vinyal, Sanjay had told Sarah the village originally existed on a beautiful site below the cliffs of Ranthambore, with an enormous banyan tree at its center and plentiful firewood, fodder grass, and water all around. The government had taken the land in the process of making Ranthambore into a national park and unceremoniously plopped the villagers down on this flat, treeless, all-but-riverless plain. True, the government had dug a well, paid what it thought was adequate compensation, and built sturdy houses on the new site. Still, it was the principle of the thing. And then the livestock ruined the ground cover, everything turned to dust, and resentment in Vinyal became about more than just principle. Things had improved five years ago when Tiger Survival built a lake, but even so, the sarpanch had little use for governmental agencies or NGOs. *Lots of promises, not much action* seemed to be his opinion.

"Unfortunately, he's not entirely wrong," Sanjay had told Sarah. "I'm forever tracking down the supervisor of thus-and-so who won't return my calls, filling out forms that turn out to be the wrong forms. You can't get a permit because you don't have an order form, but you can't get an order form without a pending permit. The bureaucracy is maddening. People think Indians are fatalistic. This is why."

The sarpanch stepped from the house just then, a small, grizzled man in white homespun. "Please, sit," he said, indicating a rough bench liberally spattered with crimson *paan* stains.

His wife disappeared inside and emerged a moment later with glass cups of tea for the three of them. Within seconds Sarah and Sanjay found themselves surrounded by several dozen men and children curious to know their business. Apparently, conversation qualified as a spectator sport. Sarah sipped her tea and did a quick assessment of the crowd over the rim of the glass. No girls over the age of ten or so.

The discussion took place half in the local dialect, half in Hindi. The sarpanch asked about government compensation for Sunil's widow. Ten thousand rupees, Sanjay told him, being processed now. Among the audience, the atmosphere shifted at the mention of money. Ten thousand rupees was about $450, and cash—like firewood, water, and every other resource with the notable exception of cow dung—was a scarce commodity in the village.

"But the money won't come," the sarpanch said. "It never does. And even if it did, eventually it runs out. Better if they offer her a job."

"I'll ask my contact if he can arrange something," Sanjay said. "Are the men wanting to kill the animal that did this?"

The sarpanch gave a noncommittal reply. Sanjay asked him to remind the men that the tiger controlled the population of boar and other crop-destroying animals.

"I think as long as there's not another accident, no one will do anything stupid," the sarpanch said.

Sanjay scanned the faces in the crowd. "*Achchha.*" He didn't look convinced. Sarah shot him a question with her eyes.

"The villagers have a lot of respect for the tiger," he told her in English. "Mostly they pray to Durga, the mother goddess, but they also pray to *him.*"

"But still they'll try to kill him if the price is right," Sarah said. "Like Sunil did, before he ended up on the other side of the equation." She knew that, in the villagers' orthodoxy, he had met with an enviable fate. A person killed by a tiger escaped the cycle of rebirth and became one with God. *Moksha* was the word for it. Nirvana. She wondered how the belief had arisen. Probably as most beliefs do, she decided: out of the need for comfort and a hedge against terror.

When she and Sanjay finished their visit with the sarpanch, a young boy led them toward the village well, down a wide dirt road where two white cows stood chewing cud, their horns painted blue. On the way, Sanjay said he felt sure there wouldn't be another accident. "In my fifteen years as a naturalist at Ranthambore, Sunil is only the second tiger accident victim," he said. "It's true that every year a body or two is found inside the park, and family members try to blame it on a tiger, but that's never the case. The rumor is that certain villagers know how to make a murder look like a tiger accident, although they would hardly need to. A day or two in the park, and the ants and vultures and jackals will dispense with ninety percent of the evidence."

Sarah raised an eyebrow. "How convenient for the murderer."

"The villages can be a little lawless," he said.

At the well, they found Padma, Sunil's widow, washing her youngest child, who stood shivering and clutching her wet clothes. They waited while Padma dried the girl and hefted her in her arms, all with the half-gone expression of the recently bereaved. When Sanjay offered condolences, she nodded dully, her eyes coming into focus only when he spoke of the compensation. Piya sucked her fingers and stared with serious eyes at Sarah, whom she seemed to remember.

"You're staying at your sister's?" Sanjay asked. "Everything going okay there?"

Padma moved her head in a way that could mean anything. Sarah surmised that *okay* might not be the right term when your husband was six days dead.

They walked with Padma to her sister's house. Piya stretched her arms toward Sarah. "She likes you," Padma said, handing her over.

"I like her, too," Sarah said. The little girl rested her chin on Sarah's shoulder and played quietly with her hair as they walked.

At the house, a silent moment passed as they considered the storage shed where Padma and her children were staying. A small patch of floor had been cleared out for their string cot and a few possessions; the rest of the shed was given over to a teetering pile of firewood, discarded odds and ends, and cow dung patties for burning. A junk slide in the making.

Sarah set Piya down. "Let's at least organize it a little," she said, wishing for a pair of thick gloves. This was going to be dirty, splintery, spidery work, but there was nothing to do about it except dive in. Padma's white sari, the traditional widows' garb, got filthy. Sarah muttered about snakes until she scratched her forearm on a piece of rusty barbed wire. She and Sanjay exchanged a glance. "Thank God for tetanus shots," she said. She pushed her sweaty hair out of her eyes with a filthy hand. This was definitely not journalism.

In an hour's time, they transformed the heap into something more like stacks, smaller and less wobbly: wooden things against one wall; plastics in the middle; rope and twine as the bookend. When they finished, they stood back and considered their handiwork. "Go, team," Sarah said brightly. She held up her hand to see if Sanjay would grasp it as he'd done on their first drive in the park, but he merely glanced at her and nodded.

Still, they'd done good work. You couldn't call it neat, but they'd lowered the junk heap's center of gravity to a presumably nonlethal level.

"Do you need anything else, Padma-ji?" Sanjay asked.

Padma stared at him and laughed in disbelief.

•

By Sarah's second week in India, it had become clear that Geeta had neglected to arrange a proper welcome dinner. William stepped into the breach with an invitation to dine with him. (She emailed Quinn: "My ten-year-old self is freaking out!")

When he opened the door, she stood grinning, a bottle of Kingfisher in each hand. "My mother told me never to show up empty-handed." She handed him the bottles and pulled off her shoes. They sat down to an expertly prepared dinner of rice, dal, saag paneer, chapatti, and small bowls of onion chutney. He poured the beer into glasses. "The last time I drank beer from a bottle," he said, "I swallowed a bee. It was rather an emergency. It stung me on the way down, and my throat swelled nearly shut."

"I can see where that would put you off bottles," she said. "If it happens again, I'll give you a tracheotomy with my Swiss army knife."

"You'd do that?" He sounded immensely pleased.

"Sure I would. One quick jab—you'd hardly even feel it."

The right side of his mouth curled into a smile. "Well," he said. "To the large-hearted gentleman. Cheers."

Sarah touched her glass to his. "To the large-hearted gentleman."

"Do you recognize that phrase?"

"Jim Corbett," she said. "I've got a 1944 first edition of *Man-Eaters of Kumaon* upstairs."

"*Do* you?" he asked. She was beginning to find his lopsided smile charming. "When I was a boy, I'd sit up beneath my sheets with a torch, reading it."

She found it lovely talking with William about Corbett's memoir, exchanging favorite tidbits of a tale they both knew. Too smart to be fearless (they agreed), Corbett was nonetheless extraordinarily brave. Tall and lanky, dressed in khaki hunting garb and accompanied by his faithful beagle, Robin, he tracked man-eating tigers into box canyons in the Himalayan foothills, following trails of bloodied clothing and human body parts, knowing every moment that the beast he stalked may have been stalking him. Yet he harbored an abiding respect for the tiger, even before his transformation from hunter to conservationist.

Sarah raised her glass and quoted her favorite passage from the memoir: "'The tiger is a large-hearted gentleman with boundless courage and … when he is exterminated—as exterminated he will be unless public opinion rallies to his support—India will be the poorer, having lost the finest of her fauna.'"

They touched glasses again. "To Jim Corbett," William said.

"To Jim Corbett." Sarah set down her glass. "So, I've been wondering. How did you end up here, working for Tiger Survival?" She scooped up a bit of dal and watched him consider his answer.

"The short version is that I'd been filming lions in the Okavango Delta and I came down with malaria. I spent eight weeks in hospital. I ended up in a coma and pretty far down the road into organ failure. The doctors didn't expect me to live." He paused. "And then I rallied. No one can say why."

She made a sympathetic sound. She supposed that explained his facial paralysis.

"I stayed on in Botswana for a time with a friend, a man named Taft who runs a big-cat rescue operation. Geeta suggested I come to India to finish recovering."

"So you knew her before you came here."

"Indeed I did. We were married once," he said dryly, surprising her. Her research hadn't uncovered the fact of their marriage, but she supposed it explained his familiar form of address. "We met when we were both living in Kenya. We moved in the same circles. After we divorced, we kept in touch through the years. When she offered me this position, she told me my primary qualification was that I knew how to build a lake." He smiled. "My first in India was at Vinyal, actually."

"That must have been satisfying work," she said.

"Less so than you might think," he said. "You would have thought the villagers would welcome it—the women spent half their days hauling water—but the men would sit and watch us, paring their fingernails with enormous knives and offering unhelpful commentary. We'd come to work in the mornings to find the track hoe and excavator had been stripped overnight. Bolts, nuts, any little part they could pry off to sell for liquor money. We'd show up for work, and they'd watch to see if we could figure out what they'd done. Usually we did, and dealt with it, but occasionally not, and then the equipment would break down and the tribesmen would laugh all the harder. In the end I had to hire armed guards."

"Talk about working against their own interests," Sarah said. "The wives, at least, must have been on your side."

"The married men would have left us alone, I think. It was the younger men doing the damage."

"Isn't that always the way?"

"Here, pass me your glass." He filled it with the last of the beer. "You know, you're quite a curious person, Sarah DeVaughan."

"Curious nosy or curious odd?"

"Nosy's a harsh word." He set the glass down. "As for the latter, I don't know you well enough to draw that conclusion, do I?"

She smiled. "Guilty as charged on the nosiness front."

"Not a bad quality in a journalist."

"When I was little," she said, "four or five, I had this assumption that I'd get to switch bodies with people every so often. I thought that was how the world worked." She paused. "I also thought I would eventually learn everything there was to know."

"Must have been a nasty shock to find out otherwise."

"I was outraged," she said. "Stuck being one person forever."

"One must admit it's a flawed system," he said. "I like your way better. I'd rather fancy being a cheetah for a day. Or a black-shouldered kite. Were animals part of your scheme?"

"Oh, absolutely. I was four, remember." She ran a piece of chapatti around her plate. "I still want to know what life is like for other people. Like Hari, for instance. I can't figure him out."

"He doesn't have much English."

"But he doesn't say much in Hindi, either."

"He does if you get him going on birds. He says it's mad to go driving about stalking the elusive tiger when there are beautiful birds to be seen everywhere you look." He sat back and looked at her curiously. "So why not still be a journalist, if you're so keen on understanding people?"

So he could give as good as he got. She liked that. "I spent ten years telling stories about wars and environmental disasters. In the end, I felt I wasn't really doing much good. As a journalist you're not supposed to influence the story or get involved. You must have faced the same thing with your films, surely?"

He considered it. "Yes and no. My films were opinion pieces, really. Built on the belief that wildlife and wild places are worth saving."

"You made a believer out of me," she said. "Young girl grows up on nature documentaries, becomes itinerant journalist. Those two things are not unrelated." She said it casually, her glass halfway to her lips, but she meant it as a gift. Though, come to think of it, she'd probably just made him feel shockingly old. "I do feel a little guilty for giving up on journalism," she added. "I'm a believer, always have been. I've always thought the journalist's job was to keep the citizens informed, and the citizens' job was to hold the politicians accountable. But now I've decided, for essentially personal reasons, to bow out."

"You feel you're shirking your duty, is that it?"

She let go an exasperated sigh. "The entire news industry is shirking its duty. No one's bothering to do real journalism anymore. Twenty-four-hour news cycle, fragmentation of the audience, blah blah blah. *You* know."

"But here you are instead. Cutting out the middleman, aren't you? Working to influence the policymakers directly. One could consider that the opposite of bowing out."

She thought about it. "When I was little, my father ran a medical clinic in Delhi. When I got older, I looked down on his work because his vision seemed so narrow. I mean, the problems are just so huge. One little clinic. A drop in the bucket."

"The trenches are a muddy place," he acknowledged. "It's hard to accept that everything one can do will always be too little. But eventually one must engage in life regardless. It ends, you know."

"So I've heard," she said. "And here I am. And here you are, too."

"Different path. But the same outcome, yes."

"Do you miss filmmaking?" she asked.

"Not the technical bits. But I do rather miss storytelling, I suppose."

After dinner they moved to the front room, where a plastic mask of a staring, stylized human face hung on the wall. She stopped to examine it, and William took it from its hook and handed it to her as they settled onto the couch. "Do you know about these masks?"

"I've heard of them," she said. "But tell me the story. Please. It would be such a treat for me."

He reddened a bit, looking pleased. "Well, then." He settled back into his seat, crossed his legs at the ankle, and rested his hands comfortably in his lap, just as he'd done in the studio shots in his documentaries. "The man-eating tiger is generally a sorry specimen," he began in that William Amesbury tone. Sarah pulled her knees up and clasped them to her chest. Daddy used to call them into the living room when one of William's documentaries came on—"Kids! Come watch!"—and they would pile into the room and plop down on the floor.

"The rare tiger that turns to human prey does so when injury or age leaves him too decrepit to hunt, or when the population of natural prey disappears. Generally speaking, man-eating is the last resort of a tiger who has run out of options. But that generality does not hold true in the Sundarbans, the vast river delta that stretches between India and Bangladesh. There, the tiger is rather more casual about the matter. As far as anyone can tell, he simply prefers the taste of human flesh."

Sarah smiled. "You've told this story before."

William twinkled his eyes at her and continued his recitation. "The five hundred tigers that live in the delta kill dozens of people every year, according to official counts, but those counts are known to be grossly underreported. Most of the men fishing the channels and gathering honey in the mangrove forests don't bother to buy permits to do so, and when a man dies while making a living illegally, his survivors rarely want that fact brought to the government's attention. Sundarbans tigers kill the unlicensed by the hundreds every year, a fact that presumably speaks not to a preference for lawbreakers but simply to their vastly higher numbers." He paused. "Some say it's the salinity of the water that drives the tigers' aggression. Some say their tastes develop around the steady supply of human corpses that float down the rivers that empty into the delta. Others say the reason is simply that man-eating always goes unpunished in the Sundarbans. You might spot a tiger as he swims from island to island; you might watch him heave himself onto the muddy shore. But three steps into the mangrove forest, and the tiger vanishes."

Sarah shivered, making William smile.

"From within the forest, he waits for the honey gatherers to come. The tiger watches from his hiding place as a group of men enters the forest, single file on narrow trails. When the time is right, the tiger attacks, always from behind. The last man in line falls victim.

"After many years of attacks, someone puzzled out that the tiger attacks only when no one in the group is looking his way. What the men needed was a set of eyes on the backs of their heads. This was in the 1980s, and it was a simple matter of manufacturing." He gestured to the mask. "Ivory faces with staring eyes, a red mouth, viperous fangs—all topped off by a silent movie–villain mustache. The honey gatherers began wearing the masks on the backs of their heads when they went into the forest. The tigers still stalked the men, but the masks stymied them. The humans had learned to face in both directions at once."

She clapped. "Well told! Oh, well told, William."

He inclined his head in a modest bow. "You're kind to indulge an old man," he said. "You know, the masks were hugely successful at first, but they never stopped the tigers altogether. A Sundarbans tiger will stalk someone wearing one of these faces for up to eight hours. And should the man remove the mask, even for a second—"

"The tiger strikes."

"Precisely."

She turned the mask, studying it. "I keep thinking about what happened to Sunil." The fear he must have felt as the tiger's jaws closed around his throat. Suffocation: not the quickest of deaths, and surely one of the most terrifying.

"Survival is a harsh business," William said. "Ruthless and impersonal. But it's astonishing, really, the fact that no organic matter ever goes unused. Perfect, in a sense."

She cocked her head at him and smiled. He was beginning to remind her of her father.

Later, when she went upstairs, she thought about their conversation. Was she engaging in life more or less, now that she had quit journalism? Day-to-day engagement felt a little anticlimactic.

Visiting villages, writing press releases, making phone calls. She wouldn't see the results of her work with anything like the regularity of journalism. In her previous life, her work appeared in the world with her name attached. Sometimes her stories and photos had an effect, and sometimes they didn't. And sometimes she learned the end of the story, but mostly she didn't.

Like the boy soldiers. They were brothers, eleven or twelve years old, who'd been made the heads of a revolutionary force. For reasons Sarah didn't understand, their followers had revered them, quite literally, as gods. Then the revolution failed. Sarah covered the story up to the point when the boys surrendered. They got starved out of their hideout and came down the mountain crawling with lice, at which point people decided maybe they weren't divine after all. Sarah wanted to know what happened to them—boys who'd been taught so much violence, who'd been granted godhood and then demoted. Did somebody take them in? Were they sold into slavery? Killed? She thought it would make an important story. But the rest of the world didn't care, or so her editor said. Nobody had the attention span anymore. Hotel checkout was at noon, he added.

"You don't have to be an ass about it, Hal," she'd said.

"Don't let yourself get soft, DeVaughan," he told her. "That's how people get killed."

She had let herself mourn while she packed, for the boys and for what she saw coming for her career. She didn't know another way to live. Then she zipped her suitcase shut, splashed water on her face, and told herself to pull it together. At five till noon, she checked out of her room. She took a tuk-tuk to the airport, boarded her plane, and left. Another goodbye to a continent beginning with the letter A. Another departure at 600 miles an hour.

She never did find out what happened to those boys.

QUINN

MOTHER HAD ALWAYS BEEN BEAUTIFUL. When Quinn was small, Westerners who met Mother said she looked like Princess Grace. There *was* something regal about her, the way she commanded a houseful of servants. The way she shopped for clothes, furniture, textiles, whatever she wanted to surround herself with: She would sweep through shops, identifying objects of desire with a graceful gesture, and the merchants would box them up beautifully and send them home with her, the spoils of an afternoon's outing.

She never gave up the shopping habit. Not after the divorce, not after the move back to the States, where her American dollars didn't have the buying power they'd had in India. Not after the bankruptcy from which Quinn and Pete had helped rescue her. Over the years, the stresses had worn at her. To Quinn's eyes, Mother looked now as Grace Kelly might have looked if she'd lived into her sixties, if she'd lost a child and blamed the cook, her husband, a teeming subcontinent. Her Serene Highness, minus the serenity.

Her shopping tracked with her anxiety levels. Shortly after Sarah left for India, Mother presented Quinn with two beautiful little coats she'd bought for the twins, navy for Nick and powder blue for Alaina.

They were at lunch at Lilly's, an upscale bistro on Bardstown Road, seated in a booth at the window. A light snow fell outside. Quinn thanked her mother uneasily. "It's too generous," she said.

"You bought them all sorts of stuff at Christmas. And they don't have anywhere to wear clothes like this."

Mother ignored her protests. When their lunches arrived, she surveyed what Quinn had ordered—soup and salad—and appeared to approve. "Do you remember when you were four and the twins were babies? You told me once that if you ate enough, you could have a twin. You were so jealous of them. You shouldn't have been. You were the best baby. Smiley and happy and beautiful with those big blue eyes and rosy cheeks."

"I couldn't help being jealous," Quinn said. "You were obsessed with them." Mother had watched the twins like a scientist, parsing their similarities (she deemed them both highly intelligent) and their differences (Sarah was the busy investigator, Marcus the contemplative observer).

At seven, Quinn had begun to grow so quickly it made her knees hurt. Ayah told her that she must be made of dough like a chapatti, and that the cook was coming to her room at night to stretch her taller. The idea scared Quinn rigid. Then she stopped growing taller and started growing thicker. Mother knelt in front of her, slim and elegant, and stuck a worried finger into the waistband of Quinn's pants. After that it was carrot sticks and cauliflower. The cook made a joyless version of masala chai with watered-down milk. At dinner one evening, Quinn reached for a slice of white bread and stuffed it into her mouth, and Mother looked away, her upper lip recoiling.

"What do you hear from Sarah?" Mother asked as a server refilled her tea.

"She said the Jogi Mahal is closed to visitors now because it's inside the park. You remember that place? The hotel where we stayed when we went to Ranthambore?"

"Beautiful building." Mother slid her fork into her quiche. "Do you remember that enormous banyan tree beside it?"

"Second-largest banyan in India. I never did find out where the largest one is."

"Calcutta, I think."

It surprised Quinn that Mother had retained these facts; she never spoke about India, and even in America, she'd never been one for nature. Mother set down her fork. "Did I tell you? I picked up an espresso machine."

Quinn arched her eyebrows.

Mother gave her a glare. "Look, it's been difficult for me with Sarah moving back to India. I buy myself nice things because that's what you have to do when you're alone."

Down that path lay bankruptcy, and they both knew it. "Why did you ever agree to go there? With Daddy, I mean?"

The question must have caught Mother by surprise. Her expression softened. "He was a doctor. When you're young, you think that means certain things." She laughed a little. "It all seemed so romantic. India. I thought I was signing up for something out of Kipling. You can't imagine the misconceptions I had. I thought I was going to be Mrs. Doctor, the mistress of the manor."

"You *were* the mistress of the manor. And you hated it."

"But I loved the idea. It sounded so sophisticated, being part of an expat community. I didn't even know what *expat* meant when I first heard it. I had to look it up."

They finished lunch over conversation about the kids. When the check came, Mother was powdering her nose. "You don't mind getting that, do you, darling?"

•

The twins woke Quinn and Pete the next morning, boinging up and down on their bed and demanding to go sledding. Bright snow topped the bare maple limbs outside their window and blindfolded the cars down in the street. Five inches, maybe six, from the look of it. Pete and Quinn exchanged a look.

It wasn't that they were fighting, exactly—more that there was a conversation waiting that they hadn't managed to have. Since the asthma attack that had sent Nick to the ER, Quinn felt on high alert all the time. She felt Pete watching her watch Nick, but when she turned to him, he couldn't quite meet her eye. It was as if only so much gaze were allowed in the family, and she was spending it all on Nick.

The development surprised her. The day she and Pete had learned the sexes of the twins, she had cried in the doctor's office parking lot. Pete listened closely as she haltingly explained how the news felt like a punishment, a reminder of her grief. The way he comforted her then seemed like a promise that when parenting the twins became too raw, he would understand the source of her hurt, would help her through the hard parts.

But now they couldn't talk about what was happening.

Pete started on toast and eggs while Quinn helped Nick with his peak flow readings—safely in the green zone—and got him going with his breathing treatment. Sledding: She didn't know. The exercise and the cold air could trigger him. But snow didn't last long in Louisville, and she didn't want to cheat her son out of a rare treat. She started a video of silly animal tricks and left him sitting on the living room floor while she went upstairs to help Alaina put her hair up. Alaina greeted Quinn at the bathroom door, chanting, "Snow day! Snow day!"

"Not exactly. It's a *snowy* day, but not a snow day."

"Why?"

Quinn sat on the edge of the tub and gathered her daughter's white-blond curls into a thick ponytail. "Because it's Saturday," she said. "A snow day is when you get to stay home from school or work because of snow."

"Humph," Alaina said. "It's snowy outside, and as far as I'm concerned, that makes it a snow day."

Quinn smiled at the joy that radiated from this pink-cheeked girl. Happy morning sounds floated up from downstairs: Pete clanging the skillet on the stove, Nick laughing at his video. "Must be pretty funny," Alaina said.

Quinn stopped brushing and listened to Nick giggle. "Stay here a minute." She hustled downstairs. Nick sat cross-legged, snorting in glee.

"Hey." She kept a smile in her voice. "Careful, Nickypants. You're messing up your treatment."

"Play it back." He giggled. White vapor escaped around the edges of the nebulizer mask.

She turned off the video. "Nick. Honey. You can't talk during a treatment. And I'm really sorry, but you can't laugh, either, not so hard that the medicine escapes. You want to play outside today, don't you?"

His shoulders slumped inside his orange T-shirt, and he gave her a wounded look over the mask. She hadn't meant it as a threat, but she could hear how it sounded. "It's okay, kiddo." She ruffled his hair. "We just need to get that medicine into you, that's all." She checked the mask's green elastic strap, gave his shoulder a squeeze, and started for the stairs.

Pete called to her from the kitchen. She backtracked and joined him at the stove.

He nodded toward Nick. "What's going on?"

"I don't know what to think," she said. "I don't know how much medicine escaped."

They stared at each other, doubtful. Nick had averaged an attack every five days since the night of the ER. "Cold weather's never triggered him," Pete ventured. "Snow'll be gone by tomorrow."

She hesitated.

"If we keep him inside, he'll think we're punishing him for the asthma," Pete said.

"Or for messing up his treatment," she said. "God, I hate this."

"By the way, I saw those boxes. What happened? I thought you weren't going to let your mother spend money on the kids like that."

"Listen, I tried," she said. "I told her she shouldn't have bought that stuff. She said it was too late to return it."

"It's always too late for her not to spend money. She paints you into a corner every time."

"Yeah," Quinn said. "And then she stuck me with lunch."

"Don't let her walk all over you, Quinn."

They'd had this discussion half a dozen times before; they both knew its contours. A familiar argument to delay, at least momentarily, a decision about Nick.

In the end, they decided to chance it. On the sledding hill at Cherokee Park, Quinn watched the skin around her son's mouth for signs of the white ring. She didn't want to think about the color he'd turned on the way to the hospital. Asthma blue.

A shock of cold slid down the back of her neck, and Alaina leapt away, giggling. "Come play, Mommy!"

Quinn chased her, careful not to get too far from Nick. She rode three times with each of the twins on the red plastic sled, handing off the inhaler to Pete to keep it close to their son. Pete was doing pretty well with this level of protectiveness, though it chafed at him, she could tell. He'd come from hearty stock, outdoorsy types who saw good health as the inevitable reward for their natural gusto.

"Warming up out here," he said as she rolled off the sled with Alaina. In the cold sunshine, his cheeks glowed red, and a drop of moisture glinted under his nose. They held eye contact for a few seconds.

"This is working, right?" she said. "I think this is good."

"It *is* good. He's doing great. Aren't you, Nick?" He called out that last part.

"What?" Nick called back from a few yards away, where he knelt, packing snowballs.

"You're a sport," Pete said.

"What's a sport?"

"It's what you are. You're up for what's happening. C'mon, let's get in one more run."

Quinn reached into her pocket. "Here." She pressed the inhaler into Pete's gloved hand.

SARAH

SHE FELT HERSELF GROWING RESTLESS. No bylines, no publications was one thing, but what was she even *doing*? Writing grants and press releases. Observing. Pitching in here and there in ways that didn't add up to much. A couple of times, she'd caught herself thinking that maybe she should call Hal. She was here, after all; why not do some stories? Make a little extra money, do something with a definable endpoint and an outcome she could hold in her hands?

She resisted the impulse. If she started down that path, she might not come back. Still, she kept up her journaling after their drives through the park, partly out of habit, partly because she might yet decide to try publishing something.

January 16, 2000

To any creature traveling through it, the grassland is another sort of forest. But what it lacks in view, it makes up for in scent and motion. Whiffs of dust and mice and sun-toasted grains. The movement of insects and snakes and, overhead, in the swaying seed heads, the lighting and taking off of tiny birds. Viewed from above, the passage of a larger animal through the grass creates an unmistakable wake.

When the creator of that wake, a tigress, steps from the tall grass onto the lakeshore, her arrival causes a stir. Tigers are the celebrities of their world, hounded by chital, sambar, wild boar—every variety of prey species, gawking and shrieking like overwrought fans. This morning, it's a troop of langur monkeys sounding a harsh alarm: Ow! Ow! And so, as usual, the whole gossiping forest knows a tiger is on the move.

The tigress—the forest guards have dubbed her Machli—makes her way around the shoreline, past water birds drawing silvery ripples in the lake's black surface. She selects a hiding spot in a stand of grass and settles in.

The sky lightens, and the forest comes fully awake. The sun breaks in a brilliant burst, and suddenly the world pops upright, or so it appears: Every tuft of grass, every pebble gains a long, crisp shadow. The monkeys move off. Machli creeps backward farther into the grass, moving in increments of millimeters. Like all tigers, she possesses a genius for imperceptible movement.

An hour past dawn, a herd of sambar deer approaches. According to Sanjay, these are the tigers' best prey: large, plentiful, and slightly lackadaisical in matters of their own survival. Sambar will ignore the alarm calls of chital and langurs, skittish creatures who'll raise a fuss about a jackal or dhole. It might be a case of species-wide overconfidence: Sambar know they're steely beasts, formidable of antler and sharp of hoof. Or maybe it's just stupidity.

The herd passes by the tigress's hiding place. She waits, motionless, till the last doe steps past. Then she charges.

A shriek of alarm calls goes up. The water explodes as sambar leap into the lake. The doe bolts. Machli gains on her, gallops alongside. With the swipe of one massive paw, she knocks the deer to her knees, and in an instant the tigress has the creature's *throat in her teeth, crushing. The doe falls. Only when the legs stop kicking and the body goes limp does Machli release her grip.*

She opens the haunch, buries her face in glistening flesh, and pulls at the connective tissue. When a tree pie ventures too close, she raises her bloodied head and snarls the bird away. After her meal, she drags what remains into thick cover to protect it from the vultures already surrounding her. If she can keep them at bay, Sanjay says, she'll dine off this carcass for three or four days.

Well fed, she drinks, then stretches out on the open lakeshore to let the sun warm her distended belly. Across the lake, the sambar graze placidly, fully aware of her but less wary now that the danger has passed.

We watch this scene, totally absorbed until a moment comes when we all realize we're hungry. We spread our picnic on the hood of the jeep and eat breakfast, observing through binoculars as Machli licks blood from her fur.

"She made it look easy," I say.

"You're a good luck charm once again," Sanjay tells me. "You've brought Machli a kill."

Is he patronizing me? I can't tell. "Happy to help," I say, but I wonder if he notices I'm a little annoyed.

She began accompanying Sanjay on school visits. Not that that amounted to doing something, but at least she was learning how Tiger Survival did its work. Sanjay opened every session with a slide presentation, saying nothing. "I want them to think about conservation," he told her, "but first they need to feel."

Here was a photo of Akbar, the big male Sarah had seen her first day in the park. He was running, his massive forelimbs reaching, his topline a long, beautiful curve. Next, a fresh pugmark in soft dirt. Akbar's regal head in profile. And a video clip of a tigress at rest in dappled sunlight, the tip of her tail thumping the ground contentedly. Sarah watched from the back of the room.

"'When you see a tiger, it is always like a dream,'" Sanjay said, looking at the screen. "The zoologist Ullas Karanth spoke those words." He turned to the children. "A hundred years ago, one hundred thousand tigers roamed all across Asia, from Siberia to Java, from China to the Caspian Sea. And how many wild tigers do you suppose there are now?"

He clicked to a photo of a construction site, captioned Encroachment. When humans moved into an area, wild lands disappeared, falling to agriculture (*click*: a mustard field) or urban sprawl (*click*: new housing). Humans poached prey species, leaving the tiger little to eat. Land development cut off natural corridors for dispersing tigers, stranding populations in disconnected patches of wilderness (*click*: aerial photo) that became genetic islands.

Click: a warehouse of stacked tiger bones and severed heads. Caption: Poaching. Gasps and shouts from the children.

"The legacy of Mao Tse-tung," Sanjay said. "Perpetrator of genocide against the tiger in the sixties and seventies. He paid for their carcasses."

The children's eyes popped at this news.

"Mao's anti-tiger policy has wiped the South China tiger off the face of the earth, except for the tiniest remnant population—thirty individuals at last count and sure to die out completely. Meanwhile Mao stockpiled the body parts of thousands of tigers for medicinal use: tiger-bone powder for pain relief, tiger brains for acne and laziness, whiskers for toothaches."

He refrained from mentioning tiger-penis soup for virility, Sarah noted, or that the Sanskrit word for *tiger* was *viagra*.

"In the 1980s, Mao's stockpiles ran out, and suddenly poaching became a crisis in India. In the early 1990s, fully half the tiger population of Ranthambore was wiped out. Half," Sanjay said. "Imagine it. And now there are only about three thousand left in the wild, anywhere in the world."

A little girl in glasses raised her hand and asked whether the tiger was doomed to go extinct in the wild.

"That is up to you," he said. "The only way the tiger will survive is if the government creates tiger-friendly laws and enforces them to the maximum. It is up to the citizens to demand that they do. The future of the tiger belongs to you. You are citizens of the largest democracy in the world. You must demand that your rightful inheritance be preserved."

"Nicely done," Sarah said on the drive back to the office.

"It's one of my favorite parts of the job," he said. "I love their idealism. I love that it's my duty to bring them hope, whether or not I can find it in my own heart."

They exchanged a smile, but then he grew silent and formal, as if he suddenly regretted their conversation. It irritated her.

"Why did you say that thing yesterday?" she asked.

He glanced at her. "What thing?"

"About me being a good-luck charm. In what scenario does my presence help Machli take down a sambar doe?"

He looked at her quizzically. "I just meant that the odds are against it. A tiger only gets a kill in something like one in every twenty hunting attempts. So Machli had good luck on that try, and we were lucky to see it. Just like we were lucky to see Akbar your first day in the park."

She wasn't sure that explanation quite answered her question, but she wasn't going to argue the point. "You're really great with kids," she ventured.

"They're my favorite kind of people."

"Do you have any of your own?" she asked.

He merely shook his head, which meant he wasn't telling the truth or he just wanted her to quit prying. Fair enough. She'd find out some other way.

She asked if they could stop by the post office. Eighteen letters this time. She could feel Sanjay's curiosity, but he didn't ask, and she offered nothing. She tucked them in her messenger bag to open at home that evening.

When she'd placed the classified ad, she hadn't considered the confusion and disappointment that would come of weeding through the responses. All were off base ("I was ayah to four children of a British family"); many told tales of tragedy ("since you left, my husband has died, and also all three of my children, and I am too crippled from arthritis to work"). Some asked for money. Sarah had supplied her own first name in the ad, but no last name and no mention of Quinn and Marcus. At the very least, Ayah would be able to give her that.

At home, she sat crossed-legged on the low sofa. One story she had never told anyone. It had happened during the liminal months after she'd decided to leave journalism and before she'd found Tiger Survival. Finishing up her journalistic fieldwork, she'd come to be a little scared of herself. *I'm not really here*, she'd thought more than once, *and I'm going to get somebody killed*.

On a hot, humid morning during her last assignment—it was in Panama—she took half a day and drove alone to a wildlife rescue center. The woman who ran it claimed she had some kind of mystical connection to the animals. Sarah had heard she had a tiger.

The woman wasn't what Sarah had expected. Brown skin wrinkled like a withered apple, white hair, about four and a half feet tall. They came to an enclosure where a beautiful young tigress, rescued from a traveling circus, lay submerged to the shoulders in a metal water trough. Flies buzzed around her eyes. She seemed at peace with her lot.

The woman asked Sarah in Spanish if she wanted to go inside.

"This one's special," she said. "You can touch her."

The tigress gazed in their direction, then looked away. Like all cats, she didn't traffic much in eye contact.

There could be no excuse for what Sarah did next. She couldn't call it immersion journalism. She couldn't call it journalism at all, just pure stupidity, the act of a woman who has lost her grip on her life. She walked into an enclosure with a tigress, thinking, Maybe this changes my life. Maybe her story would end here, in a ramshackle rescue center deep in the Panamanian jungle. Maybe that was okay.

She tried to unthink that thought. She cupped her palm around the occipital protuberance at the back of the animal's head. The tigress allowed Sarah's touch as if she knew something about her. Her hand fit that head so perfectly it made her ache.

She could just imagine how that story would go over with Geeta.

The letters lay spread out on a carved end table. Each time she opened a new batch, it surprised her how thoroughly the task drained her. She set to it with a sigh, using her finger as a letter opener.

Nothing. Nothing but an empty place that remained empty.

She could do more, of course. She could hire a private investigator, put her own reporting skills to use. But she wanted to let this play out. She had put the thing in motion. Now it was up to the universe.

•

On their days off work, William, Sarah, and Sanjay began riding in the park with a British film crew. They'd met the crew one night at the Ranthambore Regency, a gathering spot for locals who worked in conservation and ecotourism. The film crew respected Sanjay's skills as a naturalist and subtly fawned over William as an elder statesman. Sarah knew they considered her unnecessary until someone noticed they had better luck spotting tigers when she rode along—one tiger in particular. After his appearance on Sarah's first day, Akbar had apparently decided he liked the visibility. Seeing Akbar was nearly routine for Sarah—though William and Sanjay felt compelled to emphasize, each time he appeared, how unusual it really was. "He's developed a crush on you, Sarah," William joked. She shrugged modestly, but she had to admit she felt rather jaunty about the whole thing. Whatever the attraction, the film crew were happy to capitalize on it. They took hours of footage. They talked about Akbar as if they'd discovered a handsome farm boy and were about to make him a *filmi* hero.

Sarah watched Sanjay from her usual spot in the back of the jeep. He didn't have children; she'd confirmed this with William. She and William had shared a laugh with their eyes when she'd inquired. The perks of being a journalist: If you want to know something, you just ask.

February arrived. With the warmer weather, flame-of-the-forest trees burst out with scarlet flowers, painting whole valleys in brilliant swaths. Babies abounded: a litter of porcupines waddling after their mother; a newborn chital fawn practicing the delicate art of walking on long, wobbly legs. Rajbagh Lake whistled with the peeps of ducklings. One gorgeous spring morning, Sanjay spotted Machli crouching in the grass, stalking chital. Sarah raised her field glasses for her first close-up view of the tigress. Machli was particularly beautiful, she realized, with markings on her cheeks like chrysanthemum petals and a slender necklace of black that came to a point on her white chest. But her ribs stood out sharply. "She seems thin," she said.

"It's a good sign," Sanjay said. "My guess is she's nursing a litter."

"Ah, good for you, Machli," William said, with sorrow in his voice. "Her last litter didn't make it through the drought."

Sanjay lowered his field glasses. "We won't see these new cubs for a few weeks. At this age, they're easy prey for predators. Machli will keep them hidden while she hunts, and they'll stay totally silent while she's gone, unless they get hungry and cry." He paused. "It's high pressure for the mother, but otherwise these early weeks are the easy part, because she only has to hunt for herself. When the cubs start eating meat, she needs to bring in more prey, and her job gets much more difficult."

William cleared his throat. "Well. The film crew's got to be thrilled about this development. A litter of cubs provides a built-in storyline one way or the other."

Their forays through the park turned up no sign of the cubs from the Semli Valley, the ones William had mentioned the day Sunil was killed. Their absence might have meant they had dispersed. If so, they had entered the most dangerous time of their lives. Their options were limited: They could spend the next few years skulking around the park trying to avoid the resident male till they were big enough to take him on, or they could leave and try to make a living out in the prey-poor, dangerous world.

Sarah thought of Sunil, mistaken for a bullock. And of the stories Sanjay had told her of the tigers who strayed outside the park, who ended up getting hit by cars or starving to death. There simply wasn't enough food to sustain an animal so large. The previous year, a Ranthambore subadult had been found alongside some railroad tracks, 200 kilometers to the south. The autopsy had found his stomach empty but for three crickets.

•

May 3, 2000

Machli's twin daughters are about ten weeks old the first time we see them. They're no bigger than housecats, all bright eyes and stripes. She has started leading them on walks through her territory. They follow her on shaky legs, heads bobbling as they hurry to keep up. This is a classroom experience, Sanjay says. She's teaching them their world.

The weather is growing hotter by the day. Green things are burning up. Lake levels are dropping, ringing the water with mud flats that dry and break into flakes, and rivers have started to disappear entirely. Prey animals are hewing more closely to the water holes, which makes for easier kills, maybe, but poorer ones as the animals lose condition.

Machli leads her children one afternoon into a shaded glen and lies down to rest. Despite the heat, the cubs clamber over her, their hunting instincts coming into play. One hides behind Machli's head while the other flattens her ears to stalk and pounce. A swatting match ensues. Within minutes they collapse into a pile between their mother's paws and fall instantly asleep.

In the jeep we're congratulating one another on the terrific sighting when suddenly Machli senses something. She gets to her feet and stands at attention, sending the cubs to hide beneath a bush. She calls out: aaooongggh. And Akbar steps into the clearing!

They rub their heads together and turn toward the streambed. Machli summons her children, and the four of them pick their way over the dry stones of the nullah till they arrive at a muddy pool. The adults back into the water to keep drops from splashing into their eyes. The babies bound in, heedless.

The cubs keep their distance at first from Akbar, but soon the bolder one can't resist. There is a meeting of noses, and the big male chuffs deep in his throat. The cub pats her father's shoulder with her big front paws and leaps away.

Sanjay says he's never seen them together before. But he expects they'll keep up this routine as the rainy season approaches.

He asked me whether I should get credit for the sighting. I laughed and said, "Why not? I'll take it."

•

The month of June was nearly intolerable in Rajasthan. The heat refused to relent, even at night. The markets reeked of sweat and rotting food. Dust invaded every crevice, down to the faint lines at the base of Sarah's wrists.

All throughout Sawai, people carried on the same conversation. They watched the sky, talked about it, smelled the air for rain and choked on dust instead. Individually they came to realize that other people had grown stupider and more annoying. Sanjay criticized Sarah one day for yawning, and she snapped at him.

Signs of the monsoon appeared early that year. In the first week of June, clouds began to gather in the late afternoon and paced across the sky all night, obliterating the stars in restless swirls. Mornings dawned low and overcast, though by nine o'clock the gray burned off, and the rest of the day shone bright and hard as nickel.

For two weeks, the waxing moon backlit the wandering clouds, brighter each night. Thunder rumbled intermittently, far off but growing nearer, and Sarah stood listening in her doorway and thought, Come *on* already.

On the day of the full moon, the skies opened.

They were in the park when it happened, passing beneath a banyan and thus half-sheltered from the sudden downpour. Sarah held out her hands, palms up, elated to be there when the first fat drops fell through the canopy, rattling the brittle forest like a dry seed pod. The stones released their scent, and the long-dead leaves. The rain began to pelt, and for a few minutes the world seemed strangely biblical to Sarah: heaven hurling itself to earth, kicking up a furious layer of dust that mushroomed to knee height before warm, wet drops knocked it back down. Runnels gathered and coursed in thin streams topped with dust until the soil drank them in.

"Tomorrow the whole forest will be lit up lime green," Sanjay said. He nodded toward a spindly, leafless tree that Sarah had assumed was dead. "All the dhok trees will send out tiny leaves overnight. If there's sun tomorrow, they'll glow like stained glass."

Sarah studied the tree with new respect, imagining the awakening already at play beneath its dark, wet bark.

·

The rains settled in. Sarah awoke one morning to a day dark as twilight. Water poured over the eaves in sheets. A steady drip taptapped through her kitchen ceiling. She put a pan underneath it. In the front room, she picked up her copy of *Man-Eaters of Kumaon*. The cover felt cool and soft in her hand, the pages fatter than they should. Her books were swelling up.

As a child, she had hated the monsoon. She knew nothing of the way the natural world sprang to life outside the cities; to her, it meant only muddy streets and the smell of mildew advancing inexorably from curtains to carpets to the very sheets of her bed. It marooned them indoors and left them to die of boredom, maddened by neardaily power outages. Paint peeled off the walls, the bathroom ceiling turned pink with mold, and they fought, Quinn and Marcus and Sarah. They tormented one another, trying to shed their own itchy frustration by thrusting it like a dead badger into someone else's hands.

Something changed in the sound of the drip. She returned to the kitchen to discover the ceiling was bubbling. A blister of water bigger than her hand had already started to spread tentacles in three directions. There was only one thing to do: plunge a knife into the blister. Rob had taught her that trick, maybe the one useful thing to emerge from their brief marriage. The idea shocked her at the time, but he'd been right. A gouge-hole in a water-soaked ceiling is an ugly thing, but if you don't lance the boil, it spreads, creating far worse damage. She took up a kitchen knife, climbed onto the wicker seat of her least wobbly chair, and thrust. The blade hit something solid just behind the plaster surface. Bricks, she thought. She pulled it out and tried again. No luck. She changed her grip on the knife and drew it, scalpel-like, through the diameter of the blister. A cascade of milky water gushed out, splattering her hand, her face, the pan, the floor.

This was what she remembered about having cholera—the way liquid poured out of her in every imaginable way. It came out in uncontrollable shit so thin she mistook it for pee. It came out in vomit, sweat, tears, in snot dripping from her nose as she cried. Quinn found her in the bathroom and cried out for Ayah. But it was Leela, the housekeeper, who ran panicked into the room, ordered Quinn out, stripped off Sarah's filthy pants, and sluiced her down in the tub. Sarah was freezing, the water made her colder, and even in the tub she couldn't control the gush of liquid from her body. She cried and cried, humiliated. Mother appeared, her expression fierce, and Sarah braced for a tongue-lashing. "Wrap her in blankets," Mother ordered instead, and then Sarah and Marcus and their mother were in the car, Sarah clutching a bucket and vomiting clear liquid into it. There was nothing to do about the diarrhea except let it soak the blankets. The air in the car took on a fishy odor. Ravindra rolled down his window.

On the other side of Mother, Marcus slept. Sarah thought Mother had brought him along to keep her company.

The journey seemed never-ending. Flooded-out roads and broken concrete sent them doubling back. When at last they reached Daddy's clinic, the Irish nurse with the pixie cut stuck a needle in the back of Sarah's hand to drip fluids into her through a clear plastic line. "Don't you even," Mother said to the nurse, and Sarah wanted to ask, *Don't you even what?* but she was too busy examining the needle with horror. Mother had to stop her from tearing the bandage from her hand. Daddy stood over Sarah, stern-faced, asking question after question.

"Did you eat any fruit without washing it? Did you drink

unboiled milk? Did you go outside? Sarah! Were you and Marcus playing in the gully?"

"We were in the house," she said. Her words slurred and puddled. Mother sat on the bed next to her, frantically petting Sarah's hair and muttering: "The cook. The cook. The cook didn't wash the vegetables."

"What about before? Anytime in the last few days?"

Sarah looked up into her father's face, etched like a cartoon version of an angry man: forehead nothing but furrows, mouth a thin line. His eyes looked capable of shooting flames. "No," she lied. She leaned forward to vomit. A bucket appeared from somewhere, but nothing came out other than a stream of saliva.

"Did anyone give you anything to eat that you aren't sure was properly cleaned?"

She couldn't even follow that question.

He listened to her heart and took her pulse, and Sarah vaguely knew Marcus lay in the next bed. But she never heard a sound out of him, never heard him vomit, nothing, until the commotion started. Marcus's headboard began banging the wall, soft jerky sounds as if he were fighting an enemy in his sleep. Daddy dropped Sarah's wrist and leapt to Marcus's side, shouting for a tongue blade. For a moment Sarah saw Marcus's thin body jerking as the nurse pulled his head back and slid the wooden blade into his mouth. And then people began pouring into the room, and Mother flew from Sarah's side, and even though Marcus was the one in trouble, suddenly Sarah found herself surrounded by strangers wearing masks, all talking loud and fast, and her bed was moving and someone was running behind holding up the bag of fluid and they were taking her away.

She cried out for Mother and Daddy, but the strangers rolled her out of the room and parked her bed on the other side of the wall, where she could see nothing but hear everything. The smell of fish settled over her again. Daddy gave order after order to the nurses, and Mother begged, "Marcus! Marcus!" And then her begging turned to wails, filled with his name. Sarah sat up, gripping the bed rails, crying, "Daddy? Daddy?" but for a long time no one came.

At last he stepped out of the room, pulling his stethoscope from around his neck. His body sagged. He rested his forehead against the wall.

"Daddy?" Sarah asked through tears.

He turned to her. She'd never seen his face so bleak. And then a nurse on the other side of the ward called out, "Doctor!" sharp and urgent. He stood up straight and took two long strides down the hall, and then he was running.

QUINN

NICK HAD WEATHERED THE TRIP to the sledding hill unharmed. The day's casualty, instead, had been Pete's tolerance for caution. The success of the outing had been enough to convince him that everything was fine, and his gestures toward vigilance lost their sincerity as winter gave way to spring and then full summer. He thought he was humoring Quinn; she could see that, and the new dynamic eroded her confidence. He'd begun saying things she wouldn't want to admit to her friends. He knew women, he said, who let their kids play outside and didn't stand watch over them. He admired women like that, spontaneous and capable and carefree. He never said these things in an ugly way; instead he sounded wistful, as if something precious had drifted just out of reach.

The water park posed a conundrum. Given the choice, Nick and Alaina would have opted to go there every week. The best Quinn could do was space the visits out to once a month or so. On their second visit that summer, Nick survived two hours of ordinary fun only to be caught in the face with an errant blast of sunscreen from somebody else's mother.

Quinn grabbed her son by his cold, wet shoulders and pulled him out of range, shouting for Pete to bring the inhaler. She crouched on her haunches and stared up into Nick's face as he spluttered and choked. The sun caught her full in the eyes, inverting all the colors: Suddenly Nick's hair was purple, his face aqua; where the sun had been, a red-black spot. Pete ran up and slapped the inhaler into her hand. She held Nick's shoulders as he used it. The moment held a terrible intimacy: her eyes searching his face from a distance of a few inches.

"I'm fine, Mom." His voice jittered with the medicine.

"Oh, honeybun." She wiped his face. "We shouldn't have brought you here. It's too dangerous."

"I'm okay. Really. Look." He demonstrated by taking three deep breaths with a minimum of coughing. Quinn pressed her ear to his skinny chest, listening for wheezing, but could hear nothing above the warbling canned theme-park music and the rush of his heart.

They made their way to a row of turquoise plastic deck chairs and sat down, stunned and limp.

"Jesus," Pete said when she told him what had happened. "People ought to be more careful."

"They ought to be, but they aren't."

Pete's face closed when she said that.

"Not you," she said. "I'm talking about the whole world."

"You worry too much, Mommy," Alaina said, cheerfully critical.

"No, pumpkin." She pushed her daughter's wild hair off her cheek. "I worry just enough to keep the inhaler handy."

•

In the months after Marcus died, Quinn tried to guess what Daddy might want when he came home from the clinic, which wasn't often. Occasionally she guessed right, and he rewarded her with a tired smile, a hand on her shoulder.

Mother spent whole days in her bedroom when she wasn't wandering the house in her pink nightgown, which slowly faded to the color of putty. She stopped going to church. She rarely left the house at all. When she crossed paths with her daughters, she barely acknowledged them.

Sarah remained weak for a long time. *Born Free* no longer interested her. Nothing did. One day, Quinn went into the twins' room (she couldn't think of it as just Sarah's room), crawled under the covers with her sister, and began chatting about the things they would do once Sarah got her health back. But Sarah said nothing and wouldn't look at her. On the other side of the nightstand, Marcus's bed stood tidy and forlorn.

Quinn tried cuddling her, but Sarah held herself stiff. "You know what?" Quinn said, clinging tighter. "I'll be your twin now."

Sarah slapped her across the face.

On the anniversary of Marcus's death, they drove through Delhi to the cemetery where he was buried. Beneath a gloomy sky, Mother bent down to the low granite marker and pressed her finger to the dash between his birth and death dates. "That's his life, right there," she said. "That's all there was."

Sarah let out one blurting sob and began to cry. She clung to Mother's waist, sagging toward the ground. Mother grabbed her under the armpits. "Stop it, Sarah, you'll rip my dress." Then she softened and hefted Sarah into her arms. "Let's take you home. You too, Quinn. That's my good girl."

My good girl. At those words, a dirty gray memory sprang out of hiding. Quinn sat down in horror and felt it banging around inside her chest like a rat in a waterpot.

She'd seen them sneak out that day. And somehow, till just now, she'd forgotten.

She'd been deep into the book she was reading. The twins had begun making a racket, then fallen abruptly quiet. The sudden silence brought Quinn out of the world of her book, and she realized she needed to use the bathroom. She was passing by the empty kitchen as Sarah and Marcus tiptoed out of the pantry and crept to the kitchen door.

Their bodies were slim as fishes, and the door never opened more than a crack. The slightest gust of warm, wet air slid into the room as the two of them slipped outside. By the time the door clicked shut again, it was as if they had never been there at all.

"Get up, Quinn. We're leaving," Mother said, and Quinn found herself back in the cemetery, sitting on Marcus's grave. Somewhere below her, his body lay in a casket. The thought horrified her. She scrambled to her feet.

Back at the house on Cornwallis Road, they found Ayah sitting at the dining room table, her eyes streaming.

"Why is Ayah crying?" Quinn asked Mother.

That was how the girls learned they were moving to America. Ayah would not be coming with them. Neither would Daddy.

That night, Quinn went to Mother's darkened bedroom. "Please," she begged. "Don't make me leave Ayah."

Mother stroked Quinn's hair and wiped her tears. But when her sobs grew louder, Mother took Quinn's chin in her hand. "Who do you love better? Ayah or me?"

Quinn couldn't cover up the truth fast enough. Mother saw it in her face and snatched her hand away. She threw back the covers and got out of bed, lifted her white chenille robe from its hook, and wrapped it around herself. It was too late, then. Or almost too late.

"It wasn't their fault, what happened to Marcus," Quinn said. "Daddy's or Ayah's."

Mother cinched the robe at her waist. "I never said it was."

"You said if Daddy hadn't made us live in India, this never would have happened."

Mother's expression acknowledged the truth of that.

"It was *my* fault," Quinn said. "I could have kept them from getting sick."

The words skittered into the blackness under the bed and hid there, peering out. Mother's eyes locked on Quinn's. "What are you talking about?"

Quinn had counted on that question. She felt dangerous and powerful. But as she drew breath to say the words, the suspicion went out of Mother's face. "You're a child." As if that meant: *You're nothing.*

Mother shifted her weight, searching with a foot for her slippers in the darkness beneath the bed. Quinn didn't know what had just happened, but she knew she had lost.

SARAH

AT FIVE MONTHS OLD, Machli's cubs had grown to the size of cocker spaniels. They were still toddlers, romping around in compact bodies that made perfect little loaves when they tucked their legs beneath them. More often, they played and pounced, chased each other, swam, leapt, gnawed on hunks of meat from their mother's kills, and ineffectually stalked peafowl, which tolerated the cubs' attentions like long-suffering nursemaids. Occasionally the cubs would parade around single file, looking highly serious, one cub holding the other's tail between her teeth.

"They're cute before they learn how to kill," Hari said.

The comment surprised Sarah. "Everybody has to eat," she said lightly. Her Hindi was getting better.

"The world would have been better if we were all vegetarians. So much suffering, as it is."

No wonder he preferred birds, Sarah thought. But maybe not the raptors.

Just now the film crew was setting up to capture footage of Machli's family, a particularly valuable bit of filming since the park was about to shut down for the season. By the time they saw the cubs again, in three or four months, they'd be twice this size.

She had to admit, to herself if not out loud: Tiger cubs made an excellent reason to stay in India. She could put up with this amorphous work, with its frustrating lack of deadlines and bylines, a lot more happily now that tiger babies were in the picture.

Beneath an overcast sky, the cubs clambered in a tree alongside a river in flood. The forest guards had named them. The one with heart-shaped marks over her eyes was Dil, the Hindi word for *heart*. The other cub was called Lalit, for her mischief. Some distance away lay beautiful Machli, flat out on her side, fully engaged in an epic feat of digestion. Her belly looked as big as the rest of her body, as if she'd swallowed a sambar whole.

"It's the heat," Sanjay said. "She ate everything she could before it had a chance to spoil."

"Hang in there, dearest," William advised. "You'll feel better tomorrow."

Sarah turned her binoculars from the beached tigress and back to the cubs. One had abandoned the tree to stalk a peacock. The other balanced on a branch. Those paws! Like catcher's mitts. Those stubby, chunky forelegs. Sarah adjusted her focus to the cub's face to look for identifying markings, but suddenly it vanished. A blur, then gone. She lowered her field glasses. No tiger cub anywhere.

No. There she was: a bundle of striped fur being swept downriver.

In a second, the water carried the cub past the jeep and into the branches of a fallen tree, where she lodged against the trunk and disappeared beneath frothing brown water. For one split second, Sarah saw the cub's face just below the surface, and then the roil obscured it, and they were all shouting and clutching at each other. Sarah yelled, "Do something! Do something!" and when the cub did not resurface, she leapt from the jeep without thinking and crawled out onto the tree trunk.

The men shouted at her, but she could see the little face a few inches below the surface, eyes squeezed shut, paws scrambling. "Hang on, girl!" She plunged her arm into the powerful current and hauled the cub up by the scruff of the neck. The cub emerged screeching and writhing. For an instant the two found themselves face-to-face, and in that moment, Sarah knew: If she survived this, she was staying. Then the cub thrashed against her, all white-rimmed eyes, wet fur, hot breath, a slash of claws against her body. A glancing wallop caught her in the face. She heaved the cub to land, where she staggered, coughed, sprinted for her mother, and disappeared from view with the flash of a striped tail.

A shattering roar. Sarah hoped to God that Machli couldn't manage to move with her belly so full. Sanjay bellowed, "*Chalo! Chalo! Chalo!*"—*Go! Go! Go!*—as Sarah crawled back along the tree trunk, but her foot slipped, and she fell into the warm, shallow water at the river's edge. She spat out a muddy mouthful and cursed. Hari pulled the vehicle close as she scrambled up the bank, and Sanjay and William hauled her into the jeep.

She found herself sprawled facedown on the back seat, choking on river water, ears filled with the twin roars of engine and tigress until the tires found purchase and they sped away. "Are you okay?" Hari called, looking frantically in the rearview mirror as Sanjay and William pulled her upright. She started to say, "I'm fine," but a stream of red splashed from her face onto her shredded, crimson-soaked T-shirt. She saw but did not feel the long diagonal gash in her stomach. She held one hand to her cheek, one to her torso to stanch the bleeding as the jeep careened out of the park and onto the paved road. William pressed his hands to her ribcage. A garnet stream dripped down his arm.

"No death today," Hari rapped out. "No death." She wasn't sure if he meant that the tiger cub was safe or that he was worried about her.

At the hospital, they rushed her into the emergency ward. She found herself lying on a metal examining table, a doctor's beefy face hovering over her. "What have we here?" he asked equably. She didn't know whether to be comforted or pissed off by his calm.

He cut her out of her shirt, cleaned her up, sewed up her torso, and began stitching her face with black thread. "So, Ms. DeVaughan," he said. "What *have* you done to yourself?"

"Um," she said. William, Sanjay, and Hari stood behind the doctor, watching.

"Don't move the left side of your face."

"I, uh," she said out of the right side of her mouth, "I got into a disagreement with a tiger cub."

"That is rarely a good idea, madam." She supposed he thought she was crazy or at least lying. "Next you'll be telling me I should see the other fellow, eh?" The doctor pulled a stitch tight. She guessed him to be thirty-five or so, a big man sporting a prosperous belly and a *pukka* accent that sounded more British than most Brits' did. "I hope you got a good chunk out of him. But either way, you're lucky. The tiger has special feelings for you." He cut the thread with a snick of scissors. "He's given you three lovely whiskers." He was the kind of doctor Daddy had been, calm and unflappable, dispensing little jokes. Sarah raised a hand to her face. "Ah-ah. Don't touch." He nodded at William. "Hand her that glass, would you?"

William gave Sarah the mirror, and she considered her reflection. Ugly black stitches held shut the three scratches. "Tiger's whiskers are valuable, you know. Highly prized," the doctor said. "They're not so deep. Call them a badge of honor."

"Something to remember this day by," she said.

"For the next few weeks, you'll remember it more by the gash on your belly. That will hurt. And you won't enjoy the intestinal effects of swallowing river water. I'll write you a prescription for Cipro. But you'll be good as new in a few weeks. You'll have to come back for postexposure prophylaxis for rabies, of course." He smiled at her alarm. "You get the injections in the arm. It's nothing like the old days. You've had all your immunizations, of course. Tetanus?"

"Tetanus, polio, MMR, typhoid. Hep A and B."

He made a note on her chart. "Anything else I should know?

Autoimmune disorders, childhood diseases?"

"Chickenpox. And cholera." She looked up at him. "Am I going to get it again?"

"Cholera? Hard to say. But we'll keep a close watch and get you started on rehydrating fluids right away if you start showing symptoms." The doctor considered her. "I'm curious you've had it before. You don't seem the cholera sort."

She wiped her nose with the back of her hand. "I lived in Delhi till I was eight."

"Lucky girl," he commented. "Lucky girl then and lucky woman now."

"Lucky," Sanjay blurted. "She nearly died twice today. Once by the river and once by the tigress. If Machli's belly had been empty, it would have been a different story."

Sarah flinched. Her colleagues had every right to be furious.

A commotion erupted in the waiting room. The nurse planted herself in front of the film crew as they made for the ward, cameras and all. Behind them marched Geeta, mobile phone in hand, striding past the crew and through the swinging doors. Her eyes hardened on Sarah. "The park director called." She gestured with her phone hand. "I told him he must have got his story wrong because no employee of mine would do something that reckless. But it's true, isn't it? Look at you. Scratched to bits and lucky you're not killed. Rescuing a cub, was it?" She looked at the others for confirmation. "I'm to understand you got out of the jeep with a tigress within attacking distance? A tigress who saw you threatening her cubs? Have you lost your mind?"

"Geeta Ma'am," Sanjay began, and Sarah said, "It wasn't like that—"

"He's beside himself, Sarah. And I can't blame him." Her voice rose. "It's bad enough you endangered yourself. What do you think would have happened if you'd got yourself attacked? You know bloody well at least one of these men would have come to your rescue and got himself killed as well."

"Excuse me, you mustn't shout," the doctor said.

"Not to mention the danger to the tigress! If she had killed you, like as not she'd end up being put to death. My God, didn't you think for a second about the lives you were putting in danger? And don't dare to tell me the cub would've drowned. That park is not some *zoo* where nothing bad ever happens. It's nature, and animals die!"

"Madam, you must not keep shouting like this," the doctor insisted.

"I'm sorry," Sarah said. "I'm truly sorry."

"Geeta, stop," William said. "You know how quickly things develop in the field."

"You bloody well should be sorry. I *told* you! The day you arrived, I told you. Rule one: We never interfere with what happens in the park. Never! And to do it in front of a film crew!" Geeta clutched her hair with both hands. "You've ruined us. Our credibility is gone. The park director's already threatening to ban the lot of us. And how are we to get funding with this, this *debacle* on our heads? Tell me that, would you? No—don't bother. I'm sacking you. As of this minute, you no longer work for Tiger Survival. I can only hope that's enough to undo the damage you've done."

A tear slid down Sarah's cheek and lodged in black thread. It burned. She didn't wipe it away.

The doctor looked up. "Now that is quite enough. I'll not have you badger my patient. Out of my ward, all of you. Go." He turned back to Sarah as the others filed out. "Don't worry," he said. "Tears are sterile. And by the way, what you did was extraordinary."

QUINN

WOMAN RESCUES BABY TIGER.

She saw the headline over coffee, clicked on the video clip out of curiosity, and found herself watching her sister hurl a tiger cub out of a frothing river.

On the next viewing, she saw blood. Crimson stains blooming all over Sarah's white shirt.

She dialed her cell phone with shaky fingers. No answer.

Date: July 15, 2000

Subject: Are you alive??

Are you okay? Are you alive? The news clip said you were safe, but you were bleeding, I saw it. How did this happen? Answer me as quick as you can. Please be okay. I love you. What the fuck were you doing?!

She called Pete at work and waited as he watched the video. "Holy shit," he said.

"Don't tell the kids."

"Of course not." A pause. "Let me know when you hear from her, okay?"

The entire day passed without word. Sarah's reply came after midnight, in full denial mode: She was fine, just a few scratches; Quinn shouldn't worry. As if anything she said could negate the video footage. A few scratches: Quinn didn't believe it. That shirt.

Mother answered on the first ring. "Thank God," she said when Quinn relayed the news. "She could have called us before now."

"She didn't call. She emailed."

Mother fell silent. "We must seem very far away to her."

They said good night. Quinn pulled her feet up onto the couch and rested her head on her knees. She hadn't smoked since she and Pete started dating, but she wanted a cigarette. Sarah never admitted to being in danger. War zones, terrorist enclaves, countries shredded by cyclones or tsunamis: She had an answer for each of Quinn's anxieties. She was drinking only treated water, staying in the safest areas. Quinn was under orders not to worry about her. Which meant: *Shut up, Quinn. Keep your fears to yourself.*

She closed her eyes and pictured the twins creeping out of the pantry, slipping out of the kitchen. The door softly closing behind them.

Quinn clicked Reply and typed, "Sarah."

The room lay dark and silent beyond the glow and hum of her laptop. Quinn had waited seventeen hours for Sarah's reply, and the wait had left a sick emptiness in the fist of her stomach. She would only stir herself up if she tried to reply. She went upstairs, put her hand on Pete's shoulder, and whispered that Sarah was safe.

His eyes never opened, but he reached up with one warm arm and pulled her to him. He kissed her cheek. It was more tenderness than she could bear. She touched his head and left the room. Downstairs, she shut down her computer. When the screen went black, she closed her eyes and curled into a ball on the couch.

She told the twins about it before breakfast, then sent her reply while the kids ate.

Sarah,

Thank God you're safe.

The kids think it's great that Auntie Sarah saved a tiger. Remember you told them you were going to India to save tigers? And now you have. They're very proud of you.

As for me, I have to be honest. I've watched you take one risk after another. I'm tired of worrying about you, I'm tired of begging you to be careful, and I'm tired of knowing that for all your words about being safe, you seem compelled to put yourself in harm's way.

It's your life, I know. But you know what? I want my children to know you. I want you in my life for the next fifty or sixty years. I want to sit around together when we're old and reminisce about our younger days. Is that really such a terrible thing to ask? I love you, little sister. I want you safe.

Quinn

This time, Sarah's response came back before the end of the day.

Quinn. I'm sorry. I know it could have ended badly.

Geeta is furious. She says she has no choice but to fire me. My work permit is for this job, so unless I can convince her to change her mind, I'll have to leave. But I have no idea where I would go. I'm home here. I've planted a garden. I'm learning to cook.

Write to me again, even if you have to yell at me. Tell me

the truth, whatever you think the truth is. I feel very alone right now.

Tell me the truth. But what was the truth? That Quinn hoped Sarah would have to leave India? That she wanted Sarah safe, even at the cost of her happiness? What kind of love was that?

The week before, Pete had taken the kids to a birthday party and left Nick's inhaler at home. It boggled her that he could be so cavalier. It boggled *him* that she'd been so upset about it.

She should try harder with Sarah. She'd given up a long time ago on being close, but that had been a mistake. Pete could stop loving her, he could divorce her, but Sarah could never stop being her sister.

Her computer screen stared, unblinking. Sarah was alone and hurt. Her little sister.

Hey, you,

Don't be so hard on yourself, okay? You did a brave thing in the heat of the moment. You pulled a tiger out of a river with your bare hands! Who else can say they've done that?

I may not have said it before, but I'm proud of you. And no matter what happens, you're going to be okay. I've never met anyone more adaptable than you. You have a bottomless well of internal resources. And you have a sister who loves you.

Take care of yourself, Sarah Jane.

Quinn

P.S. If you have to leave India, come back to Louisville. It's home, too, remember?

SARAH

SHE SLEPT BADLY FOR TWO NIGHTS after the river rescue, gripped by stomach cramps and the knowledge that she had royally screwed up.

Five a.m. found Sarah sitting on the front porch, an overnight case at her side and a copy of the previous day's edition of the *Times of India* in her hand. A welter of bugs swarmed the porch light. Beyond the shelter of the roof, rain pattered straight to earth, no wind to slant it.

Front-page news. Front page. What had happened to journalism? Especially when the article itself was so bare-bones:

AMERICAN WOMAN RESCUES TIGER CUB

By Anjali Ghosh

SAWAI MADHOPUR, RAJASTHAN, July 15—A female American conservation worker rescued a tiger cub from a raging river yesterday in Ranthambore National Park. Sarah DeVaughan was touring the park with two male coworkers and their driver when the 5-month-old cub was swept away in the churning waters before their very eyes. While her coworkers watched from the safety of their jeep, DeVaughan leapt out of the vehicle and threw herself into the river to rescue the tiger tyke. A film crew from the U.K. captured the drama.

Neither DeVaughan nor her colleagues at Tiger Survival were available for comment. However, park director R.K. Singh said of the courageous rescue, "Of course, I can't condone any person endangering herself in the park. But I am quite happy that the cub's life was spared, and I'm grateful Ms. DeVaughan lived to tell the tale."

Meanwhile, somewhere in Ranthambore National Park, a tiger cub and its mother are no doubt grateful too.

The story wrapped up with a couple of cursory paragraphs about Ranthambore and the plight of tigers in general. As an example of journalism, Sarah judged it thoroughly mediocre, cliché-ridden and all but devoid of detail, though she knew what the reporter had been up against. She'd had little actual content to work with, due to Geeta's directive that the staff avoid speaking to the press. All the same, Geeta's media embargo accomplished little, thanks to the photo that ran with the article: Sarah on the fallen tree, holding the struggling cub by the scruff of the neck while the waters surged around them. Both Sarah and the cub had their teeth bared. It was a terrific photo, even reproduced on grainy newsprint: full of movement, good light and color, glistening water and intense facial expressions, not to mention the textures of wet skin, clothing, and orange striped fur. Sarah wished she'd taken the shot, instead of being its subject.

The landlord's door opened. Drupti, home from Jaipur for the summer, stepped out and settled beside Sarah on the bench. "Well, hello there, national heroine. How are you feeling?"

"Not bad. I haven't thrown up since last night. My abs are sore as anything, but at least I didn't pull out my stitches doing it."

Drupti smiled. "You're a bit of a mess," she observed, "but you're front-page news! Did you see the opinion piece, by the way?" She found the page and handed the paper back to Sarah. "'Why aren't Indians doing more to save the tiger?'"

"Yikes." Sarah skimmed the columns. "Partly a call to action and partly about the fact that I'm not from India."

"We like to shame ourselves from time to time with our failure to preserve our heritage. Thank goodness we've still got the Taj, at least till the pollution eats it to nothing. By the way," she said, "*I'm* waiting for a friend to take me to the library. What are *you* doing out here at five in the morning with what appears to be an overnight case?"

"I've been summoned to Delhi," Sarah said. "The assistant director, or somebody, of Project Tiger wants to meet."

"Heavens. Does this mean you're not fired anymore?"

Sarah started to laugh, sending a sharp pain through her stomach. "Unclear."

"Geeta-ji is still terribly angry. I heard her last evening in William-ji's flat." Drupti sat forward, her braids swinging. "Sorry, but it was a bit hard not to hear."

Sarah had heard, too. Geeta had called her a liability. William had called her a godsend.

"She doesn't need to be afraid," Drupti said. "Any publicity is good publicity."

"Is that what they teach you in law school?"

"Not exactly. My best friend, Chandra, is always telling me that. She's studying marketing."

"Hmm. Seems patently untrue."

"Generalizations are sloppy things, aren't they? But when the film goes public, think how much coverage it will get."

"It already has," Sarah said. "They were talking about it on the radio this morning."

"You see? Everyone in India will know this brave woman works for Tiger Survival."

"Assuming I still do."

"You'll be interviewed. Geeta-ji, too. People will see that this American woman risked her life to save a tiger, and they'll think, 'Okay, what am *I* doing? What's my government doing? Shouldn't they be doing more?' Tiger Survival will be a cause célèbre."

Sarah smiled at that. "You're making me feel better."

"Good," Drupti said. "Let's face it, Indians aren't going to stop crowding onto land that used to be tiger territory. People might feel bad about the situation, but what can they do when the problem is so big? But you've proved that one person can save a tiger. It will make people feel good, and when they *feel* good, they'll think it's possible to *do* good. They'll be inspired."

"More wisdom from Chandra?"

A breeze picked up, slanting the rain and spattering their shoes. "Wisdom from me. My family discussed it last night. We all agree that Geeta-ji doesn't need to worry. You can tell her we said so." Drupti nodded toward the road, where Hari had pulled the Sumo to a stop outside the gates.

"I'll give her the message." Sarah gathered her bag and hurried through the rain to the waiting vehicle.

•

Sawai Madhopur to Delhi was an eight-hour trip by car, from the desert where camel carts swayed down the verge to ever-widening highways and an ever-greater influx of traffic. When they crossed from Rajasthan into Haryana state, the roads improved, and suddenly the signs offered information in both Hindi and English. And by the time they crossed from Haryana into the capital territory of Delhi itself, they became one with an endless traffic jam: garlanded lorries swaying and honking, motorbikes, cars, yellow-and-green auto-rickshaws belching noxious exhaust, pedestrians, and the occasional wandering cow all surging forward in a slow, disorderly crush. Though lanes were painted on the macadam, the concept of keeping one's vehicle between the lines did not hold sway. Hari broke his silence just long enough to praise his good fortune for being a Sawai driver and not one of his unfortunate counterparts in this misbegotten mess.

When Sarah had climbed into the vehicle in Sawai, Geeta glanced at the paper in Sarah's hand and said, "Incredible," though her tone said something more like *idiot*. Since then it had been a mostly silent ride. William, seated next to Sarah, offered a kind smile from time to time and handed her a copy of *Down to Earth* to show her an article he'd found interesting. Now that they were snarled in Delhi traffic, Sarah leaned forward and tried out a version of Drupti's argument on her boss.

Geeta turned in her seat and regarded Sarah levelly, her silence accentuated by the unceasing *bap-bap* of auto horns. She had not explicitly reversed herself on firing Sarah. "Supposing you're right. The footage causes a minor sensation, and for a few weeks people get excited about the idea of saving the tiger. What good does that do? We don't get our funding from individual donors. And I don't see government bureaucrats or foundation boards getting swept up in the romance of your rescue stunt." She turned to face forward as if to declare the conversation over.

"Why not? They're human, too."

Geeta sighed, pulled down the sun visor, and pinned Sarah with a glare via the mirror. "They're policy makers. They understand the realities of the situation. The danger to tigers is not about getting swept into rivers in flood. It's a complex set of problems with no good solution in sight. And anyhow, imagine if that tigress had got hold of you with cameras rolling. Have you thought what that footage would look like?"

"Yes, I've imagined it," Sarah said. "Terrible publicity."

"Look, there's only one thing for it. I'm planning to tell the assistant director that I've asked for your resignation."

"And what if you're wrong?" William asked.

"I'm not wrong."

He smiled with the right side of his mouth. Geeta turned around and asked what he found so bloody amusing.

"I've watched you go a lot of rounds with these bureaucrats," he said. "You're too canny to make pronouncements like that. I know how you operate. You'll get a feel for their leanings before you say a word."

"I'll walk in and say my piece straight out. I operate that way, too, you know. You've seen me do it."

"All right, then. Do what you think best. Shame you haven't seen the footage, though. It's out there, for anyone who's got broadband. Which Assistant Director Gopalan undoubtedly does."

She narrowed her eyes at him. "You realize, don't you, that there's much more on the line than Sarah's position. It's your bread and butter, too. And mine, and Sanjay's. It's your lakes. Sanjay's educational program. Everything. If the money dries up, all that's finished."

"You don't know that the money will dry up," he said. "This is exactly my point. Wait and see how things play out."

"But what things? There's the Project Tiger grant we'll talk about at tomorrow's meeting," she answered herself. "And the Wildlife Conservation Society grant we'll hear about in the next few weeks. Two big indicators. Yes, I think you're right. Those grants will tell us what we need to know." She opened her bag, pulled out a can of cashews, and ate one, visibly thinking as she chewed.

"But it's not quite that simple, is it?" William said. "We might or might not get those grants regardless. You can't lay all that at Sarah's feet."

She gave him a level look. "What do you want, then, William? You're asking me to give her a chance. Fine. This is her chance. Frankly, you're so keen to let her keep her position, I'd think you'd be overjoyed I'm giving her this much rope. You know"—and here she offered him the can of cashews, as if they weren't in the midst of an argument—"five years you've been here, and this is the worst row we've had."

Sarah sat very still, the better to remain invisible.

"You can't deny she's been a good addition to Tiger Survival," William said, taking the can. "We'd been understaffed and on the verge of burnout, all three of us, for a long time." He popped a cashew into his mouth and watched Geeta as he ate it. Sarah wanted to laugh.

"She's been helpful. True enough."

They pulled up to the hotel, and the conversation paused as Hari unloaded luggage. Sarah grabbed her bag and started for the hotel. Behind her, she heard Geeta say to William, "I thought perhaps you were beginning to have feelings for her."

Sarah forced herself not to glance back, though she was dying to see the look on William's face.

"You're allowed, you know," Geeta said. Sarah nearly dropped her suitcase.

"You'd rather this was about some sort of romantic feelings, wouldn't you," William said. "You've spent your life at this work, but who'll be there to take it up when you're gone? We're the past, you and I. Sarah and Sanjay are the future."

The whole conversation amazed her. The fact that William would tell Geeta that her work would someday end. Sarah wouldn't have dared. What must their marriage have been like? She couldn't imagine.

•

"Yes," said Assistant Director Gopalan. "I've seen the footage. Most alarming. Most alarming."

"Of course, Tiger Survival is prepared to take the appropriate action," Geeta said.

The assistant director leaned back in his swivel chair. He was a soft man, and his short-sleeved white shirt had become trapped on the left side in a crease of flesh. He reminded Sarah of her high school principal, right down to the fact that everyone referred to him by his title. She found herself fighting back nervous laughter.

Gopalan tugged the fabric free and regarded Geeta down the length of his nose, ignoring Sarah and William. "The appropriate action. I see. And what would that be?"

"We cannot and do not support such recklessness in our employees. Nor interference with the tigers, obviously."

"I should think not. Shame to waste such good publicity, though. That footage. Extraordinary."

He was baiting them. Sarah could see it in the way his hand moved methodically, stroking his mustache while he talked. When his words stopped, so did his hand, the thumb and forefinger suspended on either side of his mouth. Only his eyes moved, watching their reactions.

"Actually, we haven't seen it," Geeta said.

Gopalan's eyes flared. "How is that possible? Everyone with electricity has seen it. Several times." He gestured at the computer monitor on his desk. "Come around here. I'll show you."

He offered Geeta his chair. William and Sarah stood behind her. The video loaded and the scene played out: Sarah and the cub grappling before she heaved it to land. Geeta watched, expressionless, her knuckles pressing white spots into her cheek. When it ended, she returned to her seat. "Fancy that."

"A lot of people do fancy it," Gopalan said. "It's quite sensational." He straightened a pile of papers on his desk. "In fact, it was a cheap stunt. What's more, it's something no Indian conservation worker would have done." He fixed Geeta with a glare. "Look at the people you've brought into your organization. The Englishman, first of all. Then this American woman. One lone Indian man to add the local flavor. May I remind you, Ms. Banerjee, that the tiger problem is an Indian problem, and it's Indians who will solve it."

Geeta's long body had grown still while Gopalan spoke. She smiled artificially. "I couldn't agree more. And as a responsible Indian citizen, I am doing what I can to find solutions to the problems facing the tiger."

Gopalan steepled his fingers. "No one has more respect for your conservation work than I do. But the actions of your employee are drawing the wrong kind of attention to the conservation effort."

"And what's the wrong kind of attention?"

"Suddenly everyone is asking why it's a *white* woman saving the tiger. Where are the Indians? Where is the Indian government? As if somehow the existence of this footage means we in Project Tiger are not doing our jobs."

Geeta drew herself up. "Mr. Gopalan, perhaps it's not such a bad thing the public is beginning to question the bureaucracy. A little heat from the public, and perhaps more would get done here in Delhi."

"Geeta," William warned.

"No. It needs to be said." Her voice rose. "For the past twenty-five years, our ministries have done nothing but cover up problems and inflate census counts and enact meaningless resolutions that aren't worth the paper they're printed on. Meanwhile the tiger is about to disappear for good, and the Indian government hasn't the will to stop it."

The assistant director glared at Geeta. "Are you accusing me of corruption, Ms. Banerjee? Or only incompetence?"

"I was merely pointing out that the penalties imposed under Indian law are inadequate as a deterrent to poaching. And that nothing useful is happening on the government level to curtail encroachment. And that field organizations like Tiger Survival are able to respond quickly and effectively to situations as they arise."

"Just as your American woman responded when the cub fell in the river," Gopalan said. "Which conveniently happened in front of a professional film crew. An amazing coincidence, don't you think?"

Sarah rose halfway out of her seat. "No one could have known that would happen. I know I violated a cardinal rule, but it all happened in a second. I acted on instinct." Her hair tangled in her sutures. She pushed it away.

"Lovely scars you're going to have there," Gopalan said.

"Look," Geeta said. "None of us is happy with what's happened. Ms. DeVaughan's continued employment is hanging by a very thin thread. You have my word no other missteps will be tolerated. That's the best answer I can give you."

William cleared his throat. "Mr. Gopalan, I trust you remember your last annual report mentioned Tiger Survival quite favorably. 'A fast-acting and effective organization. Consistently achieves noteworthy results on a modest budget.' This was written by your own staffers."

"That was before your executive director hired Ms. DeVaughan." He shifted his focus to Geeta. "I am frankly surprised at your choice, that's all. It makes me wonder whether your judgment is going."

"Ms. DeVaughan has proven herself a valuable asset," Geeta said, surprising Sarah again. "I trust you've read Mr. Amesbury's report. It's filled with example after example of the good work we're doing. Our lake-building efforts keep more village livestock out of the park every year. Step by step, we're helping the villagers lift themselves out of dependence on the park's resources. So I'm asking. What outcome should Tiger Survival expect in this round of grants?"

"Certainly the reports are good. But it's hard for me to tell whether your organization is beginning to lose its focus."

"And if we dismiss Ms. DeVaughan, is that the proof you're looking for of 'focus'?"

His expression turned brisk. "You'll have our decision in a few weeks' time." The assistant director stood and straightened his blotter. "Good day, Ms. Banerjee. Good day, Mr. Amesbury. Ms. DeVaughan."

Outside, Geeta turned to Sarah. "Your fate is riding on the two big grants we've got coming up. If they both come through, you can stay, assuming you behave as if you've a brain in your head. But no more stunts, Sarah."

"Yes, ma'am. Thank you."

Geeta gave her an assessing look. "I *am* glad the cub didn't die. But you must know this is a years-long battle. The life of one tiger is not the issue here. Which reminds me—I heard from the park director today. Akbar's been fighting. One of the forest guards spotted him with fresh wounds." She and William exchanged a look. "Most likely this means there's a younger male out there challenging him. Akbar didn't look too beaten up, apparently, but once a young tiger starts challenging the resident male, they'll keep fighting till one or the other gets killed. And if the intruder wins, his next job will be to kill the current generation of cubs, to bring the mothers back into heat."

Sarah blanched.

"*This* is why you don't go about endangering an entire agency for the sake of one animal." Geeta shook her head. "Serves you right you have to get rabies shots."

•

At the hotel, Sarah found herself at loose ends. Geeta and William had other business to attend to, and Sarah supposed they didn't want her company any more than she wanted Geeta's at the moment.

So here she was. Delhi.

Outside, under a thick gray sky, a line of auto-rickshaws waited for fares. She climbed into the first one, map in hand, and exchanged greetings with the driver, a small man with sleepy eyes and a copy of the sports section tucked beneath his thigh.

She gave him the address, and they were off, the racketous buzz of the unmuffled motor whining in her ears. She might as well be traveling by chainsaw. She'd never loved auto-rickshaws, the way they left your clothes and skin covered in tiny flecks of oil. She wished she had asked Hari to take her, but it was too late now. They were out in Delhi traffic, without air conditioning, without windows to shut out the auto horns, the diesel exhaust, the rain that had begun to spatter her shoes.

They traveled fitfully, stopping and going for no discernable reason. The rain picked up. Traffic stopped altogether, and the driver killed the engine and read the sports section.

What would it be like to see Cornwallis Road again, with its walled properties, bougainvillea, stately homes? Probably nothing was as grand as she remembered. She pictured the courtyard with the peepal tree and wondered if the bench would still be there. It was where she always thought of Daddy, sitting next to her, one minute cracking jokes and the next minute talking about how you owed the world something in exchange for your life.

Maybe the new owners would ask her to come in. Or maybe she should just stand outside the gate and look. Someone might have remodeled the house; she might not recognize the place.

Surely the peepal tree would still be there.

Traffic still wasn't moving. The driver had disappeared completely behind his paper. She asked what was happening. "Stoppage," he said. "Protestors have blocked the road."

"What are they protesting?"

"They're tollbooth workers. Another shooting in Delhi last week. The workers are shutting down traffic to demand better safety measures."

"Did you know this was happening?" Sarah asked.

The driver glanced back at her. "Oh, yes."

"Is there another route we can take?"

"Yes, but the other way will also be affected. The stoppages are happening all through Delhi these days."

At least they'd agreed on a price before she got in. "Any idea how long we'll be stuck here?"

He moved his head noncommittally. She glanced to her left and saw that two men in the next car were watching her. One of them grinned and gestured, an invitation to join them. She frowned and looked away. On the other side, a driver shut off his engine, propped his feet on the dashboard, and lit a cigarette.

All around them, drivers had killed their engines, and the rain was knocking exhaust fumes to earth. So at least the air was clearing up. But here she was, wedged motionless in the middle of thousands of vehicles, as close to home as she would ever be again.

She asked to go back to the hotel. Now she appreciated the auto-rickshaw's nimbleness. The driver knocked on windows one by one and convinced other drivers to back up or pull forward until, by inches, a barely navigable space appeared. He managed to steer the little vehicle between cars and onto the shoulder, then executed an illegal maneuver crossing the median.

At last they were back in motion, their speed creating a breeze in the thunderous air. They were moving—not in the direction Sarah had wanted to go, but it still beat sitting immobile.

QUINN

IN THE LAST OF THE LATE-AFTERNOON LIGHT, Quinn stood at her easel, preparing to make a quick sketch of spring-green pears on a slate tile. She'd drawn something similar at the class she'd taught that afternoon, and it hadn't come out right. This time, she exhaled deeply and shook out her shoulders before she drew, then worked fast. That method usually did the trick. But the finished drawing was lifeless. Lines on paper. She recognized that kind of work: the product of an artist who'd lost her touch but kept doggedly trying to fake it.

She placed her pastels back in their tray and did not allow herself a sigh.

If someone had asked her to draw her family life, she would have sketched Pete and the twins arrayed opposite her, wearing identical expressions of resentment. A cartoon bubble coming out of Alaina's mouth: "You're always following Nick around with the inhaler." Quinn had come home from teaching a watercolor class one day to find the three of them in a sweaty pile on the living room floor after a game of backyard soccer. She had set down the mail, taking in the grass stuck to their knees and the color around Nick's mouth. That was when Alaina made her complaint. The sentence had the ring of something repeated, something Pete had said.

That night, the elbows-and-knees man visited her in a dream. He said nothing, merely flailed across the floor in front of her, thick calluses darkening his elbows. She woke up disturbed. She hadn't conjured him that way since she'd been a teenager. Now she found herself dreaming about him several nights a week. She couldn't ignore him, couldn't make him go away. Somehow, his visits meant something about her marriage.

•

At sixteen, she had gone into treatment for an eating disorder. In the hospital, the counselors had told her over and over, till she believed it, that in order to get well, she must find ways to express her feelings: not suppress them, not use starving herself as a way to deal with the pain. Art therapy taught her how to paint her feelings, which brought them down to human scale.

The day she left treatment, on the drive home, she and her mother stopped for a meal at a carefully chosen restaurant. Quinn allowed Mother to order her a baked potato, plain, and ate half of it in silence, watching the twins slip out of the house like fishes. She set down her fork and said, "I have to tell you what happened to Marcus."

Sometime after the family moved to Louisville, they had stopped talking about Marcus, stopped saying his name.

"Eat your potato."

"I could have stopped it."

"You couldn't have stopped it, Quinn."

Like fishes from the steamy kitchen. The door never opened more than a crack. "I saw them sneak out of the house. I let them go."

They stared at each other. Her mother's eyes darted between the potato and Quinn's mouth. Quinn took a bite and chewed, making horrible faces. "You like watching me eat, Helen? Does it make you happy?"

Mother leaned forward. "Believe it or not, young lady, you are not the center of the universe. What happened to the twins had nothing to do with you." They stared at each other till Mother's face flushed. "I have spent a *fortune* getting you healthy. You ought to be grateful. Now eat that potato, and I don't want to hear another word about any of this."

The scenario had never unfolded this way when they role-played it in counseling sessions. Quinn dug a tattered notebook out of her purse and started ferociously doodling with a ballpoint pen. Apparently the feeling of being silenced expressed itself as interlocking circles and triangles, heavily inked.

"Quinn, that's rude. Put it away."

She looked up. "Seriously? Did you even talk to my therapists?" Mother glared at her. Quinn shoved the notebook into her purse.

They drove home in silence. On the way, Quinn lit a cigarette, a habit she'd picked up in treatment. "Roll down your window," was all Mother said, and Quinn knew she had won something. The buzz of the cigarette reminded her of sex, the way it felt when you held your breath when you were trying to come. Waiting for release.

That night she sneaked out of the house and met up with some girls who had a liter jug of vodka. She came home after two in the morning to find Mother waiting up. She led Quinn to the bathroom and held her head over the toilet while she threw up. She brushed Quinn's teeth and tucked her into bed, kissing her forehead.

"Ugh," Quinn groaned. "Get off me."

In the morning, Mother told Quinn and Sarah that Daddy was dead.

There was going to be a memorial. Quinn assumed she and Sarah would at least get to see their father's face, but it turned out his body had been cremated. The boy Quinn was sleeping with came to her house the night before the service and gave her a joint to take the edge off. She asked him to come to the funeral place with her (she wouldn't call it a funeral *home*; nobody lived there), and he said he would, but he didn't answer her calls after that. She stood in her room in a pair of baggy pantyhose and a too-big dress and tucked the joint inside her bra. Outside the funeral place, she ditched Mother and Sarah, stepped around the corner, and lit up. The joint burned her lips and tongue the way it always did. She didn't mind that. First the pain, then the buzz. It helped.

•

Mother began calling more often after Sarah's tiger rescue. A "rescue" was how Quinn thought of it. Mother called it a "tiger accident."

"It wasn't a tiger accident, Mother," Quinn said on one of those calls. "She wasn't attacked."

"Call it what you want. It was an accident involving a tiger."

Quinn laughed.

As the call wound down, Mother asked, "How's Marcus doing with his asthma?"

Quinn's stomach did a nasty flip. "You mean Nick," she said.

It was as if India were sucking them all back in.

SARAH

SANJAY OFFERED ONLY A SHORT GREETING when he picked her up. He'd been brusque with her since the incident in the park. Sarah threw a leg over his motorbike and rode behind him, gingerly holding his waist. Probably she should have tried sitting sidesaddle like an Indian woman. Sanjay likely found something distasteful about a woman riding astride, but she hadn't survived a tiger encounter just to get killed sliding off a motorcycle.

He parked under an awning in case of rain. When she climbed down, her limbs felt rubbery. "Here goes nothing." She laughed shakily.

"You're afraid of an injection?" He took the helmet from her and secured it to the motorcycle. "You were brave enough the other day in the park."

She didn't respond. He had every right to be angry.

His face softened, but only a fraction, as if it annoyed him to feel sorry for her. "Look, it won't be so bad. The injections aren't as painful as they say."

"Really?"

Sanjay shrugged.

"It's just that needles aren't my favorite things."

"I know. Your favorite things are tiger claws."

She supposed she deserved that.

They stepped out from under the awning and skirted the side of the low brick building. "I have to do something," she said.

"Make myself indispensable somehow."

He glanced at her as they walked. "Ranthambore has cast its spell on you, I see."

She smiled. "Ranthambore and those tiger cubs."

They entered the hospital through automatic sliding doors, past two thin brown dogs sleeping in the doorway. In the half-filled waiting room, children turned to stare at Sarah, and even the adults gave her a good long look. Sarah wondered if she owed the scrutiny to her whiteness or her sutures. Or maybe they knew what she'd done.

The nurse who had admitted Sarah the day of the accident sat behind the desk. Puja Mahar, her nametag read. She had a friendly face; Sarah guessed her to be about her own age. The nurse looked up from her paperwork and offered a good-humored smile. "So!" she said in Hindi. "Here comes the tiger woman."

Sarah glanced at Sanjay. *The tiger woman.* She hoped *that* didn't catch on.

•

A week later, he picked her up in the Sumo for her second injection. A paper bag rested on the passenger seat. "They're for you," he said. "The grocer gave me extra. No point in letting them go bad."

She opened the bag and peeked in. Three pretty mangoes. A gift, then. She glanced over at him, but his expression gave nothing away.

"I saw the film footage," Nurse Puja said when she checked Sarah in. "It's quite all right, ma'am. Plenty of people are a little mad." A slight breeze from an open window stirred the nurse's hair, and she picked up a clipboard to fan herself. "But you, you're also extremely brave. And it's obvious the tiger likes you." She gestured to her cheek, drawing three parallel lines with her fingers. "I've heard the village women talking about you," she added in a gossipy tone. "You know how they are. Superstitious. They think you have strong magic in you. Tiger magic."

Sarah glanced back at Sanjay, who seemed to be listening with great interest. She would have to ask him what, exactly, tiger magic entailed.

As a token of her admiration, the nurse gave them private mini-tours of the hospital at the end of their visits, never mind that the injections made Sarah feel dizzy and ill. Puja was proud of the hospital, a well-equipped new facility funded by a local foundation. The first tour had covered the obstetrics-gynecology ward, X-ray lab, and phlebotomy station—all at top speed, since Puja couldn't leave the front desk for long. The current itinerary ended in a wing where the walls were painted a soothing mint green, but the steamy air thrummed and clattered: the laundry down the hall to the left, the kitchen off to the right.

A girl of fifteen or so stepped from behind an unmarked door into the hallway. Sarah had seen this girl on their previous visit, sitting alone in the courtyard, embroidering. Her chin and neck were badly scarred.

"Nuri, how are you today?" Puja asked. To Sarah and Sanjay, she added, "Nuri is living here since two years. She came in with very-very bad burns on her face and chest." She lowered her voice. "Her husband's family. You know. Kerosene. When she came in, her mouth was just a hole. The doctors have done a very good job with her, don't you think? Six surgeries. And all for free."

Nuri looked at the space between Sarah and Sanjay and smiled shyly, her eyes huge and round. Sarah brought her hands together. "Namaskar, *behenji.*"

Nuri murmured a namaskar. She was hardly bigger than a child, but her back curved like an old woman's, and the hem of her sari puddled on the floor around her bare feet. She seemed as if she wanted to apologize to the world for her scars, or maybe for her existence. Sarah wondered what had made her husband's family decide she deserved to die. Too small a dowry, probably. Or she hadn't produced children. How old had she been when she was married off? Thirteen, maybe?

She thought about Drupti, studying for law exams. And about herself: divorced after a brief, ill-considered marriage; childless by choice. The entire world was hers if she wanted it. All she had to do was pick up the phone and call her editor.

She turned to Sanjay. "I don't know the words. Would you tell her I'm sorry I've been staring?"

"Not to worry." Puja waved a breezy hand. "She's quite used to it."

Sarah shot Sanjay an uncomfortable glance. He turned to Nuri and repeated Sarah's message. Nuri replied in the Vinyal dialect, and Sanjay didn't translate.

"The doctors did well," he told her. "They gave you a nice smile." Nuri dipped her head shyly, seeming pleased.

"What did she say?" Sarah asked as they walked to the parking lot through a steady drizzle.

"She said it's okay."

"No, she didn't."

He sighed. "She said everyone stares, or they don't look at her at all. She said before the surgeries, she wished she had died." He paused. "She says it's not as bad now."

Sarah said nothing on the drive back into town. The Sumo's windshield wipers slapped across the glass. Sanjay glanced at her. "It happens in the villages sometimes. They're not modern."

"*Modern*? It's barbaric."

"India is not always kind to women. In a lot of households, it's the women who run the show, believe me. But with the villagers, it's another thing entirely."

"Do *not* excuse what happened to that girl."

"I would never excuse it. I'm just telling you how it is. In the villages, sometimes people end up dead. 'She fell down.' That's what the family members tell you when you ask."

"It's horrifying," she said.

After a silence he glanced at her again. "Do you know the story of why Ranthambore became a tiger preserve?"

"I've heard it. But let's hear your version."

He told her the story. The maharajas of Jaipur had used Ranthambore as their private hunting ground. They and their entourage, riding elephants, would wait at the center of an enormous circle while hundreds of servants beat the bushes and trees at the perimeter. The animals had no choice but to flee, not knowing the beaters were driving them to slaughter. Tiger, sloth bear, python, blackbuck, jungle cat, leopard, jackal—all fell in the barrage of arrows and spears until every living being that could not fly out of range had been annihilated. The ground ran red with blood.

But the maharajas' thirst for butchery was precisely what saved Ranthambore's tigers. In order for the hunt to go well, the territory needed thriving populations of wild creatures. Hunting happened only six weeks a year, a privilege reserved for the court. The tiger population received royal protection the other forty-six weeks. A poacher discovered on the maharaja's private grounds suffered a quick and summary death.

"So what are you saying?" Sarah asked. "That somehow the attack on Nuri was actually a way of protecting her?"

"Not in the slightest. I'm saying India can be a violent place. That often the weak suffer at the hands of those who are slightly less weak."

The rain strengthened into a downpour. The air hung gray with the weight of water, though the western sky was clear. Sarah had heard the stories. The maharajas had boasted of their kills as if they'd been sexual conquests. This one had killed 112 tigers, that one, 300. What greater measure of manhood could there be than a dead tiger? They even counted the fetuses that lay curled in the womb.

"Don't hold me responsible for the history of this place," Sanjay said. "Or for what goes on in the villages. I'm only telling you. I'm not defending it."

"I know. I'm sorry. It's just upsetting."

"You know, your anger is one of my favorite things about you," he said. "It's very righteous. There's no bitterness in you."

She gave a short laugh. "Lot of good it does. All the righteous anger in the world won't keep people like Nuri from getting set on fire because her in-laws find her inconvenient. It's not going to keep poachers from killing tigers, either."

"Then why are you here? Tell me that. You came halfway round the world to make things better for the people and animals here. Don't tell me you think it's impossible."

The late-afternoon sun sank into a ribbon of clear sky between clouds and horizon, illuminating the window and casting a shadow of streaming drops onto Sarah's forearm. The effect was like film melting in a projector. Like skin in a fire. She moved her arm out of the sunlight. "Actually, I don't ask myself whether it's possible to make things right. I just tell the story so people can't pretend they don't know what's going on."

"But you're not a journalist anymore. You're here to save the tiger." He gestured to the sutures on her cheek. "A task you've taken to heart, I must say."

She sighed. "I keep fighting with myself. What should I have done? Let the cub drown like I'd been told? Or save it regardless of the consequences?"

"People do what it is their duty to do. Whether it has the outcome they want is another question." They passed a cart drawn by a camel, its head lowered against the rain. "Saving that cub was your duty, or you wouldn't have done it."

She laughed without humor. "I did it, all right."

"And you did it in front of a camera. You're going to be a tiger-rescuing celebrity."

She looked at him sidelong. "Haven't you heard? I already am."

He surprised her with a smile.

Back in Sawai, the streets had turned into rivers. Shopkeepers stood in their doorways, watching the pouring rain. Sanjay steered carefully through the flood. "You said the other day you needed a way to convince Geeta Ma'am to keep you on. She's been wanting to start a new project. Something to help the village women generate new sources of income so they can do things like buy electric cookstoves instead of burning wood they've foraged from the park. Until you joined us, we hadn't the staff to take it on."

She sat up, suddenly intent. "Does she have a particular project in mind?"

"I don't know."

"Is there money in the budget to get something started?"

"I don't know," he repeated lightly. "You'd have to ask our boss."

They stopped at Sarah's building. She stepped out of the car and turned to him. "I might have an idea."

"Don't forget your mangoes," he said.

•

Sewing would be the way to do it. The women dressed in rainbows here. Every fabric featured a block print or a gilt edge or tiny mirrors— sometimes all three. The village women knew how to sew—and embroider, too. They did it for their families. The trick would be figuring out how to scale it up into a business.

They would have to spend some money up front buying fabrics and sewing supplies. They could work out a microcredit plan, lending the women $50 or $100 each so they could buy materials, to be paid back as the goods sold.

She did her best thinking when she wasn't trying to think. In the evenings, after work, she rearranged her bookshelf, looked through her photos, ate dripping mangoes at the kitchen sink. One afternoon she decided to catch a movie at the local cinema. On the walk there, she passed a spice vendor and an electronics store, a small boy driving a wooden cart pulled by a water buffalo, a long-distance phone call store, a pig rooting in the middle of the street. A shopkeeper called out, wanting to sell her skin-care products for pretty ladies. She wondered if he was mocking her for her sutures.

She glanced up at the cinema's pink-and-white-striped façade and joined the crowd of people streaming through the doors, past the whiff of an open drain. Inside, the lobby smelled faintly of mold. Whenever she returned to Louisville, it always hit Sarah how odorless the neighborhoods were. Springtime smelled like magnolias and tree pollen, summers were cut grass and hot asphalt, but by and large, Louisville smelled like nothing, even on garbage pickup days.

She caught the manager watching her. Without thinking, she smiled at him, and he started a bit. In all her years traveling, she had never fully trained the smile out of herself, the moments of eye contact. They were dangerous habits.

The manager turned away to greet a pair of elderly women, probably a couple of aunties he'd known all his life. That's how it went in India. Everybody knew everybody. Everybody was related to everybody. It was all weddings and graduation parties and baby's first haircut. A family celebration for every imaginable rite of passage.

Some of the moviegoers stared at Sarah with undisguised curiosity. Even under normal circumstances, she would stand out in India, just for being tall and blond and white. Never mind the stitches. Never mind that people were calling her Tiger Woman. She turned her back to the room and studied a poster for a Bollywood romantic comedy coming soon to this theater.

She would never know what made her look up when she did. But she turned and scanned the crowd, and of all the people in Sawai Madhopur, Sanjay Prakash came walking through the arched entryway, his shoulders pulled down and head bent to his left. Sarah could only see him from the chest up, but she could tell he was holding hands with two children and listening to one of them talk. His face looked animated and relaxed, nothing like the frowning, stiff man he had been with Sarah lately.

Closer now, she saw the two young boys flanking him. Nephews, maybe. When she had asked William about Sanjay's status, William had described him as a devoted uncle. Whoever these boys were, their heads swiveled as they tried to take in everything at once. But the focal point of their universe, the one they kept returning to, was Sanjay. The younger boy tugged at his forearm, talking nonstop. Sanjay stopped to point something out. Ah: the bathrooms. Very practical.

A pack of teenaged boys brushed past Sarah, one of them knocking into her. She saw the sidelong glances they gave her, the looks they exchanged among one another, and knew that if she were a tourist—if she weren't living locally and known in the community for the tiger rescue—they'd be surrounding her right now, jeering at her, grabbing her body. She had lived through variations on that encounter all over the world.

If they came back, she'd tell them, "*Jao*, you little micropricks." She'd say, "Get lost before I tell your mommies on you."

They hadn't even bothered her, yet her skin prickled. It was nasty stuff, unused adrenaline.

Breathe, Sarah.

Your anger is one of my favorite things about you. She hadn't expected Sanjay to say something so generous, especially after all his disapproval.

She turned back to study Sanjay and the boys. There was something about them, the way they looked, holding hands like that, as if together they formed a single entity: a triptych, hinged by their fingers. A house with a tall, pointed roof.

His face, listening to those boys across the lobby. What would it feel like to have Sanjay Prakash look at you that way?

•

That night, she called Quinn. "I'm cooking up an idea," she said. "And I need your help."

QUINN

I NEED YOUR HELP. When was the last time Sarah had said something like that? It must have been before Marcus died. She certainly hadn't said it since.

Textiles. Quinn thought about it while she picked up Nick from a slumber party. He climbed into the back seat and buckled himself in. "What was your favorite part of the party?" she asked as she backed out of the driveway.

"When we played Donkey Kong Country," he said. His tone told her he didn't want her asking whether he'd taken his medicine. She didn't need to ask; she'd verified it with the other mother.

She turned the car onto Bardstown Road. She could picture three possibilities: Set up a shop to sell to tourists in Sawai Madhopur, find a retailer in a nearby big city like Jaipur or Udaipur, or else figure out the import-export business and sell the textiles in the States. Regardless, they would use fair-trade practices.

"There are two angles," she told Sarah on the phone the next evening as she stood in the kitchen, sorting through the mail. Bills, coupon circulars, a donation solicitation from Oxfam International. "One, the women. Supporting women who otherwise have no power in their lives. Giving them the means to make financial decisions for their families, including sending their daughters to school. And two, the tigers. If we help the women support their families, there's less incentive for the men to try to poach tigers or the tigers' prey. So here's what I'm thinking. Use your journalism skills. Write a profile of each of the women in the group. You could attach a photo of the maker to each piece, so buyers can literally look into the faces of the women they're supporting. Oh! And you can also do a photo essay on the women and see if you can't get it published somewhere."

"I don't know about that last part," Sarah said. "Most of the news outlets where I have contacts wouldn't buy a photo essay I shot of a project I'm involved in running."

In the living room, Pete turned on the TV. Quinn set down the mail and stepped out onto the deck into the warm summer evening. "Then we do an art show here in Louisville. I can talk to some gallery owners I know. And you could see about getting a show in India somewhere."

"That's a good thought. The cub rescue *was* national news."

"So piggyback on it. And when you have a photo exhibit, you have the textiles displayed right at the show, and people can buy them then and there."

They lapsed into silence, considering the possibilities.

"What do you know about import-export?" Sarah asked.

"Not a thing." She thought for a second. "But I know somebody I could ask."

SARAH

THEY FILED INTO GEETA'S OFFICE. She sat at her paper-strewn desk, a letter in her hand and a grim set to her face.

"Wildlife Conservation Society," she said, indicating the letter. "'We receive many requests for funding,' et cetera. 'Unfortunately, your proposal has not been selected.'" She looked up. "Sarah, your little romp in the park has cost us twenty percent of next year's budget. And yet much as I'd love to, I can't lay this at your door. I chose to keep you on after what happened. Perhaps if I'd sacked you right away, I'd have a different letter in my hand." She smiled a wholly unamused smile and picked up a stack of opened envelopes. "I suppose you know what these are?"

"Private donations," Sanjay said.

"They're modest amounts. But." She held up the pile. "Sixty-seven envelopes. It's extraordinary. In less than a month's time, we've gotten enough donations to cover a third of the shortfall from losing the grant. And this from school groups, women's clubs, private citizens all over the world." She shook her head. "It's shocking. Do something stupid on film and suddenly the whole world loves you."

"How long do you expect the checks to keep arriving?" William asked.

Geeta sat back in her chair. "We all know the answer to that. As long as the media keeps covering the Tiger Woman story."

It dawned on Sarah that perhaps she wasn't fired just yet.

"I don't see how that can go on much longer," William said. "Surely the news media are already onto the next thing." Except, Sarah thought, for the tabloid articles: *Tiger Woman Prowls Ancient Fortress. Tiger Woman Caught on Film Nursing Litter of Cubs.* But that kind of publicity seemed unlikely to help the cause, no matter what Drupti said.

"I've looked at the numbers," Geeta said. "If Project Tiger funds us, we can make it through the next fiscal year. But I'm not expecting that grant to come through. I'd advise you all to start thinking about your next career move."

Sarah stole a glance at the others. William wore a stoic expression. Sanjay studied his hands.

Geeta shifted some papers on her desk. "When I was a girl, my father brought me along on a trip," she said. "Jim Corbett was filming a documentary, and he'd invited Dad along. It was one of the highlights of my life. For six weeks, we camped in the foothills of the Himalayas, tracking tigers, filming all kinds of behaviors. Fights. Mating. Kills. Even then the population had been decimated, but Corbett and Dad had been around in the days when there were tigers round every corner. And now look what we've done to them."

No one spoke.

"I've spent my life doing this work," Geeta said. "And as hopeless as it may seem, I have always said that there is never no hope. There is *never. No. Hope.* But now? With the Indian population past a billion, and the Chinese slaughtering our tigers for medicine for every last ailment and moral shortcoming? Acne and laziness. The cure for limp willies." She rubbed her temples wearily. "This is the worst possible time for this organization to come crashing down."

She stood, so they all did, but she didn't dismiss them. She picked up the Wildlife Conservation Society letter, stared at it—or perhaps through it—and asked softly, "What's my life if I've failed at this?"

William said, "If Tiger Survival closes its doors, you go to work for another agency. You keep at it till you're dead, that's all."

Her eyes snapped into focus. "Damn it, William, I'm not talking about this organization. What do we do if we lose them? What if in another ten years, the only tigers left on this planet are living in zoos and rescue centers and circuses? And chained up in the odd basement by a bloody drug dealer? Would you want to keep on living in a world like that? Because I wouldn't."

Sarah and Sanjay exchanged a glance and filed out of the room. As she turned to shut the door, Sarah saw William step toward Geeta and take her into his arms. Geeta let herself slump against him.

"Hush that." William petted her hair. "Don't you let these thoughts win."

Geeta stepped out of the embrace and ran a knuckle beneath each eye. "Forgive me, William. It won't happen again."

Sarah quietly pulled the door closed.

•

She lay awake that night, trying to think of some way to offer comfort. But that was ridiculous. Geeta didn't need cheering up. She needed more funding.

Sleep finally came in the early hours. She awoke to a new idea and thought it through as she showered. At work, she found the office empty, as she'd hoped. She stepped into the back room, dialed the *Times of India*, and asked to speak to the reporter who'd covered the tiger rescue.

A few clicks and she picked up. "Anjali Ghosh."

Sarah identified herself. "I can't speak on the record. But I thought you'd like to know about an interesting phenomenon we're seeing here at Tiger Survival."

She heard papers shuffling, the click of a ballpoint pen. "Go ahead, Miss DeVaughan," the reporter said. "I'm listening."

•

The story appeared two days later:

DONATIONS, REPUTATION ON THE RISE AFTER
TIGER RESCUE

By Anjali Ghosh

DELHI, August 6—The recent dramatic rescue
of a wild tiger cub is having financial
effects for the tiger tourism industry.

American conservation worker Sarah
DeVaughan is well on her way to becoming
the most talked-about person in India,
thanks to her daring rescue of a drowning
cub last month at Ranthambore National
Park. While DeVaughan has stayed out of
the spotlight, an investigation by the
Times of India shows that the incident—
which earned DeVaughan the moniker "Tiger
Woman"—is reaping rewards for DeVaughan's
NGO employer and the tiger tourism industry
as a whole.

Tiger tourism inquiries are up 12 percent
when compared to this time last year,
according to R.K. Gupta at the Ministry of
Tourism, and DeVaughan's heroics seem to be
the reason.

"Our phones haven't stopped ringing since the
story broke," said V.H. Mistry, director of
Delhi-based Bengal Tiger Eco-Tours. "We've
had twice the usual inquiries for this time
of year, and we're fully booked for the
next six months. It's quite spectacular."

Meanwhile, donations from wildlife lovers around the world have been pouring into the coffers of DeVaughan's NGO employer, Tiger Survival. Geeta Banerjee, herself a well-known tiger advocate and the founder of the organization, said it has received "a very significant amount of support" in the form of private donations from around the world.

"What Sarah did in rescuing that cub shows that one person can make a difference," Banerjee said. "And, in fact, all the people who've been inspired to donate to our cause are making a difference too. We at Tiger Survival are humbled by their generosity and grateful for their support."

Sarah wished she'd been able to hear Geeta offer that blandly optimistic quote.

Among DeVaughan's admirers is eminent Bollywood film actress Radhika Bhagat, a regular supporter of environmental causes who visits Ranthambore regularly. Bhagat said she hopes to meet DeVaughan the next time she is there. Bhagat commented, "I have played my share of heroines in the movies. But Sarah-ji is a real-life heroine, and everyone who cares about the future of the tiger should be grateful to her."

The four of them gathered around the paper at the Tiger Survival office. "The reporter wouldn't tell me how she sniffed out this angle," Geeta said. "Brilliant journalistic skills, I can only assume."

"I take it the media embargo is off," William observed.

"It no longer serves our interests. One of our company is a real-life heroine, after all." She folded the paper. "Put it to good use, Sarah-ji."

The phone rang. The *Rajasthan Patrika*, one of Sawai Madhopur's daily newspapers, wanting an interview with Sarah. Five minutes later, it was the government-run TV channel's local affiliate in Delhi. Next, *Good Morning India* with an invitation for Sarah to be interviewed by their most popular host.

"Well, Sarah. Ready to become an ambassador?" William asked. They looked at Geeta, who humphed. Which was how Sarah found herself, later that week, seated on a living room set across from a beautiful and very famous morning-show host in Mumbai, two cups of tea on the low table between them, talking tigers. She felt completely at ease engaging the host's questions, turning the conversation effortlessly from the details of the now-famous rescue to a larger discussion of the plight of the tiger. The facts rolled out of her mouth as if she'd been doing this all her life.

Later that week, Geeta emerged from her office and sat on the edge of Sarah's desk, thwacking a pencil against her thigh. "You like being an ambassador," Geeta observed.

"I do," Sarah said. "It feels like important work."

"It must have been hard for you, giving up journalism. You'd become accustomed to seeing your name in print all the time. Now you're back in the spotlight."

Sarah waited to see where this was headed.

"You know, ambassadors get assigned to diplomatic posts," Geeta continued. "They're not always so glamorous."

Earlier in the week, Sarah had told Geeta of her idea for a women's collective. Now she eyed that thwacking pencil. "Do you have a post in mind for me?"

"I'm working on it," Geeta said.

QUINN

QUINN HAD INTENDED TO REHEARSE for her meeting on the walk down Bardstown Road, but her phone rang as she crossed the street. It was Mother, announcing she had bought a new car and needed to borrow some money. She named a figure almost twice Quinn and Pete's monthly mortgage payment. Quinn told her they didn't have that kind of money sitting around unspoken for. Mother countered, "I thought you had a line of credit. And it's just for three weeks. You won't even get charged interest."

Damn it.

A motorcycle rumbled by, spewing exhaust. The day had turned hotter than she'd expected; she should have driven the four blocks from home. As it was, she would arrive sweaty and disheveled. "I'll have to talk to Pete," she said. And Pete would get angry with her for not standing up to her mother. And then she'd have to convince him to go along with something she didn't want to do in the first place. Her stomach hurt.

"Don't tell him."

"Look, Mother, I'm walking into a meeting. I'll call you back." She hung up and took a deep breath. Standing in the coffee shop was Jane Spencer, trim and accomplished and dressed in flowing fabrics, perfect for her role as owner of a funky-but-upscale import boutique. After they got coffee and settled at a table, Quinn stammered through her explanation. It had all seemed so possible when she and Sarah had brainstormed on the phone, but she felt her certainty waning. Jane intimidated her; she always had, ever since college. They'd both been art students, but Jane possessed that small-business-owner confidence. She'd won Louisville Entrepreneur of the Year, arts category, three separate times. The plaques hung in her store.

Jane asked questions. Quinn couldn't answer them.

"You seem nervous," Jane said. "What's up?"

Quinn ducked her eyes. "I'm sorry."

"It's okay. You just don't know what this is going to be. From what you've told me, your sister hasn't put anything in place yet. Before we can talk about imports, we need specifics. The type of goods, the cost of the products, how the workers would get paid, all that. Percentages. Fifteen to thirty percent of the retail price goes to the makers if you're talking fair trade. You also have to think about whether you want to apply for certification. I have a few contacts. I can introduce you, but the plans in India need to be firmed up first."

Quinn felt herself flush.

"It's fine," Jane said. "You're information-gathering." She gave Quinn a close look and asked about her art.

Quinn grimaced. "I'm blocked. Everything I try is DOA."

"What's that about?"

She found herself confiding her worries about Nick, Pete's resentment.

"And your sister's back in India," Jane observed. "Life's gotten scary. What you need is a project. And you know what? You've got one, right here, with this women's collective. You're going over there, right?"

"What? India? Me? No."

"You should go. You'll do a better job representing the operation." She gave Quinn a sympathetic look. "Tell your sister bags and scarves are the way to go, not clothes. I'll send you some photos of designs I can sell."

Quinn thanked her. *Representing the operation.* Was that what she was doing? What did she know about the world of import-export? She was an artist, which made her an entrepreneur of sorts. But she was no Jane Spencer. And she hadn't painted anything worth keeping in six weeks.

•

"How did the meeting go?" Pete asked when she got home.

She took an apple out of the refrigerator and rested her hips against the counter. "She told me I should go to India."

Pete laughed. "She doesn't know you very well."

"I could go if I wanted."

He opened the fridge and pulled out a bottle of beer. "You've told me a million times you'd never go back. Besides, there's the kids," he said, as if he couldn't take care of them himself for a couple of weeks.

"Mother wants to borrow some money."

He opened the bottle and took a swig, asked how much. She told him. "You told her no, right? She needs to get over the idea that we're her personal bank."

"Well, she—"

"Well, nothing. She manipulates you. She does nice things for the kids and makes you feel indebted, and then she mismanages her money and wants you to bail her out. She's a financial chaos machine. We don't need to be part of her drama."

When she'd been in therapy for the eating disorder, she'd learned how to take care of herself emotionally. The art, of course. Meditation, though she hadn't practiced in years. When she'd married Pete, he'd been the kindest man she'd ever met. In their relationship, she had found a place to rest. Until this past year.

"I'm kind of excited about this project with Sarah," she said.

He nodded, but there was something abstracted about it. A pang of loneliness shot through her. They'd lost each other somewhere along the way. Something was going to have to change, but she didn't know what, or how.

It occurred to her now that she'd lost some skills. She set down the apple and left the room.

SARAH

"Vinyal?" Sarah said dumbly.

"Vinyal." Geeta sat behind her desk but seemed to take up most of the space in the room.

"Why Vinyal?"

"Can you think of another village where we need to make inroads more urgently?"

"That's not the question. They're dangerous people. They killed a forest guard two years ago." Actually, it was precisely the question. The other question was whether Geeta had singled out that particular village as punishment for Sarah's crimes. If Sarah was going to head knowingly into risky territory, she wanted to know why.

"Why do you think they killed that forest guard?" Geeta said. "Because all along they've felt the tiger conservation effort has undercut their livelihoods." She lifted a book off the shelf behind her. Sarah recognized the cover: *Tiger-Wallahs: Saving the Greatest of the Great Cats*.

Geeta flipped to a bookmarked page and read aloud, glancing up for emphasis as she did: "'No one asked them whether there should be a park here. No one warned them that entering the park to graze their herds or gather firewood as they always had would suddenly make them criminals. They're right that the park does not benefit them, at least not in the short run. It's our job to change that, to help them see that their survival and that of the park are linked, that if the forest is destroyed, their lives and all our lives will be destroyed, as well.'" She looked up. "That's a quote from Valmik Thapar. He's talking about Ranthambore." She thumped the book closed. "*That's* why Vinyal."

They stared at each other. "It's ambitious," Sarah conceded.

"There's a lot to be gained. You'll need a translator. Sanjay will be your partner on this project." She nodded briskly. "Any questions?"

That was the end of the discussion.

•

"The women already have jobs," the sarpanch said. "They work in the fields. They raise their kids."

"This project would inject cash into the village's economy," Sarah said. "The women's husbands and sons will have less incentive to break the law and do ecological harm by poaching tigers."

Sanjay translated. Around them, a crowd of men and children watched the conversation with great interest.

The sarpanch laughed without humor. "What economy? There's no infrastructure here. Half the homes don't have electricity."

"The income will let them send their children to school. Educating the people of Vinyal is the most important step you can take to lifting them out of poverty."

The sarpanch was not one for eye contact with a young white woman, but he conceded that point with a penetrating stare at her left shoulder. "How does the money work?"

"We extend small loans to the women to buy materials. They make the goods, and we facilitate exporting the textiles for sale," Sarah said. "The proceeds will be wired into bank accounts set up in their names."

"It's better to put the accounts in the names of their husbands and fathers."

"No," she said. "The women do the work; the women get paid."

The sarpanch grunted. "We have our traditions, you know. Let me think about this. Come back next week."

On the way to their vehicle, Sarah asked, "How do you think that went?"

Sanjay moved his head noncommittally.

"I feel like a politician," she said.

•

A week later, they found themselves sitting in a dirt-floored room with four of the village's best seamstresses, including Padma, Sunil's widow. She kept her head down, but Sarah thought she saw a scab at the corner of Padma's mouth and a bruise on her cheekbone. Her sister's husband had done that, Sarah guessed. Not happy to find himself housing a widow and her four children. She wondered how long it would be before he came after Padma sexually. If he did, how could Padma refuse? He had all the power. She had nothing.

The other women laughed over the glasses of tea and plates of namkeen that Sarah had arranged for them. They passed textiles hand to hand, talking of the embroidery and mirror inlays they'd do if they had the materials.

The past few days had given Sarah and Sanjay their first extended exposure to Vinyal women. It surprised Sarah how readily the women let go of their initial suspicion once they'd heard the proposal. Now Sarah and Sanjay were actually welcomed. So Vinyal women were a different story than Vinyal men, maybe.

About the sarpanch, the women agreed he could be rigid or he could surprise you. "He's leaning toward saying yes," said Anju, a graying woman with webs of wrinkles at the corners of her eyes. "Otherwise he would have told you not to talk to us. He knows we'll come around pestering him if he doesn't allow it."

"I'll pester him," said a younger woman named Rohini, raising her voice to be heard over the rain. "I want to buy a water buffalo. That old bag of bones isn't going to stop me."

"If I had the money," Padma said quietly, "I would like to buy a cow."

The conversation flowed fast, especially once Sarah got down to the business of information gathering. Where did the women get the cloth they'd be embroidering and dyeing? How much did they pay for the fabric and fasteners? Were they interested in creating new types of products they could sell outside the village, outside India, to women in America? Could Sarah buy a few fabric samples to take with her now?

At that, Sanjay stopped translating. "Geeta Ma'am will kill you if you spend money on this and the project doesn't go."

She gave him a conspirator's grin. "I'm not using Tiger Survival money. If it doesn't work out, I'll just keep the fabrics for myself. And if we do get the okay, I want to be ready to move fast."

He gave her a sidelong look. "My mother would have called you a 'leaper-inner.'"

She laughed. "I'm just ready to roll."

"I can see that."

The women watched them. "Laughing at us?" Rohini asked.

"Not at all," Sanjay said.

"We have a question for her," Rohini said, nodding toward Sarah. "Does she have children?"

Sanjay translated, and Sarah smiled. "No, but I have a niece and nephew. They're about this tall." She held out her hand. "They're missing their front teeth."

The women laughed in recognition, and the atmosphere grew light with conversation. Sanjay turned to Sarah. "They all have children. Anju has seven grandchildren. Padma says your niece and nephew are at a good age."

"They're pretty great," Sarah said. "Really funny. Curious about the world."

"She says at that age they can help with work."

"That, too," Sarah said, though she was certain Nick and Alaina weren't expected to do more than simple chores. Sarah had been there one day when Quinn showed the twins how to use a dustpan. They'd gathered around, watching seriously as she demonstrated how to nudge dirt over the lip of the pan with gentle strokes. The moment had seemed sweet to Sarah.

At the end of the visit, they stepped outside to find a lanky teenaged boy hovering nearby, wet to the skin. He stared openly at Sarah with something darker than simple curiosity behind his eyes. It wasn't until Padma spoke to him that Sarah recognized him: the boy she'd seen sitting on the ground the day of Sunil's death. His face and posture had hardened since then.

Sarah namaskared and asked his name.

"Om," the boy said. Water dripped from his shaggy hair.

"*Mera naam Sarah hai.*"

"I know who you are." He made it sound ugly.

"I will punish him for his rudeness," Padma said. "Such a naughty boy." Mother and son exchanged a complicated glance.

Sarah and Sanjay walked back to the SUV. Once out of earshot, Sanjay said, "I don't like that boy. He's too bold."

"I don't like teenaged boys, period," Sarah said.

He gave her a surprised glance.

"Too harsh?" she asked over the hood of the Sumo. "All right. Let's say I'm wary of them. I've seen boys that age all over the world, and they've got a dangerous streak. Especially the ones who know they don't have much of a future." She lifted her camera strap over her head and set the camera on the seat. "We'll keep an eye on that one."

"*Achchha.* But I'll tell you the truth. I don't trust men from Vinyal." He slid into the driver's seat and shut the door.

"So you've said. I kind of like the women, though."

A knock at Sanjay's window. Padma. Sanjay killed the engine and got out, and the two spoke intently. When they finished, Padma walked away, glancing back a few times.

"She's worried about her son," Sanjay said as they left the village. "The uncle won't let him go to school. He's making him work in the fields. It's humiliating to the boy, doing women's work. Padma says the uncle doesn't want competition as the man of the house."

"That's big of him," Sarah said.

"Om has gotten several years of education. He's been taught he can have a better life. But now, with this uncle … Padma wants to use the money from the collective to pay off her debt to him and send Om back to school."

"First we have to get the sarpanch on board," Sarah said. She sat silently, watching the muddy fields. "And there's one more complication. I want to add Nuri to the collective."

He glanced over at her. "The girl from the hospital? The other women won't want her."

"She's from Vinyal. And she could use some help putting her life back together."

"The other women will think the whole project is inauspicious. They'll want nothing to do with that kind of bad luck."

"She's been through hell. She needs help. There's nothing to discuss. What are you smiling about?"

"You're starting to sound as opinionated as an Indian woman."

She grinned. "You want to argue with me?"

"Not at all. If Sarah DeVaughan says that's the way it is, then that's the way it is."

She sat back in her seat. "I'm glad we understand each other."

His laugh sounded like a door swinging open a crack.

•

"What drew you to the Bengal tiger?" the talk show host asked.

"It's the most beautiful animal in the world," Sarah said. "And one of the most threatened by human interference. Tigers are amazing survivors, left to their own devices. And we need them."

The host interrupted her. "Isn't it true that you have an Indian connection?" He seemed very aware of his physical presence: well-built and high-cheekboned, impeccably groomed. When he spoke, his teeth flashed unnaturally white.

Sarah paused, careful to keep smiling. "My parents brought me to Ranthambore when I was a little girl. I suppose that was the beginning of it."

"In fact, you grew up here, didn't you? In Delhi."

"I did. I count myself lucky."

The host turned to face the camera. "Sarah DeVaughan, a child of India, now the face of the tiger conservation movement." He paused. "We'll be right back."

"This isn't about me," she said once they'd gone to commercial.

He shrugged. "Human interest. It's what makes the world go round."

QUINN

ON A FRIDAY AFTERNOON, Quinn sat down to check her email. A message from Sarah waited, with photos. Anju, Padma, Rohini, Sapna, and Nuri. They wore thin cotton dupattas loosely covering their hair, some of them shot through with gold-colored threads, some patterned with paisley or plaid. Every color—indigo, sugar pink, forest green—fully saturated. Beneath their dupattas, each woman's face revealed something a little different, an expressiveness or a reserve. Nuri's photo, taken from a high angle, emphasized her eyes, as if asking the viewer to consider that the burns around her mouth weren't the whole story.

In her email, Sarah reported that the other women hadn't objected to Nuri's presence as much as Sanjay had feared. Some were concerned about upsetting Nuri's family, who had refused to take her back after the attack, but Anju had convinced the women that, by disowning Nuri, the family had given up any right to be considered in matters concerning her future. "We all have to find a way to live," Anju had said, and the other women had conceded she was right. And that, apparently, was that.

Quinn knew enough to draw a general picture of what life must be for the women who lived there: early marriage, no access to birth control, raising child after child while working in the fields. Hauling water, cutting fodder grass, cooking every meal, keeping the house and children clean. She tried to imagine the arguments they had with their husbands: Yes, we *are* sending our daughter to fifth grade, because girls deserve education just as much as boys do. Quinn studied their faces. Rohini would be the one with the backbone to fight that battle. Or maybe that was just wishful thinking on Quinn's part. From what Sarah had told her, even boys got yanked out of school on a whim, and their mothers had no say in the matter at all.

The next day, she and the twins met Jane at her import store. Quinn set the children up in the pillow-and-blanket aisle—nothing breakable there, though plenty of things were knock-overable. She opened her laptop and turned the screen to Jane, who scrolled through the photos, flipping past the women's faces, lingering on the pictures of the wares they'd created.

"They've got the right idea, but they're going to have to up their quality," Jane said. "These purses need to be lined, for one thing. Have you sent them any samples? They need to really see the construction up close."

"Not yet. I'll buy a few things to send them while I'm here."

Alaina appeared at Quinn's side and tilted her bright face up at Jane. "Have you seen the video of my aunt saving the baby tiger?"

"Not yet," Jane said.

"Can we show her, Mom?" Alaina begged, and Nick joined in.

"Why not," Quinn said. The twins crowded around as Quinn searched for the video. When the search results appeared, Alaina read aloud, "Tiger Woman foils would-be poacher." She pointed at the headline. "Can we read it?"

It sounded harmless enough. Quinn clicked the link.

The web page clearly belonged to a tabloid. The familiar photo of Sarah from the tiger rescue dominated the screen, but the text had to do with a dramatic confrontation in the forest that ended with Sarah saving the day. Quinn skimmed the article. "This is just a story somebody made up about her."

"You mean she didn't really foil a would-be poacher?" Nick

asked. "What does *foil* mean?"

"To foil someone is to ruin their plans. And a *would-be* is someone who wants to be something but isn't really."

"So she caught somebody trying to be a poacher but made him stop?" Alaina asked. "What's a poacher?"

"If you poach animals, it means you—"

"Boil them in water till the whites firm up," Jane said. "Oh wait, that's an egg."

Quinn laughed. "If you poach an animal, it means you kill it illegally."

"Is it ever legal to kill animals?" Nick asked.

"Yes. But not tigers. They're endangered."

"We learned about endangered species in school," Alaina said.

"This website is kind of like those little newspapers you see in the supermarket checkout lines," Quinn said. "Most of the stories are made up."

"Why would people read it if they know the stories are lies?" Nick asked.

"Good question. I guess to some people, those stories make good entertainment."

"They shouldn't make stuff up about people."

"I agree," Quinn said.

They watched the tiger-rescue video together, the twins excitedly narrating, and then it was time to get down to business. The twins watched silently as Jane showed Quinn the bags she carried. "Tell Sarah to make sure they use colorfast dyes. They might have to order the dyes from Jaipur or somewhere. Once the women have produced some samples, have your sister send them over, and I'll check them out." She looked up. "It might take a few tries before they get the quality up to a level I can sell."

"I'll let her know," Quinn said.

"Tell them not to get discouraged. They'll get there. And when they do, I'll stock some of their products in the store and put them up on my website."

They talked about pricing, the cost of materials, labor and shipping. Quinn bought six bags to send as samples.

"How come it's legal to kill animals?" Nick asked as Jane bagged up the purchases. The twins had discovered a bin of felted-wool finger puppets and had placed little animals on all their fingers.

"Well," Quinn said, "for one thing, people eat them."

"Yuck."

"You like chicken, don't you? That's an animal."

Alaina wiggled the chicken puppet on her index finger and made it ask, "Is pizza made from animals?"

"Pepperoni is. It's made from pigs."

"You see where this is going, don't you?" Jane asked.

"I figured I had another year or so before they decided to go vegetarian." She considered her children. "This is going to make dinners complicated."

"Freezer aisle." Jane handed Quinn her bags. "You won't believe how many fake chicken products you can find."

At home, Quinn found a box for shipping the handbags and set it by the back door. Then she dug out the credit-line checkbook. *Helen DeVaughan*, she wrote on the Pay To line. Pete could convince himself that they didn't have plenty, but he was comparing their finances to the founders of the start-up where he worked, guys with seven-figure portfolios and expensive new houses. It skewed his perspective; it made him consider their bungalow life more modest than it really was.

She wrote a dollar amount and signed the check. Yes, Mother spent unwisely. But given the choice, Quinn would err on the side of generosity.

And anyway, chances were good that Pete would never find out. He pretty much left the banking to her.

SARAH

"ONE MORE AFTER TODAY," Sanjay said as they walked past the hospital's sliding doors. "And then you're through."

"It can't come soon enough for me," Sarah said.

"You Americans," Sanjay tut-tutted. "So impatient." He wore a little grin, like the one he'd given her the first couple of times they'd met.

I'll be damned, Sarah thought. He finally wants to play.

"You Indians," she said. "Not impatient enough."

"All right, then. You Americans, getting married and divorced at the drop of a hat."

She glanced at him. She wasn't sure what he knew of her history, or what he'd guessed. "You Indians, who marry people you don't even know."

He twitched, as if she'd touched a nerve. "Colonizer," he muttered, just loud enough for her to hear.

"I believe you're thinking of William."

"You're right. The bastard."

Sarah laughed aloud.

They had the waiting room nearly to themselves, aside from a young mother with a sleeping baby and a thin old farmer with a bandaged hand. Safe to say neither spoke English. Sanjay settled next to her. "It's not so terrible, arranged marriage," he said. "In your country, everyone wants a love marriage. And look how many end up divorced. Fifty percent."

A love marriage. She'd thought she had one with Rob. "I took it as a lesson," she said. "A long, painful, expensive lesson."

She hadn't told him before now that she was divorced. She thought he might apologize for bringing up something so personal. Instead he asked, "And what did you learn?"

"That what looks like safety isn't always."

"Safety? It's not a concept I associate with you."

"Why? Because I fall into rivers with tigers?" She shrugged. "At the time, I wouldn't have said I was looking for safety. I would have just told you I'd found someone mature and thoughtful, unlike the men I crossed paths with in my job."

"But later you realized you didn't want a mature, thoughtful man after all." He nodded sagely. She laughed and swatted his arm, and she saw him take note of that swat. Very familiar.

Across the room, the baby stirred. The mother began walking the infant around the room, bouncing softly on the balls of her feet. "Let's just say what I thought was maturity turned out to be something more like ... how to say this nicely? Complacency. Lack of passion."

"Of all the people in the world, I can't see you with a dull man."

"You notice I'm not with him anymore."

"But the journalists you worked with. They were too ... ?"

"Hooked on adrenaline." She grinned. "They were fun, I'll admit that. But they were all reaction."

"Indians try to be careful," he said. "We do a lot to make sure the match is right. We compare horoscopes, arrange family meetings ... "

"You look down on love marriages."

Again with the side-to-side headshake, a movement she'd begun to recognize as noncommittal. "They're considered less than respectable."

She shrugged. "Maybe you're right. Maybe it's better to marry a stranger."

"It's better to be practical. Passion doesn't last. We pay attention to the things that will."

She turned to face him. "Name them."

He grinned at her. "You think I can't? As a matter of fact, I have a theory about this."

"Do tell, Professor Prakash."

Something crossed his face, and she remembered that his father had been a professor. A nurse came to the doorway and called a name, and the farmer with the bandaged hand stood and followed her.

"First let me tell you a theory you'll hear from a lot of men in this country. The thinking goes that there are four criteria. If you're going to marry someone"—he held up his hand and ticked the items off on his fingers as he spoke—"she should be from the same state as you are, and from the same caste, and your parents should like her, and you should like her as well. What are you smiling about?"

"Nothing." She was smiling because his chatty side was reemerging from wherever he'd hidden it all these months. "Why those four things?"

"To begin with, in India, the states are like different countries. Different languages, customs, everything. The thinking is that cross-cultural relationships are too difficult ninety percent of the time, so you need to start from the same ground, literally. Second: What these guys will tell you is that if her family is from a higher caste, she's probably accustomed to things you can't provide her, and if she's from a lower caste, she might embarrass you with the way she speaks or behaves." He paused. "These are not exactly forward-thinking theories, you understand."

"Plenty of people think the same way where I come from," she said. "Even without castes, we still have class issues."

"Third. In India the parents usually live with the eldest son. If you bring home a wife they don't like? Big uproar. Everyone's unhappy. And fourth—simply that if you're going to marry her, you may as well like her."

"Wow," Sarah said. "That's quite a rubric. So what's *your* theory?"

"To me it's all about the family," he said. "It's perfectly possible to get past the state differences. And the caste stipulation just perpetuates a problem that's plagued this country forever."

"Americans can't fathom the idea of an arranged marriage," Sarah said.

He smiled. "You're so romantic, and so completely bad at marriage. You don't see that in yourselves—that's what's astonishing. Nobody ever looks at the divorce rate and says, 'Perhaps I should rethink this.'"

The nurse called Sarah's name. "Hold that thought," she said and stepped back into the ward for the dreaded shot. The needle stick was nothing, but the serum rolled through her in a cold, nauseating wave.

On the way back to her flat, she thought of half a dozen things she wanted to say, but they'd taken his motorbike, and the wind wouldn't allow it. When they got to her building, she invited him up to continue the conversation. If his friendly side showed itself this rarely, she wanted to take advantage of it.

Her mind sparked away as she filled their teacups. They settled at either end of the sofa in her front room, beneath the niche.

"Tell me about that one." He pointed to the photo of two brown boys, their serious faces turned up to the sky.

She glanced at the image. "What do *you* think it's about? I'm curious."

"They're two boys in trouble, praying for help."

"That about sums it up. They're boy soldiers. They've just surrendered."

"You captured it very well."

"Photos are tricky, though," she said. "They always tell a story, but they don't always tell the story you think they're going to. Even a totally unaltered documentary photograph can lie."

"How do you mean?"

She blew on her tea, sending up a cloud of white steam. "When you break down a situation into a sequence of isolated moments, certain moments reflect the truth, if you want to call it that, and others just don't. It's like, if you snap a picture of a person blinking, it might look like they're asleep, but they're not. And what you leave out of the frame can completely change the narrative. I could take a picture of two kids running, and you might think they're having a race. But just outside of the frame, maybe there's a tiger chasing them. Or maybe they're chasing after another kid they want to catch and beat up."

"Naughty boys."

She laughed. "And then there's what the viewer brings to the image. Everyone who looks at a photo makes up a story about it. Like you just did." She sipped her tea. "But here's what I can't fathom. Extended families living together. No privacy, no independence."

"Here's what I can't understand about Westerners," he said. "Everybody living alone. Nobody to talk to. Nobody to help you out with the things you can't do for yourself. It seems a terribly lonely way to live."

She looked at him. Sanjay lived alone, she was sure of it. They had stopped by his apartment on the way to the park one day, and she and William had waited in the front room while Sanjay got something from his bedroom. Every item in sight was recognizably his.

"At any rate," he said. "Yes, we have to put up with a lack of privacy, but we make it work. Look at our divorce rate. Ten, fifteen percent."

"Is that because everybody's so blissfully happy in their marriages?"

"Divorce isn't accepted here. Actually—" He paused. "If I were in your country, I would be divorced."

"What makes you say that? You might find some nice woman and live happily ever after."

"You misunderstand me. I mean I'd be divorced from my wife."

She looked at him, confused.

"We married seven years ago," he said. "After three years, she didn't want to be together anymore. She moved back to her parents' home."

"But you didn't divorce?"

"She refused." In a few sentences, he sketched the story. Three miscarriages. Mounting tension in the household. She had pushed him away after the third lost pregnancy, then left altogether. His parents died in a car crash the following year.

They sat in silence after he finished. "I haven't told the story outright in a long time," he said. "I'd forgotten how miserable it sounds."

"Why won't she divorce you?"

"Because it would be to her shame. She'd lose status, and she'd never find another husband. No Indian man would marry a divorced woman."

She set down her teacup, pulled her feet up onto the sofa, and wrapped her arms around her knees. "So where does that leave you?"

He spread his arms as if to say, *Right here. Just what you see.*

"Because no woman would get involved with a man who couldn't marry her," she guessed.

"More or less. I've managed to date a bit here and there, but it's always limited."

"And if you were divorced? Could *you* marry again?"

"Possibly. But it doesn't matter. I'm not divorced, so it's out of the question."

She bit her thumbnail in silence. "What's her name?"

"Lakshmi."

"I'm really mad at her for doing that to you."

"She's not a bad person. It just got to be too much. She was grieving, and I was, too. You'd think we would have been a comfort to each other, but we weren't. We made it harder for each other." He paused. "I'm not proud of that time in my life. I think leaving was her way of trying to move on." He looked at her. "You actually remind me of her a bit. Strong. Full of opinions."

She smiled. "Do you ever see her?"

"Not often. She seems to have a good life. She works as a bookkeeper in her brother's restaurant, and I help her a bit financially. She has friends, does things around town." He picked up his teacup but didn't drink. "Really, the same is true for me. It's not what I pictured for my life, but I have good companions in Geeta Ma'am and William-ji and now you. That helps."

"And you have those boys," she said. "The ones you took to the cinema. I saw you with them, across the lobby. They're your nephews?"

"They're Hari's sons. I'm an uncle to them, you could say." He paused. "You should have said hello. I would have introduced you."

"I didn't want to intrude." She could still picture how happy they'd looked that day, how comfortable with one another. "You created for yourself what life denied you. You didn't just accept your fate."

He smiled. "I think you just called me a bad Indian."

She blushed and covered her face with her hands. "You're right. How awful. I'm sorry."

"No. It's true. I'm a terrible Indian. I don't accept my fate. I don't accept what's happening to the tiger. I don't accept that those boys and for that matter hundreds of millions of people should live in extreme poverty while the lucky few live in even more extreme luxury. I don't accept that people should be consigned to their fate because of the family they were born to. I want to change all of it. But there's so little one person can do. Sometimes nothing."

"That's where you're wrong," she said. "There's never nothing."

"I suppose that's why we're both here."

"To be of use. Even if it's not enough." She sat thinking for a moment. "Do you look down on me for being divorced?"

He laughed. "Let me tell you, Sarah, I envy you. How do I say this? My situation has made me less judgmental than I used to be. And your culture is different. When you go back to America, you'll find a good man to marry you."

She picked up her cup and stared into the tea leaves as if she could read something there. "I had another tiger dream the other night. I was following it through the fog, but it was different this time. We were walking down a street with houses. It led me to an apartment building. Right up to one of the doors." She fell silent.

"What did the door look like?"

"It was blue." She looked into his eyes.

"My door is blue," he said carefully.

"I know." She climbed to her feet and held out her hand. "Here, let me take your cup. I'll get you more tea."

He followed her into the kitchen, where she stood at the stove. He stepped toward her, and she turned to him and took his face in her hands. She kissed his mouth, and when she pulled away, a droplet of moisture clung to her lower lip. He wiped it away, and her lip gave like a little pillow beneath his thumb.

He reached for her and pulled her body to his. She lifted the hem of his shirt and placed her hands on his warm bare skin, and he shuddered at her touch. She pressed her cheek to his and held still, drinking in the feel of him. He tugged her shirt up and let his hands slide across her waist and around to her back, and a current ran through them, she would swear it, moving fast and dark. And there was nothing to do in this moment except turn the lights off in the front room, pull the sofa cushions to the floor, and shed their clothing. There was nothing to do but lie still while he ran his fingers over her skin.

They touched for hours, their hands everywhere, fingertips, open palms. They whispered to each other, the words silvery on their breath. He murmured into her ear, and his words feathered and hummed at the base of her spine. He slid his fingers inside her, and she let her head fall back as she pushed against him, his knuckles hitting her pubic bone in a rhythm that made her ache. He whispered to her: that he couldn't believe her body, her skin so pliant and giving he almost couldn't feel it, like running his fingertips over the surface of a bowl of milk. They fell asleep, their bodies spooned together, her breasts to his back. When they woke an hour before dawn, their mingled sweat soaked the cushions.

He turned to face her. "My motorbike is still out front."

She nodded. "You should go."

He pulled back to look at her face. He ran a fingertip along her collarbone, around the curve of her breast. "Your skin," he whispered. "It's glowing."

She smiled. "So is yours."

"Sarah. We can't—"

She held up her hand. "We'll talk about that later," she whispered. "Go. Before William sees you."

QUINN

TIGER WOMAN TAKES A LOVER. The headline glared at Quinn from her laptop. She dialed Sarah's number.

"It says *what?*" Sarah said.

Quinn repeated the headline.

"What else does it say?"

Quinn settled onto the sofa with her laptop and read the story aloud. A tiger. It said Sarah was having a love affair with a tiger.

"Akbar," Sarah said.

"They don't know Akbar exists."

"Where do they *get* this stuff?"

"I hate to disillusion you, but they make it up."

Quinn could hear Sarah thinking on the other end of the line. "It's true, he does seem to come to me," she said. "Male tigers aren't supposed to be so visible. Females, yes. They keep to a smaller territory. Males are supposed to be elusive and aggressive. But not Akbar."

"Aww. He likes you."

"I haven't heard any rumors at all around Sawai," Sarah said. "Does Mother know?"

"I don't know if she's seen this one. She hasn't seemed too bothered by the others. Although she did buy a new car."

"Uh-oh," Sarah said. "Are you worried?"

"A little. She's been spending a lot lately. Every time I bring it up, she tells me how anxious she is about you being in India."

Sarah's sigh came down the line. "So if she goes bankrupt again, it's my fault."

And if she went bankrupt again, Pete and Quinn were out two months' mortgage payments, only Pete didn't know about it yet. "I guess we each get our turn at being the bad kid."

"Marcus didn't."

Quinn didn't know how to respond to that. "Sarah?" she asked. "Why did you go back to India?"

A pause, weighted. "That's a complicated question, oh sister of mine. But you want to know something funny? That article got it right. I *have* taken a lover."

Quinn slapped the corner of her laptop. "What! Who?"

She could hear Sarah's smile. "That's a story for another day. But I promise, he's human." Her tone turned serious. "So, listen. Geeta and William are going to Delhi on Tuesday to talk to one of our major funders. Project Tiger is about to tell us how much support they're giving us for next year, and my job depends on what they decide. By this time next week, I should know whether I get to stay or not."

"This is awkward timing, then. I sent you some sample purses."

Sarah laughed and groaned. "Oh, Quinnie. Why is life never straightforward?"

"You mean, like, why have you gotten involved with somebody when you might be leaving India any minute?"

"Yeah. Exactly like that."

"Because you're a commitment-phobe?"

"Maybe." Her voice trailed off.

"Okay, what gives?" Quinn asked.

"Nothing! Nothing gives."

"There's something you're not telling me."

Sarah laughed. "Listen, send me all the good energy you can. I'm going to need it."

They said their goodbyes. Quinn stood staring at nothing, her phone in her hand. Sarah had never let Quinn so close. Not since they were children. Not since Marcus died.

Marcus. She had actually said his name.

SARAH

SHE DIDN'T SEE SANJAY the day after their encounter. On the second day, they found themselves alone in the Tiger Survival office after William and Geeta left for a lunch meeting. He pulled her into the back room.

"You are luminous," he said. "A person would have to be blind not to see the difference in you."

"I could say the same for you, Sanjay Prakash."

"Are you okay?" He kept his voice low even though they were alone. They stood close to each other in the crowded office. She kept one eye on the front door.

"I think so," she said. "Kind of reeling. I didn't … " She let the sentence trail off. They had spent the whole night touching each other, each moment its own universe of fingertips and mouths on skin.

"You understand I'm not free," he said.

She folded her arms across her chest. "Really? Because you sure behaved that way two nights ago. I know you're married, Sanjay, but you're not *with* her."

"You can't think of it that way. India is not the West."

She wanted to argue the point, but he was right. Instead she said, "When I first came here, you seemed so familiar to me."

"Maybe we've known each other before," he said. "I do feel there's some sort of connection between us. I know it sounds strange. It *feels* strange. Even though we didn't … in the technical sense."

She nodded, watching his face.

"But I have a duty to her. The fact that we're separated doesn't change anything."

"A financial duty. Which you fulfill."

"It's more than that."

She took his hand, and there was his skin, so delicious. "So no Indian woman would have you. I'm not Indian. And you don't owe it to anyone to spend your life dying of loneliness."

He flinched a little, as if she'd named a truth he would rather not acknowledge. "All these years I thought the way I felt was what it felt like to be alive. But now I think I was asleep," he said. "You woke me up."

She took in his face: his eyes, his skin. The absence of lines she had thought were permanent. "Don't go back to sleep," she said. "You should see what you look like now that you're awake."

•

William walked past her in the office the next morning on his way to the electric teakettle. "Good morning," he said. "You're looking well loved."

She whipped around. "Excuse me?"

He gave her a strange look. "I said you're looking well."

Of course. William would never. Her mind was playing tricks.

On the day of her final rabies shot, clouds scudded high overhead. Sanjay picked her up on his motorbike. She came to him at the gate, and they looked warily at each other. Anyone could be watching. She put on the helmet and threw a leg over the seat behind him, placing her hands gingerly on his waist. She didn't know what this touch would do to either of them.

At the hospital, the familiar routine saved them. Before Sarah's nausea had quite passed, Nurse Puja bustled them off to see a small grassy courtyard where two old men in robes sat at a picnic table, playing cards. Nuri perched on the end of the bench, embroidering as she often did, and Sarah sat with her for a few minutes. They spoke together haltingly in a combination of Hindi and pantomime. Sarah told Nuri how she had called a goat a dog on one of her first trips to Vinyal, and Nuri bent her head down shyly, laughing.

Then they were through. Nurse Puja gave Sarah a bow of farewell. Sarah pressed her palms together and thanked the nurse for her kindness. Then she and Sanjay walked away beneath high clouds fraying in the wind.

"I'll miss these sessions," Sanjay said. They stood next to the motorbike, bodies separated by inches. "I wonder if you'd like to come back to my flat to wait for news." William and Geeta would be returning that evening after meeting with Project Tiger.

"Take me by the post office first?"

Twenty-four letters this time. She sighed and tucked them into her messenger bag.

The moment they stepped through his blue-painted door, the fact of their night together returned to Sarah like a presence in the room. Sanjay went to the kitchen and brought out two shallow dishes of cubed mangoes. Sarah nearly laughed: He might as well have been handing her a bowl of sex. They sat next to each other on the floor and ate the sticky-sweet flesh, and she kept that observation to herself. By the next morning, depending on the news from Delhi, they could all be out of work. Until then, they were in limbo, and why not kiss him again, feel his body rise against her? But the decision had to be his.

He seemed to be thinking along the same lines. "These past few years," he said, "self-control has become my forte."

Outside, daylight was falling away. The frogs were already singing. "It's okay, you know," she said. "That you can't be with me. It doesn't change what I feel, or what you felt when we touched. It doesn't make it any less real."

He nodded but said nothing. Maybe this would be their last

evening like this, alone together with the memory of his skin still humming in her fingertips. He had trusted her with his story. She felt she should return the favor.

She told him about Marcus, their childhood together, his death, as the air outside deepened to a smoky purple. He listened, not saying much. The intimacy of talking about it flooded her veins. Maybe it was a reckless act when the future was so uncertain. Or maybe that was exactly what made it the right thing to do.

"I haven't told many people that story," she said. "I also haven't told anyone I'm looking for our ayah. That's what all these letters are about."

"You should open them." He got up, rummaged through a drawer, and brought her a letter opener. "What will you do if you find her?"

"I don't know." She opened an envelope, scanned the letter, set it aside, and reached for the next one. Another saga of family tragedy. "Some of these are awful. And some are funny." She opened another. "And some are just bizarre. This one says that he's had a vision that I'm going to be the next incarnation of the Lord Krishna. He doesn't even know who I am. Just a name in a classified ad."

"He knows you're white. Some men are very attracted by that."

She arched an eyebrow at him. "Look who's talking."

"I'm only with you because Indian women find me unacceptable."

She cuffed him on the shoulder. "Jerk."

"It's true," he said, laughing. "There are too many of us miserable men in this country and not enough women. All the eligible women can find a man who's not been married before."

"That's a shame," she said. "Looks like you're stuck with me."

She went back to slicing envelopes. The next letter made her sit up straight. She couldn't speak except to read the letter aloud. "'My auntie was ayah to three American children in the 1970s named DeVaughan. There were two girls and a boy. The boy died. I believe you are Sarah DeVaughan, the woman on the television talking about tigers.'" She looked up at Sanjay. "He wants money in exchange for connecting me with Ayah."

"Oh, be careful. There are cheats out there."

"I know." They stared at each other. "I think I need to call my mother."

"Call her. William won't be here for a bit longer." He stood. "I'll be in the back room catching up on email."

She dug her phone out of her messenger bag.

The conversation lurched at first. It had been too long since Sarah's last call, and she had to stumble her way through Mother's stiff reserve. "I hear you're a celebrity," Mother said.

"Not really. I've been on a few shows, talking about tigers."

"I want you to be careful over there, Sarah."

She let the comment go by. "Mother? Did you ever talk to Ayah, after we left India?"

"Why would I? What would there have been to say?"

Sarah shifted on the cushion. "Don't you think she wondered how we were? Quinn and I?"

"She was probably glad to see the last of us, after everything that happened."

"She loved us."

"Oh, Christ. You and your sister. You thought the sun rose and set on Ayah, but if you could have seen things from my perspective ... "

"Why? Did she lie? Did she steal?"

"Just leave it, Sarah."

She shifted the phone to her other hand. "What was her name?"

"Manjuli. Why?"

As soon as Mother said it, Sarah recognized it: Manjuli, Ayah, smiling as she tugged down the hem of Sarah's shirt. "Manjuli what?"

"What's this about, Sarah DeVaughan? Are you planning to contact her?"

"Is there any reason I shouldn't?"

"Why do you want to stir things up? It was twenty-five years ago. We went through the worst thing that can happen to a family. Leave it alone."

"We left it alone. And look what good that did us."

"What are you talking about? We're fine."

I hear you got a new car, Sarah didn't say. She glanced down the hallway and lowered her voice. "We weren't fine. Do you remember all that stuff Quinn went through?"

"Of course I remember. She's lucky she didn't kill herself."

"What's that supposed to mean?"

"Look, you girls both suffered after your brother died. We all suffered." She sighed. "And look at you. You ended up back in India in spite of everything I did to try to keep you safe."

"I just want to do some good in the world."

"Oh, honey. You're your father's daughter."

Sarah didn't know whether to read regret or tenderness in Mother's voice. Maybe both. "I met someone," Sarah said.

She heard her mother's smile. "Is he nice?"

"Very. He's smart and kind and … he's good at his work. Handsome, too."

"Does he treat you well?"

"It's not like that," Sarah said. "I don't think this can go anywhere."

"Why not? He's not married, is he? Stay away from married men, Sarah."

"I will," she said, not really meaning to lie. "I have to go."

They exchanged pro forma *I-love-you*s and hung up. Sanjay emerged from the hallway just as Sarah heard footsteps on gravel. A quiet knock, and Sanjay opened the blue-painted door.

William entered and lowered himself to the floor before speaking. "It's good news," he said. "Full funding."

"Oh, thank God," Sarah breathed.

William recounted the scene. Gopalan had delivered the news with maximum self-righteousness, glaring at Geeta over his glasses. "In a very short time, Ms. DeVaughan has become an important resource for conservation efforts and ecotourism," he'd said. "I find it disturbing, Ms. Banerjee, to consider the damage you could single-handedly inflict on these positive trends by dismissing her."

Sanjay grinned at Sarah. "So there it is. You're safe."

"I wish Gopalan hadn't used me as a cudgel against Geeta Ma'am, though. That's going to make things a little awkward."

"Not at all," William said. "Geeta's a bigger person than that. And by the time the grant cycle comes round next year, what happened with the cub will be long forgotten."

They celebrated at a little restaurant down the street, telling stories and laughing. Since the park had closed for the monsoon, it had been weeks since they'd spent much time together. "Too long," William said. "Though you two have had plenty of opportunities, thanks to Sarah's rabies shots."

"Not my favorite circumstances," Sarah said.

Sanjay grinned. "The Tiger Woman is not so fearless when it comes to hypodermic needles. A couple of times on the ride home, I thought she might vomit down the back of my shirt."

Sarah gave him a mock-outraged look, and they both laughed, and she noticed William watching this exchange closely. She wondered if he could see it.

After dinner, she returned to Sanjay's to pick up the letters she'd left there, and the ease of the dinner party seeped away. She felt suddenly shy. They'd revealed so much to each other, shared their bodies, but now what? He drove her home on the back of his motorcycle, and she tried not to touch him more than necessary and dismounted quickly when they pulled up outside her gate. He got off, too, and propped the bike on its kickstand, catching her by surprise.

The air had cooled dramatically since sundown, and they stood facing each other outside the gate, each resting a hand on an ironwork finial. The light was on in William's flat, and she felt acutely aware of his presence. She wondered if he was watching them.

"Well, thanks for the ride," she said lamely. "I should go inside."

"Let me come with you."

It took her aback. "You're the one who told me you're not free, remember?"

"I don't know how to think about it," he admitted. "But you're right about all this loneliness. What good is it doing?"

She studied his face. "Don't play with my emotions, Sanjay. You know how I feel. You have to make up your mind."

"I know." He studied her face for a moment, and then he reached for her hand.

She took a half-step back. "Are you sure?"

He nodded.

"Okay, then," she said.

She unlocked the gate, and he wheeled his motorbike inside, tires hushing faintly over the gravel, and parked it around the corner with a soft clatter against the wall. "Quiet," she whispered. "William." They trod the stairs lightly, but she was aware of every creak and groan, of the heavy double click of her key in the door directly above William's own.

They took off their shoes, and he stepped toward her and touched her waist. Her fingers slipped through his hair, and his hand rose to her collarbone, pushing the soft white fabric back to expose the curve of her shoulder, pausing to undo one button just below the hollow at the base of her throat, another between her breasts, and on down, a quick upward pull to loosen the fabric from her jeans, his knuckles brushing the denim just over her pubic bone.

Kitchen sounds from William's flat. Cutlery, a teakettle, a crash as something fell to the floor. Sarah ran her fingertips like raindrops over the curve of Sanjay's chest and down to the metal button of his trousers, closed her fingers over the waistband while his mouth found the hollow of her neck, found the long diagonal muscle rivering down the side of her throat and traced it with his lips from its hidden source beneath her ear to the wide, slow delta at the base of her neck, over the shoal of her collarbone and into the mounting swell of her breast, his mouth riding the rise and fall while the surf of her heartbeat rushed against his lips.

The floorboards creaked as they moved from the kitchen into the bedroom. The bedsprings squeaked beneath the weight of their bodies. She clamped her fingers tight in his hair, the night breeze slipping over their bodies, the thump, thump of wooden bedframe bumping plaster wall, the sweat between their torsos suctioning their bodies together, her palm against his back, and then a creak of bedsprings beneath them, and now she couldn't contain a single soft gasp, and then another and another, soft as she could, her gasps rising and peaking and falling, and Sanjay's groan singular and guttural, grief mixed with joy.

And William downstairs. Maybe listening. Maybe hearing everything.

QUINN

THE BANK STATEMENT ARRIVED.

"I've had some unexpected expenses," Mother said when Quinn called. A hint of ice in her voice, as if Quinn had no right to ask. "I'll have it next month."

Quinn squeezed her eyes shut. "Can you pay back *some* of it before then?"

"Look, I'll cover the interest."

"It's not that." The twins had started back to school and were doing second-grade homework in the kitchen. She went into the bathroom, shut the door, rested her hips against the sink and lowered her voice. "I didn't tell Pete about it."

"Oh, honey." The news took the edge out of Mother's voice. "I'm sorry. I just don't have it. I don't know what to tell you." Her tone held warmth and regret. Now they were on the same side. God, Mother confused Quinn.

Afterward, she checked on the kids. Nick's color looked iffy, but his peak flow meter numbers looked fine. She noted it on her calendar. "Healthy as a horse," she said, falsely hearty. Nick ignored her.

She found Pete in his office upstairs, working on a database. "I need to tell you something," she said.

He turned away from his computer and looked at her expectantly. She felt sick. Pete would want her to see the loan as a terrible decision. He would accuse her of considering them rich. In a way, he was right.

She knew they had plenty, even though they didn't drive expensive cars or take extravagant vacations. In Pete's mind, those facts made them financially ordinary. Which meant they didn't agree on the basic nature of their reality. In India, farmers sometimes committed suicide because they owed a couple hundred dollars to a seed company and couldn't find a way to repay it.

Pete would also see the loan as a personal weakness, a failure to stand up to Mother. It was harder to argue with that.

Her phone rang. "It's Sarah," she said, relieved. "I'd better take this." He nodded, and she walked out of his office and answered the call. "Hey, you. It's awfully early there, isn't it?"

"Middle of the night." Sarah's voice sounded off. A little scratchy, a little subdued. "I've just got a couple things on my mind. Is this a good time?"

"Sure." Quinn slid open the door to the patio and settled on an Adirondack chair. The late-afternoon sun dappled through the leaves of the big walnut. With luck, Pete and the kids would give her a half hour.

"So I've been thinking lately about why I'm here instead of in Louisville. And why I couldn't stay married and be in one place and be happy, when you make all of that look so easy."

Quinn flinched.

"Do you ever wonder what Marcus would be like if he'd lived?" Sarah asked.

Now there was a question. She didn't, really. She saw him as a blond blur of a boy, slipping out the door. "I think about him the way he was. Maybe because my kids are that age."

"I picture him sometimes as an adult," Sarah said. "Sitting around at dinner with all of us, teasing your kids. Talking politics. Maybe we'd all live in Louisville and hang out together and, I don't know, have cookouts and stuff."

"Or maybe we'd all still live in India."

Sarah seemed to consider that. "No. Mother had had it with

India. And with Daddy. But the reason I called ... I wanted to tell you that when I left home, it wasn't that I thought Louisville wasn't good enough for me. Or that by staying, you were settling." She paused. "I talked with Mother the other night, and she alluded to some stuff from when we were teenagers. Apparently some things went on that I never knew about."

"You were three years younger than me. Of course stuff happened you didn't know about."

"She said you were lucky you didn't kill yourself." A silence, freighted with questions.

Quinn glanced into the house. The kids still sat at the table, doing homework. Pete crouched between them. "I'll tell you about that sometime."

"Do you have to go?"

"I have a few more minutes."

"Good. I have to tell you two more things."

"Is one of them about your new lover?"

"Sanjay," Sarah said.

Quinn smiled. "I wondered if it was Sanjay. You said male and human. That narrowed it down."

"He's like no one I've met before. He's completely grounded at Ranthambore, and he's on fire for this work, and it's sexy as hell. There are complications, though."

"Wait. Is he married?"

"Kind of."

"Sarah." Quinn groaned. "Be smart."

"It's not what it sounds like. He's separated. Anyway, we're keeping it quiet. But I wanted to tell you about him, and ... "

"And?"

"I may have found Ayah."

"*What?*" Quinn felt the news as a pain beneath her ribs, sharp enough to make her gasp.

"I heard from someone claiming to be her nephew." Quinn knew the next words before Sarah said them. "You should come over here."

She couldn't manage to speak.

"I've been a lousy sister to you, Quinn."

They had never talked like this. "No lousier than I've been to you," Quinn said.

"But I was always the one who left. Anyway. It's time things changed, you know? I want to make things different. Come to India."

"Can you hear yourself? You should come back *here*."

"But Ayah's in Delhi."

"According to some con man."

"We won't know till we make contact."

Damn it. Quinn glanced inside. The kids were up out of their chairs now, wandering the house like hungry ghosts. "I don't know, Sarah. We'll talk."

After they hung up, she hunched forward. "Shit." She covered her head with her hands. "Shit." Then she wiped her hand across her face and got up to fix dinner. Soy burgers were on the menu. The kids had decided they didn't want anyone killing animals, legally or otherwise, on their behalf.

Pete walked into the kitchen. "You okay?"

She sighed. "Sarah's taking stock of her life and throwing everything up in the air. It's just got me a little rattled."

"What was it you wanted to tell me?"

She managed a smile. "Nothing, hon."

SARAH

WHEN HE ENTERED HER, everything hit her at once. The way he slid inside her like that was where he belonged. The heat of him. What happened to his face: the relief and—what was it?—*gratitude* that relaxed his features, as if he could finally let go of something he'd been carrying for far too long.

The way she felt like she had finally come home.

She looked down into his face, his head tipped back against the pillow, and she thought his expression must mirror her own. A little incredulous, as if they both were asking, What *is* this? They gripped each other's hands on the mattress on either side of his head, fingers intertwined, neither of them moving much. That part could wait. Instead they let themselves sink deep into this moment when they were naked to each other, hips on hips, and he was inside her body, and forget about motion, forget about friction, right now what was washing over them was the simple fact that they were connected, at the root, at the fingers and palms, at the eyes, and the connection slammed with electricity.

"Do you feel that?" he whispered. She was certain that if he looked in a mirror he wouldn't recognize his own face, it was so alive. He never looked like this except when he was inside her. Maybe her own face was the same.

"I think so," she breathed. "What do you feel?" Like they were discovering something that had never been done before.

"Awake," he whispered.

"Exactly." Energy surged through their bodies, and what she couldn't understand was how she could feel it all the way through the circuit, all the way through both of them. "Something really strange is going on here," she whispered.

He nodded and shifted his hips experimentally, and there went another surge, high up and deep inside, and their eyes widened in the same instant as if they shared a nervous system, and without meaning to, she said, "Wow," and then, "Damn, Sanjay," and then, "Plug in and hold on," and he threw his head back against the mattress and laughed silently. He pulled her down to him and kissed her mouth, still laughing, and she dived into that kiss, the happiest kiss she had ever known. And she thought: Oh, hell yes. I *want* this. I *want* my life.

•

Water everywhere. The streets of Sawai ran with it. Water falling straight over the edges of flat rooftops, no rain gutters to catch it. The whole world had turned liquid.

Always, they came together after dark and parted before sunrise. Their sleep suffered, but the touch made up for it. They looked into each other's eyes for hours at a time, studied each other's bodies inch by inch. They spent whole nights whispering, lips next to ears, words against skin on currents of breath. During the day Sarah took pleasure in Sanjay's full-throated voice, in the resonance of his laughter, but at night she gorged on his whispers, fluid and rippling. The sound of his hushed voice in her ear sent a sweet electrical surge through her body.

"My God, woman," Sanjay murmured one midnight as they lay on floor cushions in his flat. He held her foot in his hand, examining it. "Where did you get these monstrosities?"

"From my father." She pointed her foot, admiring it. "His were just like them."

"That gap between your first and second toes! What a pugmark you must leave. I'd be able to track you anywhere."

"You don't have to track me," she said. "I'm not going to try to lose you."

"Are you sure?"

She gave him a look both chastising and tender. "You can spot a pugmark in the dirt from a moving vehicle, but you can't see how hard I've fallen for you."

"Fallen for me?"

"For everything about you."

"You're quite a one for falling, Sarah DeVaughan." With his thumb he traced the thin pink whisker-scars on her cheek. "You fell right into the water for that cub. And look what it got you."

"I'd do it again." She pushed her head into his hand.

"Are you scent-marking me?" he teased.

"'For if he meets another cat he will kiss her in kindness.'" She kissed his jaw. "'For he is of the Tribe of Tiger.' Do you know this poem? It's one of my favorites." She propped her head on her hand. "'For the cherub cat is a term of the angel tiger. For he is a mixture of gravity and waggery. For there is nothing sweeter than his peace when at rest. For there is nothing brisker than his life when in motion.'"

"That's true."

"'For he can spraggle upon waggle.'"

"What does that mean?"

She rolled onto her hands and knees and demonstrated. He laughed and took her around the waist and pulled her on top of him.

"Oh, you want to play?" She cuffed him lightly on the head, and he grabbed her wrist and held it. "What shall we play? How about you're Akbar and I'll be Machli?"

"Oh my God," he laughed. "You are scandalous."

She gave him an arch grin. "You were right, by the way. I was scent-marking you."

"So you want me for your own. *Achchha*. Very interesting. I thought you just felt sorry for me."

She gaped at him. "Sanjay Prakash, you think this is pity sex?"

"Shh!" He pointed to the wall, his landlord's flat on the other side.

She let herself fall back on the mattress and laughed soundlessly, shoulders shaking.

"You look happy," he said. "It's very beautiful."

They kissed. She pulled away and held his face in her hands. "Listen. I'm not casual about this. And I'm not with you out of pity. I'm falling in love with you, okay? Because you've lived here all your life and you're doing the work that needs to be done. You haven't let yourself go blind to the problems."

He pushed her hair back and studied her face. "It seems strange to me. You have these feelings for me for doing only the things I have to do. And Sarah. This is very fast to be falling in love."

"For doing the things you have to do, and for being the person you are. Why else fall in love with someone? *Is* there anything else?"

He lay back. "There are so many other things."

"I'm not talking about your practical marriage rubric."

"It was never my rubric. And obviously not." He placed a hand on the dip of her waist and ran his hand over her skin. "This is my portal to the universe. Your waist beneath my fingertips. Your *waist*! So strange."

"God's truth," she said. "I think most men would find another portal."

"Naughty girl."

"Hey, which of the bags do you think will be the first to sell?"

They had spent the day in Vinyal with the women, boxing up the first shipment of bags. They'd wrapped the box in muslin and watched as Anju ceremoniously sewed the fabric shut. Indian shrink wrap, Sanjay had joked. Sarah wasn't sure if this was a shipping requirement, but Sanjay had deemed it necessary before they took the box to the DHL office and sent it to the States.

"I don't know what women like to buy in America," he said. "Maybe one of Anju's."

"She does the best work," Sarah said. "Hey, I was thinking. In a few weeks, they're going to get their first payment. We need to talk to them about how a bank account works."

"Budgeting, too." He paused. "This is important work we're doing."

"We're off to a good start, yeah. But we need to figure out how to expand it. Get more women involved. Start making other products. Eventually I'd like to see something like this happening in every other village around the park."

He ran his fingers along her skin. "So this is what a love match feels like. I'm not used to so much happiness."

"You deserve to be this happy all the time."

He smiled at her. "Sarah," he said. And the sound of her name in his voice was so sweet that it lit an ache inside her, like a candle.

•

The problem with finding a portal to the universe was that it was impossible not to manifest it in the world. The next time they picked up Nuri at the hospital and drove to the village, the women greeted them with the same rumor Quinn had called her about: that Sarah and Akbar had kindled an affair.

"You saved his cub," Anju said. "And he fell in love with you in return."

It did make a certain amount of sense.

Anju told them the rumor. Sanjay did his best to translate, though Anju wouldn't say the word *bagh*, tiger, so the conversation was sprinkled with terms like *the orange man* and *the one with stripes*, but in the end, Sarah thought she understood that there were different versions of the story. In some versions, Sarah morphed into a tigress for her dalliances with her tiger lover. They took advantage of the monsoon, which had emptied the park. In the rain, she slipped along the streets of Sawai, still in human form. Somewhere along Ranthambore Road she began to run, and as she ran she changed from a tall, blond human into a golden-coated tigress. Once in the park, she roared until the male appeared. They settled together into a shaded glen and engaged in round after round of tiger sex. She lay on her stomach while he covered her, his big, shaggy head turned so he could bite the back of her neck. The rumors were very clear that this was how the mating happened.

Evidence for this version: Sarah's three whisker-scars, proof that her tiger nature could not be contained.

In other versions, the situation reversed itself: The large-hearted gentleman took on human form and visited Sarah at her flat, a tall, handsome man (like Sanjay, Sarah couldn't help thinking) bearing gifts of incense and perfume. Only his pugmarks gave him away.

"Did Anju call Akbar the large-hearted gentleman?" she asked in English.

"I threw that in," Sanjay said. "Translator's discretion."

"As rumors go, those are pretty good ones."

"Don't make light of this, Sarah. It isn't a joke."

"Are they scared of me?"

He asked the question to the group.

"We're not scared," Rohini said. "You'll protect us. It's good to have you on our side."

It discomfited Sarah to be the cause of so much tiger talk around a woman who had lost her husband to a tiger. When Padma said, quite casually, "If you'd been here earlier, maybe my husband would still be alive," Sarah felt a stab of guilt, as if she could have saved Sunil. "Just keep my children safe," Padma added. "That's enough for me."

Sarah heard herself pledge that she would try.

On the drive back to Sawai, after they dropped off Nuri, Sanjay relayed more of what the women had said as they sewed, conversations they'd pretended he couldn't hear and he'd pretended to ignore. They'd compared opinions about Sarah's body. *What do you think?* they'd asked one another. *Is her stomach growing rounder? her breasts?* Not really, they concluded. *But why* doesn't *she get pregnant? Why wouldn't she want a child?*

Because, Sapna said: *She thinks no one knows she has a tiger lover, and she wants no one to find out.*

But if she did become pregnant, Rohini wanted to know, would there be just one baby or a litter? Would it be a cub or a human? Orange-and-black, or fair like its mother, or brown like an Indian? And what if she birthed a hybrid: a little orange human with round ears, black stripes, and a tail? Wouldn't *that* be a sight to see?

Sarah sat back in her seat. "What do you think of the timing of all this?"

"Coincidence. No one knows."

"And yet anyone could have seen us going into each other's flats. You're known here. You've lived here all your life."

"And you're known here," he said. "You're the Tiger Woman. It's dangerous what we're doing."

"And is that just because you're married, or is it because you've taken a lover who's white?"

"Fifty percent each."

She shook her head. "I look at Geeta Ma'am, and there she is, an Indian woman who married a white man, then divorced him, and now works with him. And no one says a word."

"That's because she's Geeta Ma'am. The upper classes can do as they please. An ordinary middle-class man from small-town Rajasthan does not have the same latitude."

He dropped her off. She had mounted the steps to her flat when the landlord's door opened. Drupti stepped outside, gave Sarah a meaningful look, and headed toward the gate. Sarah joined her, and Drupti feigned surprise. "I'm glad to see you! Walk with me."

They chatted a bit as they walked—how Drupti's summer was going, the status of a luxury hotel going up on Ranthambore Road too close to the park. At the corner, Drupti turned right, then right again. Sarah could see no good reason to walk down this particular residential street. They stopped at a vacant lot bounded by a wall at the back of the property. A cat slunk across the lot and disappeared into overgrown shrubs.

"You recognize those flats?" Drupti asked, pointing beyond the wall.

"That's our building."

Drupti nodded. "When I was seventeen, I sneaked out my window one night and climbed over the wall just there. I met a boy. It was all quite scandalous." She laughed. "He waited for me here on his bicycle. No one saw us. I hopped on his bike and we rode away and had quite a little adventure."

Sarah gave her an assessing look. "Is that so?"

"My father pays a lot of attention to what goes on at the front of the property, but he forgets about what's back here. It's so dark and quiet. No comings and goings aside from birds and cats."

Sarah considered the wall, seven feet tall and made of brick, solidly built but not overly formidable. No barbed wire or embedded broken bottles along the top. The place Drupti had pointed out lay partly hidden by overhanging branches. "Good escape route," Sarah said.

"Easy enough to get back in, too. There's even a place to chain a bike over there." She nodded in the direction of a neem tree.

"You don't say," Sarah said.

QUINN

FOR YEARS, QUINN HAD WANTED Sarah closer. Had pursued her, really. And now? Here was Sarah, holding out her hand at last. And *we'll talk* was the best Quinn could manage. *We'll talk.*

For days after that phone conversation, Quinn had tried to picture herself flying to India, stepping back into that world she had been so heartbroken to leave. But each time she imagined going back, her body gave her its answer in the coldest possible terms. Chills across her arms and legs, floods of ice through her lungs.

Now she sat crossed-legged on the couch, laptop balanced on her thighs, staring at an email.

> Hey Quinn,
>
> I know you weren't ready to talk about it earlier, but you'd love it once you got here. You could come at the end of October and catch Diwali. Remember how much fun it was when we were kids? All over India, one big party. Think about it, okay?

Pete walked into the living room, carrying a basket of clean laundry.

"She won't stop," she said.

He paused in the doorway. "So go."

She looked up, confused.

"Go back to India. We've got the line of credit. It's worth a little debt."

Quinn flushed. Every day she resolved to tell him about the loan, and every day she convinced herself he didn't need to know. "I don't know. There's the kids. And I've got some workshops lined up—"

"Oh, is that it?" He set down the laundry basket. "You're too devoted to your family, you're too busy with your art? Or is it maybe that there's a bigger balance on the credit line than there should be?"

She felt herself pale.

"I saw the statement. Anything you want to tell me?"

"I—"

"You loaned it to your mother, didn't you? I told you specifically I wouldn't agree to that, and you went behind my back."

"It was just supposed to be for a few weeks. I thought it wouldn't matter."

"It wouldn't matter that you lied to me?"

"When I try to talk to you about things, you blow up. It's easier to just not mention them."

"Like what?"

"Like if I went to India for two or three weeks and you were totally in charge of the kids, would Nick have his inhaler with him at all times? Or would you forget?"

His face darkened. "That happened twice. In a year, I forgot his inhaler two times."

"But that's the thing. We have to be a hundred percent." She could hear the pleading note in her voice. "Remember how fast he went down that time. His life is literally at stake."

Pete did a half-turn away from her, an aborted pirouette, and clasped his head in his hands. The very picture of a man at the end of his rope. "See, this is what kills me. You treat me like I don't love our son. How can you think that?" He let his hands fall to his sides and stood facing her. "I love him more than anything. Him and Alaina both. But I look at Nick, and I see how the asthma makes his life smaller. He can't run on the soccer field with the other kids. He has to sit there on the sidelines. And you make it worse. Every time you look at him, you're checking his color, or you're coming after him with the fucking peak flow meter. Every time you do that, you make his life a little less. I can't stand to watch that."

Quinn set aside her laptop and stood to face him. "So I'm the bad guy here because I'm looking out for our son? You act like being a good sport is all it takes. Like if we all just put on our game faces, the whole problem just goes away. He *almost died*. How do you keep forgetting that?"

"No," he shouted. "We had a scare. We live five minutes from the ER, and we got him there on time."

It was too much. "You know what? If you think I'm making Nick smaller by worrying about him, you ought to see how small people get when they die. They just vanish, and it's a sick fucking joke that life goes on and on and on without them. Every second of my life since then has been an insult to him. And you know what? It never goes away. The hole he left is always there. Do you understand that? *It is still there.* It's the fucking stencil of my life."

He stared at her with bleak eyes. "You're just so goddamned damaged. It's too much." He paused. "Go to India, Quinn. I don't care about the line of credit. You've got shit you need to deal with, and God knows you're not doing it here."

The conversation was beginning to scare her. Quietly she asked, "What, are you banishing me?"

His face softened. "Look, I love you. I really do. But you're so scared all the time. You let your mother walk all over you. You're convinced our son's going to die any second. The kids need to see you let go. They need you to do something that takes guts and that's not all about them."

"You mean *you* need that."

"So what? *You* need it more than the rest of us put together. I look at you and your sister and your mom and, my God, you're so walled off from each other. You always have been."

"Don't change the subject."

"That *is* the subject. And don't think I don't know how things are between us."

She sized him up. "You hate me for being afraid."

"I don't hate you." No anger in his voice, just defeat. He wouldn't look at her again. She left the room and found Alaina and Nick huddled in the hallway, crying quietly.

"Come on." She put a hand on each of their shoulders and herded them toward the stairs. "Go back to bed."

"Why are you fighting?" Nick cried.

"Because we're sad."

"You shouldn't fight because you're sad," Alaina said.

Not two weeks ago, she and Pete had thrown a party for the twins' eighth birthday. There'd been invitations, decorations, swag bags, prizes. All that stupid mass-produced stuff, most of it now consigned to the garbage. She peered into her children's anxious faces, saw how their chins trembled, how fear made them fold their hands over their bellies.

"It's going to be okay." She wiped their cheeks and tucked them into bed, whispering, "It's okay." Then she stripped off her clothes and showered, scrubbing herself hard and crying, quietly at first, then in ragged sobs that she tried to strangle, because the twins had already heard too much.

•

The next day, Jane phoned to let her know a shipment had arrived from India. Quinn stopped by that afternoon, still wrecked from the argument. Jane stepped out from the back. "I haven't opened it yet. I thought you might want to do the honors." She frowned at Quinn. "You okay?"

"Didn't sleep," she said dully.

"Insomnia," Jane said. "I hate that."

The back room held a scatter of boxes and crates and loose baubles from around the world. In the middle of the floor sat a box sewn up in thin, off-white muslin, the address scrawled in black Sharpie—Sarah's handwriting. Someone had stapled three official-looking DHL forms to the fabric, filled out in English by another hand, not Sarah's, in capital letters written in a thin, scratchy ballpoint.

Jane handed her a pair of scissors, and Quinn cut the muslin and opened the box. A single purse rested on top, mint green and robin's-egg blue. The hope in it made Quinn want to cry. She lifted it out and opened its flap, peered inside, turned the bag over. Sturdy and well-made. Attached to the strap with a loop of twine was a cardboard tag reading, *Women's cooperative, Vinyal village, Rajasthan, India*. And a paragraph about the village, the tigers, the hopes for the bags. A second tag hung from the twine, and when she turned it over, she found herself looking at a familiar photo. Anju.

Something in her chest lifted ever so slightly. She looked up at Jane. "Thank you for letting me open it."

"It's pretty special, isn't it? I thought you should feel what it's like."

They unpacked the box and spread the purses on the floor. Thirty handbags in six different patterns, all beautifully made. Quinn's eye went back to the first one she'd unpacked, pastel green and blue. "I'm buying that one."

"I thought you might. I still have to enter them into inventory and price them, but go ahead and take that one now. I'll do the paperwork later. And then, in about eight weeks, I'll cut a check to the collective." She paused. "You should deliver it, Quinn."

"What?" she said stupidly.

"Go visit your sister. Meet these seamstresses. See the way they live and what this money's going to do for them."

The way they live. Somehow those words made Quinn think of her twins, huddled in the hallway, crying. "I can't go to India. I've got two little kids."

Jane fixed her with a stare. "And a husband who can take care of them."

"Still. It feels selfish."

"Yeah. Selfish you, helping a women's collective in rural India."

"You know what I mean."

Jane gave her a look of pity and exasperation. "Something's got a hold of you, Quinn Chamberlain. You want to shake it off, you're going to have to do something big."

Later, as Quinn was leaving the shop, Jane put a hand on her arm. "The world would be a better place if more women were selfish." Then she kissed Quinn's cheek.

SARAH

IT SEEMED, AT FIRST, just a break in the weather: a week without rain, not unheard of during the Rajasthani monsoon. But when a second week went by, and then a third, and a fourth, they knew.

They'd gotten eight weeks of rains. A little less than half a normal monsoon. Coupled with the previous year's poor rains, it made for disastrous news.

William's lakes were drying up. In his five years in Sawai, he had built reservoirs for twenty of the driest villages, and nearly half of them were in trouble. Sanjay and William traveled the district for three days, visiting the worst-hit lakes to measure their depths and consider the options. Afterward, they met, the four of them, at the Tiger Survival office to talk through the situation and work up a plan.

The meeting didn't go well. Sanjay and William seemed at odds, short with each other. Sarah studied them both. William met her gaze, unsmiling. Something in his expression unsettled her.

That night, Sanjay crept up the stairs to Sarah's flat. She opened the door soundlessly.

"I came over the back wall," he murmured.

"How was it?"

"Terrifying. The whole time I expected your landlord to step out his back door and shoot me for an intruder."

They were quiet when they made love that night. They were always quiet, but this time he put his hand lightly over her mouth.

She pushed it away and gave him an amazed look. "What's wrong?" she whispered.

He rolled onto his side, keeping his voice to a murmur, no louder than the sweep of the ceiling fan. "It's William. He knows. And he's angry. He told me if I really cared for you, I wouldn't put you in such danger."

She felt something rising, something ominous she didn't want to look at head-on. "Who does he think is a threat to us?"

"My wife's family." He looked away. "Let me tell you, Sarah. He's right. I don't like to think what happens if my brother-in-law finds out."

"Why? What would he do?"

"Tarun is not exactly a simple restaurant owner. He's friends with the district commissioner, the chief of police. When Lakshmi and I were together, he used to brag about his competitors' bad luck. Somehow their contracts were always being ruled invalid, their permits were always falling through. I suppose with me, he would go after my livelihood somehow." He ran a hand down his face. "I never thought I would be this person. A man lying in bed with a woman and talking about my wife."

"We both know this is dangerous," she said. "We've been careful."

"We need to be more careful."

A sick feeling swept over her. Every time she slid through his door and pulled it closed behind her, she felt safe, as if she'd gotten away with something. But anyone could be watching them, unseen. Likely they wouldn't know the moment of discovery. It would come not as a confrontation but as an infection, silent and unrecognized at the crucial moment, and they would know it only later, by its consequences. "William's wrong about one thing," she said. "It's not me who'd be in danger. It's you."

He didn't contradict her.

They began meeting later, in the deepest part of the night. Two hours, three, together. It was never enough.

•

The lone benefit of the failed monsoon was that the park reopened a week earlier than expected. Sarah, Sanjay, William, and Hari spent mornings there as frequently as possible, wanting to catch a first glimpse of Machli and the cubs, hoping to get a sighting of Akbar.

On an early visit, they happened upon a village man on hands and knees at the edge of a clearing, not far from a magnificent banyan tree. He didn't seem to hear the sound of their engine as they approached. Something felt off; Sarah wasn't sure what, but she raised her camera and clicked off shots. At the sound of her shutter, the man spun around and looked directly into her lens, eyes wide with alarm, then bolted into the woods.

Sanjay leapt out of the jeep and crossed to where the man had been, walking gingerly, as if he were trying not to set off a bomb. He stopped, bent over, and came up holding something. "Snare trap," he said grimly, showing them the loop of wire. He gave it a sharp tug. "Look how sturdy he's made it. He was going after tiger."

Sarah couldn't keep herself from imagining that wire biting into a tiger's leg, the tiger leaping and screaming and fighting until it gave up and lay down in defeat. And then dying in whatever way a poacher would kill a snared tiger. A spear between the ribs, probably. She felt sick to think of it but elated, too, to know that at least this once, there would be no trap. She thought she might throw up.

They radioed the forest guards and drove back to the ranger station to give a report to the police. Her horror abated slowly. She turned over her photos as evidence. "Nicely done," Geeta told her at the office that afternoon. It was the first time Geeta had praised her work.

A week later, they got their Akbar sighting. Sarah recorded it in her journal.

September 24, 2000

Akbar crouches over a fresh kill, a chital doe. He is not at his finest: thin, muddy, bedraggled, and spent. He probably hasn't eaten in days, and the hunt must have taken most of his energy. Vultures and tree pies have begun to gather, and then the intruder appears, young and thin-faced, only a year or two out of the protection of his mother. He halts three trees back in the forest, watching. Akbar, about to tear open the chital's haunch, lifts his head and snarls. The intruder holds his ground.

Akbar roars. It's a physical wallop, hard as an ax blow against the tree trunks. The intruder flinches but doesn't flee, just shifts his weight on muddy paws.

Akbar advances on him. The intruder circles, emerging from the trees a few paces downwind. He glances at the doe, licks his mouth. Akbar takes that moment to charge. The tigers engage, rearing up on hind legs to pound each other with their forepaws, claws slashing, daggerlike canine teeth bared, faces wrinkled in full recoil, ears pinned back. Their roars rip the air and set the forest shrieking with alarm calls. Birds lift off in a whir of beating wings. My heart pounds against my ribs.

Akbar is the giant in the clearing, deep-chested and mighty. He lashes his tail, gathers himself, and launches in a blur of fangs and blazing eyes, smashing blows and battering roars. He lands a wallop against the side of the intruder's skull that sends him falling to the slippery ground. On the way down, his hind leg scrapes the dead doe's hoof, opening a wound. Akbar unlooses a shattering roar and leaps for the kill.

But even wounded, the intruder is quick. He rolls to his feet and bounds into the forest, crashing through the brush. Akbar chases him a distance, then stops and gives a final bellow, quaking the leaves on the trees. He licks a long slash on his shoulder. His blood must taste hot and metallic, the same as the animals he eats.

He returns to the dead doe, chases off the vultures that have already plucked out her eyes, and sets to eating.

I know the younger male has no choice in the matter. He has survived so far by skulking and thieving, but that kind of subsistence is too meager to sustain a full-grown tiger for long. If he wants to survive, he has to take a territory in the forest for himself. So he will seek out Akbar again, even at risk of his life.

I know I'm not supposed to get attached, but I can't stand the thought of the intruder laying waste to Machli's cubs and their whole generation, all across the park. Especially not after she lost her cubs last year. It's awful to say this, but I hope Akbar kills him.

•

Something was happening between her and Sanjay. Maybe it was the drought, the stress it placed on everyone. Maybe it was the conflict in the park. Sanjay told her one night that if he were free, he would marry her. They'd just made love, and she judged him still caught up in the chemical rush.

"Really?" she said. "What would your parents have thought of that?"

He squinted, thinking. "To tell you the truth, I think they would have liked the same things about you that they liked about Lakshmi. You're both opinionated and smart. My father would have appreciated your sense of adventure. My mother loved to host journalists and professors in our home. She thought it broadened us. She would have wanted to know everything about your travels."

"But?"

"But you two would have clashed if we married. She would have wanted you to play the Indian daughter-in-law."

"Submissive," Sarah said.

"Only till you produced a son. Then you could rule the house, maximum bossy style."

She thought about that. Their son would be beautiful. His skin fairer than Sanjay's, darker than hers. He would have curls, no doubt. Sanjay would pick him up and kiss his soft, round cheek. And the neighbors would stop by with gifts because all of this family-making would happen in the open, in perfect freedom, and no one in Sawai would judge Sanjay harshly for divorcing his wife and marrying Sarah.

If only.

She could feel the want coming off him, his palpable need for a son. Was it coincidence that Sanjay had devoted his life to saving the tiger from extinction when his own family was destined for that fate? Genetically only the tiniest of lines would disappear: the one that began with his parents and ended with him. In terms of species survival, their DNA would not be missed. But she knew it saddened him that there was no one to take custody of the memories. He had told her once that his mother loved nothing better than a wedding because it gave her the chance to dress up in her best sari and dance till the sun came up. His father had taken excellent care of his possessions; he taught Sanjay to wipe down his motorbike after every ride. He tousled Sanjay's hair when he was proud of him and told him stories when Sanjay felt troubled, stories that never had anything to do with Sanjay's problem yet made him feel better just the same. Even his marriage. He and Lakshmi had had good times that first year, a period of romance and hope before the first miscarriage. Sanjay had told Sarah funny stories about his efforts to win over his mother-in-law; he talked about it like a game of strategy with a worthy opponent.

It seemed so clear that Sanjay needed to pass his memories on, needed someone to understand that they mattered. If he couldn't have a son, then Sarah would gladly do that for him.

"I wonder sometimes how you ended up here in my arms," he said.

"I think it was all the times I nearly threw up on you." She lay back against his chest. "Actually, it was the day I saw you at the cinema with Hari's boys. That was the moment I fell in love with you. I didn't realize it at the time."

"Children mean a great deal to you. The boy soldiers. Your niece and nephew." He lay silent a moment. "I want to introduce you to the boys."

QUINN

IN THE WEEKS after the twins witnessed Quinn and Pete's fight, bedtimes grew fraught with drama. Alaina became clingy, Nick quiet and serious. One night after Quinn tucked him in, he said, "Mom? Are you and Dad gonna get a divorce?"

She sat down on the edge of his bed and petted his hair. "No, honey. We've just been disagreeing about some things, is all." She kissed his forehead. "Things will get better." Once, in a fit of love blindness when the twins were babies, she had told Pete she would never lie to them. It hadn't occurred to her that there would be times she would have no idea what the truth was.

Afterward, she came downstairs and stood awkwardly at the couch, where Pete sat in a pool of yellow lamplight, staring at nothing.

"We can't let ourselves fight in front of them again," she said.

He shrugged. "They can see things aren't right. Maybe it just makes it worse if we pretend everything's okay."

"Well," she said quietly, "then let's *make* everything okay."

He looked up at her with sudden hope.

"I don't know how," she admitted. "But we'll figure it out."

He looked away again, defeated.

She rekindled her long-abandoned habit of meditating in the mornings, not really expecting it to help. The Buddha said resistance to change, not change itself, was the cause of suffering. She didn't know if she believed that. So much was unacceptable: what had happened to Marcus, what could happen to Nick. What kind of sister would she be, what kind of mother, if she accepted those things?

Meditation proved useful for identifying old hurts. The hurt, for instance, that Sarah had spent her life rejecting Quinn's overtures. And her anger at the unfairness: Now that the invitation was on Sarah's terms, Quinn should drop everything and go? Useful, too, for identifying her real agenda for sitting in meditation. She was trying to meditate her way into becoming the old Quinn, the one her husband could live with and her kids surely needed: maybe not brave, but brave enough.

Alaina accepted Quinn's practice with unconcern. Nick mocked it. "*Omm!*" he chanted at her, furious, one morning. Her sweet son, her old soul of a child. She caught him as he stomped out of the room, sat down with him, talked with him till he calmed down.

It's too selfish, she thought. How can I leave them?

She spent the next two days thinking on that question. On the third morning, she sat down to meditate. When she opened her eyes, she knew what she needed to do.

SARAH

THE SUN WAS NOSING over the horizon when Sanjay killed the engine of his motorbike outside the park gates. Sarah, sitting sidesaddle, slid off the back and lifted the boys down, and they began leaping and chasing each other, exultant with the joy of the ride.

"That was absolutely terrifying," Sarah said. "I don't know how Indian women do it."

Sanjay smiled. "Let me tell you, Indian women have nerves of steel."

"Is it a long walk, Uncle?" Mohan shouted. He was the younger boy, seven or so and missing teeth.

"It's a terribly long walk. Adventures are never easy."

Mohan and Jai grabbed Sarah's hands and swung them, and they joined the trail of worshippers heading toward the fortress. Sarah had never thought the park lacked for color, what with the parakeets, kingfishers, and peacocks, not to mention the tigers—but now, surrounded by the vivid hues of Rajasthani textiles, she felt as if she'd stumbled into a kaleidoscope.

The dusty road entered the forest, where large birds rustled in the trees and peafowl mewed, and the boys looked around, wide-eyed as any foreigner.

"Are there tigers in the forest?" Jai asked.

"Yes, but they have an agreement with Ganesha," Sanjay said. "They leave his worshippers alone."

Jai nodded seriously. "I can't believe anybody would kill a

tiger, even if they needed the money."

"Everything is connected," Sanjay said. "Protecting the tiger will protect every species of animal and plant that shares its habitat. The trees that scrub pollution from the air and the rivers that supply water to every living thing."

"So to save the tiger is to save all of nature," Jai said. "Including us."

"Well said, young man." Sanjay tousled his hair.

A forest guard recognized Sanjay and offered a ride to the base of the cliff, for which the boys clamored with relief. When the guard dropped them off, the boys tilted their heads far back to look up to the fortress ramparts a thousand feet above, glowing orange against the bright blue sky. The sun had broken above the eastern cliffs, sending daylight halfway down the western slopes.

"All the way up *there?*" Jai pointed.

"All the way up."

On the long, crowded trek upward, they passed a penitent inchworming his way up the track. "Why is he lying down with his face in the dirt?" Mohan asked loudly.

"He's going all the way to the temple just the way he's going now," Sanjay said. "Prostrating himself full out, getting up, placing his feet in his handprints, and prostrating himself again."

"Won't his mommy be angry with him for getting his clothes dirty?"

"Not at all. He's doing it because he feels the need to shed his sins."

Mohan looked confused. "He can shed his sins by crawling in the *dirt?*"

"By doing something humble and difficult."

"But why are people touching his feet?"

"Out of respect for his piety."

"Come on, Mohan, you've seen people do that at our temple," Jai said.

"No, I haven't."

"Yes, you have."

"You boys remind me of two kids I know back in America," Sarah said.

"We *do?*" Jai said, shocked.

At the top of the cliff, the earth flattened out. The boys looked around, awed to find themselves so elevated. They walked past monkeys, past a white-bearded holy man tending the Hanuman shrine. Sanjay stayed a few steps behind Sarah and the boys. "Walk with us," she invited, but he shook his head, smiling.

"I like watching you three together."

The temple yard bustled with humans and langurs. Ancient stone buildings bounded the wide courtyard, interspersed with temporary markets of scraggly timber posts roofed with blue tarp, where men sold candies and cassette tapes and garlands of marigolds. At one end of the courtyard stood the low temple, topped by a colorful striped dome against the bright blue sky.

Inside the dim temple, the atmosphere changed. A gong clanged, loud and insistent, over the hollow beat of a goatskin drum and the sounds of a flute rising and falling like a cold wind. It was as if they'd stepped through a portal into some loud, wild place high in the mountains. All this clangor to draw Ganesha's attention to the presence of worshippers.

They joined the throng shuffling to the altar in a haze of sandalwood. When their turn came, they stepped past the rail and found themselves face-to-face with the god. Ganesha sat in his niche in statue form: pot-bellied, elephant-headed bestower of wisdom and remover of obstacles. At his feet lay garlands of marigold and rose, a brass bowl filled with golden oil, powdery mounds of ochre spices.

What should she pray for? She didn't know.

Yes, she did.

The most righteous prayers were not petitions to get what you wanted. They were pleas for the grace to bear whatever came your way. She knew that. She did.

She looked straight at Ganesha and prayed: Let Sanjay be mine.

They emerged squinting into the bright blue day, the sun a coin high above. A short-horned white bullock with an extra hoof growing out of his back stood ambitionless outside the temple. Sad, Sarah thought. Or was it? Did the other cattle shun him, or did the extra hoof mean nothing? India did not hide illness and deformity. Life was so much more various here.

She looked at Sanjay, wondering if he could feel the grit of her prayer. If he knew she had claimed him.

"What do you think?" he asked the boys.

"I liked it," Jai said. "I liked having to come so far. It makes it more special."

"I like the monkeys," Mohan said.

"Be careful about the monkeys," Sanjay warned. "Sometimes they'll leap up and snatch your garland from right around your neck."

"Why?" Mohan clutched his garland.

"So they can eat the flowers."

"Stay away, monkey," Mohan scolded a nearby langur.

"And don't look him in the eye, or he'll attack you."

"Why?"

"It's considered aggressive in monkey society. It makes them think you want to fight."

"Do you think a forest guard will take us back to your motorbike?"

"I don't know. We'll have to wait and see."

"It's an adventure," Sarah reminded them. Her eyes met Sanjay's over the boys' heads, and they exchanged a smile.

Someone called Sanjay's name: a short, balding man with thick glasses. "Mr. Jain," Sanjay said. "Namaskar."

Mr. Jain looked at Mohan and Jai and particularly Sarah, clearly dying to know what was going on here. "Ms. DeVaughan is a colleague," Sanjay said. "Jai and Mohan are here today learning about the park's ecosystems."

"Always teaching," Mr. Jain said. "Since you were a boy. Well, Jai, Mohan, today will be a great education for you. Teacher uncle knows all about this park." He gave Sarah a friendly nod and said his goodbyes.

Sarah watched him walk away, pulled a five-rupee coin from her pocket, and sent the boys, whooping, to a confectionery stall nearby. She turned to Sanjay.

"He's an old family friend," Sanjay said.

"That doesn't mean he won't gossip."

"You're a colleague. It's perfectly normal for us to be together."

It was true, but it didn't feel true.

The boys came running back with a bag and showed off the boiled sweets they'd chosen. Sarah congratulated the boys on their excellent taste, and when she looked up at Sanjay, she saw that he loved her, and loved the boys, so much that it nearly crushed him.

It was so plainly visible. She wondered if Mr. Jain had seen it.

•

On their next drive in the park, they sighted Akbar lying flat on his side beneath a neem tree. Sarah raised her field glasses and watched his flank rise and fall with his breathing. Something was different; she was trying to parse it out when Sanjay, looking through his own binoculars, murmured, "Can you get us closer, Hari?"

Hari maneuvered them to a field not far from where the tiger lay. It was clear now. Akbar's coat looked scruffy and battered, torn in places. Though Hari had kept a respectful distance, the big male raised his head at their approach, struggled to his feet, and hobbled away on three legs, his head bobbing with each step. He couldn't bear weight on his right front paw. His flanks were caved in with hunger.

High overhead, a single vulture hung in midair, suspended on a thermal. They were silent the rest of the drive.

•

The knock at her door came at dawn two mornings later. She answered it in pajamas, her skin damp from sleep. William. She took in his expression.

He didn't have to say it. She already knew.

By the time they arrived, the forest guards had pulled the body from beneath the branches of a capparis shrub and collected wood for the fire.

"Oh, Akbar." Sarah knelt next to his ruined form and ran a hand over his matted ruff. It seemed impossible that he didn't flinch at her touch. He had looked so regal her first day in the park, when he had stepped in front of their jeep. Now his ribs showed through dirty, blood-matted fur, and his massive head seemed too big for his body.

"He's been fighting," Geeta said. "All these fresh scars." She crouched and picked up his paw, bigger by far than her hand, and felt among the pads. "Look at this. Puncture wound. That was what did it." She held the paw in both hands. "Akbar. You were such a good papa."

The wildlife veterinarian arrived with his kit and drew a knife from his bag. Sarah turned away as he set to work. It was a gray, shadowless day with nothing to look at, nothing to distract from the gruesome, wet sounds of a body being dismantled. She glanced at William and Sanjay, their eyes cast down. Geeta stared straight at the body, her expression unreadable.

When he finished with his work, the veterinarian straightened and flexed his knees a few times and said that barring evidence of poison in the tissue samples, in his opinion the cause of death was starvation, resulting from injury leading to the inability to hunt.

Sarah let herself look then. It was horrid. Beautiful Akbar had been destroyed. What was left looked like meat. Four forest guards hefted the butchered body and settled it onto the stacked wood.

Separately they placed the skin atop the carcass. The park director circled the woodpile, setting match to tinder. A tiger dealer would have paid thousands for the body, starved and diseased or not. Hence the fire, so the body wouldn't be looted.

Within minutes the flames took hold, sending up a stench of flesh and burning hair. They bowed their heads. Some of the forest guards prayed aloud. Some held hands, as Indian men do in friendship.

Once, Sarah had written an article about a rescue operation back in the States that housed big cats confiscated from private breeders and roadside zoos. The animals arrived skinny and malnourished, and even after they regained their health, every one of them still bore scars from the old traumas. One particular panther spent the rest of his life pacing nonstop exactly fifteen feet in either direction, the length of the cage where he had been imprisoned for years, too damaged to adjust to his larger enclosure at the rescue. The tigers' coats were a uniform dull brown, and it was impossible to tell Siberian from Sumatran because their various captors had bred them without any regard for subspecies. They were mutts. Quietly Sarah told the story.

"Your mutts will be the survivors when it's all said and done," Geeta said. "Behind bars, every last one."

The fire spat and hissed. Seven vultures wheeled in a grimy sky. The wind died, and smoke hung like a pall. Akbar had been a successful tiger, siring something like two dozen cubs in his years as resident male. Many had lived to adulthood and successfully dispersed within this small island of wilderness. So he had his legacy. A whole generation.

William wiped his eyes.

Sarah's throat ached. She wanted badly for Sanjay to hold her, but that was impossible. Instead he moved away and stepped toward William. They'd been avoiding each other the past few weeks. Now, though, they exchanged a glance. The eye contact took effort; anyone could see that. But Sanjay held out his hand, and William hesitated, then took it. They turned back to the pyre, hand in hand, and Sarah felt that what they were doing was good for all of them.

It was gritty work, burning a corpse. The forest guards prodded it with sticks and tools to break up the charred bones. The smoke carried Akbar's body into the lowering sky.

•

Late that night, Sarah unlocked her door, and Sanjay slipped into her darkened flat. She'd been crying. She thought maybe he had, too. They clasped each other close and she pressed her face into his shoulder. For a time they stood silently, unmoving. She tugged his shirttail out of his pants and unbuttoned the top few buttons, and he pulled the shirt over his head without bothering about the rest. At her bedroom doorway, they stopped and looked at each other. The headboard.

"Back here," Sarah whispered. At the far end of a darkened passage, she took off her clothing and stood naked before him. It wasn't pleasure she wanted this time; it was his skin against hers, its reassuring warmth. In the dark he fumbled with the condom.

They kept silent except for their ragged breathing and the bump of their bodies against the doorframe. She wrapped her arms around his waist and clutched him tight.

Afterward, when they realized the condom had torn, Sarah paced outside the bathroom door, madly counting on her fingers and mumbling *ohmyGod, ohmyGod.* Sanjay stood by the sink, staring at nothing. Had they never realized what a catastrophe a pregnancy would be?

"I'm so sorry, Sarah," Sanjay whispered. "I prayed to Ganesha to keep you safe."

That stopped her. "Holy shit. I prayed to him to … "

"To what?"

"To make you mine."

His eyes widened. He looked at her full on. "I want to be with you, Sarah. I want to marry you. Have children with you."

In the dimness she could barely see his face. The sudden turn in the conversation confused her. She wasn't sure if Sanjay was proposing something or merely wishing aloud, and she had the feeling that if she said one more thing about their future, she'd be setting something in motion that she didn't intend. Warily she said, "I'm not going to get pregnant tonight. I'm past the danger point."

He stood silent. "My children would have been four, five, and six if they had lived. A little younger than Mohan and Jai."

"You would have made a wonderful father."

"You don't want a family?"

She felt accused somehow. She hadn't expected to have this conversation, certainly not tonight. "We're not going to get that, Sanjay. The way we are together is the only way it can be."

He didn't respond. She stepped into his arms. Sweat slicked both their bodies. She nearly slid through his grasp.

In the bedroom she lay awake, feeling the weight of his arm curled over her hip, his fingertips resting on her abdomen.

"Hey," she said. "Are you awake?"

"I'm awake." His fingers traced the skin below her navel.

She grasped his hand and stilled it. "Sanjay, stop. I can't be your vessel."

QUINN

IT WAS AN UNSEASONABLY WARM autumn day, and Pete had just finished mowing the lawn, the last cutting before winter came. Quinn stood with him in the fresh-cut grass, staining the bottoms of her bare feet. "I've decided something."

He looked up at her, wary.

"I'm going to India." It came out sounding blunt and confrontational.

The lawnmower stood between them, all grease and metal and incipient racket. Pete produced a rag from his back pocket and crouched to wipe cut grass blades off the casing. When he stood, he looked a little hurt and a little insulted and a little hopeful and a little like he didn't believe she'd follow through.

"Please say something," she said.

He gave her an appraising look. "Good for you, Quinn. I mean it." He stuffed the rag into his pocket. "I'll make sure Nick has his inhaler."

•

After her first round of vaccinations, she drove to the eastern suburbs, where Mother lived alone in the house where the girls had grown into women. They sat facing each other on matching sage-green damask loveseats in front of the fireplace. When Quinn told her the news, Mother got up and poured them each a glass of pinot grigio, placed one in front of Quinn, and settled onto one of the loveseats. "Don't go. It's bad enough with Sarah there." Her voice was a lake in thaw: warming, but edged with brittle shards.

It hit Quinn then that Mother had lost all three of her children. They had each found their own way to disappear from her, and from one another. Marcus had had no say in the matter, but Sarah and Quinn—they chose.

"I'm sorry, Mother. I need to do this."

Mother gave her a flinty look and took a good-sized swallow of pale wine. "You know, I've always hated it that you kids call me Mother," she said. "Your father was Daddy. Why couldn't I be Mommy? Or just Mom?"

Quinn didn't know what to say. *Mommy?* She couldn't picture it. "Why didn't you ever tell us?"

She waved a manicured hand. "You can't tell your kids what to call you. But honestly. *Mother.* It sounds like someone you hate."

"We didn't hate you. We just lived different lives. Most days it was us and Ayah."

"That was my fault." She exhaled a self-mocking laugh. "That miserable little expat community. Sometimes I felt like I was living in a John Updike novel." She shook her head at some memory Quinn couldn't imagine. "That country was no place for children. I should have taken the three of you back to the States. The hell with your father." She sipped her wine and frowned as if it hurt to swallow. "Don't go back there, Quinnie. There's nothing in that place but heartache."

"There's something there for Sarah," Quinn said.

SARAH

October 3, 2000

Machli's daughters are growing bigger and hungrier all the time. She has begun to let them hunt with her, but they're clumsy and clueless, and for every time they manage to scare a boar or a chital into her path, they must botch five other attempts. It's the only way they'll learn how to judge the precise moment to pounce, the difference between a prey animal just close enough to capture and one just out of reach.

Today when we see them, Lalit stalks past Machli, grumbling to herself. They are resting on the lakeshore, and their sides look caved in, as if they haven't eaten in a few days.

Machli rises and leaves her daughters, veering away from the lakeshore and prowling into the deep forest. "She's not letting them come with her," Sanjay says. "She can't risk a mistake."

None of us say it, but I suspect we're all thinking the same thing: Something needs to change soon if the cubs are to survive.

As quietly as possible, we move to a good vantage point. Machli hides beneath the leafy cover of a bush, where she waits until a family of boars wanders into view. For a long time, they root beneath the spreading branches of a mature tree, just out of reach. She can't steal closer; there's no cover between her and them.

She holds herself immobile for more than an hour. At last the boars begin to move in her direction. When the moment is right, she explodes into attack. The forest shrieks—but the boars scatter. She stops and stares after them, breathing fast.

She returns to her cubs at the lakeshore and lies down between them. Light is fading. They will all spend a hungry night.

I wonder whether she thinks about last year's cubs, the ones who didn't survive the drought.

I know there are plenty of animal behaviorists who'd like us to believe that animals are like machines, doing whatever is necessary for survival in some sort of robotic, emotionless fashion. I can't make myself believe it, though.

Last week William finally told me the story, albeit reluctantly, after I asked. Survival (he said in his inimitable way) is always a matter of a steady stream of kills; too long a gap between meals and a tiger will grow too weak to hunt, and once that happens, the end is inevitable. For weeks last year, Machli managed to capture just enough prey to keep herself and the cubs alive. But a moment came when she must have realized she had crossed the line. The hunting was too meager, or she'd grown too weak, and she could no longer sustain herself and her three cubs. She didn't have the choice to make some sort of noble gesture, sacrificing herself to save her children. She was the family's sole breadwinner. Without her, the cubs could not survive.

So she had to make a decision: Let her cubs starve to death, or kill them herself. She chose to spare them the suffering of a lingering death. She crushed the vertebrae at the back of their necks. I try not to picture what that must have been like for her. First one, then the next, then the next. Then walking away, leaving her children's bodies behind her.

The forest guards found them beneath a banyan tree.

Machli lived to have another litter, Lalit and Dil. But I have to think she remembers her other children. I have to think she grieves for them.

QUINN

QUINN RETURNED HOME from her visit with Mother. It was early morning in Rajasthan. She pictured her sister moving about her kitchen, boiling water for tea and thinking about the coming day. Peeling an orange as the air filled with woodsmoke from ten thousand breakfast fires.

She picked up her phone.

Alaina sat at the table, drawing. "Tell Auntie Sarah we think it's really cool that she foiled a poacher."

•

That night, Sarah emailed her.

> Quinn! I'm so excited! So what if you're missing Diwali? You'll be HERE.
>
> You won't need to bring much. Fit it all in a carry-on if you can. Plug adapters, Cipro, earplugs for the flight. A camera but no binocs. I have an amazing pair you can use.
>
> For the park, no bright clothing, especially red. Khakis and natural greens are best. (If you have dust-colored clothes, all the better. You'll get covered.) What else? Money belt. A luggage padlock and a bicycle-type cable lock so nobody

can walk off with your bag in case you have to leave it alone for a minute. A whistle on a lanyard. And if you bring a purse, it should be small and cross-body style.

Bring pencils for the village kids, too.

I hope the tigers come out for you. We've seen Machli and Lalit and Dil, so we know they're still alive, but what happens next, no one knows. Either the new male will kill the cubs, or he won't. It's his decision.

Diwali is coming. Remember what it was like when we were kids? Lights everywhere. Colored powders. Firecrackers. For me it'll just be a warm-up for the real celebration— your visit.

Love,

Sarah

P.S. We have so much to talk about, Quinn. There are things I've never once said to you.

So it would be a trade, Quinn thought. One sister's secrets in exchange for the other's.

THE DEVAUGHAN SISTERS

QUINN STEPPED, EXHAUSTED, into the bustling arrivals hall, and there was Sarah, beaming like a tall blond lighthouse. They hugged and exclaimed and took each other in. Quinn looked around the bright, modern airport. "Things have changed around here."

"India is starting to boom," Sarah said. "But wait till we get to Old Delhi. We're staying there tonight. You'll recognize it." She turned to the stocky man standing next to her. "Hari, this is my sister, Quinn."

He namaskared with a touch of amusement. "Two of a kind," he said. Quinn and Sarah laughed. There was no denying it.

Delhi's old city walloped Quinn. The smells of street food and brick dust, woodsmoke and diesel, the nonstop movement of traffic and pedestrians that made her realize her memories had gone stripped-down and static. A commercial truck with multicolored pom-poms jouncing at the roofline rumbled past a wooden oxcart, a wandering white cow, and three weaving bicycles, each with an extra passenger. Shops spilled merchandise out onto sidewalks: racks of pointy-toed slippers, glinting foil packets of tobacco for sale in coiled streamers. Women wearing saris and salwar kameez shopped and worked and walked their babies in strollers; men went about their business in Western clothes or *kurta*, some with turbans, some with henna-dyed beards. Everywhere, the past showed through the overlay of the present, right down to the successively fading layers of signage on buildings: The electronics shop used to sell men's underwear and, prior to that, had housed a leatherworks. Quinn had forgotten the density of it all. It made the U.S. look flat and shiny.

At their hotel, she took a twenty-dollar bill from her wallet and held it out to Sarah. "It's from the twins," she said. "To help the tigers. They saved it up from their allowance."

Sarah took the bill. "They're good little people, those two."

"They're at an age where everything seems so clear," Quinn said. "Sometimes I envy them that."

"You and me both," Sarah said. "Nothing is simple over here. There's no doing good in one way without doing harm in another. I wish … " She shook her head. "I just wish, you know?"

"So do I," Quinn said. She watched Sarah move around the room. "You know, I thought you were crazy, coming back here."

Sarah had opened her suitcase to dig for something. She looked up at Quinn. "I've never blamed India for Marcus. Bad things happen to people, even in the States. You can't write off a whole country because of it."

Quinn considered that. "Did you know that when Daddy first told Mother he wanted to move here, she thought it was going to be like something out of Kipling?"

"Was it really that different?"

"It's not colonial anymore. I guess that's what she was imagining."

"And yet she got her big house and her personal driver and cook and nanny and security guard and housekeeper," Sarah said. "She wanted to be a *memsahib*, and she pretty much got it. Do you remember how she used to complain how hard it was to run a household staff?"

"Yeah. But think of all we had when we were kids. We benefited plenty. And anyway, *you* have a driver."

"Not like Ravindra. But you're right. I've failed to figure out how to subvert the colonial hangover." Sarah sat on her bed and wrapped her arms around her knees. "I tried to go back."

"What?"

"To Cornwallis Road. I couldn't get there. The roads were shut down." She rocked a little, lost in thought, then looked up at Quinn, her face bright. "Do you want to go?"

Quinn laughed in surprise. "I kind of assumed we would."

She called home to say she'd arrived. The conversation with Pete held more warmth than they'd shared in months. It panged her. She recognized that kind of tenderness, which felt like connection but wasn't really. More like a wistfulness at feeling the weight of the planet between them and knowing that maybe they wouldn't be able to close that distance again.

They said their love-yous, and she asked him to put the kids on. She heard the click as he turned on the speaker.

"Hi, Mommy," the twins sang.

"Hi, babies," she crooned. "It's nighttime here."

"That's so weird," Alaina said, and Nick said, "That's because of the way the earth rotates," and Alaina said, "I know, but it's still weird."

The twins reported their news. Quinn made sure to comment on everything they said, and then, when it was her turn, gave them a few impressions of India. At a lull in the conversation she said, "Okay, you two. I have to go now. Listen, I'm not going to be able to call you every day. Remember we talked about that?"

"When will you call us again?" Alaina whined.

"I'll call every three days," Quinn promised. "Four at the most," she added, suddenly struck with the fear that she'd lose track of time.

•

The next morning, Hari drove them in the direction of their childhood home, through some of Delhi's better neighborhoods. Sarah wanted to recognize landmarks, but she couldn't be sure if she did. Houses were smaller than she remembered, trees bigger.

When they turned onto their street, though, she knew instantly. The grand old brick houses, the bougainvillea-covered walls lining the street, punctuated by pretty iron gates. She remembered childhood Aprils when fallen bougainvillea petals would carpet the ground in rose red.

A block from where they'd grown up, she and Quinn got out of the vehicle and walked in the shade of mellow brick walls. Off to the left, a ribbon of woods still stood behind the houses, sheltering the creek that ran through the neighborhood in the rainy season.

At the gate, they stopped and wrapped their fingers around the sun-warmed iron bars. There it was: the house they'd grown up in. A circular driveway surrounded the peepal tree, the asphalt a bit crumbled but still neatly lined with pea gravel. No car in the driveway. A watchman came striding across the courtyard, stopped opposite them inside the gate, and inquired politely about their business. When they told him, he nodded, wished them a good day, and retreated to the far side of the courtyard, where he pretended not to watch them and they pretended not to notice his watching.

Their bodies knew that house: the bumpiness of the ivory-painted stucco, the way the sunlight poured through its tall, graceful windows and spilled onto warm hardwood floors, the view from that second-story window in the corner, where the nursery had been. The only noticeable change was that the landscaping around the house was different now, an assortment of small ornamental bushes where they'd had sprawling hibiscus.

The peepal tree had grown even more beautiful. Thick-bodied and muscular, its smooth gray trunk curved in and out on itself. To Sarah it looked like a gathering of people crowding close together, their arms raised high and spreading out to shade the courtyard. The tree had put down new prop roots since they'd last seen it, straight down from branch to earth, and some of those roots had merged with the trunk. Its heart-shaped leaves quaked subtly on slim petioles as if the tree were breathing.

"*Ficus religiosa*," Sarah said. "It's not hard to see why it's called that."

Quinn gave her a puzzled glance.

"That's its scientific name. Didn't you know that? Also known as the Bodhi tree, the tree the Buddha was sitting under when he gained enlightenment."

"So everybody knows this kind of tree is special," Quinn said. "All this time I thought it was just us."

It was the best tree, Sarah thought: so clearly alive and full of friendly spirits. Someone had tucked a marble Ganesha into the incurving between two roots. The wooden bench was gone, but someone had replaced it with a wrought iron bench in exactly the same location. Roots bumped up through the dirt. The day Marcus had put a snake down her shirt, she'd taken off running, tripped over a root and fallen on her face. If she'd been bigger and heavier, she would have squashed the snake. As it was, the thing wiggled out her armhole and slithered away at top speed, hissing.

"Look how much bigger around it is," Quinn said. "Twenty-six years."

Sarah considered it. "We couldn't get our arms around it then. I wonder if we could now, as adults. All of us, I mean."

"Hold out your arms." Quinn reached the fingertips of her left hand out to meet the fingertips of Sarah's right, and as the watchman looked on, they both stretched out the other hand and tried to gauge the circle they could have made if they'd had Mother and Daddy, Marcus and Ayah to complete it.

•

That night, they bought the fixings for gin and tonics, then hit up the hotel bar for ice made from purified water. "The perfect medicinal drink," Quinn said, mixing her cocktail with her finger. "With quinine for malaria!"

Sarah raised her glass. "Here's looking up your old address."

"Didn't we just."

They sat on Quinn's bed, Sarah cross-legged with Quinn's right foot in her lap, painting her toenails lime green and doing an increasingly sloppy job of it, thanks to the cocktails. "You and I have the exact same feet," Sarah said. "Wide as bear paws."

"Better that than Mother's bunions."

"You got her hands, though," Sarah said. "Long and elegant. I got Daddy's square ones." She dipped the brush into the bottle and painted a stripe. "Do you remember Ayah's last name?"

Quinn shook her head.

"Singh."

"I wonder if I knew that," Quinn mused. "All Sikhs are Singhs, but not all Singhs are Sikhs."

"They always told us that, growing up, but guess what? It's not true."

"Are you kidding me? I've spent my entire life believing that."

"Turns out all *male* Sikhs are Singhs. Female Sikhs are Kaurs. Though I don't think everyone even abides by that tradition anymore."

"But Ayah was a woman, and her last name was Singh."

This was a difficult problem. They both thought on it. Quinn had almost drifted to sleep when Sarah said, "I think that means she must not have been a Sikh."

"She was definitely not a Sikh," Quinn said. "She was Hindu. I remember praying with her."

"Mmm," Sarah said. "I think I'm falling asleep now."

"You'd better cap that nail polish."

"Good idea." Sarah capped the bottle and slid off of Quinn's bed and into her own.

"Sleep tight," Quinn said.

"*Lala salama.*"

"What's that mean?"

"It's Swahili. It means 'sleep safe.' Or 'hope for tomorrow.'"

"*Lala salama.* That's pretty."

"*Faire de beaux rêves.*"

"Cut it out, show-off."

Sarah responded with a loud fake snore.

In the morning, they ate fried potatoes and toast for their hangovers, drank French-press coffee, and downed bottles and bottles of water to dispel their headaches before leaving on their next errand: Mother's request.

Marcus had been buried at a pretty site in the British cemetery, tucked into a hillside beneath ornamental trees. Quinn and Sarah stood side by side, staring down at the little granite marker. Quinn held a bouquet of yellow dahlias, the kind Mother had grown in the garden on Cornwallis Road. Marcus had once landed in trouble for decapitating a handful of them with a stick when he'd been practicing his swashbuckling.

Quinn knelt and settled the flowers at the base of the gravestone. Marcus Whitaker DeVaughan. His birthday, the same as Sarah's. Then a dash, and the date of his death.

"I don't remember the funeral at all," Sarah said.

Quinn looked up, surprised. "You weren't there."

"Are you kidding? They made me stay home?"

"You were still sick, I think. Daddy stayed with you."

Sarah stared at her. "*Daddy* didn't go to Marcus's funeral?"

It had rained that day. The mourners had huddled together under a canvas tent, Mother standing behind Quinn, clutching her like a pocketbook as they lowered Marcus's beautiful white casket into the ugly red hole.

The house was quiet when they came home. Sarah must have been asleep. Daddy sat in his mustard-colored recliner in the den.

He'd been crying. "How was it?" he asked through the open door. In the hallway, Mother stopped in the act of lifting off her black rain hat and glared at him.

"'*How was it?*'" she said. "I buried our son. How do you think it was?" She threw her hat into the closet and stalked down the hall.

"There was water in the bottom of the hole," Quinn told him, and Daddy nodded, his eyes far away.

A breeze ruffled the cemetery's ornamental trees. Quinn smoothed down her hair. "Do you remember how they fought?"

"I remember Mother yelling at him. 'You think you're a saint for helping the goddamned less fortunate.' I'd never heard her swear before."

"She kept saying the cook didn't wash the vegetables." Quinn tucked a piece of hair behind her ear. "I feel so sorry for Mother sometimes. She doesn't have anyone."

"She has you," Sarah said.

Quinn looked out across the headstones. "I'm just the consolation prize."

They fell silent, considering the little gravestone with the bright bouquet. Sweet Marcus. The empty space in the middle of all their lives.

•

They arrived in Sawai past dinnertime. A newspaper clipping lay on the floor just inside the front door. Sarah picked it up and read it, then handed it silently to Quinn. A handwritten note in blue ballpoint in the margin: *Thought you'd want to see. Wm.* And a circle around a small notice:

```
ARRESTED. Hemraj Meena, Vinyal Village,
Sawai Madhopur District, on a charge of
attempted   poaching   inside   Ranthambore
```

```
National Park. Police stated the arrest was
based on photographic evidence showing the
detainee setting a snare trap.
```

"That's good, right?" Quinn asked.

"It is, except that I'm the one who took the photos. I won't be the most popular person in Vinyal."

In the kitchen, Sarah opened a bottle of beer for each of them. They stood at the counter while they drank. "It always drove me crazy," Quinn said. "All the risks you took as a journalist. I always thought you were going to get yourself killed."

"I know. You always said that thing about *The Year of Living Dangerously*. But do you remember who died in that movie? It wasn't the white people, I'll tell you that." Sarah took a sip of beer. "There's a certain level of protection that comes with being white in a non-Western society. People tend to treat your life like it's worth more. Punishments are harsher for crimes against white people."

"That's not exactly a pretty truth," Quinn said.

"Nothing pretty about it."

They ate a cold dinner of leftovers out of Sarah's refrigerator and afterward put down some blankets and pillows and stretched out on the floor. Quinn told Sarah about the state of her marriage.

"Crap. I'm sorry," Sarah said. "I had no idea."

They lapsed into silence. Quinn was floating somewhere smoky gray when Sarah said her name.

"Yeah?"

"What did Mother mean when she said you were lucky you didn't kill yourself?"

Quinn stared at the ceiling. "I tried to, once, when I was sixteen. Pills."

"How come I never knew about it?"

"You were away somewhere when it happened. Like, for weeks."

"Camp. I would have been thirteen." She fell silent. "You really went through hell."

Quinn sat up and rearranged the pillows. "The good thing about screwing up as a kid is that you get therapy. You learn different ways to channel your feelings. But then, my painting's gone to crap in the past few months."

Sarah rolled onto her side to look at her sister. "Cause or effect?"

"I wish I knew."

•

They got up before dawn for a drive in the park. Now Quinn felt the best part of her visit could begin. Delhi was too fraught. But Ranthambore! She remembered the family trip here vividly: the Jogi Mahal, the clifftop fortress, banyan trees so big you could drive a car between their aerial roots. They arrived in the dark and patrolled for ninety minutes without seeing much beyond boars and langurs, then stopped and spread out a picnic breakfast on the hood of the jeep: vegetable cutlets and hardboiled eggs and masala chai out of a thermos.

Afterward, they drove back to Rajbagh Lake just as the sun established itself over the trees, and there was Machli, lying at the lakeside, regal in repose. Shaggy and thin as she was, she was still glorious. She blinked lazily and elevated her chin as if contemplating her own magnificence. How satisfying, she seemed to say, to be so splendid. Quinn did a quick ink drawing of the tigress, her image reflected in the lake. Machli's daughters lay nearby, gnawing on the remains of what must have been an enormous animal.

"Nilgai," Sanjay said. "A feast."

Quinn had been relieved to discover she liked Sanjay very much, though it felt odd sizing up a married man as boyfriend material for her little sister.

After leaving the park, they stopped by the hospital to pick up

Nuri. Sarah walked with Nuri to the car, their heads close together, smiling and laughing about something. They settled into the Sumo. "Next stop Vinyal," Sanjay said. "Are you ready?"

Quinn hesitated. "That man they arrested for poaching ... "

"You don't have to go if you don't want," Sarah said. "We can drop you off at my apartment. Or we can go, and if it doesn't feel right when we get there, we just leave."

Not very reassuring. It seemed selfish even to take a chance, with the twins so young. But *they need to see you do something brave*, Pete had said. And she couldn't tell Jane she'd gotten this close but hadn't had the guts to finish the journey. She glanced over at Nuri, at her scarred face, and remembered Sarah's words. *There's a certain level of protection that comes with being white.* Hot shame flooded her. She had no right to her fears.

When they arrived, the atmosphere felt welcoming enough. The women and children seemed to find the sudden appearance of a duplicate Sarah highly amusing, and it was hard to stay tense in the midst of their laughter. In Anju's courtyard, they sat on the ground, eating homemade chapatti. The women were shy around Quinn until she told them how she had unpacked the box of their handbags and seen each of their faces on the tags. "You saw our work in America?" Rohini asked.

Quinn brought out photos—the bags hanging on the wall, Jane smiling next to them. They passed the snapshots around, all looking a little dazed at the idea of their handiwork in such an exotic location as Louisville, Kentucky.

"How does it feel to be international businesswomen?" Sarah asked.

Nuri cried when she saw her photo. Padma, sitting next to her, patted her hand and whispered something into her ear, and Nuri smiled and wiped her eyes and sat up straight.

"We made something for your children," she said. The other

women watched her, seeming to radiate encouragement. Apparently Nuri had been appointed spokeswoman for the group. From somewhere, Nuri produced two small, bulging, hand-sewn bags. "Dolls for your little girl and animals for your boy. We made them from leftover fabric. Here." She handed the bags to Quinn.

Quinn peeked into the bags at the toys inside. "They're wonderful!" she exclaimed. "The kids will love these." She looked up. "I brought you all something, too, but it's already yours."

Rohini pressed her hands to her chest. "Did you bring our money from America?"

Quinn nodded toward Sarah, who reached into her bag and pulled out a stack of rupees she'd converted from dollars before they left Delhi. In an instant, the women were on their feet in a tight circle. Sarah passed the earnings to Anju, who touched the notes to her forehead. "Every girl should go to school like Rohini did. Every girl needs to know how to read and do maths so she can run her own business." She turned to Rohini. "You should do this."

Rohini clasped the bundle of banknotes ceremonially in both hands. "We took some fabric and made it into bags. The bags turned into rupees. And now the rupees can turn into whatever we want. Pretty good magic, if you ask me."

Quinn had never seen a happier payday. Rohini counted the money carefully and gave a stack of cash to each woman. "This is what happens when women do more than just work the fields and tend to the house and babies," Anju said, raising her money and giving it a victorious shake. "It's better for everyone."

"Better for women, anyway," Sapna said. "The men are going to have to watch out."

"That's long overdue." Anju tucked her banknotes into her sari. "Sorry, Sanjay, but men have had it their way long enough."

"Fair enough," he said.

Padma gripped her cash in two hands, blinking back tears. "My cow." She grinned so hard her eyes watered. "*Now* let that toothless old dog tell me I'm not worth anything!"

Quinn looked at Padma's shining face and thought: This is what a brave woman looks like.

•

That evening, Sarah made chamomile tea, and she and Quinn sat on opposite ends of the sofa. Quinn studied the photo of Marcus and Sarah, then set it aside.

"I have to tell you something," she said quietly. "The day I caught you and Marcus coming into the house all wet—" She paused.

Sarah watched her, guarded.

"I've never told you this, but I saw the two of you sneak out. I could have stopped you."

Sarah's face gave away nothing, which was almost more than Quinn could bear.

"I'm sorry. I think about it every day."

Sarah frowned, as if puzzling something out. "I always wondered how we managed to sneak out without getting caught." She looked up. "Do you even know what happened that day? I tricked him into going outside. I told him some made-up story to get him down to the creek, and then I pushed him in. It was a few days after he put the snake down my shirt. I wanted to get back at him."

"But you *both* came back all muddy."

"He held out his hand like he wanted me to help him up. I thought we were even, so I reached out, and he yanked me in. Which I deserved."

So Sarah had been the instigator. Somehow Quinn had never asked herself which twin took the lead; she'd thought only of her own failure to stop them. "You were seven years old. You didn't know any better."

"I *did* know better. Mother and Daddy talked about germs all the time. But I couldn't think of a better revenge than pushing him into the creek, and I wasn't going to let the germ part stop me. I guess I thought he might get a little sick." She paused. "I don't feel guilty about it. We were little kids. But you've carried it around with you all this time."

Tears prickled Quinn's sinuses.

"Look. Don't," Sarah said. "You need to let that go. This is who we are. Two sisters whose brother died a long time ago. You think you could have stopped us? You couldn't have stopped us. We were going to get out of that house one way or another. If not that day, another day. We had cabin fever like crazy."

"No. Any other day and the servants never would have let you get past them. But they disappeared for a while that day, remember?" Quinn said. "I've asked myself over and over why I let you go. It was the monsoon. You two had been making a racket sock-skating in the hallway, and I was tired of listening to you do that stupid chant."

Sarah smiled. "'Ladies and gentlemen, take my advice. Pull down your pants and slide on the ice.'"

"That's the one. When I saw you slip out, I thought, 'Finally. Some peace and quiet.'" She fell silent. "I don't know. We kids were all upset by whatever went on that morning with Mother. I always wondered where everybody went. The whole time I was bathing you, I thought Ayah or somebody would come in and make a huge fuss that I was doing a servant's work. Which I barely managed to do as it was."

"I think they left."

"No, what's weird is that they were there *somewhere*. Ayah was, anyway. After I bathed you, she came in and dressed you."

"*You* dressed us. I remember because you were looking for pants in the shirts drawer, and I couldn't believe you didn't know how our dresser was organized."

"No, Ayah came in and made you promise never to sneak out again."

They stared at each other, full of doubt.

"And God only knows where Mother was," Quinn said. "Whenever I ask her about it, she just deflects."

"But you know what?" Sarah said. "It happened the way it happened. We might as well blame Marcus. He's the one who put the snake down my shirt. Sneaky little shit," she added, and Quinn blurted a painful, wicked laugh and hid her face behind her hands.

"Can you forgive me?" she asked.

"There's nothing to forgive," Sarah said. "I wish you could see that. We can call it fate, we can call it a freak accident, we can call it what happens when somebody makes a bad judgment call. But those are all just stories we tell ourselves. Does it matter which one we choose?"

Quinn lowered her hands from her face. "I think it matters more than anything."

They sat in silence for a moment. "Hey," Sarah said. "Aren't you supposed to call your kids tonight?"

Quinn started guiltily. "What's today? Friday?" She took a shaky breath and blew it out. "I think I'd better wait till tomorrow."

•

The next morning, Sarah got up early and put a pan of milk on the stove. Quinn had expected Sarah to blame her; that seemed clear. But divvying up the blame had never been the point. They needed to talk about the past so they could move on. Forward was the only direction that made sense. She tossed cardamom pods, black peppercorns, and cloves into her mortar and was grinding them by hand when Quinn wandered, pajama-clad, into the kitchen.

"That smells fantastic," Quinn mumbled, her voice groggy.

"Hey, sleepyhead. Go call your kids," she said lightly. "I'll have masala chai ready by the time you're done." They exchanged a smile. They would be all right, Sarah thought, although it might take a day or two for the tenderness to wear off. That was okay. They had a whole week ahead of them.

They returned to the park the next morning at dawn, and every day after that. Most days, they sighted Machli and the cubs. Sanjay arranged a tour of the Ranthambore School of Art, where the headmaster spontaneously invited Quinn to give the students a drawing lesson. It went so well, she went back twice to do it again.

As their week in Sawai drew to a close, Sarah observed a fragile peace take hold of her sister. As for herself, a thread of adrenaline began humming through her veins. They were going back to Delhi. Back to Ayah, or so they'd been promised. She knew it could all be a fraud, but she couldn't fend off a growing sense of hope. Ayah, after all these years.

When the day arrived, they left before dawn for the long car ride to the city. The plan was to meet on the maidan that afternoon. Sarah had insisted that they meet in a public place. She wasn't convinced that this so-called nephew—Rajit, he called himself—was the real thing. True, he knew things about the DeVaughan family circa the early 1970s, which meant he knew Ayah, probably. But in India, there were aunties and aunties. The latter category included more or less every older woman you knew.

Sarah had named the date and place of the meeting, and Rajit had written back to her post office box, okaying the time and date but suggesting that they meet instead at his house, where Manjuli would be waiting. Sarah wrote back to say she would be at the maidan at the appointed time.

They arrived twenty minutes early and found seats on a bench not far from the cricket pitch. The afternoon was sunny and crisp; women wore cardigans over their saris and salwar kameez. Ayah: Would she look more or less the same, or was she ancient now? How old *was* she? Fifty-five? Seventy? Sarah wondered if she would recognize her. Ayah would no doubt recognize Sarah and Quinn by their coloring alone.

An hour ticked by. This was inauspicious. If Rajit wanted his money, why didn't he show up? He knew where to find them; he knew they were carrying cash.

Or maybe the tollbooth workers were protesting again. There were a hundred reasons for them not to show.

Quinn blew out her cheeks.

"Let's give them a few more minutes," Sarah said.

A man approached wearing dress slacks, a light-blue button-down shirt made of shiny synthetic material, and a thin gold chain. He strode up with harried strides, namaskared, and launched into an apology: *The roads, terrible, terrible, but what a pleasure to meet you, I've heard so much about you.* He smelled of hair oil. He looked younger than Sarah had expected. Twenty-five at most.

The sisters glanced at each other and stood. Quinn murmured a hello and then managed to efface herself to a remarkable extent, as if she could turn invisible through sheer force of will. Sarah fought down the impulse to confront him.

"It's a pleasure." She checked his waistband for the bulge of a gun. "But I'm surprised. I thought you'd be bringing Mrs. Singh with you?"

"No, ma'am," he said. "Auntie has been at home cooking since the past three days. She's preparing quite a feast in your honor. Come, we should go. She'll be fretting."

Sarah arranged her face into a facsimile of a pleasant look. "It's been such a long time since we've seen Mrs. Singh," she said. "Do you by any chance have a picture of her?"

"A picture?" Restrained insult, real or calculated. "No, I'm afraid I do not carry a picture of my auntie with me."

"But you understand why I ask."

"I understand, yes, but I am sorry you don't trust me. You call me a liar."

"She didn't call you a liar. We don't know you," Quinn pointed out in a surprisingly firm voice.

"*Achchha*. This is true. Well." He thrust his hands in his pockets. "My auntie has been talking a great deal about Dr. DeVaughan and Mrs. Doctor. She told me your mother played tennis."

Sarah gazed at him. All the white ladies played tennis.

"Your mother didn't care for India. And you father was a great believer in oranges for good health."

Sarah and Quinn exchanged a glance.

"*Achchha*," Sarah said to Rajit. "What's your address? We'll take an auto-rickshaw and meet you there."

•

They arrived at a modern high-rise apartment building and took a tiny elevator to the sixth floor. Quinn and Sarah exchanged a glance on the ride up, as if to say, *What happens now?* and *I guess we're about to find out*. In the narrow hallway, Rajit unlocked a forest-green door and swung it open, calling, "Look what I found on the maidan!"

They stepped inside.

Hurrying through a doorway from an interior room, there she was, unmistakably Ayah: the way she moved, the way she wiped her fingers on the dishcloth and exclaimed and put her hands to her own cheeks, then to Sarah's, then Quinn's, exclaiming, "My girls! My girls!" and they were laughing and chattering, and it was painful, somehow, to be so overjoyed.

They'd grown taller than Ayah, and she'd grown rounder and older, obviously, but was still vigorous. She wore a tangerine salwar kameez, her hair in a long black braid shot through with silver. "And what did you think you were doing with that tiger, young lady? Lucky you didn't get yourself killed! And now you're a celebrity because of it. Such a crazy world."

Ayah made introductions. Her daughter, Gitanjali, a librarian, a bit older than Quinn and Sarah, which meant Ayah had left a young child at home when she took care of the DeVaughan brood.

Gitanjali's husband and their two lanky little boys, and Ayah's sister Prema, who was Rajit's mother, and Ayah's husband, Arjun, whom they had always heard about but never met. He was bald on top with longish sideburns and looked a little like Salman Rushdie.

It was easy to believe Ayah had been cooking for days. They started out with bowls of chaat and progressed through pakora and samosas, baingan bharta and saag paneer, naan and dal and chana masala and aloo gobi and mattar paneer and towering piles of rice. A feast on the order of Thanksgiving dinner.

Ayah had not heard the news that Dr. DeVaughan had died long ago, so there was that shock to get through. "Such a good man," she said, wet-eyed. "A heart like a giant." She asked about Mrs. Doctor somewhat warily, and then about Quinn's family. Quinn had brought pictures; Ayah said they should wait till they were done eating to look at them but then decided she didn't want to wait. She wiped her hands carefully, took the photos, and looked up, bright-eyed, at Quinn. "So much like Marcus and Sarah!"

Sarah's marital status was tut-tutted over. "And you in India all this time and didn't look me up," Ayah added, scooping up dal with a piece of naan.

"I tried," Sarah said. "I put an ad in the *Times*."

Ayah hadn't seen it. "When I saw you on the TV, I thought I might fall down dead from shock. Sarah." She shook her head affectionately. "Sarah and Quinn. To have you here now, in front of me." She pinched her nephew's cheek. "It's lucky Rajit found you."

Lucky indeed.

When they finished eating, Ayah folded her hands beneath her chin and smiled fondly at them, as if they were still little girls. "You were such smart children. So curious about the world. Quinn, you were the artist. And Sarah, with all the questions. To this day, no one has made me think harder than you. And Marcus." She shook her head. "I've always wondered how he was reincarnated. What life he's living now."

"I don't think of him that way," Quinn admitted. She'd eaten too much. She'd never known Ayah could cook like that.

"How *do* you think of him?"

"As he was. As a little boy."

Ayah clucked her tongue. "You cannot stay stuck in the past. The world is change. We've no choice but to let it carry us forward." She took a sip of chai and turned to Sarah. "And you? How do you think of him?"

"Like … " she hesitated. "Like someone who was granted only a little time. But he changed us all."

Ayah set her cup down with a deliberate gesture. "You still feel guilty," she said to Quinn. Her voice rose. "You girls were not responsible, neither of you, for what happened to Marcus. How many times did I tell you that? That was *my* duty. The very reason I was part of your household was to look after you children."

There was heat in her voice. Quinn shifted uncomfortably. "But I was the one to give them a bath the day they sneaked outside."

Ayah folded her arms. "I am not sure you girls realize that, in fact, I wasn't there that day."

"I thought so," Sarah said, just as Quinn said, "Yes, you were."

They exchanged a look. "I was always confused about that," Sarah said. "I remember you served us breakfast, but then … "

"You had to have been there," Quinn said. "You dressed them after their bath. You made them promise never to sneak out again."

Ayah looked at Sarah. "*You* have a very good memory, young lady. I *was* there for breakfast. I brought you children your toast and eggs and sat with you while you ate. But later that morning, your mother sent us all home."

She turned to Quinn. "What you're remembering, when I made them promise not to slip out again—that happened the next morning. I was helping them dress, and I found their dirty clothes all crusted with dried mud in the hamper. I realized what must have happened the day before, with none of us there to stop it."

It took a moment for Quinn to make sense of it. "Wait," she said. "You were supposed to be watching us, and she *sent you home*? Why would she do that?"

"For that, you will have to ask your mother. But enough of this. The past is past. This day is a celebration." She picked up her napkin, folded it with emphasis, and plunked it on the table. "Now. I remember two little girls who couldn't get enough of kheer. Who is ready for some now?"

The rest of the visit hewed to sunnier territory. Gifts exchanged and declarations of affection. Promises to keep in touch. Rajit ferried them to their hotel, and Sarah pulled an envelope from her money belt. As they were leaving, she handed it to him. He took it and not very discreetly counted the money, then smiled and bowed and said it had been a great, great pleasure and he hoped to see them again.

At the hotel, Sarah wanted to chatter about their visit. But Quinn walked into the bathroom, stared at herself in the mirror, and walked out again with brimming eyes. "She left us to the wolves."

Sarah was perched on the edge of the bed, removing her shoes. She looked up. "What?"

"Mother. She sent Ayah and the others home, and then she, what, climbed back into bed with one of her trashy novels or something? She didn't watch us! She had to have heard what was going on. I mean, what happened? She was having a bad day and just couldn't cope? She basically said, 'Here, universe, here are my children, do what you will.' And then had the nerve to blame the cook for what happened! Where the hell was *she*? Where *was* she?"

Sarah set her shoes down. "Quinn."

"When I go home, I'm finding out what the hell happened."

"Quinn."

"What?"

"It isn't going to help. Whatever the answer is, he's gone. It happened the way it happened. We can divvy up the blame any way we want, but does any of it help?"

"Yes. It would help me to know why nobody was watching us. And why nobody even bothered to tell me I was in charge! The truth is supposed to set you free, so let's have it. All of it."

Sarah studied her sister's face. "You've got part of the truth now. Do you feel any freer?"

"I feel like shit, is how I feel."

Sarah picked up a pillow and offered it to Quinn. "Punching bag?"

"Can I punch Mother instead?"

Sarah patted the bed next to her. "Come here, Quinnie. Sit with me." She scooted over, and Quinn climbed up next to her, and they sat side by side, cross-legged. Sarah put her arm around Quinn and gently tugged her closer. Quinn let her head rest on her sister's shoulder. "So, aside from shit?" Sarah asked.

Quinn's throat ached. "I just feel tired."

"I bet you do." She kissed the top of Quinn's head. "You can set it down now."

QUINN

AT THE AIRPORT, after clearing security, Quinn found a grimy public computer, wiped it down with hand sanitizer, and wrote the email she'd been composing in her head for days, since her last phone call home. Since before that, if she was honest with herself. Since the day she'd decided to go to India.

Dear Pete,

Do you remember the day we found out the sex of the twins? Afterward, I cried because having a boy and a girl felt like my punishment for letting Marcus and Sarah sneak outside. When I told you what I'd done, you begged me to forgive myself and said you loved me anyway.

I took that as a promise that when things became painful for me as a parent, you'd be there by my side. But instead you've opposed me and undercut me ever since the night Nick nearly died of an asthma attack. I will talk about it that way even if you don't like it.

I think you've decided to let me be the one who's scared, so you don't have to be. You get to nudge the kids behind my back and say, "There goes Mom, freaking out again."

This trip to India has made me realize it's not you I'm afraid of, when it comes to Nick. It turns out, I'm afraid of me. Afraid I'll make some split-second decision like I did the day Sarah and Marcus slipped out of the house, and our son will die because of it. And I've been unfair to you, treating you like you're too casual about Nick's safety.

But it's unfair and unloving of you to hold me in contempt.

You criticize me for letting Mother walk all over me. Can you see that you walk all over me, too? The morning after that trip to the ER, you told me to argue with you if I saw you were missing the warning signs. You told me to insist on taking his symptoms more seriously. And every single time I've done that, you've dismissed me.

Maybe the damage we've done to our relationship is too much to repair. If so, we can end this marriage. Or we can decide it's not too late, and fix it. We get to decide. We HAVE to decide.

I am sick about all of this. But I do still love you.

Quinn

She sent the message before she could change her mind.

SARAH

SHE SAID GOODBYE to Quinn at the airport and Hari at the railway station—he was staying on in Delhi an extra day—and returned to Sawai alone. At the station in Sawai, she found William waiting for her. She'd been expecting Sanjay.

They took the long way home, stopping at a bridge over the river to watch two mahouts on a sandbar, washing their elephants with buckets and scrub brushes. Sarah and William stood side by side, leaning their forearms on the railing. He was holding something, an object wrapped without ceremony in paper. He was working up to saying something, she could tell.

"I've decided you should have this," he said.

She opened the paper to find the Sundarbans mask staring up at her. "William, no. It's too special." She tried to hand it back to him, but he wouldn't accept it.

"I want you to have it. Please. It appears you need it more than I do."

That sounded worrisome. She looked around to make sure they were alone. The mahouts on the river couldn't possibly hear them.

He kept his eyes on the mask. "Look, it's really none of my business, but I find myself in a position where I have to warn you. I saw Sanjay's brother-in-law the other day. He asked about you."

The hair on her arms rose. "What did he want to know?"

"You can imagine. About the rescue and so on. Just general inquiry, I suppose. But it doesn't matter. It's the fact that he asked."

"He's watching me."

"I don't like to think what would happen if he looked too closely into your private affairs," William said. It seemed to cost him something. "This is a dangerous place, Sarah. You're something of a celebrity now as a conservationist. I've been in that position. It doesn't always make one the most popular person."

"Wait. Are we talking about my private life or my public life?"

A pair of cormorants flew over the bridge. William tracked their flight till they disappeared around a bend. "Look, this kind of conversation is not my strong suit," he said, and suddenly she saw that he felt something toward her. They had become friends, but he was still her childhood hero. She liked him immensely. But she had never caught sight of his feelings.

"You're kind to talk to me about this," she said.

He smiled at her, rather sadly. "Be careful, my dear. He's a powerful man."

In her flat, she sat on the low couch, holding the mask between her palms like a vinyl record, studying its staring eyes. The honey hunters in the Sundarbans went into the forest every day knowing they were stalked by a predator they couldn't see. Now she found herself in someone's sights. Someone with a capital S: the hard-hearted gentleman. But, unlike a tiger, this Someone had chosen to reveal himself.

Her bag, still packed, sat by the front door. She could buy a ticket and leave, just like that. She could walk away from it all.

She thought of Sanjay. And of Machli, doing her best to protect her children from the new male who would kill them if he could.

·

November 12, 2000

She must know he is gone. It's been weeks now. Still, I imagine she calls for him each night: aaooongggh. *Silence meets her roars, but she can't stop herself.*

Her cubs are growing. If the intruder lets them live, they will stay with her another year. Everything depends on his patience.

Today in the park, from the next valley over, we heard the voice of another tigress calling and calling. Weeping for her children, and refusing consolation, because they are no more.

What must it be like for Machli, protecting her daughters from the intruder? Today she surprised us all. It happened like this:

He comes to her as she's resting beneath a ficus tree. She rises to her feet and faces him, growling a warning to her children, who retreat. The intruder makes no move to menace them, and maybe it's this fact that emboldens her to do what she does next.

She takes a step toward him. They stand face-to-face. The intruder looks a bit unsure of himself, and, lacking any other plan (so it seems), he chuffs a hello. She greets him with a touch of her nose.

Then she turns her back to him, settles to the ground, and shifts her tail to one side.

He mounts her, and they mate briefly. Afterward he plops down in the clearing not far from her. A few minutes later, they do it again.

If they were going about the business of creating a litter, they would mate for three or four days before she sends him away. But this appears to be a transaction of a different sort. They couple three times, and then she snarls, leaps to her feet, and slashes him across the nose. He shakes off the blow and stands watching her as if she hasn't made herself perfectly clear. She hisses, body tensed to attack. Left no choice, he turns and walks down to a deer path at the side of the stream. She watches him go till he disappears around a bend.

For an hour she stands watch, in case he should return. At last she allows herself to turn away and calls her children to her side.

•

That night she stole outside and descended the stairs silently, willing herself invisible as she slipped past William's flat. She walked a few blocks to an anonymous neighborhood, where Sanjay picked her up on his motorcycle. They ate a late dinner of leftovers from his fridge.

Near midnight, they sat together on his floor cushions. She felt exhausted but strangely wakeful. The plaster against her back felt chalky through her shirt. They watched moon shadows brush the wall opposite the window.

"What is it?" he whispered into her hair.

"Your brother-in-law. He asked William about me," she said.

His body stilled. "That's not good."

She got to her feet and crossed to the window, making sure to stand where she couldn't be seen from the street. Bats swooped across the dingy yellow sky. He came up behind her and put his arms around her waist. She turned to him and they crashed their bodies together. She felt their time together coming to an end. Judging from the desperate light in his eyes, he felt it, too. They stumbled to the bedroom and undressed only partly before her hands groped for him. She pressed a palm against the flat of his belly and searched his eyes.

"I want you," he said.

"You have me."

"I have no one." His voice was sharp. "No family. I can't have you."

His belly burned beneath the palm of her hand. The decision was right there before them, demanding to be recognized. She saw him see it in her eyes. "Fuck it," she said. "We want to change things, let's change them."

His pulse beat against her palm. The nightstand held a stash of condoms, but she pulled her hand away from his stomach and he wrapped his arms tight around her and buried his face in her neck. She clenched him to her, kissed him hard, let herself call his name out loud.

QUINN

AT THE AIRPORT in Louisville, she looked for Pete, afraid to find him.

There he was. She felt something lift inside her and nearly cried from relief to realize she was happy to see him.

He'd brought the twins, beautiful and fresh-skinned. To Quinn's eyes, they seemed visibly bigger than when she'd left. Or maybe it was just their sturdiness she was seeing. Her children were Shetland ponies compared to the Indian kids she'd seen. They jumped up and down, flung their arms around her waist. Pete hugged her tightly. "I'm glad to be back," she said into his ear.

He pressed his cheek to hers. "We're glad you're back, too. A couple of people around here have missed you."

She pulled back. "A couple?"

He smiled with the right side of his mouth, a complex smile, unfamiliar. It reminded her of William's. "Three people, actually."

They gazed at each other, both looking for something.

The drive home disoriented her. It was less the fact that cars drove on the opposite side of the road and more that she could hardly grasp the orderliness of the expressway. No one honked, every car kept to its lane, and she saw not one bicycle or auto-rickshaw or cow, not one single man getting a haircut by the side of the road. Office buildings slid by, shiny and blank. Not a hint of the past anywhere. When they walked into the house, she was shocked to find it so enormous and spare.

She'd brought tiger-themed souvenirs: stuffed animals and stickers for the twins, a Ranthambore ball cap for Pete. The kids gleefully hugged the stuffed animals and lobbed questions at her. She told them yes, she'd seen a tiger, a beautiful tiger with a coat the color of turmeric.

"What color is that?" Alaina asked.

"Picture Cheetos," Quinn said.

Later that night, she tucked the twins into bed, then emailed Sarah to say she'd made it home. Downstairs, she found Pete waiting for her on the couch. He lifted one arm, inviting her to slide in next to him. She closed her eyes and nestled against the warmth of his chest.

"I guess we've got a lot to say to each other," he said.

"I'm too tired to have much of a conversation right now, though."

"I figured. You've covered a few miles today."

She yawned enormously and fell asleep.

SARAH

BACK IN HER APARTMENT, she sank to the floor. Twelve days, thirteen, before her next period was due. She hadn't even counted before she threw her body open to Sanjay.

She placed her hand on the soft tissue just above her pubic bone and tried to gauge whether it felt any different. This could be the moment of conception: *Right now.* Sperm and egg coming together. And after that, a zygote, floating free as a planet for a few hours or days, soon to be tethered. She had heard women say they just knew. Quinn said that, when she got pregnant with Nick and Alaina. She just knew. Sarah had never asked her when, exactly, or how.

What would it mean for Sarah to be pregnant in Sawai? She was already the foreigner, the anti-poaching activist, the reason a man was in jail. But a pregnancy: That would suddenly make things unbearably personal for the Sawai community. It would take no time for them to figure out Sanjay was the father. They wouldn't accept the child, or Sarah and Sanjay for making it. Tarun could very well kill Sanjay for their crime.

Let's change things. What had she been thinking? How could she have been so foolish?

But wait: Sanjay's wife. She had forgotten their story. The thought threw her free of her trance, and suddenly she was pacing, chewing ferociously at her thumbnail. Because that changed things, didn't it? They'd tried to get pregnant and failed. Tried for three years and never—

So the chances were slim that—

No. They had made a baby. Babies. But lost them.

An hour ago, in the moment of decision, she and Sanjay had both been willing to change their lives. But if it came down to it, could he leave Sawai, the park, the tigers? Sarah had never met anyone so connected to a place. He was made of it. She couldn't ask him to leave Ranthambore. She would have to leave without him, to keep him safe. She'd go somewhere with good health care. London, Paris. Someplace a woman with a child could thrive on her own.

Twelve days. Thirteen. She didn't feel any different. But she did. What if. What if.

This was crazy. Sanjay would never give up being with his child. He would insist that they start over together somewhere else. They could move to Delhi. To Cornwallis Road. The thoughts flashed like lightning and tilted the room till she had to reach for the wall. And what if there were *two* worlds spinning inside her, orbiting each other like curious dogs at the park? A boy and a girl. Like Nick and Alaina. Like Marcus and her.

She lowered herself to the sofa and tucked her feet up under her.

Sanjay would make such a good father. He radiated kindness. She saw it in the creases at the corners of his eyes, in the set of his shoulders, which sometimes slumped softly forward. He often stood with his arms crossed, not in defiance or defensiveness but when he was considering something. His head tilted softly to one side, and his crossed arms became a shelf for his heart to rest on. A man giving himself over. She didn't know if anyone else understood that about him.

And maybe she wasn't pregnant after all. What then?

Then—life would go on, like before. But somehow that didn't seem possible. Something had already changed.

Her phone rang. Sanjay. This day was never going to end.

"I am so sorry, Sarah." His voice low. "Where are you?"

He was asking about her cycle. "Right in the middle."

"We have to think."

"We have to sleep first."

"This is my fault." There was wonder in his voice, as though he didn't recognize the man he had become.

"If it's anyone's fault, it's mine." When he didn't reply, she added, "Things became impossible."

He said nothing. And she no longer knew what was in that silence.

QUINN

AUTUMN RAIN spattered her windshield as Quinn, still jet-lagged, drove to Mother's house. They sat together at the glass-topped kitchen table, the room dimmed by the gray day outside. Quinn drank coffee and showed photos from India on her laptop. She included a picture she'd taken of Marcus's headstone but no photos from their visit with Ayah.

"You went to Cornwallis Road," Mother said. "It was a beautiful house, I'll give it that."

"Mother? There's something I need to ask you."

Mother's face did not invite whatever was coming next.

"Before Sarah and Marcus got sick ... there was a day when Ayah wasn't there."

Mother got up from the table and retrieved a bag of potatoes from the cabinet. Quinn watched dumbfounded as she began briskly peeling them, flicking ribbons of beige skin into the sink. "I'm supposed to make a dish for my women's club tonight," Mother said.

Quinn strode to the counter. "The day I'm talking about. Why did you send the servants home?"

The knife paused, its tip balanced on the cutting board. Mother turned to her. "Who told you that?" She pointed the knife at Quinn. "You *saw* her. You and your sister *saw* Ayah. Didn't you?"

Quinn eyed the blade. "Sarah found her. We went to her apartment."

Mother's eyes fixed on hers. "What did she tell you?"

"What do you mean?"

"I mean, what did she tell you! Damn it, Quinn, tell me what she said."

"Holy crap, would you put the knife down? You're scaring me."

Mother let her arm fall to her side. Quinn took the knife, set it on the cutting board, and led Mother back to the table as the wind flung handfuls of rain at the window. "She said you sent her home. She didn't say why. I swear that's all. But Sarah and I ... there are things we still don't understand. Maybe if we knew what happened that day, it would help."

"'What happened that day' should have never happened." Mother drew a breath. "Look. Quinn. I should have told you girls this a long time ago. I almost took you kids and left India. Before, I mean. When the twins were five." She looked away. "Think what I could have spared us."

A wind gust rattled the panes. The lights went down and came back up, and the clock on the stove began blinking. "I would have been eight," Quinn said. "The year we went to the Taj. Wait. You were going to leave Daddy? Why?"

"I didn't realize how lonely it would be. He was married to his clinic. I couldn't do it anymore." She collected herself. "He begged me to stay. He swore he'd do better. So I stayed, but nothing changed. But now if I was lonely, I had no one to blame but myself." She looked up at Quinn. "You kept trying to tell me it was your fault, what happened to Marcus. And every single time, without fail, I told you it wasn't. So now you understand. We were in the wrong place, living the wrong lives, and that's my fault, not yours."

Quinn started to cry, which infuriated her because she wasn't sad; she was just jet-lagged and confused, and it was too cold and raw outside and she should have waited to come here till she had her feet back underneath her. "Why didn't you tell me this before? When you told me it wasn't my fault, it felt like you just wanted to shut me up. Like what I'd done was too horrible to be acknowledged."

Mother folded her hands. "That was never what I meant. It was complicated. Not the kind of thing you can explain to a ten-year-old."

Quinn got up and flung her cold coffee in the sink. "You could have explained it to me when I was sixteen and starving myself. You could have explained it when I was in the psych ward after I swallowed a bottle of pills. Those things were pretty goddamned complicated, too." She stood at the counter, holding the empty mug in front of her like a shield.

"I'm sorry. I wanted to protect you."

"To *protect* me? What the hell, Mother? You sent Ayah home that day, and you won't say why. Fine. But where were you? When you sent Ayah and all the other servants away and left me in charge, only somehow you forgot to tell me that little fact? *Where were you?*"

Mother met her eyes. "I left the house."

Quinn set her cup down hard on the counter. Tears sprang to her eyes. "You did *what?* How could you do that to me?"

"There's no excuse, all right, Quinn? I made the worst mistake of my life that day." She stood and crossed the room to look into her daughter's face. "But I was the adult, not you. I never meant to make you suffer."

"But you did."

"I know. I'm sorry."

Quinn's tears were flowing fast now, but she no longer cared. "Can you at least tell me where you went?"

"Oh, Quinnie." Mother reached out to cup her face, but Quinn shied away. "It's something I have to live with, but you don't. Count yourself lucky." She let her hand drop, left the room, came back with a tissue, and handed it to Quinn. In a brisk voice she asked, "Was Ayah's husband there? Arjun?"

"Yes. He seemed nice." She wiped her cheeks, folded the sodden tissue, and stuffed it into her pocket.

"I always liked him," Mother said. She picked up the knife and another potato and went back to work.

SARAH

ON A COOL, WINDY MORNING, Sarah, Sanjay, and William rode through the park with the film crew. In the hour before the sun broke over the hills to the east, they spotted chital deer, sambar, langur monkeys, wild boar, and an iridescent flash of blue as a kingfisher crossed their path. At midmorning they stopped for a quick breakfast. As they packed up, they heard voices in the core area, the tones suggesting argument.

On the far side of a hill, they found a dozen Vinyal herdsmen facing off with three forest guards while cattle and water buffalo snuffled the dirt for fodder. A guard raised a radio to his mouth. A herder brandished his stick.

The film crew got to work. One of the herdsmen stepped up to the camera and spoke directly into its lens. Sanjay quietly translated. "'What do they want us to do? Our lake is dry. Our animals are dying of hunger and thirst. This is the only fodder and water near our village. We have no choice.'"

"Hey, lady." A nasty catcall, loud, in Hindi. Padma's son, Om. He caught Sarah's eye and blew her an ugly kiss. "My friend's father is in jail because of you," he called.

She stared back at him to show she wasn't scared. "This is fucked up," she muttered. "We need a dredger to dig out that lake."

Back at the Tiger Survival office, they worked the phones for hours. Geeta and Sarah put out calls to other NGOs and government agencies, trying to round up emergency funding. Sanjay and William called their construction contacts in search of earth-moving equipment, though with the ground baked so hard, the equipment might prove useless. At the end of the day, they gathered for a briefing. "The best we can do is start in ten days' time," William said.

"And until then?" Geeta asked.

"I can think of only one solution. Bring the water in by tanker."

"Expensive," she said. "*And* insufficient. But I don't see a way around it."

Sarah said nothing. Her period was due to begin that day. When they left the office, Sanjay fell into step with Sarah. She could feel his question.

"Nothing yet," she said.

•

Three days passed. At the village, the sun shone on a listless crowd. They'd been waiting for more than an hour, empty tin waterpots dangling from their fingers. Some of the women had turned the pots over and were using them as stools, chins in their hands, dupattas dragging the ground. The sarpanch skirted the crowd. "You promised water. Where is it?"

Four o'clock. The tankers should have been there. Sarah glanced at the Sumo, gauging how quickly they could reach the vehicle if things turned ugly. Dust hung like a scrim in the air.

A few days before, Quinn had emailed with the news that Mother had almost taken them back to the States when she and Marcus were five. It would have been a completely different life.

Sanjay pulled out his mobile phone and called the dispatcher in Jaipur. Afterward he scanned the crowd. "They're not far. A half hour, maybe."

The congregation grew, all eyes on the road. Like churchgoers, Sarah thought. Or refugees. She found herself making eye contact with the wife of the man arrested for poaching. The woman strode to her, clutching a baby to her chest. Sarah might not have understood the words, but there was no mistaking the woman's finger poking Sarah's chest, the aggrieved and rising tone, the gestures she made to her baby and the children arrayed around her, who stared at Sarah with sullen faces.

"Do you want me to translate?" Sanjay asked after the woman marched off.

"I think I got it. I've ruined their lives, right?"

"More or less."

"We didn't do anything to help her," Sarah said. "Her husband's in jail, and we didn't invite her to join the collective. We should have done that in the first place."

"She might not be interested," he said. "If I were in her shoes, I might not want help from an organization named Tiger Survival."

Tiger Survival. She could understand how that name must sound like a taunt. "It's not supposed to be a zero-sum game."

He looked over at the woman, clutching her dupatta miserably. "But you can see how it would look that way to her."

They stood silently, waiting.

In a low voice, she said, "I was thinking I could go to Delhi. Stay with Ayah, maybe."

"Forever?" he asked, dubious.

"I don't know."

They watched the sun slide toward the western horizon.

"What if you came with me?" she asked.

He said nothing.

In the distance, a line of dust appeared. A murmur went up, the first hopeful sound Sarah had heard in weeks. The dust grew into a cloud. Sunlight glinted off metal skin. And there they were: three water tankers, their silver bodies shimmering in the afternoon light. They turned off the paved road and rumbled into the village center, cabs and bumpers garlanded with pink and orange plastic flowers, tailpipes spewing exhaust. The ubiquitous words HORN PLEASE were hand-painted in Hindi and in square-lettered English on the bumpers. The tankers turned off the track into a stubbled field, where the drivers killed the engines, climbed down from the cabs, and cranked open the spigots. Gleaming water began to gush into tin pots. Hundreds of people crowded, jostling and hopeful. Even the cows and goats looked interested. Dogs circled beneath the taps and lapped at the forming puddles.

She and William exchanged a small smile. "It's not a solution," he said, "but it's a start."

But something was happening. Sarah lay a hand on William's arm and nodded at the nearest tanker. A skinny teenaged boy was climbing its ladder. She recognized him instantly: Om. "This water," he shouted when he reached the top, "this water is nothing. A pot for each of us when we should have a lake." He turned his head and spat, hitting someone below. People in the crowd shouted up at him. Padma, looking furious and scared, ordered him to come down.

Sanjay translated Om's words. "You *meenas* are content to go along, even if it means we all die of thirst. But we should be at Ranthambore. We belong there. Are we worth less than a bunch of wild animals? Are our cattle worth less than the tiger that killed my father?"

Most of the people weren't listening, instead scrambling around the spigot, filling containers and staggering away under their loads. "Listen to me!" Om shouted. He climbed down the ladder, grabbed the handle, and threw his weight into it, heaving till water poured out hard enough to slap buckets from hands and soak the people standing nearest. An old woman slipped and fell. Precious gallons soaked into the ground as the throng stood watching and yelling. The sarpanch pushed through the crowd, grabbed the handle, and heaved. Metal squealed as the torrent narrowed to a stream, then a drip, then nothing. The crowd cheered.

A man strode up behind Om and hit him hard on the back of his head, knocking him to his knees.

Padma cried out, "Mandeep, no!"

Mandeep slammed a fist into Om's eye and kicked him in the stomach. Om fell over and curled into a ball. Padma ran at Mandeep, but he pushed her to the ground and began kicking her. Sarah started toward them, but Sanjay caught her arm and stopped her with a look. A dozen people shouted at Mandeep, but no one stepped forward to stop him.

Mandeep drove his foot into Padma's back. "You should be killed for raising such an idiot! You think it's funny he disgraces me?" With the next kick, his sandal flew off, and he shifted position and drove his bare foot hard into Padma's belly. She cried out in pain.

Om, back on his feet, tackled his uncle and knocked him to the ground.

"You little dog-fucker. I'll kill you," Mandeep shouted, but Om straddled his uncle's chest and wrapped his hands around his throat, shouting, "I hate you! I hate you," until his uncle's face turned purple and his tongue protruded.

The sight of that tongue seemed to shock Om. He hauled his uncle to his feet, walked him to an upturned bucket, and sat him down. Mandeep held his throat, heaving for breath.

"Listen to me, Uncle," Om shouted. "You will never, ever touch my mother or me again, or any of our family. If you do, I will kill you. I promise you that." His uncle glared up at him. "And starting tomorrow, I'm going back to school."

Sarah helped Padma to her feet, trying to determine whether she needed medical help, but Padma's sister waved her off and led Padma away. Sarah walked alongside, uninvited, gesturing for Sanjay to come translate. "Padma-ji, you need to see a doctor," she said. "You could be bleeding inside. Let us take you to the hospital." But already Padma was glancing back at Mandeep.

"It would just make him angrier," she said, and her sister ushered her away.

Sarah watched them go. She turned to Sanjay. "How long do you think this water will last?"

He tilted his head side to side.

•

Weeks passed. She mailed off a package of Christmas gifts to the twins, strung some lights in her apartment, stared at the calendar on the wall.

She arrived at Sanjay's flat as the air was filling with woodsmoke from breakfast fires. She didn't have to say anything. She wore the news on her face.

They sat on cushions in his front room. He couldn't stop staring at her belly. "So this is it," he whispered. "You have to leave."

"I could have an abortion," she said grimly.

"Sawai is too dangerous for you now. You should be seeing doctors. If you go to an obstetrician here, everyone will know by the end of the day."

She looked up at him. "Sanjay." As in: *Pay attention.*

"Is that really what you want?" He looked sick.

"What I *want*?" Her eyes reddened. "It's the only way I could stay here with you. With the work. But it would ruin everything between us." She looked up at him. "You do have a say in this."

"You know what I want."

She did know. To her surprise, she wanted it, too. Before Sanjay, she'd never even considered having children. She looked down at her hands. "I could still lose this baby, you know." He looked away, and she wondered if he thought she was hoping to lose it, or that she was making a dig about Lakshmi's miscarriages. She took his hand. "We can figure this out."

He shook his head. "I don't know what my dharma is anymore.

I have a duty to Lakshmi. But how can that mean I don't have a duty to you now, and to our baby?"

"Come with me," she said. "It's only complicated because we're making it that way." Which was pure wishful thinking; they both knew it. Sarah could work anywhere. For Sanjay, the choices were limited. "You could teach," she said. "Or, I don't know, work for another NGO."

"I wouldn't be free. I couldn't marry you. I will always be bound to Lakshmi."

"So you live out of wedlock with me and our baby. We'll scandalize everyone. So what?"

He stood and crossed the room. "Do not treat this lightly, Sarah. This is India. We'd be outcasts. We wouldn't be able to rent a flat. No one would hire us. No one would want us even shopping in their shops. I would fear for your safety. For both of you. For all of us."

"Then we go to America."

"I don't have that kind of money."

"Then Vietnam or Argentina or Tanzania. Somewhere."

He sat back down next to her. They fell silent, thinking.

"We have time," she said. "I won't start showing till February. We're smart people. We can figure this out." She let her head tip back and allowed herself a deep groan. "God, Sanjay. I would have stayed here. The park. The collective. The tigers. Instead I did the one thing that makes that impossible."

They sat in silence for a minute. "If you went to America, where would you go?"

"I think Louisville. You'd like it there."

"I'd be a foreigner in a country with no history, no tigers. Not a single memory that belongs to me." He paused. "It's a very long way from here."

"But it's the only family I've got."

•

India wouldn't let her stay, and it wouldn't let him leave. She lay in bed with him, thinking. Round and round till she was out of ideas.

The room was dark, the sheets cool. The lovemaking was frantic, raw. Afterward they lay in a sweaty heap, chests heaving, eyes focused on the blank spot where their futures should be.

"There are Hindu ceremonies for the pregnancy and afterward," Sanjay said. "Promise me you'll do them."

She sat up and stared as if he'd slapped her.

"The first one is at three months into the pregnancy, *punsavana*. It's to protect the fetus."

She shoved him hard in the shoulder. "Are you giving up on me, you jerk?"

He caught her hand. "I just keep trying to see how to make it work, and I can't. I'll keep trying."

She glared at him. "You'd better."

•

The new year arrived: 2001. Sawai Madhopur marked the occasion with fireworks and parties. Sarah couldn't bring herself to celebrate. It only meant one day closer to the end of everything.

Another night, another bout of anxiety-fueled sex. Fuck the future, Sarah thought as they drove their bodies together. Afterward she felt sticky and sore and half-drugged by the hormones and chemicals racing through her bloodstream. Their heads lay side by side on the pillow. They stared up, panting.

"I want to name him after you, if it's a boy," she said.

"We don't do that here," he said. "It's forbidden in Hinduism, actually. We'll come up with something that suits him, after we've met him and gotten a chance to see what he's like." He fell quiet. "I want to raise him here, with you as my wife. I want us to take him to the park together and show him how the tigers' stripes work as camouflage for hiding in the tall grass."

An idea was beginning to form in her mind, right on the threshold of words.

He lay his head against her chest. "Tell me everything is going to turn out all right."

She petted his hair absently, listening for the thought to coalesce.

"You could come back," he said. "You could stay in Delhi or Jaipur."

That was it. She threw back the sheet and paced to the window. Sanjay sat up, watching her. "We're thinking about this wrong," she said. "Let's look at it logically. What's the nature of our problem?"

"I can't leave. And you can't stay."

"Because?"

"Because I'm married to someone else."

"Exactly," she said. "I need to talk to her."

·

Two days later, they met at a café in a distant part of town, where no one was likely to know Lakshmi, even if they recognized Sarah. Lakshmi, clad in a spring-green salwar kameez, seemed perfectly composed. She was attractive in a quiet way, with an attentive face framed by neatly bobbed hair. She'd known who Sarah was immediately when she'd called the day before to arrange the meeting.

They were seated at a small table overlooking the courtyard. When the server left their table, Lakshmi placed her napkin in her lap and said, "Your call came as a surprise. How can I help you?"

So it would be down to business right away. "You know I work with your husband," Sarah said.

"I'm aware of that."

Sarah drew a breath. "Our relationship isn't just professional."

For the merest moment, Lakshmi looked startled. She recovered quickly. "So this is a personal conversation we're having, then."

"Yes." She struggled not to look away.

The server returned and set down hot tea in small, handled glasses, along with a bowl of sugar cubes. Lakshmi added sugar to her tea and stirred with a small spoon. "And what is it you want from me? You're here to ask my permission?"

"I'm here to ask what it would take for you to agree to divorce him."

The merest flicker of surprise crossed Lakshmi's face, barely there before it disappeared. She sat silently for a moment, then folded her hands on the table and leaned forward. "And why am I talking with you instead of Sanjay?"

"Because I insisted, basically," Sarah said. "Because I'm divorced myself, and I know that the conversations between a husband and wife can fall into a rut and never find their way out."

"You're divorced," Lakshmi said. "And how has that affected your life? Are you treated poorly because of it? Did you lose all your friends and end up isolated back in your parents' home because everyone thinks you're an embarrassment?"

It was a hard-edged question, but Sarah met Lakshmi's eyes and held her gaze until something softened in the other woman's face. "Did those things happen to you?"

"Every one of them, as a matter of fact. And I'm not even divorced, just separated—but in this town, that's bad enough."

"You've sacrificed a lot in order to live apart," Sarah said.

"I assume he told you about the miscarriages," she said. "It was just too much sadness, year after year. Too much disappointment." Her face had gone sorrowful, but she looked steadily at Sarah. "And what about you? What's your story?"

Sarah shook her head. "Nothing like yours. We just chose poorly. In the end, I wanted to keep living my life and he wanted to keep living his, and there didn't seem any point in being together if we weren't going to build a life. Getting divorced was hard, but the consequences were nothing like what you've gone through. I lost more friends when I left journalism, to tell you the truth."

Lakshmi watched Sarah with her jaw cocked. "So you just"—she flicked her wrists as if shaking water off her fingers—"moved on."

Sarah nodded.

"Here in Sawai, it would be impossible. Everybody knows everybody in this rotten little town."

It was the tone of Lakshmi's comment that made Sarah say, "Would you like to live somewhere else?" She hoped she hadn't just blown it. She half-expected Lakshmi to tell her to fuck off.

Lakshmi laughed and looked up at the sky through the bars of the window. "Every single day."

Sarah leaned forward. "What would it take to get you the life you want?"

Lakshmi looked at her for a moment and laughed in disbelief. "Are you seriously asking me that?"

"You hold the key to my happiness. Maybe there's something I can do for you."

"You're proposing a trade."

"We could call it that. Why not." Sarah lifted her tea glass and looked Lakshmi in the eye. Almost, but not quite, a toast. Lakshmi noticed the gesture and the corner of her mouth lifted. Almost, but not quite, a smile.

•

Two days later, Lakshmi's number appeared on Sarah's phone. She sat on the low sofa and answered.

"The women's collective you've started in the village," Lakshmi said. "You're selling their goods in the States, aren't you?"

"That's right."

"I want three things," she said. "I want to move to Mumbai, where I can start over as an unmarried woman. I want an arrangement that makes me the India-operations manager of your U.S.-based business.

And I want to be financially independent enough that I'm out from under my brother's control."

"Wow. That's complicated." Sarah thought for a second. "There are people who'd have to sign on to those ideas. Especially the one about the business."

"Of course. You'll talk to them. We're not in a hurry, are we? And we have to arrange this without my family knowing. I won't tell them until everything's one hundred percent in place. It must be done in strict secrecy."

Sarah hesitated. "Before we get started on this, you need to know that I'm pregnant."

Sarah heard Lakshmi breathe in sharply, followed by a long silence.

"Are you still there?" Sarah asked.

"How far along are you?"

"About seven weeks."

"I see." She cleared her throat. "I lost my three at the end of the first trimester."

"I'm sorry," Sarah said softly. "I'm not telling you this to hurt you. You need to know in case it changes anything for you with our arrangement."

On the street outside, a truck rumbled by, the growl of the engine peaking, then diminishing till it faded to nothing. Sarah realized she was holding her breath.

"It doesn't," Lakshmi said.

"Please keep this news between us. We haven't figured out yet what we're going to do."

"Well, you can't possibly stay in Sawai," Lakshmi said. "I hope you know that."

"We know," Sarah said.

QUINN

A BRIGHT, COLD Saturday morning, the kids both out on playdates, the house to herself. After Sarah's phone call the night before, she couldn't sleep. Now she sat on the sofa, trying to meditate, but she kept losing track of her breath. Pete had gone to the gym for a game of pick-up basketball; he'd be home any minute.

She rose and fixed a cup of coffee. Drummed her fingers on the countertop. Watched the driveway till his car pulled up.

He entered the house in a waft of cold air and woodsmoke. When he registered her state, he stopped halfway out of his jacket. "What is it? Are the kids okay?"

"They're fine. I have to tell you something. Come sit down."

He gave her a worried look and hung his jacket on the hook by the door. She led him to the couch, and he sat forward, elbows on his knees.

"It's Sarah," she said. "She's—she's okay, but she needs me."

"What do you mean? You're already helping her. You were just over there."

She looked him in the eye. "She's pregnant."

"Pregnant!" He sat stunned. "How far along?"

"Not very."

"What does she need you for?"

She told him what Sarah had proposed, watched him flinch when she said the amount out loud.

"Okay, stop," he said. "I can see where you're going with this, but come on. That's a ton of money."

"It's not a ton. It's, like, a midsized car."

"Which is a ton of money! We don't have that kind of cash lying around. Not even in the credit line. Is that your big plan? The credit line?"

"I'm taking it out of my retirement fund, and I'm loaning it to her."

He stood as if propelled. "Are you crazy? There are penalties for that."

She didn't like the way he loomed. She stood and faced him. "There are penalties for letting your sister's life come apart when you could have helped her keep it together."

"So it's your moral duty to help Sarah and her illicit lover run off into the sunset and live happily ever after? Come on, Quinn, you know your sister. She doesn't settle down. And anyway, she's an adult. She got herself into this; she'll get herself out."

"It's not just her now."

"Yeah, it's her married lover who knocked her up. Who is this guy, anyway? What kind of man lets a woman pay for his divorce?"

"Would it be more palatable to you if the gender roles were reversed?" She crossed the room and turned to face him. "Anyway. It's a loan."

"I don't care," he said. "I'm not going along with this. That's our money. You and me and the kids."

"Actually, it's for you and me and *not* the kids, thirty years from now. And this is a crisis happening right now in my sister's life. I can't stand back and watch everything go to hell. And"— she inhaled shakily—"it's my money."

He shook his head incredulously. "You always fall for this. Your mom shakes you down, now your sister's shaking you down—"

"Pete, listen. I'm not asking your permission. But I *am* telling you about it, before I do it, like you asked me to." Her voice grew firmer. "You can hate me if you want to. You can tell me you're leaving me. But at least give me credit for not hiding this from you."

He looked away. "What the hell, Quinn. I never said anything about leaving you. And I don't hate you. God."

"You treat me with contempt. It's the same thing."

"I treat you that way because I get sick of watching you let people walk all over you."

"Nobody's walking all over me. Sarah asked me a favor, and I decided to come through for her. And I'm telling you about it before I do it. There is nothing here for you to pass judgment on."

"What about the other part of it, your friend Jane? Am I understanding right that this woman is demanding a stake in Jane's company?"

"She wants to open up a branch in Mumbai. Jane's open to having a discussion about it. She said there could be benefits to it. Obviously Jane won't do it if it doesn't make sense for the business."

"What about what makes sense for our family? This is a huge financial decision. You should have consulted me."

"She's my sister. I'm the one who had to make the call."

His expression hardened. "You've got an answer for everything, don't you? Look at us. Once again you're being perfectly reasonable, and I'm the jerk here." He strode into the kitchen, yanked his jacket from the hook, and pulled it on. "I'm honored you so graciously decided to share your news with me." A corner of his collar was turned under. He tugged it free. "I'm going for a drive."

He pulled the door open, letting in a wedge of chill air that raised goose bumps on Quinn's arms, and then he was gone.

SARAH

SANJAY HAD RESISTED THE IDEA AT FIRST. It wasn't right, it wasn't honorable.

"It's not charity," Sarah had argued. "It's a loan for the cost of beginning our lives together." They fought about it until she said, in a fit of exasperation, "What the hell, you'd take it if it were my dowry, wouldn't you?" and they both laughed.

For about eighteen hours, he couldn't look Sarah in the eye. Then the idea of freedom began to take hold. She saw it straighten his spine, expand his chest. "It suits you," Sarah told him. "Dare I say you're glowing."

Without revealing any other details, he mentioned to Geeta that Lakshmi was interested in getting in on the women's collective, selling their work in Mumbai. He'd half-expected a grilling about it, but Geeta hadn't asked a single question. In fact, she had thought it was excellent news. The more outlets they had, the more rural women they could bring into the business. They could expand beyond Vinyal, even.

But after a day or two, his restlessness transmitted itself to Sarah. "You're going to resent me," she told him. "You're going to find yourself in some strange city, in some strange apartment with me and a squalling baby, and you're going to think about Ranthambore, and you're going to hate me for making you leave."

He looked up from his notebook and set down his pen. "Actually, what would you think about going to Kanha? It's a huge park. Different from Ranthambore, but still beautiful. Tigers, all the same animals, plus barasingha. I could get a job there. So could you."

"How would that be any different from Sawai?"

"The conservation community there is different from here. More international. I think we could be accepted there."

"Almost like being expats," she said. There was hope in his face. She sat down with him. "Tell me about Kanha."

·

She was beginning to feel pregnant, her abdomen heavy. She had somehow sidestepped morning sickness, but now she had to pee every hour.

Monday morning, they picked up Nuri and went to Vinyal to coordinate the next shipment. On her first drives with them, Nuri had kept silent, but now she made occasional comments, remarking on a temple they drove past or the brick kilns in a field. In the village, they met with the women in Anju's courtyard around a blanket piled with fifty or sixty freshly sewn bags. It was wonderful, really: Rohini radiating assurance as she updated the inventory list in her composition notebook, Padma and Nuri and the others wrapping their creations with care in crinkling sheets of ivory newsprint. Padma's bruises had faded, and her mood seemed surprisingly good. "I don't know if the government is ever going to pay what they owe me," she said to the group when they'd finished their packaging. "But when we get our next payment for this work, Nuri and I will put our money together. I can pay the bank enough to get my house back, and Nuri will come live with us."

The other women looked at them in surprise. Anju said, "Well, now! That is wonderful," and the rest of the conversation revolved around the news. Sanjay didn't translate the entire discussion, but Sarah thought she got the general shape of it: happiness, inflected with wonder that such a decision was possible.

When they finished, Sanjay loaded the bags into the Sumo. Padma stepped away from the other women and gave Sarah a meaningful look. "You have a secret," she said, grinning widely.

Sarah looked at Sanjay, who translated in a careful monotone.

"No," Sarah said brightly. "No secret. I'm so happy you're getting your house back, Padma-ji."

"I can't wait," Padma said. "But you're trying to change the subject. You've definitely got a secret. For now. In a few weeks, everyone will see it."

"*Chalo*, Sarah," Sanjay said. "Let's go. We're late."

He didn't translate Padma's last words till they climbed into the vehicle. Sarah blanched. "How does she know? Do I look different to you?"

"To me, yes. But maybe that's because I know."

"I think I smell different. My sweat. My pee."

"To me you are more delicious." He seemed jaunty, a man anticipating his freedom.

He dropped her at her flat. Later that evening, he phoned her. "Guess what I'm holding in my hand."

"What?"

"I am holding the business card for one V.J. Chowdhury, Esquire. Lakshmi's lawyer." She could hear his grin. "She told me to have my lawyer call him and get the paperwork going."

"Wow," Sarah said. "She wants out. How long will the divorce take?"

His hesitation came down the line. "Longer than it will take you to grow this baby." Into her silence, he said, "Don't be sad. I'll be there before he even figures out how to roll over."

But there was something in his voice. "I worry," he admitted. "Tarun. Lakshmi's brother. He fancies himself her protector. He'll be furious at both of us—Lakshmi and me. He'll try to talk her out of it. Maybe more than talk."

There was something more he wasn't saying. She waited.

"And he'll try to intimidate me," he said. "If he can find something to hold over me, he will."

"Then we need to make sure he doesn't find out I'm pregnant."

•

The next morning, the two of them filed into Geeta's office and sat. She looked warily from one to the other. "I don't like the look of this."

Sanjay explained. Geeta listened blank-faced. "Don't suppose the two of you've ever heard of condoms." She leaned forward, forearms on her desk. "You understand you've put yourselves in serious danger, the both of you. No one must know, outside this circle, and William, of course. You haven't seen a doctor here, have you? Don't. Go to Jaipur."

She vigorously straightened a stack of papers, banging their edges against her desk. "You've really upset the apple cart, you two. Half my staff walking out on me. *You*," she said to Sarah, "I can do without, though you've done well enough with the collective. But *you*." She leaned forward and tapped an index finger at Sanjay. "How do you propose I find a replacement for you? There's no one in Rajasthan who does everything you do."

"I'll be here till the divorce goes through," he said. "A year, at least. And I'll help you find someone. I still have friends at the Bombay Natural History Society. There are good naturalists right here in Sawai, and I know plenty at other parks."

"I need someone who knows *this* park. And here in Sawai, no one's half the naturalist you are, much less the hundred other things you do. Are you sure about this decision, Sanjay? Your life is here. The tigers. The park. Your family, forever. You're a mud hut, you know; you're made of this place."

"I know, believe me. But my duty has changed. I'm sorry."

Geeta regarded him. "I suppose I'm better off, really, if you do go. You'll be ruined for this work, forever wishing you were off in your love nest with *that* one." She shook her head. "You were the best asset we had. And we're the best hope the tiger has. A critically endangered top predator, the linchpin of entire ecosystems. But I understand, truly I do. This is what happens when people procreate."

She looked from Sanjay to Sarah and let go an exasperated sigh. "I suppose I should congratulate you. Our Sanjay is very good with children, you know," she said to Sarah, and her eyes grew unexpectedly bright. "The two of you will raise up a proper little conservationist."

They thanked her and stood to go. Geeta cleared her throat and said, "One more thing. If the pregnancy doesn't stick, what then? Do you stay?"

The question was so very Geeta, Sarah couldn't even take offense. "Yes. We stay."

"But then you two are back to square one, carrying on an extremely dangerous affair. Better if you end your romance in that case. It's the only way you can both stay here safely." She looked from one to the other. "Tell me you understand that."

Very little work got done that day. Sanjay made calls about water tankers. William arrived to check on the status of dredging equipment for the Vinyal dig-out, but Geeta called him back to her office and shut the door. When he emerged, he avoided all eye contact and went straight to his desk.

Sarah couldn't stand the tension. After he finished a call, she went to his desk and said, "She told you."

"Yes." He wouldn't quite look at her. He was embarrassed for her, she realized. *Embarazada*, the Spanish word for *pregnant*.

"I'll miss you," she said.

He shifted some papers and cleared his throat. "Let's have this conversation another time, shall we?"

That evening, exhausted, they went out to dinner as a group. It was a subdued occasion, everyone staring into their plates. Sarah felt exposed now that Geeta and William knew. Padma had seen she was pregnant just by looking at her. Sarah wasn't showing, but apparently it showed anyway.

When they finished, she stopped in the bathroom, a separate structure at the far end of a courtyard. She emerged to the sound of voices, Sanjay and someone else, unfamiliar. She stepped into the shadow of a neem tree. William and Geeta waited at a distance, outside the restaurant door. Sanjay and the man stood in a quiet corner of the courtyard, close enough for her to hear their conversation.

She shifted her weight and craned her neck. There they were: Sanjay and, oh God, his brother-in-law, looking immaculate as always with his perfectly groomed hair, his custom-fitted suit. She'd seen him once at his restaurant, but she had forgotten how large and powerful he looked. She could see the barely contained fury in the set of his shoulders. His voice was a low, pressured growl. "Are you trying to ruin her? I will not allow it."

"This is a business transaction between Lakshmi and me," Sanjay said. "We have every right as husband and wife. You have no say in this matter."

"I don't give a fuck about the legalities. You will not hurt my sister again. Let this idea drop, or trust me, you're going to wish you had."

The men stared each other down, and then Tarun looked up and his gaze landed directly on Sarah in the shadows. "Ah," he said, and paced toward her as if Sanjay had suddenly ceased to exist. His gaze on Sarah was strange, predatory; he stared through her like a tiger about to strike. "Ms. DeVaughan," he said.

She stepped from the shadows, and he gave her a leisurely head-to-toe scan, calculated to intrude. "Mr. Thakur," she said.

"You're looking well." His gaze swiveled between her body and her face. *You're looking well loved.*

"Good evening." She turned on her heel and crossed the courtyard.

From behind her came Tarun's voice: "Does Lakshmi know about this?"

And Sanjay's: "I don't know what you're talking about."

•

"He knows," Sarah insisted.

"He doesn't know," Sanjay argued. "He knows you're the one, but not about the baby. How could he possibly?"

"How did Padma?"

He had no answer for her.

Tarun knew. She had seen his eyes rove up and down her body as if he owned her. She had seen him see. She didn't want to think about what he might do to Sanjay.

The weekend came and went. Monday, at the office, frequent trips to the bathroom. William and his crew would begin dredging the Vinyal lake in three days, but they needed water now.

"I talked to the park director," Geeta said. "The district is pressuring him. Livestock are dying of thirst in every village, and there sit those three beautiful lakes, or what's left of them, smack in the middle of Ranthambore." She pinched the bridge of her nose. "Damn this drought."

•

At 1:00 a.m., Sarah's phone rang. She bolted up, heart pounding.

"The park director called," Geeta said. "It's happening sooner than expected. First thing in the morning. We'll come by at five to pick you up."

"I'll be ready."

"Get some sleep," Geeta said. "This is going to be a disaster."

•

The moon had set. It was the darkest part of the night when Sarah heard the jeep at the gate. She made eye contact with her colleagues one by one as she slid into the back seat. Defeat on every face.

"It sickens me to think it's come to this," Geeta said.

"Can't be helped," William said.

"It could have been helped if the government had done what they should have done when they established the park and ensured all the surrounding villages had reliable water. It's a shit job they've done. A shit job."

The world was still black and starry when Hari pulled the jeep to a stop before the park gates. The village men had not yet arrived. A forest guard raised the gate, its metallic yawp harsh in the waiting dark. Four police officers watched them pass. Hari pulled to the shoulder and killed the engine.

A few minutes later, the film crew arrived. They exchanged tense nods. No one spoke.

The sky was beginning to gray as the first villagers turned off the main road. Sarah counted two hundred head of livestock before losing track. The column flowed on and on, silent men surrounded by bleating goats, lowing cattle, water buffalo. Emaciated, every one of them, and sunken-eyed from dehydration. Thirty minutes passed. A thousand, maybe two thousand, and the end of the column nowhere in sight. The park director had told Geeta he expected ten thousand head of livestock before it was over. Sarah began taking pictures despite the low light. She wanted a record of this day.

The guards raised the creaking gate again, and the first lot flowed through. Twenty-five men, and something like a hundred head of livestock. Then six forest guards blocked the entrance, and the gate clanged down. A hundred head at a time, and ten thousand animals to water. It seemed impossible.

The sun broke in a rosy blaze, striping the world with long, thin shadows. The guards let in a new group of men and animals every ten minutes, but the numbers waiting only swelled. Sarah couldn't see the back of the crowd.

The animals were the first to grow restless. Then the men.

There was no signal, no shout, but an uprush of tension set the animals bawling. Men pushed past the guards. The police drew their guns, pointed at the sky, fired. A cadre of men wrested the gate from its hinges and threw it to the ground, and herders and livestock poured through the gap.

The jeep sat directly in their path. Sarah clicked off shots nonstop.

Without a word, Hari pulled onto the track, ahead of the flood, while the film crew's jeeps rolled alongside the mob, recording. A sudden *tunk*: rock on metal. *Tunk. Tunk.* A young village man scooped stones from the ground and hurled them at the film crew, his face contorted in anger. The film crew jeeps picked up speed, but the sound rang out again from a different direction. *Tunk, tunktunktunk.* Like hail, pelting, and suddenly Sarah realized there must be twenty-five men stoning the film crew. The jeeps roared away down a side track.

William and Sarah exchanged a glance. She lowered her camera and capped her lens. Hari moved to follow the film crew, but Geeta said, "No. We'll stay ahead of the herdsmen and see what happens."

"Are you mad?" William asked.

"They're not stoning *us*. Anyway, it's a bit of a moot point. There's no getting back through the gate now."

Hari drove on as instructed, the set of his back radiating disapproval.

The livestock surged down the road, enveloped in a dust cloud of their own making. Chital deer bounded away, tails high. The herders' faces relaxed into blankness, and they ambled on with their animals as if this march into the park were an ordinary event. Langur monkeys watched from the trees. One kilometer. Two. A disaster unfolding at walking speed.

The forward edge of the throng crested a hill. Rajbagh Lake lay below, shrunken and weed-choked, the summer palace stranded high above the diminished shore. Still, the animals smelled water. At the front of the pack, a goat began to trot. A white cow with a high hump broke into a rickety run, and the animals behind her followed. "There they go," Geeta murmured as Hari drove to the far side of the lake and stopped at a vantage point where they had sometimes watched Machli and her cubs.

The animals reached shore at a dead run. Momentum carried the leaders into the lake and pushed them into deeper water as the herd behind them kept coming. A white cow fell, floundered, and sank out of sight. She did not reappear.

Sarah's hands flew to her mouth. She should have been taking pictures, but instead she wanted to look away, to protect her baby from this sadness. Was that what motherhood would do to her? Make her no longer willing to bear witness?

"Sickening, isn't it," Geeta said. "But some of these animals were going to die anyway." She said it not to dismiss the loss, Sarah thought, but as an offering, the only words she could think of that might console them all.

"Look," Sanjay said, pointing. "Machli."

It took Sarah a minute to locate her with her binoculars. From a thicket of bushes, the tigress looked down on the lake. Sarah couldn't imagine how strange this day must seem to her. Machli wouldn't recognize the creatures that had overrun her territory. They were not the animals of the forest; they were heavy and stupid and lost. Their smell was thirst and fear mixed with the scum of the lake. Individually, they would make for easy prey, but Machli couldn't possibly understand herds so large. They didn't belong in her world.

The tigress stood alert. Her cubs pressed against her. But she rounded on them and snarled, and when they cowered behind her, she lunged, snapping and hissing till she chased them away.

·

Not many animals drowned, really. A dozen, two dozen. Most kept to the shallow water, drank their fill, and were herded away.

The throng of men and animals filled the lakeshore and kept advancing till they surrounded the jeep, making Sarah feel both claustrophobic and exposed. Geeta stood on the seat and scanned the scene, muttering about the film crew. "Where *are* they? This needs to be documented."

In one motion Sarah took up her camera, framed a shot, and pressed the shutter as Sanjay called, "Sarah, no!"

Their eyes met, and she realized her mistake. She lowered the camera to her chest, hoping no one had seen, but a teenaged boy shouted, "No pictures!" and every herder in sight turned to stare. The boy stormed up to the jeep and demanded, "Give me the camera! Are you trying to get us all arrested?"

William planted himself in front of Sarah, but the herder swung his stick and cracked it into William's head, and William jerked back, and the boy climbed over him. Sarah ripped the memory card from her camera and thrust it at him, shouting, "Here! Take it!"

The herder snatched the card, hurled it to the ground, and reached for Sarah's throat with both hands. Not for her throat: for the camera strap. He jerked it, pulling Sarah half out of the jeep over William's lap. The sound of glass shattering. A sharp pain flashed in the back of her neck, and her lungs went still for a sickening few seconds, the breath knocked out of her by William's knee. When she could breathe again, her camera lay wrecked on the ground. The boy was gone.

She pushed herself off William's legs and dropped back into her seat, one hand tracing the raw stripe where the camera strap had scraped nearly the whole circumference of her neck, one hand on her belly, trying to judge the damage. She felt winded but nothing worse. Sanjay caught her eye, but she shook off his concern and turned to William.

At the sight of his face, she gasped. Blood dripped from his temple, a lurid crimson. A gash ran from his scalp to his cheekbone, missing his eye by a centimeter. "I'm all right," he said, unconvincingly.

Geeta handed him a clean white cloth. "Just blood," she said, her eyes locked on William's. "Ears ringing? Tell me what you see, have you got double vision?"

He shook his head, grimacing. "This old loaf's too hard to crack."

"Sarah, you're all right?" she asked.

Sarah nodded.

"I want us far from here, Hari," Geeta said. "But I still want to see the lake."

"We shouldn't be here at all," Hari said, but he steered the jeep farther into the park, tapping the horn as animals and men milled around them.

•

William's face did not stop bleeding. Flies buzzed around the cut. The air smelled of barnyard—dust, sweat, manure, the bitter odor of horns and hooves. Tufts of hair wafted through the air and stuck to Sarah's skin. A kingfisher flitted past, an iridescent flash of beauty on this ugly day.

Hour by hour, the lake changed. Thousands of cloven hooves punched deep holes into the sucking muck of the shoreline. Egrets and ibises settled onto the backs of wading cattle. The water level dropped as if someone had opened a drain at the bottom of the lake. Without her camera, Sarah felt useless, craven. Not a witness: a voyeur.

Toward noon, the atmosphere turned oddly ordinary. Livestock wandered past the jeep. Men stood patiently beneath the sun, close enough that Sarah could see sweat beading on their upper lips. No one bothered them again. Sarah thought they were lucky in that regard—lucky as opposed to smart or strategic. Hari was right: It was madness, being there without even a forest guard for protection. She glanced at William and followed his gaze out over the scene. All these people, all these cattle and buffalo and goats. The havoc they were wreaking on this delicate ecosystem. All of it necessary if the animals—and the villagers who depended on them—were to survive.

"The trenches are a muddy place," she said.

They sat beneath the noonday sun, its faint heat providing a strange bit of comfort.

A tall, bone-thin man approached the jeep, the lower half of his face covered with a green bandanna. A bullock was down, he said, crowded over the edge of a ravine. It was lying with its head downhill, unable to get its legs underneath it. They needed a rope.

Sanjay climbed out of the jeep, swung open the tailgate, and pulled out a coil of sturdy line. He hoisted it over one shoulder, seeming relieved to have something to do.

"I'll go with you," Sarah said.

"You will not," Geeta said. "I forbid it."

Sanjay turned to her. "Stay here where it's safe."

"Where it's *safe?*" she said. "I love you. I am not letting you walk into this chaos by yourself."

Geeta reached for the radio and thrust it into Sarah's hands. "Whatever you do, do not get separated."

Sanjay held out his hand and helped Sarah to the ground. Their eyes met. They turned to follow the man through the throng of cattle. Ranthambore was unrecognizable, as if the wind had lifted a bustling marketplace and set it down in the middle of the park. They were passing by Vinyal men, Sarah noticed. Om stood nearby on one foot, leaning listlessly against Padma's pregnant white cow.

They crested a rise. Off to the left, a cluster of men stood near a narrow wash, looking as if they had important business. Sarah nodded toward them. "This must be our bullock."

The animal lay quietly on his side in the ravine, head resting below his legs. His tongue protruded. He was not far from death.

They needed to roll him, get his legs below his head. The owner crouched, murmuring into the animal's ear, while the men worked the rope around his legs. Sarah moved to help with the rope, but her eyes caught Sanjay's, and she stepped back. She didn't need to chance a blow from flailing hooves.

Eight men got into position on the far side of the wash and began to pull. The bullock's legs rose into the air. His eyes widened as he flipped onto his back and then rolled fully over. He rose to his feet and began to scramble up the incline, but the rope tripped him, and he fell to his knees, thoroughly hobbled. Now they were in dangerous territory. If they couldn't free him, they would have to leave him there to die.

The animal lay still as two men released his forelegs. Sarah held her breath as Sanjay reached for the loop of rope around his back leg and tugged.

When the rope came free, the bullock kicked out. A flash of movement, and Sanjay was flying.

She ran to him in the wash. He lay limp on his back, eyes closed. For a second she thought he was dead. Then his eyes flickered, and he began to turn his head but stopped short and cried out in pain.

Two men reached for him. "Don't move him," Sarah said.

"I think it's my collarbone," he said. "Maybe a rib." He reached for her with his good hand, and she caught it and held it, but in a practical way, as Geeta or William might have done. She put her ear to his chest, and he groaned. She closed her eyes, listening for a punctured lung, but it was a useless effort. She was no medic.

She lifted her head. "I'm going to get help. Don't try to move. We'll get some forest guards and get you out of here."

She climbed out of the wash and raised park headquarters on the radio, but the voice on the other end told her there was nothing they could do. All the forest guards were arrayed between the park entrance and Rajbagh Lake, "handling crowd control."

She would have laughed at the absurdity if she weren't so scared. "We need to get him to a doctor. Something's broken."

Silence. She counted off two minutes. Then the voice again. "We'll send someone, but it will take time."

She glanced back at Sanjay. It could be hours before help arrived. She'd go back to the jeep instead, to Hari and Geeta and William. They could splint Sanjay's collarbone and drive him out of the park.

She whispered a quick explanation to Sanjay and took off running through the crowd, though it was more of a duck and shuffle, like trying to run down a crowded Delhi sidewalk. She kept her eyes trained on the ground. A rocky outcropping forced her to the right, then farther right. When she looked up, she found she was at the top of the rise, alone in a declivity between two low cliffs.

Below her, a curtain of dust hung in the amber air. The lake was gone, sucked down to a pocked expanse of soupy mud, sodden with trampled lake grass. Crocodiles dispatched drowned animals' corpses. A serpent eagle dropped from the sky to the lake bed and lifted off, a fish writhing in its talons.

Someone stepped in front of her, blocked her way. She looked up into his face.

"No," she said. "Don't. Please."

•

It happens the way it happens in nightmares. She can't get away.

His hands feel like flame on the raw skin at her throat.

When her vision goes, the world becomes a pounding, pulsing red. The sound of time beats, slowing, in her ears.

A blue-black wave builds on the horizon and rushes at her from afar. Hissing, it closes over her and tumbles her down into the deep and roaring dark.

Time slows.

The man on top of her shrieks and leaps and vanishes.

A wild face appears above her. Gold eyes stare down into her own.

Machli dips her head and licks Sarah's forehead with a sandpapery tongue. Looks into her face and chuffs, *Hello, you.*

QUINN

WHAT? IS THE FIRST QUESTION, the one said in a gasp as the hands fly to the mouth. It's the panicked, shocked question, the one that means *No.* The one that makes you hear the news a second time.

And then, *When?* The helpless, urgent question. The one that means *I didn't feel it. How could I not have felt it?* It would have been morning in the States when it happened. Quinn and her family have lived out an entire ordinary day and gone to bed, oblivious.

And then, *How?* But she can hardly follow Geeta's reply.

It's past the hour for phone calls, and Quinn is sitting on the edge of the bed in her nightgown, staring into blackness in the corner of the room. Pete has wrapped his arms around her in an embrace made awkward by the phone pressed to her ear.

"I'm sorry it's taken this long to call you. We couldn't find your number." Geeta's voice rasps with fatigue. "Mrs. Chamberlain, I should tell you that a tigress was with Sarah's body when she was found."

Quinn sucks in her breath. Don't picture it, she commands herself.

"It's not what you think," Geeta says. "The police aren't treating this as a tiger accident."

She understands the implication but can't say it aloud. She is too engulfed in the only news that matters. When they hang up, she looks into Pete's face. "Sarah," she manages, though he already knows.

He whispers, "I'm so sorry."

They say a country goes strangely quiet before an earthquake, and that's how Quinn feels, that something terrible is coming, but for now there is just this quiet place where she's been thrust, waiting. She had been with Sarah just weeks ago, a heartbeat of time. They'd become sisters again. And now: gone, all of it. Stolen.

She remembers the day Sarah told her she was going back to India. She remembers her response: *All right, you. Go save those tigers.*

This is how we fail each other, she thinks. We try to love the best way we know how. The day she'd said those words, Quinn thought she was being kind.

Down the darkened hallway, the children sleep quietly, their bodies perfect and unbruised. Alaina's breath whispers as Quinn bends down and gathers her in her arms. She mumbles, "Mommy, what's happening?" and Quinn says, "Shh, you're going to sleep in our bed tonight," and Alaina asks, "Why?" and Quinn can't answer.

Pete stands in the doorway, and she asks him, "Get Nick?" and he says, "Quinn," but she asks him again with her eyes, and his face tells her he'll do whatever she needs him to do. He hefts their son and murmurs reassurance when Nick wakes up. They settle the twins into the bed between them, and across their children's breathing bodies she and Pete lie facing each other, arms stretched out, touching each other's shoulders, rubbing their hands over that warm, known skin for reassurance. In the gray darkness she can just see that his eyes are open. For a time she watches him watch her. But the news is still unreal, and she's not ready for his gaze. So she closes her eyes and tells herself, Sarah is dead, but it feels like a lie. And she tries to rehearse an answer for the question the twins will ask: *Why did she have to die?* But she can think of no answer at all.

Alaina sighs and flings her arm above her head, knocking Quinn's cheek with the back of her hand. Nick kicks out and catches Alaina in the leg, and she makes a little cry of protest. Before long the twins are engaged in a slow-motion, somnolent fight, limbs lifting and landing heavily. They are eight years old. Eight, the end of real childhood. Their bodies are poised to change. They're used to their own beds, and the feel of being surrounded makes them rebel. She bears the blows and thinks, I have my twins. I have my twins.

And she thinks: Mother.

•

When Mother opens the door, wrapped tight in her blue silk dressing gown, Quinn can manage only to say her sister's name, but it's enough. Mother crosses her arms over her abdomen and bends forward, wrapping herself around the emptiness where her babies were formed. The sound she makes is low and loud. Her mouth stretches open around it.

Quinn brings Mother to her house and leads her to the kitchen table, where she sits and stares at nothing. She must be thinking of her three shining children, of everything she poured into making them; birthing them; raising, teaching, loving them. Where did all that love, all that energy, go when they died? Was it just lost?

And what is the word for being the last child left alive? Not *orphan*. But something like it.

Quinn and Pete sit their children down at the table and tell them Auntie Sarah is dead. The twins' faces change at the news. This is the end of their childhood, although they don't know it yet. And it enrages Quinn; it sickens her. She doesn't want them to have to live through what she did. She doesn't want them to watch their family disappear, piece by piece.

•

Night falls, but she cannot sleep. And she refuses to meditate. She has no interest in accepting anything right now.

The light in her studio stabs her eyes. There's a primed canvas on her easel, and she grabs for a tube of cobalt. She uses her palette knife to shove the pigment up and down, blotting out everything. Tonight she rejects all white.

She opens a tube of ultramarine and buries a new canvas in it, using her stiffest brush to apply the pigment thick as clay. Next she switches to orange for tigers, and when that's gone, to black, reveling bitterly in the pigment's thick oiliness, the way it gives back nothing at all.

But this is all going too fast, and the night is dishwater yellow outside her window. Morning is far away. She never expected Sarah to die in India. She thought she'd be safe there, after all her years traveling the world. She thought her sister had settled down.

She picks up a half-spent tube of burnt sienna and stares at it, then retrieves her smallest brush and some water to thin the paint.

Henna tattoos are for weddings, but the patterns are intricate and organic—tiny leaves, flowers, vines—and they take hours of careful attention. By the time Pete finds her in the morning, she has painted her entire left hand, front and back, and her arm up to the elbow.

He studies her there, sitting on the strewn floor, staring hypnotized at her own hand. "You didn't sleep," he says. She shakes her head.

He kneels beside her, tucks his chin into the crook of her neck. Places a kiss just below her ear and whispers, "I know. I know." And she loves him for that, even though he doesn't know, and she hopes to God he never will.

•

William meets her at the station in Sawai and lets her into her sister's apartment, where she spends the night in Sarah's bed, lying awake and trying to open herself to any filament of energy that might remain.

In the morning, he brings her the obituary from the *Times of India*. The lead paragraph refers to Sarah, as she knew it would, as "Tiger Woman" and weaves the expected tale. She was, depending on whose viewpoint you subscribe to, a mystic, a human/tiger hybrid, the Dian Fossey of the tiger world; or a typical American, foolhardy, sentimental, with enough money in her bank account to follow her fancies no matter the cost to herself or the Indian government or the tigers she so mawkishly adored.

The obituary mentions the tabloid stories. *Tiger Woman Stalks Villagers. Tiger Woman Caught on Film Nursing Litter of Cubs. Tiger Woman Rescues Baby from Flood.* And a drawing of a feline figure with a human face, carrying a dark-haired infant by the scruff of its neck.

Quinn sets the paper aside and looks up at William.

"A few days ago, I looked through my records." He pulls a small green notebook out of his shirt pocket, flips it open, puts on his reading glasses. "In the months before Sarah's arrival, we sighted a tiger on average one day out of seven. But on the days she accompanied us, it was one out of two, and then, in that last month, it was nearly every time." He removes his glasses. "You expect an increase in sightings during the dry season, as animals hew closer to the water holes. But even so, her percentages were extraordinary. Hari once told me she was blessed by Durga. Sanjay suspected pheromones. I told myself it was coincidence, remarkable luck."

In the tree outside Sarah's window, a whirring of feathers. "But I think now it was simply the fact that she drew animals to her. We know that that phenomenon exists. The fact that science hasn't yet explained it doesn't make it untrue. So I believe it comes down to this. The tigers came out for Sarah because she was Sarah." He looks closely at Quinn. "Do you see what I'm saying? It was the tigers who made her Tiger Woman."

•

It's a small service, held in the park, in a meadow near the ranger station. Sanjay, arm in a sling and eyes burning in their sockets, looks as if he can barely stand. Hari tells Quinn his boys have been mourning Sarah; they considered her a friend.

The park director and a handful of forest guards attend. The ambassador from Delhi, seeming out of place in his stylish charcoal suit. The women of the collective in brightly colored *lehenga choli*. Sarah's landlord and his family. Reporters and television crews. Quinn asks the media crews to respect their privacy and, astonishingly, they pack up their equipment and leave.

The service takes place beneath a clear blue sky. A light breeze rustles the dry grass and blows songbirds from tree to tree. As they eulogize her sister, Quinn can't stop thinking about the other service, the one for their brother. How it rained that day in Delhi. How Mother clutched Quinn to her like a pocketbook.

Afterward, the women of the collective gather, talking intently and looking at Quinn from a short distance away. They approach her, and Anju offers condolences on behalf of the group, adding, "We should be happy. She achieved *moksha*." Sanjay barely manages to choke out the translation.

Rohini turns to Sanjay and asks, "What happens now?"

"I don't know," he admits. "This was her project."

"You've always been an equal part of it," Anju argues.

"Look, we're very-very sad about Sarah," Rohini says. "She was our friend. But we've got families to feed. We all need the income. Padma-ji is about to get her house back. Nuri will have a place to live." She nods toward Quinn. "Why can't *she* help?"

Quinn explains that she lives eight thousand miles away. The women are undaunted by that fact. The conversation ends with no promises. Quinn knows what she needs to do, but she is too flattened by grief to make the commitment yet. The women turn away, and someone official hands Quinn a small, flimsy cardboard box, heavy for its size.

It's shocking how little remains of the body after cremation: a heap of pale, sandy bone you could hold in two cupped palms. Quinn carefully shakes half of the ashes into a bronze urn for Mother and closes the box on the rest. Hari drives Quinn and Geeta, William and Sanjay into the park's tawny interior, where they scatter Sarah's ashes in the dry, stony bed of the river where once she rescued a tiger cub.

•

That night, William invites Quinn to eat with him. She brings the Sundarbans mask, and he places it on the table, a silent dinner guest. When they finish the meal and the washing up, she turns to face him and rests her hips against the speckled yellow countertop, and he looks at her standing in this posture, and she can see she's reminding him of Sarah. He picks up the mask. "It was meant as protection from threats that stalk from behind," he says. "But it wasn't the past stalking her, it turns out."

Quinn is not so sure. Lately she has begun to think of the past as a vast place, dark and mysterious as a forest. Always decaying, collapsing in upon itself, only to bring forth new growth in the most surprising of places. She thinks of Mother, of Ayah. In those last months before Sarah's death, Quinn began to see that the past is a place we think belongs to us, but we are wrong. We are only ever visitors there.

Maybe she would have recognized that truth long ago if she and Sarah had not lost each other for so many years.

William's pale blue eyes shine with tears. "She didn't have to die."

"Sanjay needs your friendship," she says. "Even if you're angry with him."

"I loved her, too. I never told her that." A jagged laugh catches in his throat. "Brave of me, isn't it, to tell you this now that it's too late for it to mean anything."

"You gave her that mask, William," she says. "She knew."

•

For three days, she dogs the police commissioner. He tells her repeatedly that his men are doing everything they can, which seems to mean interviewing villagers. She makes Geeta and William and Sanjay recount their memories of that day in minute detail. She invites Drupti to dinner at Sanjay's brother-in-law's restaurant, as if being there, and possibly seeing him, will tell her anything. Tarun, tall and leonine, comes to their table in his French-cuffed shirt and ruby cufflinks to offer condolences and pick up the tab. In other words, to let Quinn know he knows who she is.

From Sarah's flat the next morning, she calls the embassy and ends up speaking with a foreign service officer she's never met. She tells him about her encounter with Tarun. His voice goes tight with alarm. He advises her in the strongest possible terms—that's the actual phrase he uses—to avoid contact with anyone involved in the case. He tells her she should leave this matter with the embassy. He strongly urges her to return to the States.

After she hangs up, Geeta arrives with a copy of the *Times of India*. "Have you seen it?" They sit at the dining room table while Quinn reads the story, the terra cotta tiles cold against her feet.

EVEN IN DEATH, MYTH OF TIGER WOMAN LIVES ON

By Anjali Ghosh

SAWAI MADHOPUR, RAJASTHAN, January 24— Two weeks ago, Sarah DeVaughan, known internationally as "Tiger Woman," was killed while heroically protecting tigers during an uprising in Ranthambore National Park. But whispers in the surrounding villages suggest her myth did not die with her.

DeVaughan gained fame last summer when footage of her tiger-cub river rescue went public. But in nearby villages, her notoriety took on a different flavor. After the incident, a variety of rumors cropped up, including one linking the Tiger Woman to a tiger lover. Legends of shape-shifting tigers are common among tribal communities throughout India.

The latest rumor arose from an incident that occurred Tuesday, when a would-be poacher fell from a cliff while attempting to set a snare trap inside the park. The poacher, who broke both legs in the fall, is said to have seen a mysterious tiger with an unusually fair coat—similar to DeVaughan's blond hair—and a humanlike face vanishing into the forest just before he fell.

It is not clear where the rumor originated. But in the villages surrounding Ranthambore, people are saying the ghost of the Tiger Woman is afoot, working in death as she did in life to protect the tigers of the park.

She looks up at Geeta. "People really believe this kind of thing?"

"In the villages, yes."

Quinn nearly smiles. "I think Sarah would have loved it."

Geeta crosses her forearms on the table. "I'll tell you, I don't have much confidence that Sarah's death is going to receive more police scrutiny. No one has come forward with any information, and trust me, they won't. The villagers protect their own."

"You think it was a villager," Quinn says. "I keep coming back to Sanjay's brother-in-law."

"It's true he's a bit of a tough," Geeta says. "But I can't imagine he was in the park that day."

"So what do you want me to do?" Quinn asks. "Either way. Tarun or one of the villagers. Should I say it's okay that the man who killed my sister gets to live out the rest of his life in peace?"

Geeta ignores her tone, and for that matter, her question. "Look, I have to ask. Are you planning to bring suit against Tiger Survival?"

"*What?*"

"As director of this agency, I hired Sarah. I'm the reason she came to Ranthambore, and, to that extent, I'm the reason she ended up dying here."

Quinn can hardly speak. "You think I've come here to *sue* you?"

"Please remember I barely know you. I can't afford to make assumptions about what's motivated you to come back here."

That word, *afford*, enrages Quinn. "My sister is dead. What's *your* stake in this?"

"Tiger survival," Geeta says.

Quinn cannot manage to speak.

After a wordless interval, Geeta clears her throat. "I apologize for upsetting you. But you must prepare yourself for the fact you may not find what you're looking for."

Quinn squeezes her eyes shut. "All right. You're dying to tell me what to do. So say it."

Geeta's face holds not smugness but regret. "Go home, Quinn. You'll not find justice here."

•

The next morning, word comes from the chief of police that Mandeep, Padma's brother-in-law, has been arrested for Sarah's murder.

"A Vinyal man. It doesn't surprise me," the police chief says. "Vinyal is a very rough place."

•

Quinn arrives in Louisville exhausted and sleeps for the better part of two days. On the third day, she wakes to snow, a couple of inches on the ground and more floating down from a white sky.

After Pete and the twins leave for school, Mother calls and asks if she can come by. Quinn can hear in her voice that she has something to say. When she arrives, Quinn takes her coat as Mother smooths snowflakes from her hair.

Outside the window, snow gathers in the bark on the north side of the walnut tree. "I would like so much to believe in some sort of afterlife," Quinn says. "Heaven. Reincarnation. *Moksha*. I would love that comfort."

"So you don't believe she has an afterlife, then."

But Quinn does believe it. Sarah is still alive because they love her: Quinn and Mother, Sanjay and William, Pete and the kids. And because halfway around the world, women are selling textiles for a living wage, thanks to Sarah. And because there are people in the villages who believe her spirit is still alive, guarding the tigers of Ranthambore. Burning bright.

"I'm glad you girls reconnected."

"I'm sorry we waited so long."

"I should have been different with her," Mother says. "I should have found a way."

Quinn looks at her straight on. "It felt like you left us after Marcus died. We never got you back."

Mother blinks and composes herself and says, "I'll tell you what happened that day, if you still want to know. But it's not going to make you any happier. So you have to ask yourself whether you want this information, because it will be a burden to you."

Quinn feels her body still. "I think it will help."

"I hope so. For your sake." Mother takes a breath, tucks her hair behind her ear. "Your father should have married someone adventurous. I wasn't cut out for that life." She squares herself to Quinn, but her eyes drop.

"You had an affair," Quinn guesses. "With the pastor," she adds on a hunch.

Mother's mouth sags. "No. I found out he had gotten involved with someone. One of the nurses."

Quinn squints at her. "Pastor Mark had an affair with one of the nurses?"

Mother gives her a look. "I'm talking about your father, Quinn."

"*Daddy?*"

"A few days before the twins got sick, I caught him on the phone talking with her. They worked together at the clinic. The old cliché."

Quinn thinks back. "I remember a party at our house."

Mother nods. "I found out about it not an hour before the guests arrived. I was too upset to be hosting a houseful of people, but it was too late to cancel. So I put on a big smile, and I pulled it off."

"But I saw you crying," Quinn says. "On the stairs, with Pastor Mark."

Her mother pauses. "I'd forgotten about that," she says quietly. "But I recovered, well enough to play hostess for the rest of the night. I remember standing in the doorway with your father, waving goodbye to the last guests. The next morning, he went to the clinic, and I sat by myself in our bedroom and—" She looks up. "I couldn't bear it, Quinn. I'd stayed in India for him. I'd kept you kids in India. He knew I couldn't take it. He should have let us go."

Quinn is silent, taking it all in. "You sent all the servants home that day. And then what? Where did you go?"

The furnace kicks on. Mother keeps her eyes on her hands. "I went to church."

"To *church?*"

"To talk to Pastor Mark."

"You couldn't have just *called* him?"

Mother's body goes still. When she speaks, her voice is small and weary. "I was scared."

"Of what?"

She keeps her eyes lowered. "Of what I might do."

Quinn stares, wanting to ask Mother what she means but afraid she couldn't bear the answer. "You didn't tell me you were leaving," she says gently. "You left me in charge, and you never told me."

"There's no excuse. I'm sorry, Quinn. I told you this story wouldn't make you happy. But you asked for the truth, and now it's yours. I'm sorry."

Quinn stands, goes to the counter. So here is her answer, and it feels meaningless, no better or worse than any other answer. This is how people's lives grow uglier. Like the fact that Mandeep killed Sarah: That feels meaningless, too. He was an angry, frustrated, violent man, and in a moment of chaos he vented his rage, and Sarah died for it. She died pregnant and hopeful and just about to cross the threshold into real happiness at last, and those things were not enough to save her. And why should they be? The world has never worked that way.

Outside, the snowflakes fly.

Sarah once told Quinn that on the train to Sawai, when she'd first arrived in India, a spiritualist from Mumbai had asked her why she was so passionate about tigers. She tried to explain it—how she'd been fascinated when she was young, how the experience of touching a tigress at a rescue center had been important to her at a vulnerable moment. She said those things, and then she stopped because all of those facts were true, but none of them really explained anything. The man saw her hesitate, and he said to her, "Passion. You can explain to yourself *how* you came to be passionate about something, but you can never explain *why*." And then he said, "It's just as good to go chasing after tigers as it is to go chasing after God."

How strange that he said those words to Sarah, and that a tigress watched over her body in the hour of her death. Quinn would like to believe that in her sister's last moments, she looked up into those wild gold eyes and saw them transformed. That she found herself gazing into the face of God, or into the young blue eyes of her beloved lost Marcus. She would like to believe those eyes greeted Sarah and welcomed her home. That she reached out to the face of her beloved and felt its softness at the center of her palm.

Quinn prepares a pot of coffee, braces her hands on the counter, and lets her head drop as the water begins to grumble and sigh. Heat condenses on the window. Outside, the flakes come down bigger and faster. Reflected in the window, Mother sits, shoulders bowed, like a crumbling statue. The snow passes through her as if she's not even there.

In her memory Quinn sees her mother back on Cornwallis Road, young and lonely and living the wrong life. She sees her as a grieving mother in a stale pink nightgown, haunting the hallways, smelling of dirty hair.

And now she sees something she almost doesn't recognize, an indistinct haze of black and gray. Her ultrasound. A boy and a girl, just like Marcus and Sarah. She hasn't thought of this in years, but now she remembers that she apologized, weeping, to Mother when she told her the news.

And Mother held her and whispered, *Don't be sorry. I'm happy for you.*

EPILOGUE

MACHLI'S DAUGHTERS ARE GROWN NOW. Since the last full moon, they have left her, each dispersing to a new territory she has granted them, small in size but rich with game.

Left alone, she grows discontented. One early morning, she rises. The birds have woken and are singing in the trees. The black lake dimly reflects stars. On this patrol, the scent she leaves is an invitation. When she is done, she settles into a glade near the lake and waits.

Toward late morning, she feels the vibration in her chest. He calls to her and she answers: *aaooongggh.*

He appears at the edge of her glade, his nose crisscrossed with old scratches, evidence of his couplings with other females. His body has grown heavier. A ruff of fur rings his face.

She rises and walks to him. They greet each other with rubs of the head. He circles her, and she drops to her belly and shifts her tail to one side.

He covers her with his body. He bites the back of her neck.

Author's Note

The plight of the tiger has been closely watched in India since the 1970s, when the decimation of a once-thriving population was recognized. In recent years, India and other countries have experienced a rebound in numbers thanks to a global conservation initiative known as Tx2, which in 2010 announced its intent to double the world population of tigers by 2022. As of this writing, World Wildlife Fund estimates the global tiger population at about 4,000. More than half of those tigers are found in India. The rebound, however, seems to be self-limiting. There can only be as many tigers as there is territory and food to support them and corridors they can use to disperse to new territory. Bringing back tiger numbers without increasing the amount of wilderness available to them is an impossible task. And, as tiger numbers grow, human-tiger conflict increases as well.

More worrisome yet, in October 2018, the Chinese government rescinded a decades-old ban on tiger body parts. While the new policy applies only to farmed tigers, it is effectively impossible to tell the body parts of a farmed tiger from those of a poached wild tiger—and poached tigers potentially offer far more profit for dealers than do farmed cats. Conservationists fear the lifting of the ban will prove catastrophic to the world's remaining wild tigers. While China temporarily reinstated the ban in November 2018 due to pressure from environmental organizations, conservationists concerned about the world's remaining wild tigers are fighting fiercely to have the ban permanently reinstated.

Machli is based upon a real tigress by the same name, born in 1996 or 1997, who ruled the lakes region of Ranthambore in her prime. She was glorious. I was privileged to witness her there during a trip I took with my mother to Ranthambore and the Sawai Madhopur district in January of 2006, during what we were told was the deepest cold snap in seventy years. When I encountered Machli, she was accompanied by two subadults, somewhere around fifteen months old. She died of old age in 2016 after having raised five litters of cubs. Her body was strewn with flowers, given a funeral procession, and cremated in observance of Hindu rituals.

The village of Vinyal is based partly on villages I visited in the Sawai Madhopur district, and partly on secondhand accounts, though the name of the village is invented. When I traveled to India, my guide, Vipul Jain, and several other people I interviewed mentioned an uprising in which villagers drove thousands of head of livestock into the park during a water crisis. Everyone who mentioned the uprising told me, in effect, "It didn't happen the way you heard." They said this without asking what I'd heard. Presumably, they knew the version of the story that had gone public. I took that as permission to write about the episode the way I imagined.

Organizations such as WWF-India, the Indian arm of the World Wildlife Fund, have led the effort to protect tiger populations for decades. You can read more about the efforts of WWF-India at https://www.wwfindia.org/about_wwf/priority_species, or visit the World Wildlife Fund's U.S. website, which maintains a tiger page at https://www.worldwildlife.org/species/tiger. The U.S.-based organization Panthera focuses on saving wild cats of all types; its tiger page is at https://www.panthera.org/cat/tiger.

Some of the incidents described in the book sprang from my imagination (notably the river rescue). The text that Sarah reads during her first visit to the park, which begins, "The Aravalli Hills are the oldest in the world," is credited to an unnamed natural history book, but I actually wrote this passage based on the history I learned during my visit to Ranthambore.

Many other descriptions and incidents in these pages are based upon my observations of tigers at Ranthambore, Kanha, and the Sundarbans, and on stories I heard while interviewing naturalists, wildlife veterinarians, and others involved in conservation and ecotourism. Other incidents are based on events related in natural history books and are credited below. Those books have educated and enlightened me and have informed my work, though any errors are my own.

Although tigresses are sometimes forced to kill their offspring or let them die, to my knowledge, the real Machli never killed any of her cubs.

The scene of the aftermath of a tiger accident was inspired by the book *Of Tigers and Men: Entering the Age of Extinction*, by Richard Ives, which is also where I first encountered the myth of human-tiger hybrids, or were-tigers. William tells Sarah the story of Sundarbans tigers and the masks local fishermen and honey hunters use to protect themselves from tiger attack; I read many accounts of the Sundarbans tigers and these masks, including in Sy Montgomery's haunting book *Spell of the Tiger: The Man-Eaters of Sundarbans*. The phenomenon of forest animals broadcasting the movements of a tiger is colorfully described in Stephen Mills's excellent book *Tiger*.

Noted tiger expert Valmik Thapar recorded instances of a Ranthambore male cooling himself at a water hole with a tigress and their cubs in his book *The Secret Life of Tigers*. An instance of a tiger eating so much it apparently couldn't move is documented in Stephen Mills's *Tiger*.

"No one asked them whether there should be a park here ... all our lives will be destroyed, as well" is a quote from Valmik Thapar, quoted in Geoffrey C. Ward and Diane Raines Ward's book *Tiger-Wallahs: Saving the Greatest of the Great Cats*.

The text that Sarah recites—"For if he meets another cat he will kiss her in kindness ... For he can spraggle upon waggle"—is from "Jubilate Agno," by Christopher Smart, originally published in 1759. The story of the real Machli mating with an intruder, presumably in order to convince him to spare her cubs, is recounted in *Tiger*, by Stephen Mills. Finally, in one of Sarah's journal entries, she includes a quote from the Bible: "Weeping for her children, and refusing consolation, because they are no more" (Matthew 2:18).

ACKNOWLEDGMENTS

Early on in the first draft of this novel, I realized I needed to go to India in order to have the faintest hope of writing authentically. Without hesitation, my husband, Jeff, encouraged me to do so, sending along an audio player loaded with daily messages to keep me company during my travels. In the years that followed, he graciously supported my absences from home, sometimes for weeks at a time, as I researched and revised this book. He has also been the best sounding board I could hope for. Among the great pleasures of writing this novel have been the evenings spent sitting with him, utterly absorbed in conversation about imaginary people and events and the truths that might emerge from the fiction. Jeff, you are my large-hearted human, and my gratitude is boundless.

For financial help, I thank the Elizabeth George Foundation, which funded my trip to India; Louanda McClure Kynhoff and the Juanita McClure Scholarship for generous support; the Kentucky Foundation for Women; and the Kentucky Arts Council, whose Al Smith Fellowship Award for artistic excellence helped fund the final stages of revision. Special thanks to Ashland Creek Press and JoeAnn Hart for awarding this manuscript the Siskiyou Prize for New Environmental Literature.

For invaluable space and time to write, I owe thanks first and foremost to the Kentucky Foundation for Women, which offered me a literary home at Hopscotch House, an airy, art-filled farmhouse, over the years I worked on this novel. I'm also grateful to the Kimmel Harding Nelson Center for the Arts; the Mary Anderson Center; Crosshatch, for a snow-filled writing residency in the North Woods of Michigan; and Playa, for the gift of quiet and community in a vast and magical landscape.

Beyond the obvious boons they granted, the individuals and organizations mentioned above gave me the heart to keep writing when it would have been far easier to stop.

My deepest thanks to Vipul Jain, my guide at Ranthambore, who introduced me to the flora, fauna (notably Machli), geography, history, and people of that awe-inducing place. Thanks to Allan and Kristy Blanchard at Tiger Trails, who arranged my trip to India and who connected me with Vipul. Without the help and guidance of these three people, this book could not have been written.

Thanks to fellow traveler Alan Ivens for stories around the fire, and to Tarun and Dimple Bhati of the Kanha Jungle Lodge for warm hospitality. For patiently and thoughtfully answering questions that arrived by email from a total stranger, I thank conservation workers Debbie Martyr and Neil Franklin. Thanks to poet and professor Satyapriya Mukhopadhyay for introducing me to Calcutta, and to Glenny Brock for introducing me to Professor Mukhopadhyay.

Loving thanks to my mother, Laura Kahl, for raising me to be an animal lover, a traveler, and a reader, curious about the world. Thank you for traveling to India with me despite your initial misgivings, Mom. I am so happy we got to share those experiences.

Numerous readers gave me invaluable feedback on these pages. Much gratitude to these smart and talented friends. For notes and advice on early drafts, love and gratitude to Beverly Bartlett, Julie Brickman, Megan McKenzie Conca, K.L. (Kenny) Cook, Charlotte Rains Dixon, Laura Kahl, Katrina Kittle, Karen Mann, Linda Busby Parker, and Deidre Woollard. For reading and providing feedback on later revisions, love and thanks to Cindy Corpier, Kristin Matly Dennis, Lia Eastep, Carolyn Flynn, Marjetta Geerling, Jacquelin Gorman, Bridgett Jensen, Maryann Lesert, Sena Jeter Naslund, Elaine Neil Orr, Lori Reisenbichler, Julie Stewart, and Jeff Yocom.

Thanks to Mimi Mondal for offering invaluable insights and advice. Surekha Kulkarni of the Beaded Treasures Project helped me understand the workings of a women's collective. Dorian Karchmar and Wendi Gu provided helpful notes along the way.

Lesléa Newman told me the story of a deer who lay next to Matthew Shepard along the Wyoming fence line where he had been left to die. That image inspired an important moment in this novel.

For particular kindness and encouragement, I'm grateful to Kenny Cook, Elizabeth George, Richard Goodman, Leah Henderson, Silas House, Cathleen Medwick, Sy Montgomery, Lesléa Newman, Elaine Neil Orr, Molly Peacock, and Keith Reddin, who told me I had to keep going. For encouragement and help in a variety of forms, a big thank-you to Susan Campbell Bartoletti; I'll keep the particulars just between us. For always believing and for helping me celebrate, thanks to Renée Croket and Sherry Hurley. For making a home for me in their hearts, love to Cindy Corpier, Lia Eastep, Marjetta Geerling, Jackie Gorman, Bridgett Jensen, Maryann Lesert, Terry Price, Lori Reisenbichler, and Julie Stewart. Much love and gratitude to Brady Yocom, who cheered me on from the start, and to Kiki Briggs, Kristy Urman, and Kassie Fedrick, who believed in this book and in me. And lifetime love and thanks to Hester George, who was the first person in my life to tell me that someday I'd write a book.

Heartfelt thanks to Sena Jeter Naslund, who first made me believe I could be a creative writer, and to Karen Mann, who, along with Sena, created a literary home for me and hundreds of other writers in the Spalding low-residency MFA in Writing program. Much gratitude to my colleagues in the Spalding program over the years: Sena and Karen, Kathleen Driskell, Ellyn Lichvar, Jason Hill, Gayle Hanratty, and Lynnell Edwards, for support and encouragement, and for graciously allowing and putting up with my absences. And warm thanks to the rest of my Spalding MFA family—students, faculty, and alumni—for their kindness over the years in inquiring, "How's the tiger novel going?"

Awestruck gratitude to my literary agent, Lisa Gallagher, for championing this book with a magnificent tenacity and expertise. I can't imagine a better guide and partner on this journey. Thank you, Lisa. Your belief in this book was a life raft.

Giddy thanks to JoeAnn Hart, who selected my manuscript for the Siskiyou Prize for New Environmental Literature. And joyful appreciation to Midge Raymond and John Yunker of Ashland Creek Press, who have dedicated themselves to publishing literature that grapples with humanity's relationship to the animals with whom we share this fragile planet. They saw in these pages a story they thought deserved a place in the world, and they offered this novel a home. Thanks also to Midge Raymond for a smart, clear-eyed copyedit that made this book better; to Jackie Dever for her expert proofreading; and to Matt Smith for creating a knockout book cover that thrills me every time I see it.

I will end the way I began, with love and appreciation to my spouse and partner, Jeff Yocom, who introduced me to Jai, Mohan, and Leela, which is how this story began.

ABOUT THE AUTHOR

Photo credit: Terry Price

Katy Yocom's fiction, poetry, and essays have appeared in *Salon*, *The Louisville Review*, *decomP magazinE*, *Midlife at the Oasis*, and elsewhere. Her short fiction has been nominated for the Pushcart Prize and her poetry has been translated into Bulgarian. Her debut novel, *Three Ways to Disappear*, won the Siskiyou Prize for New Environmental Literature and was a finalist for the Dzanc Books Disquiet Open Borders Book Prize and the UNO Press Publishing Lab Prize.

Katy is a 2019 recipient of the Al Smith Fellowship Award for artistic excellence from the Kentucky Arts Council. She has received grants from the Kentucky Foundation for Women and the Elizabeth George Foundation as well as writing residencies from Kimmel Harding Nelson Center for the Arts and Crosshatch Hill House. She holds an MFA in writing from Spalding University, codirects the Spalding at 21c reading series in Louisville, and serves on the board of the Kentucky Women Writers Conference. She lives with her husband and animal companions in Louisville, where she is associate director of Spalding's low-residency MFA in Writing program.

Ashland
Creek
Press

Ashland Creek Press is a small, independent publisher of books for a better planet. Our mission is to publish a range of books that foster an appreciation for worlds outside our own, for nature and the animal kingdom, for the creative process, and for the ways in which we all connect. To keep up-to-date on new and forthcoming works, subscribe to our free newsletter by visiting www.AshlandCreekPress.com.